BLOODSTONE

The Brother Athelstan Mysteries from Paul Doherty

* available from Severn House

BLOODSTONE

Being the Eleventh of the Sorrowful Mysteries of
Brother Athelstan

Paul Doherty

CRÈME de la CRIME

This first world edition published 2012
in Great Britain and in the USA by
Crème de la Crime, an imprint of
SEVERN HOUSE PUBLISHERS LTD of
9–15 High Street, Sutton, Surrey, England, SM1 1DF.
Trade paperback edition first published
in Great Britain and the USA 2012 by
SEVERN HOUSE PUBLISHERS LTD .

British Library Cataloguing in Publication Data

Doherty, P. C.
  Bloodstone.
  1. Athelstan, Brother (Fictitious character)–Fiction.
  2. Priests–Fiction. 3. John, of Gaunt, Duke of Lancaster,
  1340-1399–Fiction. 4. Relics–Fiction. 5. Serial murder
  investigation–Fiction. 6. Great Britain–History--
  Richard II, 1377-1399–Fiction. 7. Detective and mystery
  stories.
  I. Title
  823.9'2-dc22

ISBN-13: 978-1-78029-016-4 (cased)
ISBN-13: 978-1-78029-520-6 (trade paper)

All Severn House titles are printed on acid-free paper.

Severn House Publishers support The Forest Stewardship Council [FSC],
the leading international forest certification organisation. All our titles that
are printed on Greenpeace-approved FSC-certified paper carry the FSC logo.

Typeset by Palimpsest Book Production Ltd.,
Falkirk, Stirlingshire, Scotland.
Printed and bound in Great Britain by
MPG Books Ltd., Bodmin, Cornwall.

To Joe, Edel, Patrick and Ciaran Monahan of Leytonstone for their courage and good humour during a very tough period. Brother Athelstan would be very proud of you!

PROLOGUE

'Murdrum: Murder.'

Sir Robert Kilverby was about to be murdered. Of course
he did not know that, ensconced so comfortably in his
warm, snug chancery chamber, its costly linen panelling
gleaming in the dancing light of the candle spigots. True, the
fiery glow of the pine logs crackling in the mantled hearth
sent the shadows swiftly fluttering. The gargoyle faces carved
on either side of the hearth assumed a more sinister look whilst
the grisly scenes of Archbishop Alphege's martyrdom on the
painted cloths above the panelling took on an eerie life of
their own. Nevertheless, Kilverby felt safe and secure in this
fortified chamber, its heavy oaken door bolted and locked. The
oriel windows high in the pink plaster walls glowed with
the dying light of the December day though they were too
small for any footpad to break through. Kilverby hitched his
fur-lined cloak closer about his bony shoulders. He stopped
gnawing on the plume of the elegant quill pen and placed it
down on the pewter writing palette. Distracted, he gazed around
at the sprigs of evergreen pinned to some of the gaily coloured
cloths by his beloved daughter Alesia. She had gone out into
the frosted garden and plucked holly, ivy and mistletoe,
reminders of the evergreen Christ and the imminent arrival of
Christmas. Soon Advent would be over. The fasting and the
chanting of the Dirige psalms finished. The great 'O Antiphons'
would be sung to the 'Key of David', 'Lion of Judah' and
'Ever Mighty Counsellor'. Christmas would soon be celebrated
but not as it had been before – that's what Alesia was quietly
hinting at – in those glorious days when Kilverby's first wife,
Alesia's mother Margaret, was alive.

Kilverby ignored his growling stomach. The rich Cheapside
merchant picked up his rosewood Ave beads and threaded
them through his bony fingers. He quickly recited a Pater and

placed the beads back down. He had truly made a mistake when he'd married Helen Rauliffe. 'Helen of hell' as Alesia now called her stepmother; his daughter was right and he was wrong. He had been seduced by Helen's fine figure and beautiful, hard face. So eager to recapture former joys both at bed and board, he had, like the old fool he was, rushed to exchange vows in the porch of St Mary Le Bow, only to find the trap had been sprung. The fowler had cast his net and he was caught. Hard of heart and bitter of tongue was the fair Helen. She carried her head like a priest would the monstrance. In fact, she'd turned his life into a living hell. Kilverby stirred in his great chancery chair and took a deep sip of the dark red claret. He stared sadly at the loving cup, a gift from Alesia, and breathed in deeply. How could he escape judgement? Kilverby grasped his Ave beads again. He had gone to St Fulcher's. He had listened to the warnings from Sub-Prior Richer who had heard the confession of that old reprobate, William Chalk. Kilverby beat his breast. He had done wrong. He had financed those depredations in France. He was partly to blame for the theft of that sacred bloodstone, the Passio Christi. Kilverby wanted absolution. He had cut himself off from the Wyverns, who'd been responsible for the theft. He had bribed Abbot Walter with good gold and silver to ensure further reparation was made. Above all, Kilverby had read that book! He had reflected on the curses and wondered if the death of Margaret and his second marriage were all part of God's judgement against him. What if the curse spread to include his beloved daughter Alesia? Kilverby swiftly crossed himself. He would continue to make reparation. He would, eventually, take the Passio Christi to St Fulcher's and then continue his pilgrimage of reparation to Santiago, Rome and Jerusalem. Kilverby paused in his thoughts at a knock on the door.

'Who is it?' he called.

'Father,' Alesia replied, 'I'm here with Crispin.'

'Go to bed,' Kilverby retorted. 'God be with you. I shall speak to you in the morning.'

Kilverby heard the footsteps fade and returned to his reflections. He was certain of what he had to do. In the meantime he would ask for God's help as he always did every Friday. When the Angelus bell tolled, he'd leave his counting house near the Standard in Cheapside and crawl on hands and knees to prostrate himself before the great rood screen in St Mary's. He had done the same at St Fulcher's, aware of the curse pressing close. He had much to say about 'Helen of hell', much to judge and much to condemn but what was the use? Kilverby picked up the quill pen, nibbling at its end again, as he always did. Helen would brook no opposition. She wanted this and she wanted that and, if he refused, she'd glare at him and turn for comfort and counsel to her so-called kinsman Adam Lestral. Kinsman! Were they really lovers? Was Alesia correct in her suspicions? Kilverby stopped nibbling at the rich plumage on the quill pen and put it down for the second time. He truly must leave here! His merchant days were over, his gold and silver salted away with goldsmiths in Cheapside and Poultry. Everything was ready. His will was drawn up, witnessed by no less a person than Sir John Cranston, Coroner of London – that portly, red-faced, gloriously bewhiskered old soldier would keep an eye on Alesia and her beloved husband Edmund. A good man, Kilverby mused about his son-in-law, as long as Edmund stayed away from the hawk lords at Westminster. Kilverby sipped at his claret. Times were certainly changing. Old King Edward had died in his dotage, alone, except for his mistress, Alice Perrers, who'd stayed long enough to strip the old King's corpse of anything which glittered. The King's son, the illustrious Black Prince, had already died of some loathsome, lingering pestilence contracted in Spain. Now a child ruled the kingdom.

'*Vae Regno cujus Rex est Puer*,' Kilverby whispered. 'Woe to the kingdom where the ruler is a child.'

Richard was a boy king; real power lay with his cunning uncle, the Regent, John of Gaunt. Nevertheless, even Gaunt, chief amongst men, was beset daily by the Commons, whilst behind them in the shadows clustered the hawk lords, greedy for any rich pickings.

Kilverby groaned and rose to ease the pain in his belly. He stamped his feet against the onset of a sudden coldness. He must leave all this! He stood listening to the sounds of his great mansion settling for the night. Crispin, his faithful steward and secretarius, would still be busy. Kilverby sighed. He truly wished Crispin could come with him on pilgrimage to Santiago, Rome and Jerusalem but that was not possible. Nevertheless, Crispin would be well looked after. Kilverby, on his clerk's behalf, had negotiated with Abbot Walter at St Fulcher-on-Thames. In the end Crispin would take care of everything, even tomorrow's journey to St Fulcher with that precious bloodstone, large as a duck's egg, the Passio Christi. Kilverby glanced at the small coffer where, for most of the time, he kept the bloodstone secure. He recalled the relic's remarkable history and singular powers; he absent-mindedly fingered the silver chain around his neck carrying the keys to the coffer. The Passio Christi had been with him for years. Kilverby wondered guiltily about its former owner, the Abbey of St Calliste outside Poitiers in France. Sub-Prior Richer had constantly reminded him about all that; even today the Frenchman had asked to see the bloodstone when he visited with Prior Alexander. Kilverby really needed no such reminder. He had done wrong. He fully understood the curses which the bloodstone could bring down on those who abused it. He had distanced himself from the Wyvern Company: Wenlock, Mahant and the rest. One of them, William Chalk, had confessed during his final illness to be living proof of the warnings contained in the '*Liber Passionis Christi* – The Book of the Passion of Christ'. He was so glad not to be taking the bloodstone to St Fulcher's on the morrow. Crispin, faithful as ever, had promised to do that. And why not? Crispin himself hoped to benefit from the curative properties of the sacred bloodstone, especially during this holy season. True, he would not go tomorrow, but once he began his pilgrimage Kilverby intended to leave the precious relic with the Benedictines. That would satisfy his conscience.

The merchant rose and moved across the chamber. He stared down at the wooden polished coffer with its three locks singularly crafted to hold the sacred ruby. He also glimpsed the silver chased dish of sweetmeats the Benedictines had brought him as a gift. Kilverby pulled back the linen cloth. He picked one up and bit half of it, relishing the rich cream and marzipan. He put the other half down and returned to his desk, his mind teeming like a box of ants. He grasped the quill pen and gnawed at its end again before weighing this in his right hand. He peered at the ink stains on his fingers, rose, crossed to the lavarium and dipped his hands in the still-warm rose water. Kilverby groaned again at the pain in his belly. The icy constriction in his legs intensified. Something was wrong! Kilverby glanced swiftly at the locked and bolted door and staggered back to his stout chancery chair, clutching his stomach as he lowered himself into it. The pain was now intense. He forgot about everything, even his beloved Alesia. He was ill, tormented by the assault in his belly, that creeping coldness seeping through his legs. Kilverby's head snapped back, mouth open in a silent scream, eyes popping as his death engulfed him.

On that same night, the eve of the Feast of St Damasus Pope, the year of our Lord 1380, Gilbert Hanep, former master bowman in the Wyvern Company, also rose to meet his own violent death. As usual Hanep had found sleep impossible in his narrow chamber in the main guest house at the Abbey of St Fulcher-on-Thames. Hanep had fallen asleep for a while but his soul had been tormented by demons. He had woken from a dream that the cold air around him was black with devils waiting to drag him to hell. For a while Hanep sat on the edge of his cot bed and stared at the fiery red glow of the charcoal in the small braziers now turning into a sea of white, feathery ash. Hanep quietly cursed mumbling monks like Sub-Prior Richer and his influence over the likes of poor old William Chalk. Hanep shivered. He swiftly donned his war cloak emblazoned with a striking red Wyvern. The heraldic device brought memories rushing back like water gushing from a spilt cask. The past returned. Memories of the hard-fought battles in France, the bitter fights. The white fog of chalk and lime surging up in clouds from crudely whitewashed shields. The strident screech of sword, club, dagger and mace. Arrows like angry black hornets streaking the blue sky in their thousands. The grating of steel against bone. The constant spray of hot, fresh blood. The shriek of armour against armour, the hideous yells, horrid cries and blasphemous curses of men locked in deadly combat. Banners all gaudily decorated moving through the fog of battle . . .

Such memories would never go away, whilst lodging in this abbey did not help the soul. Sub-Prior Richer said the Wyvern Company and all who supported them would go to eternal damnation. They'd be herded into a rough, murky prison full of stench, filth, dark shadows and verminous demons. They'd be punished along with all the other tribes of sinners through an eternity of torture. They'd be imprisoned in dungeons of fire, eating the harsh crust of hell and drinking the cup of everlasting bitterness. Hanep took a deep breath. But what did that frosty-faced, self-styled man of God know? Hanep rose to his feet and filled a pewter goblet from the flagon. He moved over to one of the braziers, plucked out the narrow white-hot poker and pushed its tip into the wine until, in the light of the lantern horn, he saw it bubble. Hanep put the poker back and, grasping the goblet in his two hands, drank greedily. Once satisfied, he thrust his feet into the rough thick-soled sandals, walked across, pulled back the shutters and stared out through the lancet window at the gathering gloom. Memories were like a ravenous host just waiting to gain entry. Hanep, a veteran of many bloody combats, was used to them. He would wake suddenly in this grey-stoned, hollow-sounding abbey and the days of blood flooded back though, after a while, they would turn sweet as other memories surfaced: the days of glory when he and his companions had swaggered along the roads of France taking what they wanted, be it a flagon of wine or some plump French wench to be enjoyed despite her squeals and warbling. Oh yes, sun-drenched days, or so it seemed, when flowers covered the world, the sky was always blue and the trees remained a cluster of thick green. They were heroes then, Hanep reflected bitterly. They had shattered the power of France, the gorgeous, thundering cavalcade of the Valois. Now it was different. The King at Westminster was a child. The armies of England had retreated, forced back into the enclave of Calais. The realm was fearful of the black-prowed French galleys who threatened the passage to Dover and roamed the

Narrow Seas, their crews making sudden landings along the south coast to pillage and burn. So much had changed! Here he was, he and the rest, given a corrody at this lonely, haunted abbey, living out their lives as Mahant had said, 'like stabled cattle, waiting for the slaughter'.

The fate of old William Chalk certainly proved that: his death had been long, lingering and painful. If it had happened in France, Chalk, the defrocked priest beyond all hope of physic, would have received a mercy cut from a razor-edged misericord dagger to put him beyond all pain. Instead they had to visit him in the infirmary day after day, week after week, month in month out. They had to listen to his lamentations about the past, the sins they'd committed and the reparation they should all make. Now, thank God, old William Chalk was gone, buried in the Strangers' Plot in the great sprawling abbey cemetery. Perhaps he should visit William's grave, go out and brave the cold and say a prayer, if that merited anything. He could not stay here. Hanep had to, as he often did, walk this abbey in the early hours when the monks were snoring in their dormitories before the first bell of the day roused them to sing matins. He'd be warm enough in his thick serge leggings and stockings. He moved to the door and smiled. He'd forgotten the oath, the great pledge following the mysterious attack on Wenlock. He must remember that's why his war belt now hung ready on a peg. He took this down carefully moving both sword and dagger in their intricately brocaded scabbards. Hanep circled his waist, pulling the belt tight and securing the buckle. He felt more comfortable, younger and stronger. Mahant was correct. The warrior path of cold steel and the sheer joy of battle, conflict and resolution, was everything.

Hanep picked up the shuttered lantern, opened the door and stepped out. The night was freezing cold in its blackness. Already a frost dusted the sills and carved faces of both saints and gargoyles. A deathly silence hung like some invisible pall pressing down, smothering all sound. Hanep walked along the narrow path which took him into the main cloister: a maze of stone, soaring pillars, sills and doorways fretted in the dog-tooth fashion. Cresset torches flared, their flames leaping in the stiff, freezing breeze. Holy men and demons glared ghostly down at him. The paving stones he walked were scrubbed and dusted with dry herbs which crackled beneath his sandals. Shadows darted. A spirit-thronged place, Hanep reflected. One hand on the hilt of his sword, Hanep went round the cloister garth, out under an archway following the path which skirted the great abbey church. Hanep paused before its yawning, cavernous porch. He stared up at the tympanum above the door, garishly lit by flaring torches. The darting flames brought to life the cluster of carvings depicting the damned and the saved, angels and hellish creatures all transfixed by the dominating figure of Christ in judgement. Hanep felt his conscience prick. How many years had passed since he had been shriven? Sat in the pew taking absolution from a priest? Chalk had urged him to reflect on that yet it was impossible to remember. Hanep again stared up at the Last of Days sculptured so graphically. He remembered the only words of scripture he'd ever learnt so many, many years ago in the dusty aisle of St Mary's Church at Leighton in Essex. He'd always, like some talisman, quoted the verses before battle: 'The Lord is my help,' Hanep whispered, 'whom should I fear? The Lord is the fortress of my life, before whom should I cower?' But now in this midnight darkness did he, did the others, believe in all that? Were not their souls weighed down by thick, rich, oozing layers of sin? The women he had taken, the deaths he had inflicted, the plunder seized, the drinking and cramming of his belly with the food and wine of others? The Wyvern Company had acquired a fearsome reputation as a deadly, hostile horde from the havens of hell. They had waged war with fire and sword, having no respect for anything under the sun.

Hanep ground his teeth. That was the problem. They were old lions like those in the royal menagerie at the Tower, caged and kept close. Of course there were distractions like Abbot Walter's comely niece who resided with her guardian in the abbot's luxurious guest house. Both women were a source of good gossip, as was the anchorite bricked up in his anker house in the abbey church. Rumour had it that he was a painter who became the Hangman of Rochester. According to whispers amongst the black garbed brothers of St Benedict, the anchorite had fled his grisly job after being plagued by the ghosts of some of his victims. Mind you, Hanep chewed the corner of his lip, it didn't stop the anchorite still acting as the abbot's hangman. Was the man really haunted? Was it true that the anchorite's dead wife had once begged for help from himself and others in the Wyvern Company, only to be refused? Some story about outlaws in the Weald of Kent, who were later captured and hanged from the battlements of Rochester keep? The anchorite had laid such an accusation against them. Wenlock said he vaguely remembered it, Hanep certainly didn't. Was the man madcap, his wits all fey? Indeed, Hanep felt a secret sympathy for that recluse; after all, didn't the dead visit him as well, greyish-white shapes with blood-filled eyes and gaping maws to plague Hanep's sleep? What could he do about them? Was it really too late to change? Wenlock said it was. They had discussed going on pilgrimage to Outremer and visiting the cave which served as a burial vault for Abraham, Isaac and Jacob, not to mention Adam and Eve. They had planned to see the cavern where the form of Aaron's bed could be traced, the pillar of salt which had once been Lot's wife, the house where Elijah had been born and the site of the thorn tree that had later been cut down to form the true cross. Hanep shivered. In truth they'd been more eager to feel the hot sun on their backs and sample the food, wine and other pleasures of Outremer. They certainly had to leave St Fulcher's, at least for a while. Hanep felt uncomfortable, particularly with that sub-prior, the young Frenchman, Richer. Did Richer know the truth about how the Wyvern Company had plundered St Calliste outside Poitiers and stolen its brilliant bloodstone, the Passio Christi? Hanep and his comrades had claimed it as their own. The Crown had decided differently, ordering the bloodstone to be held in trust by one of its principal bankers and goldsmiths, Sir Robert Kilverby, on the understanding that he would pay monies into the royal exchequer as a pension for Hanep and his companions. Was the Passio Christi the reason why Richer hated them so much? Was he really here to seize it back? But that would be futile, surely? The bloodstone was securely held by Kilverby, who brought it to the abbey every Easter as well as on the feast of St Damasus. In fact, Kilverby, or his emissary, was due to arrive here tomorrow. He should bring the bloodstone for the Wyvern Company to view, as it had been agreed by solemn indenture, but Kilverby, although he still visited the abbey, now kept his distance from them. Wenlock claimed that was due to Richer's influence. And yet, Hanep stamped his feet, Richer had proved very compassionate to old Chalk on his death bed. Had that old rogue confessed all his sins? Did Richer know the full truth? Mahant was certainly worried about that. Hanep stared up at the sky. Snow clouds were gathering. He heard a sound and whirled round.

'Who's there?' Hanep peered anxiously through the murk, fingers stroking the steel coiled hilt of his long, stabbing dagger. He must move on. The sacristan would soon appear with his retinue of acolytes, candles burning, lanterns swaying, keys jangling. Hanep hurried on. He reached the cemetery lychgate, lifted the latch and slipped through the musty entrance into sprawling God's Acre with its jumbled mounds, tumbled crosses and decaying tombstones. Here the silence was broken by the scurriers of the night. The hush-winged owl, rats scraping from beneath the stone-canopied tombs, as well as foxes foraging for any scraps amongst the thin layers of dirt which covered the dead. Hanep gazed around. Was this the thronging place of the ghostly dead, the stalking ground of the *Custos Mortuorum*, the Guardian of the Dead, the soul of the last person buried here? Hanep smiled grimly; that would be his boon companion, William Chalk. William, however, had been buried deep. He and Hanep had shared many a girl and a wassail-cup, and sung all the glee songs they knew, but that was in the past. Hanep put the lantern down and followed the pebbled path snaking around the crumbling monuments of the dead. He staggered and slipped over the occasional briar and trailing bramble. The breeze seemed to be stronger here, colder with a knife-edge cut. He pulled at his hood and tucked up the muffler of his cloak. He strained both eyes and ears. He had not forgotten that earlier sound, an alien one in the deserted silence of this place. Hanep, both sword and dagger now drawn, walked on. He passed the soaring cemetery cross with its stone figure of Christ in agony and continued on to

Chalk's grave, a freshly dug mound now glistening with hoar frost. The cross had slipped sideways. Hanep knelt, swiftly blessed himself, put down his weapons and made to straighten the cross. He heard a sound and whirled round, one hand going for the hilt of his sword – too late, too stupid! The hooded figure, black against the poor light, was already swinging back his great sword, a flash of shimmering light as it sliced deep into the side of Hanep's neck . . .

ONE

'Mummer: an actor wearing a mask!'

'For my sins, truly I know them,' Athelstan breathed as he plunged the rough rag back in to the bucket and splashed the herb-drenched water on to the last grey flagstone which lay before the door to his priest house.

'My sin is always before me,' Athelstan continued, 'against you and you alone have I sinned . . .' Once he'd finished washing the flagstone, Athelstan, Dominican friar and parish priest of St Erconwald's in Southwark, proudly gazed round on what he'd achieved on this the Feast of St Damasus twenty days before the great celebration of the Nativity. He'd cleaned the house thoroughly. He had scrubbed and polished every nook and cranny. The small bed loft was all clean and sweet-smelling, its linen sheets, bolsters and blankets had been changed, and not a pewter dish or copper pot had been missed by him. After that Athelstan had turned his attention to what he mockingly called his solar, the great flagstone kitchen with its whitewashed walls and rough-stone hearth. Everything had been cleaned, from the tongs and pokers in the hearth to the large oaken table which served as both his supper bench and chancery desk.

'What do you think, Bonaventure?' Still kneeling Athelstan joined his hands in mock prayer and gazed fondly at the great, one-eyed tom cat sprawling before the crackling hearth like the Grand Cham of Tartary on his gold-encrusted divan. The cat, the prowling scourge of the needle-thin alleyways round St Erconwald's, deigned to lift his head; he gazed sleepily at his strange master then flopped back as if the effort had proved all too much for him.

'I know what you are waiting for, my friend.' Athelstan scrambled to his feet. He emptied the pail of water, wrung out the cloth and walked back into the kitchen. He crouched before the hearth next to Bonaventure and stared hungrily at the blackened copper pot hanging by its chain above the darting flames. He closed his eyes and smelt the warm savouriness of the bubbling oatmeal, hot and sweet with the precious honey Athelstan had stirred in.

'We'll eat well, Bonaventure.' Athelstan stroked the cat's silky fur. 'But not yet – God waits.'

Athelstan stripped, shaved, washed then dressed quickly in woollen leggings, drawers and the hair shirt he always wore beneath the black and white robes of a Dominican friar. He buckled the straps of his stout sandals. Going over to a corner he took out the polished dish, a gift from a parishioner, which also served as his mirror. Athelstan stared hard at the face which gazed back at him: the close-cropped black hair, the rather long, serious face with its furrowed cheeks, the wrinkles round both mouth and eyes. Did the face portray the soul, he wondered, or was it just the eyes? In which case Athelstan reflected ruefully, God help him, his eyes were dark and deep set. He practised that hard stare he often used on some of his parishioners.

'Lord forgive me,' he prayed, 'I have to; otherwise they'd lead me an even merrier jig.'

The thought of his parishioners made Athelstan hurry around. He doused the few candles, banked the fire, gazed proudly around his 'new swept kingdom' and, grasping his psalter, left the priest house. He secured the door and began what he called his daily pilgrimage. He walked carefully; a hard frost shimmered on the path leading up to the dark mass of St Erconwald's. All lay quiet. He crossed to the stables, pushed open the half-door and smiled at Philomel, his mount, sprawling on the thick bed of hay Pike the ditcher had so carefully turned the night before. The old war horse lifted his head, neighed and snatched at the fodder net. Athelstan sketched a blessing in the ancient destrier's direction and continued on. He stopped by the newly refurbished gate to the cemetery, opened it and stepped into God's Acre. He quietly thanked the Lord for winter because in summer this was a favourite trysting place for his parishioners and others so much so, as Athelstan had wryly remarked to Sir John Cranston, on a midsummer's day more of the living lay there than the dead. Now it was murky, forbidding and frostbitten. Only a meagre light gleamed from the ancient death house where the keeper of the cemetery, the beggar Godbless, lived with his constant companion, Thaddeus the goat. Athelstan murmured a prayer of thanks for both of them. Young lovers lying down in the long grass of summer were not so troublesome as the warlocks, sorcerers and witches who plagued the cemeteries of London with their midnight rites to summon up the dark lords of the air. The ever-curious, garrulous Godbless, with his equally curious goat, would put any practitioner of such forbidden ceremonies to flight. Godbless, called so because of his constant use of that benediction, would talk them to death whilst the omnivorous Thaddeus would chew any grimoire of spells to shreds.

'Benedicite,' Athelstan called out, '*Pax et bonum.*'

'God bless you too, Father,' came the swift reply.

Athelstan passed on up to the church. He fumbled with the key ring, opened the battered corpse door and stepped inside. He wrinkled his nose: despite his best efforts to scrub the floor, the mildewed air of the old church caught his nose and mouth. Athelstan peered through the gloom; the charcoal braziers still glowed like welcome beacons fending off the cold mustiness. Athelstan took out a tinder from the pouch on his cord. He lit the candles paid for by the Brotherhood of Rood Light, a wealthy group of local merchants who used St Erconwald's as their guild chapel. In return they generously supplied the church with tallow and beeswax tapers. Athelstan lit those in front of the Lady chapel as well as the candles before the statue of St Erconwald. He gazed up at the severe face of the Saxon bishop of London who'd founded the first church here. Huddle the painter had elegantly regilded the statue, delicately picking out the scarlets and whites of the bishop's vestments. Athelstan, ignoring the scurry of mice in the far corner, lit some of the sconce torches. The friar noticed the tendrils of mist seeping under the corpse door as if they were pursuing him and shivered.

'God bring us spring soon,' he murmured, 'for swarms of bees and beetles bringing in the soft music of the world, for heavy bowls of hazelnuts, sweet apples, plums and whortleberries.' Athelstan turned to go up into the sanctuary when he glimpsed Huddle's new painting on the far wall above the leper squint. Athelstan wandered across. Huddle had been busy sketching out in charcoal the Seven Deadly Sins. Athelstan thought the painter would begin with 'Lust', which all the parish council wanted. Instead Huddle, who gambled and was desperate for income, had decided on 'Avarice'. The painting was graphic enough, bold and vigorous, an eye-catching vision of startling colours and images. A goldsmith of Cheapside was Huddle's incarnation of the deadly sin: a shrivelled up old man, bow-legged and palsy stricken, with a head as bald as a pigeon's egg, a beard as bushy as a tangle of brier, skimpy loose cheeks, goggling eyes either side of a nose pointed and as sharp as a hook. The goldsmith was being attacked by two shaggy demons that were dragging him away from his money bags. One of these hellish creatures, all hoofed and horned, had wrapped his goatskin legs around the banker and forced his bald head down so as to clamp his wolf fangs into the back of his victim's exposed neck. The other demon was clawing the goldsmith's belly, ripping it open to spill out the man's black and red innards. Gossips, and that was virtually everyone in the parish, claimed Avarice was no less a person than Sir Robert Kilverby, city goldsmith, former alderman and an acquaintance of no less a person than Sir John Cranston, the King's coroner in London.

'Sweet Lord, I hope not,' Athelstan murmured, 'or Cranston will have Huddle's head. I just wish our painter would paint and leave the cogged dice alone.'

Athelstan plucked at his waist cord and fingered the three knots symbolizing his vows of poverty, chastity and obedience. Cranston could be genial but, like all law officers in London, watchful and wary of any dissent or mockery of authority. Winter was proving very harsh. The price of bread and other purveyance remained high. Defeat abroad and piracy in the Narrow Seas made matters worse, especially in London where The Upright Men, leaders of the Great Community of the Realm, were plotting bloody revolt to turn the world upside down. Huddle should be careful of whom he mocked. Athelstan went back to the corpse door and picked up his psalter from the stool near the collection of leaning poles. He moved under the rood screen, stood at the bottom of the sanctuary steps and stared up at the Pyx dangling on its chain, shimmering in the glow of the red sanctuary lamp hanging close by. Athelstan genuflected then busied himself, taking out the palliasse from the small alcove where any sanctuary man in flight from the law could settle. Thankfully there was no one. Athelstan unrolled the palliasse at the bottom of the steps just outside the rood screen. He prostrated himself on this, intoned psalm fifty then confessed his sins, a litany of weaknesses: his failure to love, his irritation with Watkin the dung collector, his short temper with Ursula the Pig-woman and her godforsaken sow which followed her everywhere, including into Athelstan's vegetable patch. The friar caught his temper and smiled. If he was not careful he would be sinning again, yet behind all these petty offences gathered greater shadows: the death of his beloved brother, Francis-Stephen, and his secret love for the widow woman Benedicta, though she was not his only distraction from matters spiritual. Even more so was Athelstan's fascination for hunting down killers, assassins and murderers who believed they could snuff out another's life as easily as they might a taper, wipe their lips and, like Pilate, wash their hands of any blood and guilt. Athelstan let his mind drift deeper into the gathering darkness to confront more threatening shapes which questioned his very vocation and basic beliefs.

'So much evil, Lord.' He prayed. 'So deep the wickedness. The rich wax stronger and more powerful whilst the poor, like naked earth worms, are crushed and stamped even deeper into the mud. Why, Lord?'

The friar recalled the words of his own confessor, the venerable Magister Ailred at Blackfriars, the principal Dominican house in London. 'Evil is not a problem, Athelstan,' Ailred had advised. 'If it was a problem, like those we confront in philosophy or logic, it could be resolved. No, Athelstan, evil is a great mystery which can only be confronted. Christ did that during his passion, singing his own hymn of love as he journeyed into the very heart of evil to confront it. He became one of us to experience that same mystery. Look at the crib at Christmas, the Holy Rood on Good Friday . . .' Athelstan sighed, crossed himself and rose to his feet. He wandered down to the main door and stared at the crude but vivid crib set up by Tab the Tinker, Crispin the Carpenter and others. Athelstan smiled. He had imitated the Franciscan idea of the Bethlehem stable and the chanting of the 'O Antiphons' instead of the planned mystery play about the Nativity. He'd had a bellyful of that after Watkin, relegated to being one of the shepherds, had furiously assaulted two of the Wise Men. Athelstan sighed noisily and shook his head in admiration of the large gold star Huddle and Crispin had nailed above the crib. He recalled his own secret passion. On a clear night, he'd be up on the church tower observing the stars, but the dire weather froze even birds on the wing whilst threatening clouds blotted out heaven's gems.

Athelstan doused some of the torches and returned to lie before the rood screen. He intended to recite a psalm but, as usual, he drifted into sleep until roused by a hammering on the locked main door. He struggled awake, pulled himself up, quickly rolled up the palliasse and returned it to the recess. He glanced up at one of the windows and groaned as he noticed the grey dawn light. He had slept too long! The door rattled again. Athelstan hurried down, turned the great key, slipped back the bolts and swung it open. Benedicta, hooded and muffled, and Crim the altar boy almost threw themselves into the church.

'Sorry, Father, sorry, Father,' the boy yelped, jumping up and down. 'It was so cold, we thought we'd die. We wondered what had happened . . .'

Athelstan peered behind them at the freezing mist boiling over the great cobbled expanse in front of the church. Night was over and a chilly day had dawned.

'Day has come,' Athelstan murmured, 'and so we must continue our journey.'

'Father?'

Athelstan smiled over his shoulder at Benedicta. She looked truly beautiful: a simple grey wimple under a cowl framed her olive-skinned face. Benedicta's lustrous dark eyes, full of life, reminded Athelstan of the frescoes celebrating beauty in the great cathedrals of northern Italy, but now was not the time for reflection on such matters.

'Never was and never should be,' Athelstan murmured to himself.

'What?' Crim was still jumping up and down, as agitated as a box of frogs.

'It's never the time for certain things,' Athelstan smiled. 'So come.'

There was, in fact, little time for further conversation or greeting. All three hastened under the rood screen, up the sanctuary steps and into the whitewashed sacristy to the left of the high altar. Athelstan unlocked the vestment chest and the coffer holding the sacred vessels, cloths and bread and wine. Candles were brought out and lit. The sanctuary glowed into light. Manyer the bell clerk, all cowled and visored against the cold, hurried in to sound the bell for the Jesus Mass. The clanging echoed out. At short while later Athelstan's parishioners, bustling and chattering, coughing and spluttering, filed into the church: Watkin the dung collector; Pike the ditcher with his narrow-eyed wife Imelda constantly on the search for insult; Godbless accompanied by his goat; Ranulf the rat catcher who always brought his two prize ferrets, Ferox and Audax; and Ursula and her sow, the great pig's flanks and ears all flapping. The sight of so much luscious pork on the hoof, and so vulnerable, made people pause, stare and wet their lips. Basil the blacksmith always sat next to the sow so, as he put it, he could savour its warmth, though many noticed how the blacksmith's fingers never wandered far from the stabbing dagger in his belt. Moleskin the boatman came along with other members of his coven: Merrylegs the pie-maker, Joscelyn the one-armed former pirate and keeper of 'The Piebald' tavern, Mauger the hangman and Pernel the mad Fleming woman who, in anticipation of Christ's nativity, had dyed her wild tangle of hair red and green.

'Green for the eternal Christ,' she had screeched down the nave. 'Red for his blood.'

They all congregated within the rood screen. Some squatted on the floor; others used the leaning poles. Athelstan, dressed in the purple and gold vestments of Advent, left the sacristy, approached the high altar and made the sign of the cross.

'I will go unto the altar of God,' he intoned, and so the Mass began sweeping towards its climax, the consecration and elevation of Christ's body and blood under the appearance of bread and wine. The singing bread was distributed, the *osculum pacis*, the kiss of peace, exchanged, the Eucharist given. Athelstan delivered the final blessing.

'The Mass is finished,' he declared. 'Go in peace, but not just yet.'

Athelstan ushered his parishioners out into the nave. He dramatically pointed to the small, self-standing cubicle of oak which stood near the small Galilee porch on the far side of the church.

'Remember,' he declared, 'on one side is a pew for the penitent. On the other, separated by a partition with that lattice grille in the centre, is the seat for the priest.' He paused. 'Crispin and Tab built that; it's our new shriving pew. We must use it. We must all go to confession.' He smiled at the red, chapped faces of his parishioners, mittened fingers scratching their hair or tugging at ragged cloaks against the cold. 'I shall be hearing confessions every evening during the last week of Advent to shrive you of your sins.' His smile widened. 'I hope to journey to Blackfriars to have my own pardoned.'

'Do you sin?' Watkin shouted. 'You, a friar?'

'Friars especially,' Athelstan retorted, 'then monks and even coroners. By the way, Huddle, I must have a chat with you about your most recent painting. Now,' Athelstan hurried on, 'as you know there'll be no Nativity play. You also know the reason.'

He glimpsed Imelda dig Pike viciously in the ribs.

'I will not rehearse the sorry reasons why. We took a vote and decided to form our own choir. Now, I have translated the "O Antiphons".' Athelstan gestured at the bell clerk, who officiously began to distribute the stained, dog-eared but precious scraps of parchment. 'I know some of you cannot read.'

'All of us!' Tab joked.

'Perhaps.' Athelstan clasped his hands. 'However, we've been through the words, we have learnt them. Now let us arrange ourselves in the proper voices.'

The usual confusion ensued but at last Athelstan had his
choir ready. The gravel-hard, deep voices of Watkin, Pike
and Ranulf at the back, the clear, lucid singers of Benedicta,
Crim and Pernel at the front with the others in between. Once
he had silence the front line, under Athelstan's direction,
began:

'Alleluia, Oh Root of Jesse thrusting up, a sign to all the
nations.'

The line of singers behind repeated it, and so on. Athelstan
caught Benedicta's eyes and smiled in delight.

'Wonderful,' he whispered as he directed them with his
hands. These poor but grace-enriched souls sang so strong, so
passionately, with all their hearts the great hymn to the Divine
Child. Athelstan felt the tears prick his eyes. The antiphons
continued.

'Oh, Morning Star . . . Oh, Key of David . . .'

When they had finished, Athelstan shook his head in
wonderment.

'All I can do.' He opened the wallet on his cord and took
out a silver coin, a gift from Cranston. He twirled this between
his fingers. 'The labourer, or rather in this case,' he proclaimed,
'the singers, deserve their wages. Merrylegs, your pies are
baked fresh and piping hot . . .?'

Athelstan's parishioners needed no further encouragement.
The coin was snatched and Athelstan had never seen his church
empty so swiftly.

'Was it so good, Father?'

'Benedicta, even the angels of God must have wept.'
Athelstan walked over and grasped her hands, warm in their
black woollen mittens. 'Benedicta, I am starving. Would you
please look after the church and put the vessels back in the
fosser?'

With Benedicta's assurances ringing in his ears, Athelstan
left by the corpse door. Bracing himself against the cold, the
friar walked back up the lane to the priest house. He opened
the door and stared at the huge figure seated on the stool, horn
spoon in one hand, crouched over a steaming bowl of oatmeal.
Beside Athelstan's guest, watching every mouthful disappear,
was Bonaventure, waiting so when Sir John Cranston, Lord

High Coroner of London, finished the bowl he could lick it really clean.

'Judas,' Athelstan whispered. 'Cat, your name is Judas.' He raised his voice. 'My Lord Coroner, what is the penalty for stealing a poor friar's breakfast?'

'Murder.' Cranston, wrapped in a Lincoln green war cloak, a brocaded beaver hat of the same colour on his head, turned, his rubicund, white be-whiskered face wreathed in a smile. 'Murder, my little friar! I have left enough for you then we must go. The sons and daughters of Cain await us.'

'The eyes of the dark robe of night. The shadow lands which stretch past evensong, these are all part of my story . . .' The enterprising taleteller, perched on an overturned barrel at the end of the lane leading on to the thoroughfare down to London Bridge caught Athelstan's attention. The friar plucked at Cranston's arm and paused to catch the dramatic words and colourful images which he hoped to use in a future sermon.

'There,' the teller of tales bawled, 'the larvae of human souls wander whispering like bats twittering in a cave, for this truly is the realm of the screech owl . . .'

'Come on, Friar.' Cranston, face almost hidden behind his muffler, pointed to where his principal bailiff Flaxwith with his hideous-looking mastiff Samson stood waiting ready to clear a way before the coroner. 'Come on,' Cranston repeated, 'I've got a better tale to tell you.'

Athelstan dug into his wallet, dropped a penny into the storyteller's box and, cowl pulled well over his head, joined Cranston to battle through the surging crowd. Despite a cutting breeze from the river and the stench of uncleared refuse on the slippery paths, London's citizens had flocked out hacking and sneezing in the freezing air, oblivious to the leaden, brooding clouds which threatened more snow. They hurried down to the tawdry markets around the bridge to gawp, purchase or just gossip. The more vigorous also thronged around the stocks close to the river to fling refuse at Guillaume Lederer, who sat imprisoned for calling Bertram Mitford 'a covetous snot, a vagabond, a wagwallet' not to mention, 'a side-tailed knave'. Guillaume's name and crime were proclaimed on a placard around his neck, which also invited passing citizens to hurl abuse as well as anything else they could lay their hands on. Further down a more serious business was drawing to an end: the hanging of two women, Dulcea and her companion Katerina, who'd feloniously murdered Alice Willard of Rotherhithe – strangled her, no less, during a pilgrimage to Canterbury. The crowds swirled around the execution cart which abruptly pulled away just as Athelstan and Cranston passed. Both women were left to dance in the air as they slowly strangled on the hempen noose dangling down from the sooty, four-branched scaffold.

Death, of course, especially executions, was good for business and Athelstan was constantly distracted by the charlatans who always emerged on such occasions. One conjurer who, despite it being bleak midwinter, loudly boasted that the small pouch in his right hand contained three bumble bees which he could summon out, one by one each by their own name, as given to him by an angel he'd met on the road outside Havering-atte-Bowe. Other cozeners and conjurers had given up their tricks to plunder the corpses of the hanged and sell their ill-gotten items for a profit. A few of these knights of the dark just hoped the macabre scenes would influence the minds of those they hoped to cheat. Outside the Chapel of St Mary Overy a journeyman, his black capuchon, cotehardie and chausses embroidered with gold stars and silver moons, proclaimed how he, John Crok of Tedworth, had in the scarlet-blue fosser beside him a man's head in a book. He proclaimed how the head was that of a Saracen. How he had bought it in Toledo in order to enclose a certain spirit which could answer questions about the future. Apparently the said spirit had not informed him about the approach of the coroner. One look at the burly Flaxwith and the equally fearsome Samson sent John Crok of Tedworth, his precious fosser clutched under one arm, fleeing through the crowds. Cranston just grunted noisily and muttered about some other time.

They passed under the gatehouse to the bridge, its crenellations ornamented with long poles bearing the severed heads of executed traitors, pirates and other criminals. On the steps leading up to the gatehouse sat the diminutive Robert Burdon, the keeper surrounded by his brood of children. Burdon was preparing another head, all pickled and tarred, to decorate the end of a pole. He glimpsed Cranston and Athelstan, shouted a greeting and continued with his macabre task of combing the long hair on the severed head.

Athelstan was now finding it difficult to keep up with Cranston's stride. He still wasn't sure where they were going or what they were doing. Cranston had told him little except that his wife, the diminutive Lady Maude, and their two sons the poppets were all 'in fine fettle'. Then he added something, just as they left the priest house, about the mysterious death of Kilverby the Cheapside merchant as well as the gruesome slaying of one Gilbert Hanep at the great Benedictine Abbey of St Fulcher-on-Thames. The coroner also mentioned John of Gaunt, a precious bloodstone called the 'Passio Christi – the Passion of Christ' and that was it. Athelstan was curious for more but decided he would have to wait, especially here on London Bridge with its crowded shops, booths and stalls. The houses packed on either side soared up against the grey sky, forcing them and others to push up the broad narrow lane between, already packed with carts rattling on iron-bound wheels, braying sumpter ponies and apprentices bawling, 'What do ye lack, what do ye lack?' The sheer crush, the rancid stench of unwashed bodies, the clatter of waterwheels and the pounding of the angry river against the starlings of the bridge were a stark contrast to the silence Athelstan was accustomed to. He felt slightly dizzy as if he'd not eaten, even though he had. Cranston, thankfully, had not devoured all the oatmeal. Athelstan crossed himself and murmured the 'Veni Creator Spiritus'. He certainly needed God's help. He was about to enter the meadows of murder, creep along the twisted alleyways along which padded the silent, soft-footed assassin. The age old duel was about to begin; as always, it would be 'lutte à l'outrance, usque ad mortem – a fight to the death'. Would it be his? Athelstan wondered. Would he draw too close, make a mistake?

Athelstan touched Cranston's arm for comfort; the coroner pressed his hand reassuringly and they left the bridge, entering the wealthy part of the city. The streets, paths and alleyways

here were packed with fatter, fuller bodies encased in gaily
caparisoned houppelandes, capuchons, cloaks, poltocks and
tabards. Merchants, shimmering in their jewellery pompously
paraded, accompanied by wives bedecked in gorgeous clothes
and elaborately decorated headdresses. Knights in half-armour
on plump, powerful destriers trotted by. Lawyers, resplendent
in red silks, hastened down to the '*Si Quis*' door at St Paul's.
The stalls and booths were open and business was brisk.
Merchants and traders offered silver tasselled dorsers and thick
woollen cushions for benches. Priests and monks, armed with
cross and thuribles, processed to this ritual or that. The air
was rich with the many smells from the public bakehouse as
well as the fragrance of the vegetable stalls stacked high with
onions, leeks, cabbages and garlic. Next to these the fleshers'
booths offered suckling pigs and capons freshly slaughtered
and drained of blood. Pilgrims to the shrine of Becket's parents
rubbed shoulders with those fingering pardon beads as the
Fraternity of the Salve Regina made their way down to one
of the city churches.

Squalor and brutality also made themselves felt. Beggars,
covered in sores and garbed in rags, clustered at the mouth
of alleyways and the spindle-thin runnels which cut between
the mansions and shops. Outside the churches the poor
swarmed, desperate for the Marymeat and Marybread given
out by the parish beadles in honour of the Virgin. Fripperers
pushed their handcarts full of old clothes, ever quick to escape
the sharp eyes of the market bailiffs. A clerk, who'd begged
after hiding his tonsure with cattle dung, was being fastened
in the stocks, next to him a woman who'd stolen a baby so
she could plead for alms. The noise, bustle, smell and colour
deafened the ear and blurred the mind. The forest of steepled
churches continuously clanged, their bells marking the hour
for Mass or another recitation of the divine office. Smoke,
fumes and smells from smithies, cook shops, tanneries, fullers,
taverns and alehouses mingled and merged. Dung carts
crashed by, full of ordure collected from the streets.
Night-walkers, faces the colour of box-wood, were being
marched, manacled together, to stand in the cage on the Tun
in Cheapside. Children, dogs and cats raced through gaps in

the crowds, spreading their own noise and confusion and drowning the shouts of tinkers and traders.

Athelstan, who'd taken to fingering his Ave beads, sighed with relief when Flaxwith, Samson trotting behind him, abruptly turned into Rosenip Lane, leaning towards the great mansions of Cheapside. Each of these stood behind its own towering curtain wall, their rims protected by shards of pottery and broken glass. The noise, stench and clatter died away. They stopped before one mansion. A porter let them through the smartly painted black gates and into the broad gardens where small square plots of herbs, shrubs and plants lay dormant in the severe grip of winter. Athelstan gazed around. There were clumps of apple and other fruit trees, their branches stark black whilst the large stew pond was nothing more than a thick sheet of ice. Athelstan hurried to keep up with Cranston as he strode along the white-pebbled path leading towards an enclosed porch built around the main door.

A grey-haired, grey-faced, grey-eyed servant, who introduced himself as Crispin, Sir Robert Kilverby's secretarius or clerk, ushered them in. Athelstan had been struck by the gorgeous wealth of this red-brick mansion with its blue slated roof, glass-filled windows and soaring chimney stacks. The interior was no different. Athelstan and Cranston walked across tiled floors of black and white lozenges. Drapes and tapestries decorated the pink-washed plaster above gleaming wooden panelling. A gorgeous riot of colours: emeralds, deep blues, argents, purples and gleaming reds pleased the eye. Beeswax tapers glowed on spigots and candelabra, shimmering in the sheen of oaken sideboards boasting gold and silver gilt cups, mazers, dishes and goblets. Thick turkey cloths covered some floors whilst heraldic devices decorated the walls of the broad staircase they climbed. The air was fragrant with the smell of scented woodsmoke as well as the perfumes from small heated herb pots pushed into corners or on sills, a pleasing mixture of black poplar, green grape and elder oil. Nevertheless, Athelstan detected a tension, a watching silence beneath all this opulence.

Crispin eventually ushered them both into the magnificent solar, assuring Sir John that Master Flaxwith would be made most comfortable in the kitchen below. The group of people seated on chairs, stools and settles before the roaring fire rose to greet them. Lady Helen, Kilverby's widow, was dressed in a sumptuously green and gold gown with a white lace headdress. Beautiful but as hard as flint, Athelstan thought, with a temper sharper than the panther's tooth. Adam Lestral, whom Lady Helen introduced as 'her kinsman', was pasty-faced with shifting eyes and a weak mouth, his long black hair sleek with nard. A man of dark design, Athelstan considered, full of arrogance, kinsman Adam dismissed both Cranston and the friar with a look of flickering contempt. Alesia, Kilverby's daughter, was fair-headed with crystal-grey eyes and cherry lips. She kept smoothing down the gem-encrusted stomacher of her long, tawny gown whilst glancing across at her imperious stepmother with a venom Athelstan considered to be past all understanding. The introductions were finished. Mulled spice wine and wafer thin doucettes were offered and taken. Cranston emptied his small silver dish and downed his wine in noisy gulps whilst he stood with his back to the fire, stamping his feet. Athelstan sipped his wine partly to hide his smile. Cranston, as ever, was acting the bluff, hearty old soldier as he offered his condolences to the family. The coroner refused to sit down and gestured at Athelstan to undo the leather satchel containing his writing tray.

'My Lady,' Cranston began, 'your husband's corpse?'

'Left in the chancery chamber,' Alesia replied before her stepmother could, 'on the floor. I thought it was best.' She motioned at Crispin. 'My father's secretarius, Crispin, found him.'

'Found him?' Cranston barked. 'When?'

'Lamp lighting time,' Crispin replied sonorously. 'Just before dawn, I knocked . . .'

'Let us see.' Cranston interrupted harshly, all bonhomie draining from his face. He pointed at Crispin who shrugged and led them out of the solar, along a gleaming, wood-panelled passageway and up a short flight of stairs.

'My father's chancery or counting house,' Alesia called from behind them.

Athelstan turned and stared at the group from the solar.

Alesia, Helen, Adam and Crispin. He sensed the rancid hatred and resentment curdling in this family. Even though Sir Robert lay dead they were all determined on their rights, certainly Mistress Alesia and Lady Helen were openly competing over who exercised authority now.

'We'll need help.' Cranston stepped back. The heavy oaken door had been snapped off its hinges, causing severe damage to the surrounding lintel. It now blocked the entrance to the chancery.

'It had to be done,' Lady Helen declared. She pointed back down the gallery where a group of servants clustered. 'My husband would not answer. The door was both locked and bolted from the inside. It had to be forced.'

'I had it placed back,' Alesia added sharply, 'to seal the chamber. My father, Sir John, did not die. He was murdered.'

'Nonsense,' Lady Helen whispered, 'who would . . .'

Athelstan came back down the steps. 'Whatever is the cause, that is why we are here.'

Athelstan and Cranston waited until the servants moved the door. They then told the household to wait outside and walked into the chamber. Athelstan stared round that comfortable, luxurious room. He crossed himself then knelt and removed the sheet over the corpse lying on its makeshift bed of turkey rugs. Kilverby, an old man with scrawny white hair, had certainly died in agony: eyes popping, throat constricted, his partly opened lips had turned faintly blueish. The skin of his face was slightly liverish, the flesh swiftly hardening.

'Has he been shriven?' Athelstan called.

'No, Father,' Alesia retorted falteringly.

'Or a physician called?' Cranston added.

'Yes.' Lady Helen came up into the doorway and stopped at Athelstan's sign to remain outside.

'Master Theobald the physician, but he has been detained.'

Athelstan fished inside his leather satchel, took out his stole, put it round his neck then brought out the small phial of holy oils. Lady Helen walked away whilst Athelstan swiftly murmured the '*Absolvo te*' into the dead man's ear. Afterwards he anointed the corpse on the brow, eyes, nose, mouth, hands and feet as he intoned the funeral prayer: 'Go forth Christian

soul . . .' Once completed Athelstan undid the man's clothing.
Pulling up the quilted jerkin, cambric chemise and linen
undershirt, Athelstan felt the belly, hard like a ball of old
string. He also noticed the blueish-red stains on the stomach
and lower chest.

'Poison?' Cranston, who'd been wandering the chamber,
came back to stand over him.

'I think so, Sir John, of the garden variety.' Athelstan took
off his stole and put the items back in his satchel.

'Hemlock, henbane, belladonna are the most powerful
potions and, at the same time, the easiest to disguise.'

'Well, it's not in the wine.' Cranston brought across both
the half-filled flagon and the loving cup, still quite full.

Athelstan sniffed at these. 'No trace, no odour,' he murmured.
He knelt back down and smelt the dead man's mouth. He
caught a highly bitter, rather sour tang.

'Any food?' He glanced up.

'Only these.' Cranston brought across the small silver dish
of sweetmeats. He pulled back the linen covering. 'One is half
eaten.'

Athelstan picked this up and examined it. 'Nothing but
sweetness. I wonder?' He stared down at the corpse. 'Was it
really poison or just a seizure?' He crouched and swiftly went
through Kilverby's pockets and belt purse but found nothing
untoward. He rose and went round that chamber, a jewel of a
chancery with its broad oaken desk, side tables, high-backed
quilted chair and stools. Shelves fastened against the walls
alongside cunningly crafted pigeon-hole boxes were used to
store manuscripts and rolls of vellum. Fossers, chests and
coffers stood neatly stacked. Cranston seemed more concerned
with these, trying lids and locks. Athelstan crouched before
the hearth. The fire was nothing more than white ash but the
chafing dishes and small heating pans, perforated to emit spiced
smoke, were still warm. Wrinkling his nose, Athelstan
uncovered the chamber pot kept in the corner; it contained
nothing but urine, no trace that Sir Robert had vomited or
been caught by some stomach seizure. Athelstan put this back,
washed his hands at the small lavarium and sat down on the
chancery chair. The desk in front of him was littered with

blank scraps of vellum. The writing tray, a pallet of exquisitely carved silver, contained three luxuriously plumed quill pens, all used. Nearby ranged pots of red, green and black inks, pumice stones, a parchment knife, a sander and scraps of sealing wax.

'Sir John?' Lady Helen, eager to exert her authority, reappeared in the doorway.

'Not yet, my Lady.' Cranston pointed at the sheeted corpse. 'Though your husband's corpse can be taken away, perhaps to your own bed chamber?'

A short while later Crispin and a few servants entered. Cranston supervised the removal of the corpse whilst Athelstan studied the tapestry hanging above the wainscoting. A vision of hell rich with gory scenes of the avaricious swallowing fiery coins, vomiting them up, then being forced to re-devour them under the supervision of a wrathful goblin. A synod of demons watched this torture. They all sat in council around Hell's dread Emperor enthroned under a purple-black awning. On either side of him clustered night-hags and hell-hounds.

'Wait!' the coroner ordered. 'Don't move the corpse yet.'

Athelstan broke from his reverie.

'Lady Helen, Mistress Alesia?' Cranston called.

Both women, Adam Lestral slipping in behind, entered the chamber.

'My ladies,' Cranston made a bow, 'once again, my condolences. However, His Grace the Regent is not only concerned about the mysterious death of Sir Robert but the safety and security of the Passio Christi.'

'He kept it here.' Alesia declared. 'Always in this chamber. The room is so secure. You've seen the door?' She gestured at the small oriel windows filled with painted glass. 'Those are too small for entry, and there are no secret entrances or closets.'

'And which coffer or casket holds the bloodstone?'

'This one.' Crispin crossed and picked up a small iron-bound casket with a barrel-shaped lid, three stout locks ranged along its lip.

'And the keys?'

'Three separate locks each with its own unique key,' Crispin muttered.

'And?' the coroner demanded.

'Only Sir Robert kept them.'

'I know where.' Athelstan smiled, recalling the jingling as he examined the dead man's belly. Athelstan crossed to the stretcher, each of its poles held by a servant. He ran a finger round the dead man's neck and pulled free the chain, undid the clasp and gently drew it away.

'That should be done . . .' Lady Helen gasped.

'This shall be done by the King's coroner,' Cranston snapped, and took the keys. After a great deal of trial and error, he inserted each into its appropriate lock. Whilst the coroner was busy, Athelstan studied Kilverby's household gathered in the doorway then gazed round that opulent chamber. He was certain of this: under the cope of night, murder had slipped like some silent fury into this locked chamber and snatched Kilverby's soul. The Apostate Angel hovered in that wealthy house, brushing them all with his wings. Murder had certainly unfurled its dark banners but how had this bloody mayhem been so cunningly executed? He half expected Cranston's cry of surprise, echoed by the others, as the coffer lid snapped back.

'Empty!' Cranston whirled round. 'The Passio Christi has gone!'

'Impossible!' Crispin blurted out. 'It was there yesterday, I and others were present when Sir Robert showed it to the two monks from St Fulcher's. We were there later in the solar when he put it back. I . . .'

Athelstan glanced at the others. Alesia stood, her mouth gaping. Helen, face in her hands, peered through her fingers. Kinsman Adam just stared at the open coffer and the empty dark blue samite which once held the bloodstone.

'His Grace will not be pleased,' Cranston muttered. 'He'll claim treason and vow that someone will hang for this.'

'We have not taken it,' Alesia cried.

'Taken what?' a voice shouted from the stairwell. Theobald de Troyes, the local physician, shoved his way in coughing and spluttering as he apologized for his tardiness. Unaware of the confusion in the chamber, Theobald pulled back the shroud and stared down at the cadaver.

'He's dead!' he bellowed. 'And that will cost you five shillings.' He turned to go but Cranston caught at his costly, ermine-trimmed robe and dragged him back.

'Master Theobald,' he said mockingly, 'good day!'

'And good day to you, Sir John. I . . .'

'I am not in the best of tempers,' Cranston bellowed. 'You . . .' he jabbed a finger at the terrified-looking Crispin, 'take the corpse to your mistress's bed chamber. You, master physician, examine it most carefully then come back here and you,' he gestured at the others, 'wait for me in the solar.'

Once they'd all gone, Cranston slumped down on the stool cradling the empty casket.

'Well, Friar?'

'This chamber was certainly locked and bolted.' Athelstan gestured round. 'No secret passageways, no window to be forced yet, some stealthy night-shape, some shadow-stalker gained entry. If our evidence holds true, this assassin poisoned Sir Robert, forced that casket, stole the Passio Christi, relocked the coffer and put the keys around Sir Robert's neck. Sir John, what exactly is this bloodstone?'

'In a while, in a while.' Cranston's blue eyes were now hard as glass. 'This surely is only the beginning of our troubles. Look, Friar,' the coroner put the coffer down between his feet. 'Sir Robert Kilverby is – was, a merchant with fingers and toes in every pie in the kitchen. He traded in everything, silk, spices and salt. His stalls and shops displayed dazzling armour, precious silver belts, pouches and scabbards. He brought in leather goods from Cordova, linens from Genoa, scarlet silks from Lucca and Florence. He was both banker and money changer. He gave generously to the old King and his sons so they could go on chevauchee across the Narrow Seas to plunder the French . . .'

'I know of Sir Robert,' Athelstan intervened. He picked up the quill pens and examined them carefully. He sniffed at all three plume tails and cautiously licked them with his tongue, running each of the quill pens through his fingers.

'Monk?'

'Friar, Sir John.' Athelstan smiled. 'I thought these might be tainted but they're not. Anyway, the Passio Christi?'

'The Passion of Christ.' Cranston glanced at the wine jug and smacked his lips.

'I wouldn't, Sir John.'

'True.' Cranston sighed. 'Well, the Passio Christi or the Passion of Christ is a precious bloodstone. When Christ died on the Cross, drops of his blood and sweat trickled down to miraculously form a precious ruby. Joseph of Arimathea took this sacred jewel and . . .' Cranston shrugged. 'Well, it passed from hand to hand, from one generation to the next until it ended up in the Abbey of St Calliste near Poitiers in France. Now, after the Black Prince's great victory there, a cart found near the abbey was plundered by one of those free companies who fought for the Crown, the Wyverns, a company both feared and fearful.'

'I've heard of such companies,' Athelstan intervened, chewing his lip. 'I've also seen their handiwork,' he added sadly, recalling his own youth.

'Ah, well.' Cranston continued in a rush, glancing at Athelstan out of the corner of his eye. He just prayed he was not stirring harsh, cruel memories in the little friar's soul. 'Now, a group of these Wyverns, master bowmen all, allegedly found the Passio Christi and claimed it as legitimate plunder of war . . .'

'But surely the abbey, the church objected?'

'Oh, our noble archers were very cunning. They maintained they'd found the bloodstone, along with other precious items, in a cart on a trackway near the abbey. You know the proclamations, Athelstan. Let's be blunt. You've served in France. Stealing from a church could earn you a hanging but something found on a cart in a country lane . . .? Of course the good monks, their abbot and the local bishop could sing whatever hymn they wanted but, in this case, however fictitious their story might be, those who find do keep. Now, the bloodstone couldn't be divided or kept by one of them whilst the Crown also demanded a share.'

'The Wyverns would not be too pleased with that? As you said, those who find, do keep?'

'Precisely. In the end an indenture was drawn up: the Passio Christi would be held by a responsible third party.'

'In this case Sir Robert Kilverby?'

'Correct. He would keep it safe and provide a pension, on behalf of the Crown, to the exchequer for each master bowman.'

'How many?'

'Oh, not the whole company – five or six I believe – only those who actually found the bloodstone.' Cranston sighed. 'If they survived military service, and they did, the former soldiers would also be provided with corrodies: comfortable lodgings at some great monastery. This occurred, in their case the Abbey of St Fulcher-on-Thames.'

'And when they all died?'

'Good question, Friar, for that may relate to our next mystery.' Cranston shook a gauntleted hand. 'All will be revealed in God's good time. To answer your specific question, once all the finders of the bloodstone were dead, the precious relic would revert to the Crown who'd pay Kilverby, or his estate, one tenth of its market value as recompense for his good services.'

'And why was it held here?'

'Everyone trusted Kilverby. He was too rich to be tempted. Anyway, I believe the indenture was modified slightly so that twice a year he would show the Passio Christi to both the exchequer at Westminster as well as all relicts of the Wyvern Company residing at St Fulcher.' Cranston squinted at Athelstan. 'I am sure it was twice a year, at Easter and the Feast of St Damasus.'

'Which is today.'

'True, true.' Cranston fidgeted on the stool.

'And now something has also happened at St Fulcher's.'

'Horrid murder!' Cranston retorted. 'One of the Wyverns, Gilbert Hanep, was found headless near the grave of an old comrade.'

'He was beheaded!'

'Clean and neat as you would cut a flower.'

'Why . . .?' Athelstan was interrupted by Physician Theobald storming into the chamber, in one hand a piece of bread in the other a cup of claret, which he downed in one gulp before glaring at Cranston.

'Poison!' he almost shouted. 'Definitely poison, very powerful, water hemlock perhaps. So, my Lord Coroner, I'm done.'

'Not yet.' Athelstan got to his feet. 'Good and learned physician, I want you to help us search this chamber for any trace of poison, be it smeared on a handle or anywhere else.' He pointed at the chamber pot. 'And you can re-examine that.' Athelstan tapped the silver dish of comfits on the desk as well as the wine jug and loving cup. 'You are to take these away and scrupulously search for any trace of poison.' Athelstan caught a flicker of annoyance in the physician's greedy eyes. 'You'll be paid. Now, my Lord Coroner, let us search.'

As they did so Athelstan asked Cranston to send for Flaxwith and to tell him about Kilverby and his family. Sir John, moving around the chamber, chattered about how he and the dead man were old acquaintances, though not quite friends. How he was one of the executors of Kilverby's will, adding that in the event of Lady Helen not giving him a child, the bulk of the dead merchant's wealth, including this fine mansion, would go to Sir Robert's only daughter, the recently wedded Alesia.

'Her husband is also a goldsmith,' Theobald offered. 'Sir Robert had ceased his trading days. He was getting ready to leave . . .'

'Leave?'

'Aye. Leave all this in the trusting hands of Alesia and her husband Edmond Pulick whilst Sir Robert went on pilgrimage to Santiago, Rome and Jerusalem though, some say,' Theobald lowered his voice, 'he was fleeing from the hellish Helen and her shadow, kinsman Adam.' He paused as Crispin knocked on the lintel and enquired how long they would have to wait in the solar.

'For as long as it takes,' Cranston snapped. 'Send up Master Flaxwith; he's filled his belly enough.'

'Oh, by the way, Crispin,' Theobald called, 'your eyes?'

'Just the same,' the clerk replied. 'We're all growing old, master physician.'

Cranston waited for Crispin's footsteps to fade then clapped his hands.

'Friar, we've finished here, yes?'

'We certainly have and found nothing,' Athelstan agreed. 'Only the wine, the flagon, cup and sweetmeats remain. Master Theobald, don't forget to take them away.'

'And eat them?' the physician protested.

'Nonsense.' Athelstan laughed. 'You have a cellar plagued by rats? Put the sweetmeats and the wine down there, you'll soon discover if they are tainted. Oh, by the way, did you examine Kilverby's fingertips?'

'Nothing but ink and wine,' the physician replied wearily. 'No trace of any noxious potion.'

Flaxwith appeared in the doorway.

'Ah, Flaxwith.' Athelstan waited until the physician, carrying jug, goblet and silver bowl, stomped off, grumbling under his breath about payment. 'Flaxwith, with Sir John's permission, I want you, whilst we are questioning our hosts in the solar, to have this door repaired. Once it is, I want it locked, barred and firmly sealed with the Lord Coroner's signet so that no one can enter. Do you understand?'

'Athelstan?' Cranston queried.

'Nothing is to leave this chamber. No one is to enter once Sir John and I have adjourned to the solar. Come on.' Athelstan waved. 'Sir John, the hours pass.'

A short while later Cranston, Athelstan sitting beside him, stared round this wealthy family. Edmond Pulick had now joined Alesia. He was friendly-faced with sandy hair and a snub nose above a smiling mouth. Pleasant and discreet, Athelstan considered, though with sharp eyes. The precise way Pulick acted showed he was a merchant through and through, ready to assess and weigh everything in the balance. Athelstan studied the rest. Each nursed their own soul, which was full of what? God's grace or murder, hatred, revenge or even just the love of killing? Certainly one of them was an assassin. Athelstan then smiled and mentally murmured 'Mea culpa' for his rushed judgement as Cranston's first question revealed that others may well be involved.

'Who gave Sir Robert the dish of sweetmeats?'

'Not us,' Crispin replied swiftly. 'Sir Robert, God assoil him, entertained Prior Alexander and Brother Richer from St

Fulcher's yesterday afternoon. They brought the comfits as a gift. I even ate one.'

'Why did they visit Sir Robert?'

'Business,' Crispin replied. 'The Passio Christi was to be taken to St Fulcher's today – they came to fix the hour. There were other matters. Sir Robert also confirmed that I would be given good lodgings when he began his pilgrimage at the beginning of Lent.'

'And who,' Cranston interrupted, 'would have looked after Sir Robert's affairs when he was away?'

'Edmond and I,' Alesia replied, throwing a hateful glance at her stepmother. 'Matters would be in safe hands.' She grasped her husband's arm. He simply smiled, eyes watchful for Cranston's next question.

'And the Passio Christi, what would have happened to that when Sir Robert left?'

'We would have kept it secure.' Alesia didn't seem so certain now. 'After all, Edmond is a very respected member . . .'

Kinsman Adam suddenly sniggered. Athelstan glanced sideways. Sir John's eyes were growing heavy; he was slumping in the great chair brought up in front of the roaring fire.

'Sir John is weary.' Athelstan paused at the furious knocking from down the gallery. 'Your father's chamber is being made secure and sealed. No one, and I repeat no one, on their allegiance to the Crown, is to enter that chamber. I repeat.' He ignored all their protests, especially from Lady Helen. 'No one is to enter.' He pointed at Alesia, her red-rimmed eyes now dry in her long, pale face. 'Mistress, your father was murdered – undoubtedly poisoned.' He waited for the gasps and cries to subside.

'But how?' Edmond demanded. 'We had supper with him last night. Sir Robert was in good spirits when he left the table.'

'Then?' Cranston abruptly drew himself up in the chair, smacking his lips, fingers impatiently beating against the arm rest. 'What happened then?' he repeated.

'He adjourned to his chamber.' Crispin spoke up.

'Did you go with him?'

'No, Sir John,' Lady Helen replied. 'My *husband*,' she

emphasized the word, 'said he wanted to reflect. I don't know why, we don't know why, he simply asked not to be disturbed. He had his wine and those sweetmeats, to which he was partial. He bolted and locked the door and never came out.'

'And no one visited him?'

'Nobody,' Crispin declared. 'Once Sir Robert had decided to be alone that was it.'

'I wished him goodnight,' Lady Helen declared. 'I called through the door.'

'As did I,' Alesia added.

'And Sir Robert replied both times?'

'Of course, Brother. If he hadn't, we would have been alarmed.'

'And the Passio Christi?'

'I saw it,' Alesia declared. 'Crispin, Edmond and I were here after the monks had left. He showed it to us and put it back in the coffer. Crispin and he took it back to his chamber. I saw him lock the casket and put the keys back on the chain around his neck.' Alesia wetted her lips, slender fingers rubbing her brow. 'Sir John, Brother Athelstan, my father kept the bloodstone in that coffer in his chancery. I . . .'

'Mistress,' Athelstan soothed, 'after supper your father retired for the night about what hour?'

'He went to the garderobe first,' she replied. 'It's a little further along the gallery. He made himself comfortable. I think it must have been . . .'

'About compline,' Crispin interjected, 'the bells were ringing for compline. I remember glancing through the window and saw the beacons flaring in the church steeples. The streets below were quiet.'

'And Sir Robert definitely stayed in his chamber?'

'Yes, yes.' They spoke together.

'So,' Athelstan cradled his leather satchel rocking gently backwards and forwards. 'No one goes into that chamber. It is bolted and locked from the inside, and this morning?'

'I went there,' Crispin replied. 'I knocked, then I hammered and shouted.'

'I came down,' Lady Helen leaned forward. 'Kinsman Adam and I also tried.' She pulled a face and one, Athelstan

reflected, not so full of grieving. 'By then the entire house
was roused. The door was forced and Sir Robert,' she tried to
create a tremor in her voice and dabbed quickly at her eyes
with the long hem of her cuff, 'lay dead on the floor but, apart
from that horrid sight, nothing else was disturbed.'

'And nothing was?' Athelstan queried sharply. 'Nobody
touched anything?'

'Nobody,' Alesia agreed. 'I was so shocked I just stood in
the doorway. Master Crispin scrutinized the chancery table
and asked me if the casket holding the Passio Christi was
secure. I did. It was undisturbed. Sir John, you discovered
where my father kept his keys?'

For a while there was silence.

'One more thing.' Athelstan smiled round. 'Let's go back
to something you have mentioned. Yesterday afternoon,
Tuesday the eve of St Damasus, you were visited by two
monks from St Fulcher's – Prior Alexander and Sub-Prior
Richer, yes?'

'True,' Crispin murmured, 'we've explained that.' Crispin's
eyes were blinking so furiously Athelstan recalled Physician
Theobald's earlier question and wondered if this old secretarius
had a serious ailment of the eyes.

'Who met them?'

'My father,' Alesia declared. 'Crispin, Edmond and I were
also present.'

'They brought gifts?'

'Yes, delicious sweetmeats. They asked to see the Passio
Christi.'

'So what was the purpose of their visit?'

'I've explained already,' Crispin answered. 'They had
business in Cheapside dealing with other merchants but,' he
fingered the cap of the inkhorn strapped to his belt, 'Sir Robert
also wanted to see them.'

'What I mean is this,' Athelstan paused, 'I understand the
Passio Christi had to be taken to St Fulcher's to be shown to
the members of the Wyvern Company. Your father would have
taken it, so why see the monks yesterday when a further
meeting was planned for today?'

'I shall answer that,' Lady Helen declared fiercely.

'Shall you, mother dearest?'

'Alesia!' Helen's face was a mask of fury. 'My husband also confided in me, Sir John.' Lady Helen apparently considered Athelstan beneath her notice; she hardly glanced at him. 'My husband was a devout man. He did not ask to hold the Passio Christi, which he regarded as a precious relic. He did not like the Wyvern Company. More importantly, he resented taking the Passio Christi out to them.'

'So he asked the monks to come here?'

'Brother, you have it wrong!' Lady Helen snapped. 'My husband may have done wrong, been harsh, but he did penance for all that. At the same time he continued to do his duty here in London. You see,' Lady Helen forced a smile, 'the bloodstone still had to be taken to St Fulcher's today for those old soldiers to see whatever happened yesterday.'

'So?'

'I was to take it!' Alesia declared.

'As was I.' Crispin rubbed his hands on his gown. 'Lady Helen is correct. My master hated taking the Passio Christi to St Fulcher's. He did not go last year and he certainly didn't intend to this year. The Passio Christi was to be taken by me, Mistress Alesia and Master Edmond. We planned,' he controlled the quaver in his voice, 'to leave at first light this morning, which is when I tried to rouse my master.'

'So why did the good brothers visit here?' Athelstan insisted. 'The Passio Christi was a curiosity but why else?' He smiled apologetically. 'I know I have asked this before but I want to clarify matters.'

'My eyesight is failing,' Crispin explained. 'I have been examined by skilled oculists. When my master left on pilgrimage I was to be given comfortable lodgings at St Fulcher's, in the abbot's own guest house. Prior Alexander, who used to be infirmarian and skilled in physics, would look after my eyes.'

'And you wanted that?'

'Oh, yes,' Crispin confessed. 'I would be distraught about my master's leaving but one day he would return.'

'And the Passio Christi?' Athelstan asked.

'You are persistent, Friar,' Crispin murmured. He glanced

around. 'I must tell the truth.' He paused. 'Sir Robert was tired of holding the Passio Christi. He wanted to give it back.'

'To whom?' Cranston asked.

'Why, the Abbey of St Fulcher,' Alesia replied. 'Father truly disliked those old soldiers. He'd always thought the bloodstone was taken as the legitimate plunder of war but, in the last few years, he began to wonder whether they had stolen it – an act of sacrilege. Of course he liked to go to the abbey itself. He was a generous benefactor and often visited the brothers.'

'For what?' Cranston asked.

'To retreat, to pray, to fast, to cure his soul.'

'And would the exchequer have agreed to the Passio Christi being given to the abbey?' Cranston asked.

'My father . . .' Alesia's voice faltered, she looked askance at Crispin.

'Oh, for heaven's sake tell them the rest,' Lady Helen almost shouted. 'Sir Robert intended to leave the Passio Christi at St Fulcher's and let the Crown fight its own battle. The Abbey of St Calliste outside Poitiers was Benedictine. Sir Robert couldn't return it there but he could at least hand it over to the Benedictines in this kingdom. True?'

Athelstan glanced at the others, who murmured their agreement.

'Very astute,' Athelstan murmured. 'Once Holy Mother Church seizes something, it is very difficult to force her to relinquish it, especially when she can claim rights in the first place. So,' he drew a deep breath, 'nothing else was discussed? You're sure the Passio Christi was still here when the good brothers left?'

'We all saw it,' Edmond replied. 'Brother Athelstan, I know what you are thinking.'

'Do you?' Athelstan smiled. 'Then you are a better man than I.'

'I suspect you are wondering whether we allowed the Passio Christi to be taken by our visitors, but that would have been highly dangerous. The Crown would have blamed us, yes?'

Athelstan nodded.

'What Edmond is saying,' Alesia spoke up, 'is my father

would have taken the bloodstone to St Fulcher's on the very day he left for Jerusalem. It would be his decision, his responsibility, not ours. Brother,' Alesia waved around, 'look at our great wealth. My father was a hard but honourable man; in his last days he turned more and more to God. Sir John,' she appealed to the coroner. 'Would you like to be the custodian of the Passio Christi? A sacred relic possibly pillaged from the sanctuary of an abbey?'

'But why the change?' Cranston asked. 'After all the bloodstone was in his care for decades, yes?'

'In years past my father would take it to the exchequer at Westminster where one or all of the Wyvern Company would always be present. He simply viewed that as part of his many business relationships.'

'And recently?'

'Four years ago the Wyverns were given lodgings at St Fulcher's. It was agreed that the twice a year journey would take place whilst they were there.'

'Why?'

'The soldiers were growing old; William Chalk became frail. My father also had considerable business with the abbey. All parties agreed to that so the indenture was amended accordingly.'

'And Sir Robert's attitude towards the Wyverns?'

'At first they were simply one group amongst my father's many commercial acquaintances. However, once they were at St Fulcher's, my father's attitude towards them changed. I suspect that as he grew more devout, he began to question whether they really had stolen it. He grew to resent them.'

'Why did he change?'

'I've told you, there are two accounts: first that the Wyvern Company found the Passio Christi, the other that they'd stolen it. My father began to believe the latter.'

'Did he have proof for that?'

'I don't know.'

'When your father visited St Fulcher's, which monk was he friendly with?'

Alesia moved her head from side to side. 'From what I gather . . .' She glanced at Crispin.

'Abbot Walter,' the old clerk replied. 'Prior Alexander as well as the young Frenchman, Sub-Prior Richer.'

'Did any of them,' Athelstan asked, 'give your father ghostly advice?'

'He spoke to all three – I don't really know.'

'So,' Cranston declared, 'Sir Robert Kilverby came to dislike those old soldiers; he also resented holding the Passio Christi. He didn't like what he'd done or what he was doing. He turned to God. He was preparing to leave on pilgrimage and that raises a further possibility. Did Sir Robert himself decide to get rid of the Passio Christi?'

'What?' Adam Lestral's voice was thin and reedy. 'Sir John, are you saying that Sir Robert took the Passio Christi and cast it down the privy or threw it into the street?'

Despite the petulant, strident tone Athelstan recognized the logic of the question. If this company were to be believed, and on this Athelstan certainly did, Sir Robert regarded the Passio Christi as a most sacred relic to be securely kept, not thrown away like a piece of rubbish.

'We would all go on oath,' Alesia said quietly. 'The Passio Christi was here last night long after those monks had returned to their abbey. Look at my father's chancery chamber; there is no hiding place, no window to open even if he wanted to throw something away.'

'I agree,' Athelstan intervened. 'When he died Sir Robert truly believed the Passio Christi was still firmly in his care. So,' he shook his head, 'what really happened remains a mystery.' Athelstan sat, allowing the silence to deepen.

Cranston gently tapped the friar's sandalled foot with the toe of his boot. Athelstan got to his feet and both he and Sir John took their leave. The friar was now fully distracted, eager to escape and reflect on all this murderous mayhem and the mysteries which surrounded it . . .

oOoOo

TWO

*'Corrody: pension paid to an abbey
for someone to stay there.'*

n the Abbey of St Fulcher-on-Thames Ailward Hyde, former
master bowman and a member of the Wyvern Company,
stood fascinated by the wall paintings in the south aisle
just near the Galilee porch. Ailward was also agitated. He'd
taken the oath. He was pledged to the company. He was an
experienced swordsman, a warrior yet poor Hanep! Ailward
had visited the bloody remains of Gilbert Hanep laid out in
its coffin on a trestle in the abbey death house. The infirmarian,
the keeper of the dead, had done his best, sewing on the severed
head with black twine, yet the sheer horror of seeing a comrade
like that! Ailward swallowed the bile at the back of his throat
and caressed the hilt of both sword and dagger. Who had
committed such a horror? Surely it could not be one of them,
yet who could overcome a skilled master of arms such as
Hanep, and take his head as clean as snipping a button? Hanep
had died like some hog slaughtered out there in the bleak,
cold cemetery. Now he, Ailward, had come here to collect his
thoughts, pray and perhaps plot. Ailward just wished Fulk
Wenlock, their *consiliarius*, an ever-perpetual source of good
advice, was here but he and Mahant had gone into the city
yesterday to roister as well as to do other business. He recalled
Wenlock's nut-brown face all creased in friendly concern when
they'd strolled through the maze, that subtle conceit built by
a previous abbot. They had been discussing Chalk and the
lingering days of his death. Wenlock had gripped Hyde's arm
with his maimed hand and spun him around.

'Ailward,' he urged, 'Chalk's death has changed nothing.
You'll see, everything will calm down.' He had then taken
him to meet Mahant, their serjeant-at-arms. Mahant, his hawk-
like face as harsh as ever, had confirmed Wenlock's words:

Chalk was dead. He could speak no more; all would be as it always was. Nevertheless, Ailward was still unsure. Wenlock had given him further words of comfort promising how everything would turn out well.

'I just wish you were here,' Ailward whispered.

Wenlock was always reassuring; after all, he had survived. Once a fighter, a master bowman, the most accurate of archers who could send a grey goose-feathered shaft into any target. The French had captured Wenlock and hacked off the bowman fingers on each hand. Wenlock bore his infirmity well and always comforted the others. Yet he and Mahant had still not returned and probably would not be back until later. So Ailward had come here to be distracted, as he always was, by the vivid array of wall paintings which dominated the south aisle. A collection of stories demonstrating the power of God over Satan and all his works, especially when the forces of hell confronted the black monks, the followers of St Benedict. Some of these wall paintings, or so he was given to understand, were the work of the anchorite, that mysterious person who had once been an itinerant painter as well as the Hangman of Rochester, a service he still carried out for the abbot. Ailward was always fascinated by such frescoes, especially those which celebrated events from the history of St Fulcher's such as the former abbot who had foiled an evil spirit stealing wine from the abbey cellars. Ailward smiled as his fingers traced the story. The abbot had sealed all the taps of the barrels with holy chrism oil as a trap for the demon. The next scene showed a black-limbed, red-faced devil, fiery charcoal eyes glaring, green horns twitching, glued to one of the barrels. A further story, depicted in glowing colours, narrated how a young novice monk was tempted and threatened by a demon who flung his hellish cloak over the novice's tonsure, burning his head and blistering his skin. The painting then showed the young novice on his knees begging St Benedict to assist him, which the great saint did in a blaze of shimmering light. Ailward closed his eyes and turned away. In truth he had also come here for help, for assistance, to pray, but who would listen to him? A former soldier whose soul was sin-burdened, sin-scorched, buried deep in all kinds of crimes against both God and man?

'Corpse-maker, slave of hell, ravenous hell brute, coward!'

Ailward almost screamed at the voice which rang like a trumpet blast through the greying light, echoing under the ribbed-vault ceiling.

'Slash of blood, raging demons, bloated and dangerous, battle-scarred. Terrors gather amongst us . . .'

Ailward relaxed, tapping the pommel of his sword for comfort. He recognized the sepulchral voice of the anchorite in his cell built further along the south aisle. Once a small chantry chapel with altar, ambo and sanctuary, the entire closure had been bricked up except for a small door and a ledge in the front.

'Mad as a barrel of crickets!' Ailward whispered reassuringly as he made his way along. He reached the anker house and stared through the aperture. In the poor light he could only dimly make out the anchorite's tangled hair, the frenetic eyes glaring back.

'Good morrow, Brother,' Ailward grated.

'Good morrow to you too.' The anchorite's voice was surprisingly soft and clear. 'Frightened are we, soldier, of the jabbing daggers, the swish of smooth swords? Oh yes, I've heard about the harrower of the dark who crawled through the gloaming and captured one of your kind. You lived for the arrow storm; you'll die in the arrow storm.'

'And you,' Ailward taunted back, 'live in fear of ghosts?'

'We all have wolfish souls and hate-honed hearts,' the anchorite retorted. 'Guilty, God cursed.' The anchorite breathed out noisily – a gust of air through the aperture. 'And you, soldier, don't the spirits gather around you? The ghosts of my wife and child?'

'I've heard your fable,' Ailward snapped, 'your family's blood is not on our hands. You rant and rave. You chatter like some earth-bound spirit but no one listens.'

'I do,' the anchorite whispered. 'I listen to all the tales, especially about your comrade's death.'

'What do you know about Hanep's murder?'

'The good brothers gossip like women around the well. You should be careful, all of you! More walks this abbey than you think.'

'Such as whom?'

'She with that wicked face,' the anchorite's voice changed, 'with slimy hair. Hanged her I did yet still she walks. Hush!'

Ailward felt a prickling fear. The anchorite, despite his ranting, was right. The soft slither of sandal echoed through the stone-hollowed darkness. The brothers were out in the fields or tending to other duties. The abbey church should be deserted now, that's why he had come here. Ailward lifted a warning hand towards the anchorite. He moved to stand behind one of the great drum-like pillars; a sculpted fool's face grinned down at him from the acanthus leaves carved around its top.

'Horror from the great darkness,' the anchorite's voice boomed, 'horror on all sides! A hideous oppression fills the soul with dread.'

Ailward ignored him; the mysterious intruder would also do likewise. The anchorite's doom-laden pronouncements were common enough. Ailward peered round the pillar. A shape moved near the Lady chapel. Ailward could make out the garb of a black monk, hood pulled forward. Something clattered to the ground. The figure pushed back his cowl as he stretched out to pick up the sword, its blade blinking in the dancing light of the tapers. Ailward recognized him – Richer, the sub-prior, the Frenchman! Why was he carrying a sword and creeping about so closely cloaked and cowled? Richer had once been a monk at St Calliste which formerly housed the Passio Christi. Hadn't Henry Osborne, another of the Wyvern Company, also remarked about Richer's strange recent comings and goings? The sub-prior, in charge of the library and the scriptorium, had shown little love for the Wyvern Company ever since his arrival. Hadn't he, chattering in French, once dismissed Ailward and his companions as tail-bearing Englishmen worthy of hell fire? Although to be fair, Richer had proved to be most compassionate to that old reprobate Chalk. Had he done that to squirrel out secrets? Had he been successful? Wenlock claimed he had. Curious, Ailward now decided to follow the sub-prior. The monk had disappeared. Ailward followed swiftly, his soft-soled boots making little noise.

Outside in the freezing cold, Ailward glimpsed the black

gowned sub-prior go around a corner and across the monk's
bowling yard where the good brothers played nine-pins.
Ailward drew his dagger. He kept this low as he pursued his
quarry across the frozen gardens, through the apple yard and
into Mortival meadow which stretched down to the watergate,
usually a desolate spot especially at the height of winter.
Ailward followed using the bushes and small copses to hide
himself. Richer strolled boldly on. Now and again the monk
would turn and glance back but Ailward was skilled in subterfuge and concealment. Hadn't he and his comrades done
similar work against so many French camps and strongholds?
Ailward was now absorbed, his former unease and fear
dissipated. Mahant was correct. The prospect of battle and
conflict solved all misery. Ailward felt he was young again,
heading towards the enemy. He was aware of the gathering
river mist, the sharp breeze and the oppressive silence which
seemed to shroud this lonely abbey. There again he had experienced the same many times in France. Ailward gripped his
dagger. Richer was now near the lychgate in the curtain wall.
The Frenchman abruptly paused. He put down what he was
carrying and called out, a strident cry like that of a bird. A
reply echoed in from the river. Richer picked up what he was
carrying and hurried towards the watergate. Ailward made to
follow but paused at the sound of dry wood snapping behind
him. He turned round, dagger out; nothing, only the thickening
mist billowing and shifting. He glanced back. Richer was now
through the watergate. Ailward followed. Ignoring the stench
of fox and other vermin, he pushed the gate open and stared
through the crack. Richer stood further along the narrow
quayside. He was crouching down beneath the soaring three
branched scaffold handing a package to a man hooded and
visored standing in a ship's boat alongside the quay. The
conversation was hushed and swift but Ailward caught
the occasional French word. The man on the boat took the
oilskin pouch Richer handed him. Ailward tensed. Was Richer
a spy? What could he be handing over to some foreign ship?
Something for the French or some other power? Ailward fought
to control his excitement. He calmed himself, drew his sword
and peered again. The monk had disappeared. Nothing was

there but the boat, the figure in it now squatting down. 'God go with you.'

Ailward turned and almost fell on the sword of the cowled figure cloaked all in black. Ailward gagged as the sword dug deep, its razor-sharp blade slicing his innards. He screamed again, a long, harrowing cry choked off by the blood welling through both nose and mouth . . .

Athelstan caught his breath as he and Sir John hurried along the byways and alleyways leading off Cheapside down to the river. The day was drawing on. Bells tolled for the Angelus and noon day Mass as well as the sign for traders to break their fast in the cook shops, pastry houses, inns and taverns. Athelstan roughly shouldered by a pedlar of old boots with an assortment of footwear hanging from a stick, swiftly dodged one of St Anthony's pigs, bell tingling around its neck, as it charged across an alleyway pursued by a group of ragged urchins armed with sticks. He crossed himself as a funeral cortège went by with bell, cross and incense. A young boy carolled the Dirige psalms while a group of beggars, clothed as penitents and fortified with bread and strong ale, staggered behind the purple-clothed coffin, funeral candles drunkenly held. Cranston and Athelstan crossed Fish Street. They passed St Nicholas Coe Abbey where the Brotherhood of the Beggars was feeding lepers on mouldy bread, rancid pork, slimy veal, flat beer and stale fish. Athelstan glanced away in disgust at the loathsome platters set out on a tawdry stall. He also felt guilty. He and Sir John had left Kilverby's mansion. They had braved the importunity of the two beggars who haunted Cheapside – Leif and his associate Rawbum who'd once had the misfortune when drunk to sit down on a pan of burning oil. After they had coaxed their way by this precious pair, Cranston and Athelstan went into the warmth of 'The Holy Lamb of God', Cranston's favourite 'chapel' since the merry-mouthed, rosy-cheeked landlady had taken over from the old harridan who had once resided there. Minehost had been preparing Brouet de Capon. The tap room was enriched by the fragrance of almonds, cinnamon, clove, peppers and grains of paradise. They'd eaten and drunk well. Now, faced with all this desperation, Athelstan paused. He opened his purse and went back to distribute coins into the bandaged hands of the ever-desperate lepers.

'Dangerous,' Cranston observed when the friar returned, 'the contagion could catch you.'

'Nonsense,' Athelstan retorted, 'there's no real harm to be had from that. A silly fable, Sir John. You have to live with these poor unfortunates perhaps months, years before the contagion takes you.' Athelstan was about to continue but he noticed a well-known foist approaching so he gripped his leather satchel more tightly and urged Cranston on.

A short while later they reached Queenshithe Wharf and hired a covered barge to take them down to St Fulcher's. The river was swollen and dark; a freezing fog had rolled in to cloak the Thames in a deep greyness. Shapes of other craft emerged then swiftly faded. Lantern horns placed in their prows glowed as beacons whilst along the banks similar warning lights flared from the steeples of St Nicholas, St Benet and other churches. Cranston had refilled his miraculous wine-skin at 'The Holy Lamb of God'. He took a generous swig from this, settled himself more comfortably against the cushions in the stern and offered Athelstan a drink. The friar shook his head and stared fearfully across the river, a forbidding thoroughfare he reflected, full of mystery and sudden terrors. He recalled the Fisher of Men who, with his little band of swimmers led by Icthus, combed the river for corpses which, at a price, could be collected from his chapel, the 'Barque of St Peter'. Even at the height of summer this river reeked of danger and Athelstan recalled some of the ghoulish tales narrated by Moleskin the boatman.

'Dangerous weather,' Cranston murmured. 'These sea banks of fog float in and the French war cogs use them. A fleet of privateers prowl the Narrow Seas; they could slip into the estuary to pillage and burn, but,' he sighed, 'such thoughts darken the mind. Now Athelstan, Kilverby, there's a family of choice souls?'

'That does not concern us, Sir John.' Athelstan steadied himself as the barge rocked violently. 'Not yet. Let us move to the arrow point, to the conclusion then argue backwards.

According to the evidence, Sir Robert Kilverby, in good health, locked and bolted himself in that chancery chamber. He never left, no one entered. No trace, as yet, of any noxious substance has been found in that room, but Sir Robert was definitely poisoned.'

'Could that have happened before he went in?'

'No. I suspect the potion he took grew in its malignancy. We deduced from those who knocked on the door later that evening that Sir Robert remained hale and hearty. No, that rich man was poisoned by some malevolent potion growing within him. But how and why I do not know. Even more mysteriously, someone took those three keys from the chain around his neck, opened the casket, removed the Passio Christi and put the keys back.'

'Kilverby could have admitted someone during the evening; such a person could have brought the poison.'

'But how, Sir John? The wine, the sweetmeats – we have no proof that these were tainted?'

'She or he could have offered a poisoned cup or a dish of savouries, then taken them away?'

Athelstan steadied himself again as the barge rose and fell on the swell. The four oarsmen, capuchined against the stinging wind, quietly cursed as the surge broke the even beat of their rowing. 'We have no evidence for that, Sir John. Surely Sir Robert would be suspicious of anyone entering with wine and food? He'd already supped whilst he had his own flagon. He'd insisted on being left alone and, as we heard, he was not to be disobeyed. Moreover, how does that explain the disappearance of the Passio Christi? In addition, Kilverby's chamber is on a gallery close to the solar; anyone approaching, entering or leaving that chamber would easily be seen. No, Sir Robert was not disturbed. Indeed, knowing the little I do about that family, they would scrupulously watch each other; they all confirm nobody entered or left that room.' Athelstan sighed. 'Kilverby was mysteriously poisoned. The Passio Christi was stolen, not violently but by using those three keys which Kilverby guarded so zealously.'

'And why?' Cranston murmured. 'Why has he been murdered now?'

'That,' Athelstan retorted, 'is another mystery. Nor can I detect a suspect. Alesia is wealthy; her father's death would enrich her further but why hasten it? In truth, she seems a dutiful daughter whilst Lady Helen certainly did not benefit from her husband's death, nor is Master Crispin scarcely helped by such a dramatic, murderous change in the family's fortunes.'

'Did the assassin use the chaos which ensued when the corpse was found to mask their bloody handiwork?'

'I cannot see how,' Athelstan shook his head, 'as I said that family watch each other. Any untoward action, I am sure, would have been observed.'

Cranston took another swig from the miraculous wineskin and began to hum an old marching tune under his breath. Athelstan looked across the river, fascinated by how the curtain of mist would suddenly part to reveal a wherry crammed with goods making its way up to one of the city wharfs or a fishing smack lying low in the water. On one occasion a royal barge broke through, lanterns glowing on its carved prow, the royal pennant of blue, scarlet and gold flapping in the breeze, the oarsmen all liveried, six on either side, bending over their oars, archers clustered in the stern with arrows notched. The mist would then close again and the silence descend. Was that a pale reflection of the spiritual life? Athelstan wondered. Did the veil between the invisible and visible thin, even part? Athelstan closed his eyes and murmured a prayer. He relaxed as the rocking of the boat lulled him into a light sleep and fitful dreaming about what he'd seen and heard that morning.

As soon as they reached the watergate at St Fulcher's, they recognized some dreadful act had recently taken place. Lay brothers clustered around the quayside or just within the watergate. Cranston leapt from the barge, helped Athelstan out and immediately tried to impose order on the brothers, who gathered around him like frightened chickens. Eventually a young man, face bronzed by the sun, his dark hair neatly cropped to show the tonsure, made his way through the throng. He pushed his hands up the voluminous sleeves of his black gown and bowed.

'Sir John Cranston, Brother Athelstan, *pax et bonum*. I am Sub-Prior Richer, librarian and keeper of the scriptorium.

Welcome indeed to St Fulcher's. We have been expecting you but the murder of poor Hanep has been overtaken by another slaying, Ailward Hyde.' He ushered them through the watergate and pointed to the great black stains on the frozen ground then the splashes of blood on the curtain wall. 'Murdered most recently – we've just removed his corpse to our death house.'

'How?' Athelstan asked.

'A fatal sword thrust to the belly.' Richer swallowed hard. 'A killing cut which sliced his vital organs. His screams were terrible. The good brothers working in the gardens have never heard the like before. Father Abbot, indeed our whole community, is most disturbed. Lord Walter and Prior Alexander are waiting for you.' He led them across what he called Mortival meadow. Athelstan stared around with a pang of nostalgia. The great field with its rolling frozen grass and mist hung bushes and copses evoked memories of his parents' farm at this time of year, of him running wild with his brother and sisters. How he used to stop to watch the peddler with his emaciated horse come along the trackway at the bottom, followed by the warrener with his sack of rabbits or foresters with a deer slung on their poles.

'Enter by the narrow door!'

Athelstan broke from his reverie.

'Sir John?'

'I was quoting scripture,' Cranston whispered, plodding behind the fast-paced Richer. 'We are, my good friend, about to enter the halls of murder yet again. Pray God we enter the narrow door and leave just as safely.'

They continued on up into the abbey precincts. Athelstan caught his breath at the sheer magnificence of the buildings, dominated by the great church with its scores of windows, most of them filled with coloured glass. Soaring buttresses and elaborately carved cornices with balustrades and sills closed in around them. Saints, angels, demons, satyrs, babewyns and gargoyles stared down at them with a variety of expressions on their holy or demonic carved faces. They crossed the sand-packed bowling alley, through gardens of neatly laid out herb and shrub plots, all contained within small red-brick walls, the path winding around them covered in packed white pebbles. Richer pointed out the dormitories, chapter house, guest house, refectory, infirmary and the rest, a bewildering array of grey stone or pebble-dashed buildings. Bells chimed and the stony corridors echoed with the slap of sandals and the murmur of voices. Snatches of plain chant trailed. The air grew rich with a variety of smells, odours and fragrances: incense, sandalwood, burning meat, fresh bread, candle wax and tallow. The tang of soap and the powerful astringent the brothers used to scrub the paving stones permeated the great cloister. They crossed baileys and stable yards, went around duck and carp ponds, hen coops and dove cotes. Athelstan tried to recall what he knew about St Fulcher's. All he could remember was that the Benedictine abbey, like many of the houses of the black monks, had waxed rich and strong over the centuries, generously endowed by kings, princes and all the great ones of the land. He tried to make sense of his surroundings but his heart sank. The abbey was as intricate and complex as any labyrinth of runnels and alleyways in Southwark. An assassin's paradise, Athelstan mused, with stairs and steps leading here and there, alcoves for towel and linen cupboards, passageways and narrow galleries abruptly branching off in all directions. Dark recesses and tunnels yawned, ending in broad open spaces full of light. He was increasingly aware of hedges, walls, gates and postern doors as well as steps and stairs leading down into the cellars and crypts. Oh yes, Athelstan thought, a flitting place of many shadows where a killer could hunt and slay as stealthily as any assassin in the darkest forest.

At last they were free of the main abbey buildings and entered a walled enclosure guarded by freshly painted gates. A garrulous lay brother bustled out from the small lodge saying he was the abbot's doorman and porter. Richer just ignored him. At the far end of the enclosure rose a stately manor house of beautiful honey-coloured Cotswold stone with a black slated roof, chimney stacks and broad windows of mullion-coloured glass. Steps of sandstone swept up to an impressive door with gleaming bronze metal work. A small bell hung in its own coping, its rope, white as snow, attached to a large clasp. On either side of the main house ranged other two-storied buildings – those to the left of the gate were the abbot's own kitchens, scullery, buttery and bakery. On the right, with its elegant paintwork and glass-filled windows, stood the Lord Abbot's guest house for his own special visitors. The door to this opened. A young woman dressed in russet cloak over a samite dress, a white veil around her auburn hair, came out, one arm resting on an older, grey-haired, severe-faced woman garbed in a similar fashion. They both paused and drew apart to pull up their hoods. Richer led his guests along the paved path which cut between neatly cultivated garden squares. He paused in front of the women and bowed.

'My ladies, these are Lord Walter's guests, Sir John Cranston and Brother Athelstan.'

The young woman, plump and pretty-faced, smiled and nodded; her older companion simply glared. Athelstan guessed there was little love lost between the sub-prior and the lady whom he introduced as the Lord Abbot's sister, the younger woman being his niece. The two women walked away as Richer took Athelstan and Cranston up into the luxurious manor house, smelling delicately of polish and the fragrance of crushed flowers. Dark, wooden panelling, balustrades, wainscoting and floor planks gleamed in the light of many candles. The abbot's own chamber was an elegant, oblong-shaped room boasting finely carved furniture. Striking black crosses hung against two of the smooth walls, brilliantly coloured tapestries and turkey rugs covered the others whilst the intricately tiled floor described a map of the world with Jerusalem at its centre.

Abbot Walter and Prior Alexander were sitting in chairs before the great mantled hearth. They rose as Cranston entered. The coroner and Athelstan immediately genuflected to kiss the abbatial ring. Once introductions were finished, they were ushered to the waiting chairs, each with a small table beside it holding a goblet of white wine and a bowl of sugared dry fruit. They made themselves comfortable after the freezing river journey. Athelstan basked in the heat from the flaming logs whilst quickly studying the abbot. Lord Walter was a small, plump man; his black robe was of the purest wool, thick buskins on his feet and a precious pectoral cross hung around his fat throat. Soft and comfortable, Athelstan considered, Lord

Walter was portly with a shining, balding pate, his gloriously rubicund, clean-shaven face glistening with perfumed oil. Nevertheless, a stubborn, determined man. Athelstan noted the pert cast to Lord Walter's thick lips and the shifting eyes ever so quick to wrinkle in a smile as if the abbot was wearing a mask to face other masks. Prior Alexander was different, tall and gangling with a slight stoop to his bony shoulders, his closely cropped red hair emphasized a long, pale face, sharp green eyes with a beaked nose over a thin lipped mouth. Simply by watching them Athelstan sensed the tension between abbot and prior; they hardly looked at each other when they talked whilst their gestures were off hand, as if they were fully aware of some resentment between them. Richer, however, urbane, cultured and soft spoken, seemed to be well liked by both, especially Prior Alexander.

Cranston, sipping his wine, noisily cleared his throat to speak when the door abruptly opened and the largest swan Athelstan had ever seen waddled pompously into the chamber. The bird's webbed feet slapped the polished floor, its long elegant neck arched, the oval-shaped head of downy white and black-eyed patches ending in a yellow bill which opened to cry eerily as the bird fluffed snow-white feathery wings. The swan headed straight for the abbot. Cranston made to rise. The swan turned, hissing furiously, glorious wings unfolding.

'It's best to sit down,' Prior Alexander declared wearily. 'Leda only answers to Father Abbot.'

Cranston resumed his seat and the bird continued on to receive food from the abbot's hand before nestling on soft cushions in the corner. Cranston just glared at the bird as Abbot Walter explained how Leda had been his special pet since a hatchling.

'A change from the monkeys, apes and peacocks,' Prior Alexander breathed, 'not to mention the marmosets, greyhounds and lap dogs.'

'All God's creatures,' Abbot Walter commented cheerfully, 'all gone back to God.'

'There's even a small place in God's Acre for God's own creatures.' Prior Alexander could not keep the sarcasm out of his voice.

'All God's creatures,' Cranston echoed sharply, 'and there's two more for God's Acre, former soldiers who lodged here, Gilbert Hanep and Ailward Hyde brutally despatched to judgement before their time and,' Cranston now had the monks attention, 'I bring you the most distressing news. You expected the Passio Christi to be brought here this morning by Sir Robert Kilverby's steward Crispin, together with his daughter and son-in-law?'

'Yes, we wondered . . .'

'Murdered!' Cranston retorted. 'Sir Robert was foully poisoned in his chamber and the Passio Christi has disappeared.'

Abbot Walter almost choked on his wine. Prior Alexander sat back clutching the arms of his chair, mouth gaping in surprise. Richer stared in disbelief at both Cranston and Athelstan then glanced away, shaking his head. Once they had recovered, Cranston, ignoring their questions, pithily informed them what they had learnt at Kilverby's house.

'So,' Cranston concluded. 'Did Sir Robert share with you his intention to leave the Passio Christi here at St Fulcher's on the very day he left on pilgrimage?'

'That,' Abbot Walter waved a hand, 'may have been in his mind but,' his fat face creased into a smile, 'I cannot comment on what Sir Robert intended or what might have been. Sir Robert is now dead. The Passio Christi is missing, then there are the deaths here.'

'Murders,' Athelstan broke in. 'Father Abbot, two of the Wyvern Company have been foully slaughtered in your abbey.'

'My Lord of Gaunt has heard of the first death,' Cranston added, 'when he hears of the second, not to mention the murder of Sir Robert and the disappearance of the Passio Christi, his rage will know no bounds.' Cranston's words created a tense silence. His Grace the Regent was not to be crossed, even by Holy Mother Church.

'I would not be surprised,' Cranston added softly, 'if His Grace did not honour you with a visit, Lord Walter, but now, reverend fathers, these murders?'

Prior Alexander replied. He assured Sir John how the Wyvern Company were happy, as they had been for the past four years. They'd claimed the Passio Christi was their find, so twice a year they were allowed to both view and hold it. For the rest, Sir Robert paid the abbey through the exchequer a most generous amount so the former soldiers enjoyed very comfortable lodgings.

'Until now?' Athelstan declared.

'Yes, early this morning just after first light, Brother Otto who tends the cemetery went for his usual morning walk. Gilbert Hanep's corpse was found near the grave of his old comrade William Chalk.'

'Another death?'

'By God's good grace, in the order of nature,' the prior replied. 'William Chalk was sickening for some time from tumours in both his belly and groin.'

'So Hanep rose in the middle of night to pay his respects to this dead comrade?'

'Brother Athelstan, Hanep, like his comrades, was a veteran, a warrior, a professional soldier. He was restless, much given to wandering this abbey at night.'

'And someone who knew that was waiting? His assassin must have followed him down to the cemetery and killed him?'

'Took his head, Brother, a swinging cut; those who found him were sickened by the sight.'

'And no indication or evidence for the murderer?'

'The ground was awash with blood,' Prior Alexander retorted, 'but no one saw or heard anything untoward.'

'And late this afternoon, Ailward Hyde was murdered near the watergate.'

'A vicious wound to the belly,' the prior replied, 'the poor man's screams rang across the abbey. By the time our good brothers reached him he was dead, soaked, almost floating in his own blood.'

'Why?' Cranston asked. 'Why now?'

'Sir John, we truly don't know.'

Was there a link? Athelstan reflected, staring at the carved figure of a seraph carrying a harp on the right side of the fireplace. Was Sir Robert's death, the disappearance of the Passio Christi and the murder of these two unfortunates all connected, or was it something else? Athelstan shivered.

He recalled a lecture by Dominus Albertus in the schools so many years ago. How every evil act like seed in the ground eventually blooms to manifest its own malevolent fruit. Wickedness was like a tangled bramble, cruel and twisting, breaking through the soil, stretching out to create its own trap. Kilverby had enjoyed the reputation of being a hard-fisted money lender, notorious throughout the city and Southwark. Members of the Wyvern Company had killed, pillaged and plundered, even seizing a precious relic for their own greedy uses. Was this their judgement day, 'their day of wrath, the day of mourning' as described by the poet Thomas di Celano? Had the victims of all these murders been caught out by their own wickedness sown so many years ago? 'Everything sown will be reaped', or so ran the old Jewish proverb. Had harvest time now arrived?

'Brother Athelstan?'

'Sir John.' Athelstan rose to his feet. 'I have other questions but they will wait. We should view the corpses and question the Wyvern Company. After all, the day is drawing on and my parish awaits.'

'Your parish?' Prior Alexander's voice was harsh. 'Brother Athelstan, we know of you, a Dominican sent to do penance . . .'

'Then if you know,' Cranston declared, getting to his feet, 'there's little point in retelling it.' He bowed perfunctorily in the direction of the abbot. 'Reverend Father, if we can view the corpses?'

Richer led them out of the abbatial enclosure and into the main cloisters. The day was drawing on and the monkish scribes working in their carrels around the cloister garth were collecting their writing equipment in obedience to the bell tolling for the next hour of divine office. Athelstan drank in the sights, watching the scurrying black-robed monks, as organized as any cohort in battle array, prepare for the next task. Other brothers were coming in from the field, doffing their aprons, shaking off their hard wooden clogs and gathering around the different lavaria to wash and prepare themselves. Athelstan wanted to speak to Cranston but Richer kept close as he led them across the abbey. At last they reached a deserted, cobbled yard. Richer ushered them into the whitewashed death house where two coffins rested on trestles beneath a crude black crucifix nailed to the wall. Six purple candles on wooden stands ringed each coffin. Beneath these, fire pots containing crushed herbs exuded a pleasant smell to counter the reek of corruption and decay. A gap-toothed, balding lay brother, hands all a flutter, came out of a shadowy recess to introduce himself. Richer curtly ordered him to raise the deerskin coverlets drawn over both corpses. Once done Athelstan gazed down at both cadavers. Hanep's head had been sown back on with black twine but the face seemed to have shrunken and shrivelled like a decaying plum. Hyde's cadaver was still cloaked in congealing blood, the great slit across his belly crammed with scented linen rags.

'I've yet to wash him,' the keeper of the dead declared mournfully.

Athelstan leaned over and studied the gruesome wounds.

'Friar?'

'Sir John, look,' Athelstan pointed, 'here's the gash, the death wound but look, another piercing here.' He motioned further up the belly. 'The assassin made a sweeping cut, turning the blade of his sword to skewer his victim's innards, a killing cut but then withdraws the sword and plunges it again.'

'And?'

'The assassin must have enjoyed that, for one slash would have been enough. Hyde's screams were immediate yet the killer stays for a second thrust.' Athelstan stepped back; his boot caught something beneath the trestles. He stooped down and dragged out the war belts, swords and daggers in their sheaths.

'The victims,' Richer declared.

'Wearing sword belts in an abbey?'

The sub-prior made a face.

'When Hyde's corpse was found, were his weapons sheathed?'

'He was holding both sword and dagger,' the keeper of the dead offered. 'I was there when we found him slumped against the curtain wall near the watergate.'

Athelstan carried the sword belt into a pool of lantern light. He drew both weapons; their blades were clean though flecks of blood stained the hilts where Hyde must have held his weapons close. Athelstan placed the war belt back.

'And Hanep carried weapons?'

'Yes,' the keeper replied, 'but I do not know whether they were sheathed or not.'

'And why should Ailward Hyde go down to the watergate?'

'I don't know, Brother,' Richer was quick to answer, 'but his presence there might indicate that his killer came from the river rather than the abbey.'

Athelstan had seen enough. He put down the perfumed pomander the lay brother had thrust into his hand and walked back into the darkening day. He stood listening to the different sounds of the abbey whilst Cranston took a generous sip from his wineskin.

'You will meet the members of the Wyvern Company?' Brother Richer's dislike of the former soldiers was obvious; his handsome face was twisted in contempt, his English almost perfect except for the slight accent now coming through.

'They're all assembled in the refectory of their guest house where they will, as usual, be slurping their ale and boasting about their sins.'

'Brother, you must resent these men? You come from the Abbey of St Calliste near Poitiers. You believe your abbey was plundered by these men?'

'Before my day,' Richer dug his hands up the sleeves of his robe, 'long before my day, but yes, I resent them. They are pillagers, ravishers, sacrilegious miscreants. If they'd not been on the side of the victors they'd have been hanged out of hand. Brother, why talk here in the freezing cold?' Richer led them away from the gloomy death house, back into the main buildings. He waved them into a small visiting chamber warmed by two braziers and lit by a huge lantern-horn; they sat around a small table, Richer pulling one of the braziers closer.

'Brother Athelstan, Sir John,' Richer smiled, 'I'm French through and through. I do not believe that the English Crown has any right to that of France but,' he held up a slender hand, 'I'm also a Benedictine. Our houses stretch across Europe and beyond. Here at St Fulcher are English, French, Bretons,

Hainaulters, Castilians and Germans. One thing binds us: we have all put away our former selves and donned the black robes and accepted the rule of our master St Benedict.'

'But why are you here?'

'Because I'm a scholar, Sir John, a bibliophile, a peritus – how do you say? An expert in the care and use of precious manuscripts. I have visited the great libraries of Rome, Avignon and St Chapelle. Three years ago Abbot Walter asked my superiors in France for assistance with the great library here and *çela*,' he spread his hands, 'I am here.'

'I'll be blunt, Richer. Did you come here with secret orders to seize the Passio Christi?'

Richer grinned. 'I'm a Benedictine, Sir John, a librarian. True,' he conceded, 'I would love to take the Passio Christi back to St Calliste but, if rumour is true, that was about to happen anyway. I mean, if Sir Robert left it here before journeying on pilgrimage, it would have only been a matter of time before our precious bloodstone passed back into the rightful hands.'

'You apparently don't believe the story how the Wyvern Company found the Passio Christi on a cart, along with other precious items, on a deserted road near the Abbey of St Calliste?'

'No, Brother, I certainly don't and I suspect, neither do you. A farrago of lies! I was a novice at St Calliste. I followed my vocation there. I've heard the stories. The battle at Poitiers was truly a disaster for the power of France. In the days following, English free companies roamed the fields and highways pursuing their enemies and helping themselves to whatever they wanted. St Calliste should have been sacred but a group of ruffians wearing the Wyvern livery scaled the walls and wandered the abbey. The Passio Christi was kept in a tabernacle in a small chantry chapel to the right of our high altar.' Richer's face grew flushed, his voice more strident. 'It should have been safe there, a sacred relic in a most holy place! The House of God, the Gate of Heaven! Yet it was stolen, along with other precious items.'

'Have you ever confronted the Wyverns with their crime?'

'Of course, Brother Athelstan, just once. I was mocked and

ignored.' Richer snorted with laughter. 'Do you think these ribauds are going to confess to sacrilegious theft? I told them if they were guilty of that then they incurred excommunication, *ipso facto*, immediate and swift. You know, Brother Athelstan, such an excommunication can only be lifted . . .'

'After three steps have been taken.' Athelstan recalled the relevant decree. 'Restitution, reparation and an absolution by a priest.'

'*Tu dixisti!*' Richer quipped. 'You have said it, but those ribauds will never confess the truth.'

'And Sir Robert, he often visited St Fulcher for spiritual consolation?'

'Four or five times a year.' The sub-prior shook his head. 'Sometimes I'd talk to him, a strange man much taken up by the state of his soul. Of course I cannot speak about that. I am sorry to hear he died un-shriven but I can say little. He did most of his business with either Abbot Walter or Prior Alexander. If he spoke to me it was on spiritual matters and that is my concern.'

'And the Wyvern Company – have they changed recently?'

'If they have, I've hardly noticed. They keep to themselves. Prior Alexander might help.'

'When Hanep and Hyde were murdered they were still wearing their sword belts – why should they go armed here in a peaceful abbey?'

'Very observant, Brother Athelstan.' Richer wagged a finger. 'By the way, we have heard of you here, an indefatigable seeker of the truth.'

'Praise from a Benedictine is praise indeed,' Athelstan retorted, keeping an eye on Cranston, who looked on the verge of sleep. 'But my question?'

'I don't know. Perhaps they feared each other. Perhaps some relict from their past outside this abbey has intervened.'

'You mean,' Cranston shook his head, smacking his lips, 'someone from outside is responsible for their murders? Surely a stranger would soon be noticed here?'

'Not at the dead of night, Sir John, or on a dark December afternoon with the river mist curling around the abbey. Even worse if the assassin donned the black robes of a Benedictine.'

Richer rose to his feet. 'Perhaps some ancient, unresolved blood feud, God knows. Such men must have made enough enemies in life. Come, let them tell you themselves.'

They left the petty cloisters, darkness was falling. Athelstan plucked at Cranston's cloak. 'We should be gone!'

'In a while.' The coroner seemed evasive, lost in thought and strode swiftly after the sub-prior. Most of the brothers were now in the abbey church. Silence lay like a pall across the precincts and gardens. Athelstan paused at the welling sounds of voices chanting a psalm from the divine office: *Vindica me Domine et judica causam meam* – Vindicate me Lord and judge my cause'. Aye, Athelstan thought, do so, Lord, for this truly is a maze of lies and deceit. They passed the Galilee porch; a coffin stood there. Athelstan recalled what he'd glimpsed in the death house. He paused and abruptly asked Brother Richer to show them where both men had been murdered.

'Must we?' the sub-prior protested. 'Brother, this day has proved hard enough.'

'Please?' Athelstan glanced quickly at Cranston. 'The coroner is supposed to view the place of death.'

'The King's coroner has no jurisdiction in an abbey.'

Cranston stopped, grasped the sub-prior by the shoulder and gently turned him. 'My friend,' Cranston pushed his face close to Richer's, 'trust me on this if nothing else. I do have jurisdiction here for if the Lord Almighty John of Gaunt wants it, then that is the law!'

Richer swiftly apologized and led them across into the gloomy cemetery. He showed William Chalk's grave with its raw mound of earth. Above it a wooden funeral cross on which were carved the former soldier's name and date of death with the words: *Requiet in luce* – Let him rest in light', etched beneath a crude carving of a dragon-like creature.

'Gilbert Hyde came here.' Athelstan crouched. 'He did what I am doing now.' He then turned, straining his neck, his outline clear in the faint light. The assailant was undoubtedly a professional swordsman, a master-at-arms. He took Hyde's head in one clear cut. 'Come.' Athelstan rose, pulling his cloak closer about him.

Richer, grumbling under his breath, led them out of the cemetery across the abbey and into Mortival meadow. The broad field now looked bleaker in the gloaming, the mist still swirled, crows called raucously from the trees. The wind had turned sharper, more vigorous tugging at hood and cloak; the frozen, icy grass scored their ankles.

'A field of ghosts,' Athelstan whispered.

They reached the watergate. Athelstan crouched to study the place where Hyde had died, his blood flecking the curtain wall.

'Why was he here?' He peered up at Richer. 'Why was an old soldier armed with a sword down here at the watergate? To meet someone? Did his assailant come by boat, kill him then flee? Or did someone in the abbey follow him down here and strike the killing blow? Yet there were two assailants, I'm sure of that, two not one, but how did the assailants kill and escape?' Athelstan couldn't make out Richer's face; the monk's cowl and the poor light made it difficult to discern any expression. Athelstan touched the wall, then went through the watergate on to the mist-hung quayside, a bleak place especially with the black three-branched gallows soaring above them. Glowing braziers shed some light. Athelstan crouched, peering at the ground, scratching it with his fingernail, then he walked back stopping now and again to do the same. He swiftly recited the '*Veni Creator Spiritus*' and stood up.

'Very well, I have seen enough . . .'

The Wyvern Company, all four of them, were assembled in the beam-raftered, whitewashed refectory in the main guest house, a long room with a roundel window at the far end; lancet windows pierced one wall whilst a narrow hearth stoked with fiery logs stood in the centre of the other. The floor was covered with green supple rushes. A common trestle table ran down the centre of the refectory with benches either side. The former soldiers sat grouped at the top of the table, whispering amongst themselves as they shared a jug of ale and a platter of bread and cheese. They hardly moved when Richer entered and introduced Cranston and Athelstan. Rugged, hard men, all four looked what they were – veteran soldiers who'd served the god of war for many a year, their furrowed, clean-shaven faces burnt by sun and wind, narrow-eyed, thin-lipped, heads shorn. They ate and drank slowly, savouring every mouthful, eyes watchful. They were dressed alike in thick woollen jerkins and cambric shirts. War belts lay close to their soft, booted feet.

'Well, my paladins of old, if you don't want to stand as a courtesy for Holy Mother Church,' Cranston leaned all his considerable bulk on the end of the table, 'I suggest you do so for the King's High Coroner, confidant of His Grace, John of Gaunt and former veteran of the illustrious King's, not to mention his equally illustrious son Edward the Black Prince's wars against the French.' His voice rose. 'By the grace of God, Sir John Cranston, Officer of the Crown.'

One of the company raised a badly-maimed hand, grunted and rose slowly to his feet; the rest followed. They all clasped Cranston's now outstretched hand, nodded at Richer and Athelstan then sat down, their insolence barely concealed by their reluctant courtesy. Cranston took Athelstan to the other end of the table. He sat on the high stool with Athelstan and Richer either side, forcing the soldiers to turn and shuffle awkwardly towards them.

'The day is dying,' Cranston smiled, 'and we are all waiting for the dark which comes sooner or later. Well, you know who I am. Who are you?'

Richer swiftly introduced the four former soldiers: Richard Mahant, Fulk Wenlock, Andrew Brokersby and Henry Osborne. Once he had their attention, Cranston briefly described what had happened in the city – the mysterious death of Kilverby and the disappearance of the Passio Christi. All four were shocked and surprised, although Athelstan suspected that since they'd already told the abbot such news would spread swiftly in an enclosed community.

'It does not affect us really.' Fulk Wenlock raised his right hand, the two forefingers savagely cut off at the stump. 'The Passio Christi was surety for our comfortable quarters here, but I am sure my Lord of Gaunt will honour the Crown's pledges.'

'True, true,' Cranston considered. 'But where were you all yesterday – here?'

'No,' Wenlock retorted, 'not all of us. Mahant and I left in the afternoon for the city.'

'Why?' Athelstan asked.

'Our business, Friar, but if you want to know to roister, to drink and I had petty business with a goldsmith in Poultry.'

'His name?'

'John Oakham.'

'Which tavern did you lodge at?'

'The Pride of Purgatory.'

'I know it well,' Cranston replied. 'Large and sprawling. Minehost is famous for his stews.'

'And you returned?' Athelstan asked.

'Late in the afternoon. We immediately heard the news of poor Ailward's death.'

'And you?' Athelstan turned to Osborne and Brokersby. 'Where were you when Hanep was murdered?'

'Asleep in our beds, Friar.'

'And when Master Hyde was murdered down near the watergate?'

'We were here together.' Osborne's voice portrayed a strong burr. 'We were eating a slice of venison pie and a dish of vegetables.'

'So why was Hyde wandering Mortival meadow?'

'We don't know,' Brokersby retorted, 'nor do we know why Hanep was murdered out in the cemetery. For God's sake, Priest,' Brokersby brought his hand down flat against the table, 'we truly don't know. Hanep could never sleep; he loved to wander at night.'

'That's true,' Richer intervened. 'Master Hanep's nightly pilgrimages around this abbey were well known.'

'Yet both men were murdered,' Athelstan continued remorselessly, 'executed by a skilled swordsman. Indeed, Master Ailward may have been murdered by two assailants. Why?'

'We don't know,' Wenlock spoke up, 'we truly don't. Matters between us were most amicable. We have served together for decades. We have fought, starved, been threatened and survived.'

'We come from the same manor in Essex,' Brokersby explained, 'Leighton, on the way to Wodeford. We became master bowmen and joined the Company of Edward the Black Prince. We took the Wyvern as our livery . . .'

'Continue.' Athelstan smiled.

Brokersby described how he and his companions, at least two score in number, fought in France under the Wyvern banner, about their allegiance to Prince Edward and their undying adoration of him. Athelstan warned Cranston with his eyes to remain silent, for these men needed little encouragement to wax lyrical about their exploits in the Poitiers campaign when they had shattered the power of France. Brokersby mentioned how he'd once been a scholar, a would-be cleric, educated in the local church of St Mary's. Indeed, he added, he was writing his own chronicle of events. This caused surprise even amongst his companions. So, as darkness descended and the bells sounded for the next hour of divine office, the old soldiers reminisced. Athelstan listened and closely studied these grey-haired warriors with the archer braces still on their wrists. Once these were the scourge of France, men who feared no enemy. He also concluded that Mahant was their leader, Wenlock their adviser. More ale was supped. Cranston joined in with his own memories as Richer politely excused himself and withdrew. Once the Frenchman had closed the door behind him Cranston tapped the table for silence.

'So we come to the Passio Christi,' the coroner declared. 'Did you steal it? Of course if you did you are excommunicated, cut off from the church. You shouldn't even be here in these hallowed precincts.' He sighed. 'Naturally you'll deny that. Anyway, tell us, how did you find the bloodstone?'

'To be as blunt,' Wenlock retorted, 'after Poitiers we swept the fields like a windstorm, the very fires of hell.'

'In other words you plundered and pillaged?' Cranston barked. 'I was there, you know. I took part in it. Our army was full of vagabonds, runaways, rascals and ribauds, the scum of our prisons who came from slums so horrid even the rats hanged themselves.' Cranston's words were greeted with silent disbelief until Wenlock beat the table with a maimed hand, bellowing with laughter.

'True, Sir John.' He glanced around his companions. 'Come

on, that is the truth! We had cozeners, tumblers, ape-carriers.'
His words won nods of approval. 'However, we were master
bowmen,' all the good humour drained from Wenlock's face,
'and the Passio Christi was found in a casket on a cart along
a leafy country lane.'

'By you?'

'By us, Friar.'

'And what else was in that cart?'

'Some cloths.' Wenlock paused. 'Cups, mazers, a few
manuscripts.'

'And you surrendered all of this to Edward, the King's son?'

'We did.'

'And?' Athelstan persisted.

'An indenture was drawn up. You can study it at the
Exchequer of Receipt . . .'

'I have,' Cranston interrupted.

'We were given an allowance every month. The jewel was
to be held by Kilverby, the Prince's treasurer. You know the
rest so why should we tell you?'

'How long have you been here?' Athelstan asked, fighting
off the weariness of the day.

'About four years. We came from France then did guard duty
at the Tower, Sheen, Rochester and King's Langley. Five years
ago we petitioned the Crown. We were promised corrodies here.'

'And why St Fulcher's?'

'Ask Father Abbot, Sir John. The old King and his son,
before they left London for Dover and their chevauchées
through France, stopped here to light tapers. They arranged
for Masses to be sung to Christ, Our Lady of Walsingham,
and all the saints that God would favour the Leopards of
England. The old King even founded a chantry chapel here
dedicated to St George.' Wenlock pulled a face. 'St Fulcher
received other gifts and endowments from the royal family.'
Wenlock gazed over his shoulder at the capped hour candle
on its stand in the far corner of the refectory. 'Sir John, Brother
Athelstan, the day goes and so must we.'

'Richer,' Athelstan moved his writing tray, 'do you find him
hostile? After all, he is from the Abbey of St Calliste which
once held the Passio Christi?'

'They claim they once held it,' Wenlock replied. 'We have no real proof that the bloodstone we found belonged to that abbey. I mean, if it was,' he smiled, 'why was it outside the abbey on a cart?'

Athelstan gazed at these former soldiers. He recalled how he and his brother consorted with such men, practical and pragmatic without any real interest in religion or indeed anything else outside their own narrow world. Wenlock's blunt language was typical.

'Was the cart abandoned?' Athelstan asked. 'What happened to its escort?'

'By all the saints,' Brokersby exclaimed, 'that was years ago! What does it matter now?'

'Because, my friend,' Cranston shouted back, 'if it was proven, even now, that the Passio Christi was stolen from the Abbey of St Calliste that renders you excommunicate, whatever the number of years. You would still be proclaimed public sinners and stripped of everything. You might even hang. So tell us,' Cranston added quietly.

'We found it in a cart,' Wenlock answered coolly.

'No escort?'

'Nothing, just plunder of war waiting to be taken.'

Athelstan sighed noisily. 'That is your story.'

'We are our own witnesses,' Mahant declared. 'Who else is there?'

'Tell us,' Cranston asked, 'why should two of your company be so barbarously slain?'

'We don't know,' Osborne declared.

'We are old soldiers serving our time,' Mahant added.

'So why go armed in this abbey?'

'Because Sir John, this abbey is not what it appears to be.' Osborne threw off Brokersby's warning hand.

'You think these good brothers are united in prayer? Well, look at the facts. The abbot hates the prior who responds with as much loathing. The prior loves the Frenchman Richer with a love not known even towards women. Our Lord Abbot is more concerned about that nasty swan than he is about the rule of St Benedict. He keeps his beloved niece, if that is what she really is, in the guest house guarded by that old harridan.

Meanwhile Richer slips in and out of this abbey like a rat from its hole. We've seen him wander down to the watergate. Was he there when poor Ailward was murdered?' Osborne breathed in heavily, wiping the white flecks of foam from his lips on the back of his hand. 'Then there's that anchorite, mad as a March hare, in the abbey church, screaming that he is haunted. He has grudges against us, as do Prior Alexander and others who, I am sure, have great sympathy for the Great Community of the Realm and their leaders the Upright Men. Now two of our comrades are foully murdered, certainly not by us. Why not make your enquiries amongst the brothers: Abbot Walter, Prior Alexander, Richer the Frenchman? After all, we've seen military service, but they've also done their fair share of spilling blood. They can wield swords.' Osborne's voice trailed off in a fit of coughing and throat clearing.

'Do you see Richer as your enemy?'

'No, Brother, but he may view us as his.'

'So why are you armed?'

'Because,' Wenlock intervened, 'three weeks ago, just before the beginning of Advent, I was attacked out in the abbey grounds. I have a passion for herbs and shrubs – I always have. I visited the gardens and afterwards I went for a walk. Nearby runs a maze, its high hedgerows, all prickly, laid out in a subtle plan. A former abbot had built it so those who could not take the cross to Outremer to fight the infidel could crawl through its maze of narrow paths to the centre where there is a Great Pity surmounted by a cross. I entered but dusk was creeping in. I was about to leave when a figure charged out of the gloom, hooded and masked, sword and dagger whirling. I was petrified; all I carried was a pilgrim staff.' Wenlock grimaced. 'The forefingers of both my hands are maimed, the French, God curse them. I cannot pull a bow but still, albeit clumsily, wield a weapon.'

'You fought your assailant off?'

'I was out looking for Wenlock,' Mahant spoke up. 'I heard the shouting, the slash and clatter. I answered Wenlock's cries of *'Aux aide! Aux aide!'* By the time I arrived his assailant had fled; from that time on we decided to go armed.'

'And you reported all this to Father Abbot?'

'I might as well have talked to his stupid swan!'

'And you have no idea of your attacker?'

'No, he was dressed all in black, cowled and masked.'

'Or why you were attacked, at that time, in that place?'

'None whatsoever.'

'Have any of you,' Athelstan persisted, 'relatives outside this abbey?'

'Not that we know of, we are old soldiers. Some of us were married but now our wives are dead.' Mahant's voice turned wistful. 'Whatever children we had lie cold beside them.'

'As do two of your comrades?'

'Brother, Sir John?' Wenlock's voice turned pleading. 'We are finished, surely?'

'I would like to inspect the chambers of the dead men.' Cranston rose swiftly to his feet. 'And that includes William Chalk's.' Cranston gestured towards the door. 'Now, sirs. With you or without you . . .?'

The anchorite, whom the old soldiers described as mad as a March hare, stared calmly through the aperture of his anker house on the south aisle of the abbey church. The monks had finished their hour of divine office. They'd left in a soft slither of sandal and the bobbing light of lantern horns. A cold breeze now seeped through an opened door to whip the remaining glow of candles and tapers. Gusts of sweet beeswax and incense still trailed. Here and there the silence was disturbed by the scurrying of mice and rats sheltering in this forest of stone against the savage cold outside. The anchorite wondered what he might see tonight. He'd heard of Hyde pricked to death near the watergate. The anchorite had tried to warn him. He'd seen Hyde leaving in pursuit of some monk – was it the Frenchman Richer? Then another shadow followed him – a monk, surely? The anchorite was certain of that. He'd seen the flitting blackness through the dark. He glimpsed the glint of steel, but that was life, was it not? Violent and turbulent, full of tension and strife, that's why he sheltered in these sacred precincts with his precious manuscripts, his box of treasure and pallet of paints. He was an anchorite but an exceptional one. He performed one service for the Lord Abbot which few painters did. The abbot was a Grand Seigneur with all the powers of a lord, of Oyer and Terminer, of being Justice of Assize. He had the power of axe, tumbril and gallows and the anchorite served as the abbot's hangman. In return Lord Walter had been good, allowing the anchorite, when the church was deserted, to leave his cell and paint visions of the life hereafter on the walls and pillars around his cell. Yet she, Alice Rednal, the sinister haunter of his life, had followed him here. The anchorite was sure of that. He'd seen Alice Rednal's hard face pressed up against the aperture, features all ghoulish, hair as tangled as a briar bush, but that couldn't be, surely? He'd hanged Rednal at the Elms in Smithfield. He had tolerated her taunting as they rattled along in the execution cart but he'd then watched her die. The anchorite moved back to his small carrel and chancery stool. He sat, picked up his quill pen, opened his journal and began to describe the nightmare which always plagued his sleep. Was this, he wondered, the cause of the recent horrid apparitions?

'Suddenly, without warning,' he whispered as he wrote, 'I saw the witch, yes I did,' the anchorite glanced towards his cot bed, 'climbing on to me. It greatly shocked me. I was so terrified I could not speak. In one hand the harridan carried a wooden coffin and in the other a sharpened scythe. She put a foot upon my chest to restrain me.' The anchorite pushed his journal aside and crept back towards the aperture. He peered through at the painting on the far pillar, the evocation of his own nightmare which haunted him day and night, awake or asleep. He had executed that. At the time he'd been proud of it, and so had the good brothers who'd called it a vivid 'Memento Mori'. Now the anchorite was not so sure as he gazed out in the juddering light of a torch fixed in an iron sconce above the painting. He had depicted Death as that night-hag, her face gnawed away to gleaming white bone. He'd intended to paint black hollow eye sockets but instead he had given her red glaring eyes, her teeth jutting up loose in a large jaw, arms stretched out like scaly bat wings. The anchorite turned away then froze at the rustling of a robe and the slither of soft buskins. He hurried back to the anker slit. He was sure she was there – Alice Rednal had returned to haunt him. The anchorite wanted to scream but he could not, he dare not.

'Go back to hell!' he whispered hoarsely. 'Go back I sent you there! Go back! In the name of the Lord and all that is holy I adjure you to return and stay there.' He grasped the stoup of holy water which stood just within the doorway and feverishly threw a few drops about, but the cold pricking of his spine and the nape of his neck only deepened. She had come. The anchorite closed his eyes trying to summon up images of the Virgin and Child but he could not. All he could picture was a chamber full of flames and filth where venomous demons danced.

'Hangman of Rochester, I promised you would see me again. Alice is here.' The woman's voice sounded like the hissing of a curling viper.

'What do you want?' the anchorite pleaded. 'In God's name, what do you want?'

'Your soul!'

'That is the Lord's.'

'Then your blood money.'

The anchorite glanced at the small silver-hooped casket crammed with precious coins.

'Never!' He turned, looked and recoiled at the face leering through the aperture, chalky white with glaring eyes.

'Remember me?' the voice hissed. 'At the hanging tomorrow I will see you there, perhaps?'

The anchorite grabbed the pole he kept near his bed and turned to thrust it through the gap, but the phantasm had disappeared. The anchorite closed his eyes and fell to his knees, sobbing in prayer . . .

oOoOo

THREE

'Forsteal: a violent affray.'

'The day of their destruction draws near,
Doom comes on wings towards them . . .'
The melodious chant of the black monks of St
Fulcher rose and fell in the taper-lit darkness of their great
oak-carved choir close to the high altar. Athelstan leaned against
the raised stall and tried not to be distracted by the
images clustering around him. The sculptures, the vivid wall
paintings, the shimmering colour of stained-glass windows, the
darkness brooding at the edge of flickering light, not to mention
row upon row of black garbed monks, their faces hidden by
cowls – all of these were a constant temptation to gaze around.

'I have sharpened my flashing sword,' the choir sang.

Athelstan smiled at the words of the psalmist. Coroner
Cranston had decided to curb his sharpened thirst in the refectory of the guest house, though not before telling Athelstan
that they would not be returning to the city that evening.
Athelstan had reluctantly agreed. He wanted to return to St
Erconwald's. God knows he had enough work there but the
business here was compelling. This great abbey absorbed him.
In itself it was a small stone city. At its centre stood this
hallowed cathedral with its transepts and arches, pillars and
plinths, its great rood screen carved in the same fine oak as
the latticed woodwork of the chantry chapels dedicated to this
saint or that which ranged along each aisle. Athelstan would
love to bring his parishioners around this church, show them
the exciting wall paintings and frescoes, the great table tombs
of former abbots, the elaborate pulpit surmounted by a
gorgeous banner displaying the Five Wounds of Christ. Perhaps
the swan-loving abbot would grant such permission? A
Christmas treat with a feast of bread and ale in the abbey
buttery? But not now!

Athelstan let his mind drift. He had visited the narrow chambers of all three dead men. A sad experience. He and Cranston had gone through a collection of paltry possessions: badges, scraps of letters, weapons, clothing and pieces of armour, be it a wrist brace or an ugly-looking dagger. Nothing remarkable except in William Chalk's, those pieces of parchment bearing the crudely inscribed words, '*Jesu Miserere* – Jesus have mercy on me', repeated time and again. Athelstan had asked Wenlock the reason for this. He simply pulled a face and said that Chalk, like any man, was fearful of approaching death. For the rest . . .

Athelstan stared up at a statue of St Fulcher. Those bare, whitewashed chambers with their pathetic possessions intrigued him. Something was wrong, Athelstan reflected. Ah, that was it! He smiled. Yes, they were far too neat and tidy, as if someone had already searched the dead men's possessions – to remove what? Any suspicion about their past, the Passio Christi or some other bloody deed they'd perpetrated during the long years of war . . .?

'Then would the waters have engulfed us.'

Before the leading cantor's words could be answered by the choir, a voice low but carrying echoed through the church.

'And they have engulfed me,' the voice continued. 'Yea, I am caught in the fowler's net and the trap has been sprung.' The voice faded.

'The anchorite, God bless him,' the monk next to Athelstan whispered. 'He has to hang a man tomorrow.'

The cantor, now recovered from his surprise, repeated the verse and the plain chant continued. Athelstan peered down the church and quietly promised himself a visit to the anchorite sooner rather than later. At the end of compline Athelstan expected Father Abbot, seated in his elaborately carved stall, to rise garbed in all his pontificals and deliver the final blessing. Instead a strange ceremony ensued, the likes of which Athelstan had never seen before. The monks sat down in their stalls, cowled heads bowed. A side door in the nave opened. Four burly lay brothers, armed with iron-tipped staves, brought in a man dressed in a black tunic, feet bare, hands bound, his face hidden by a mask. Immediately the cantor rose and began

singing the seven penitential psalms as the prisoner was forced
to kneel between black cloths set over trestles. Athelstan had
noticed these when he had first come under the rood screen
into the choir. As the monks chanted, Prior Alexander left his
stall and thrust a crucifix into the prisoner's bound hands.
Other brothers wheeled a coffin just inside the rood screen
whilst the almoner brought a tray carrying a flagon of wine
and a platter of bread, cheese and salted bacon. Athelstan
recalled the coffin he had seen and the gallows near the
watergate. The abbot must have seigneural jurisdiction.
The prisoner now before them was undoubtedly condemned
to hang on the morrow though not before his soul was shriven
and his belly filled with food. Athelstan whispered a question
to the monk in the next stall. The good brother broke off from
chanting the '*De Profundis*' – and swiftly answered, before
the prior coughed dramatically in their direction, how the
prisoner was a convicted river pirate who'd murdered one of
their lay brothers. The felon had fled to a church further up
the Thames to claim sanctuary but eventually surrendered
himself to the abbot's court. He had been tried and condemned
to hang from the gallows after the Jesus Mass the following
day.

The penitential service finished. The good brothers filed out
of their stalls, past the prisoner who now sat in his coffin,
ringed by guards. Athelstan followed the others and, once out
of the abbey church, he joined the rest in washing his hands
and face in the spacious lavarium near the great cloisters.
Afterwards, led by a servitor, Athelstan joined Cranston for
supper in the abbot's own dining chamber, a magnificent
wood-panelled room warmed by a roaring fire. Thick turkey
rugs covered the floor and skilfully painted cloths hung over
the square, mullioned-glass windows. The splendid dining
table had been covered in samite and a huge golden Nef or
salt seller, carved in the shape of a war cog in full sail, stood
at its centre. The platters, tranchers and goblets were of pure
silver and gold. Napkins of the finest linen draped beautifully
fluted Venetian glasses to hold water drawn from the abbey's
own spring. The wines, both red and white were, so Abbot
Walter assured them, from the richest vineyards outside

Bordeaux. Athelstan wasn't hungry but the mouth-watering odours from the abbot's kitchens pricked his appetite whilst Cranston, now bereft of cloak and beaver hat, sat enthroned like a prince rubbing his hands in relish. Other guests joined them: Prior Alexander, Richer and the ladies Athelstan had glimpsed earlier. The young, fresh-faced woman was Isabella Velours, the abbot's niece; the older one Eleanor Remiet, the abbot's widowed sister. Isabella was dressed for the occasion in a tight fitting gown of green samite, a gold cord around her slender waist, her fair hair hidden beneath a pure white veil of the finest gauze. Mistress Eleanor, however, was garbed like a nun though in a costly dark blue dress tied tightly just under her chin, a veil of the same colour covering her hair and a stiff white wimple framing her harsh, imperious face. Unlike Isabella she wore no rings, brooches, collars or necklaces. Both women bowed to Cranston and Athelstan, then as soon as Abbot Walter delivered the '*Benedicite*' they sat down on the high-backed chairs, grasped their water glasses and whispered busily between themselves. Occasionally Athelstan caught Isabella throwing coy glances at Richer, who always tactfully smiled back. The door to the kitchen opened in a billow of sweet fragrances. Leda the swan, wings half extended, waddled up to the top of the table to receive some delicacies from the abbot. Prior Alexander audibly groaned and loudly muttered that perhaps the swan could be served up in another way. The cutting remark was not lost on Abbot Walter, who grimaced and seemed about to reply in kind but then the first course was promptly served: dates stuffed with egg and cheese, spiced chestnuts, cabbage and almond soup, lentils and lamb, strips of beef roasted in a thick sauce and slices of stuffed pike. Servitors refilled wine goblets and water glasses. For a while the conversation was general: the state of the roads, French piracy in the Narrow Seas, the demand from the Crown for a poll tax and the growing unrest in the city and surrounding shires. The conversation turned to the emergence of the Great Community of the Realm, that shadowy, fervent movement amongst the shire peasants and city poor, threatening revolution and preaching the brotherhood of man. The name of the Kentish hedge-priest John Ball was mentioned as being one

of the Upright Men. Judgements were made on him and opin-
ions passed. Athelstan kept his head down as if more interested
in his food. The friar quietly prayed that his views would not
be asked. Many of his parishioners were fervent adherents of
the Great Community; Pike the ditcher for one sat very close
to some of the most zealous of the Upright Men. Cranston,
wolfing down his food, caught the friar's unease and deftly
turned the conversation to what Athelstan had told him about
the prisoner condemned to hang the following morning.

'A notorious river pirate,' Abbot Walter pronounced, feeding
Leda whilst smiling at his niece.

The abbot went on to describe other depredations of this
well-known felon. Athelstan just picked at his food, secretly
wishing he could take the entire banquet back in baskets for
his parishioners. The friar lifted his head and quickly gazed
round. He was certainly learning more about this abbey. He
caught the mutual dislike between Abbot and Prior, which
he recognized as truly rankling. Isabella, the abbot's niece,
seemed rather vapid and flirtatious. Athelstan wondered about
her true relationship with the abbot yet the more he stared
at her his conviction only deepened that a strong blood tie
existed between the two. The elder woman, Eleanor, was at
first tight-lipped but, as the wine flushed her face, she relaxed,
becoming quite chatty, a highly intelligent woman, sharp-witted
with a keen mind, who shrewdly commented on different
matters. However, Athelstan noticed that the more she talked
the more Cranston seemed fascinated by her, staring across the
table as if trying to recall something. Athelstan took advantage
of the servants clearing the table for the final course of sweet-
ened tarts crowned with cream, to pluck at the coroner's sleeve
and whisper what was the matter?

'I know her,' Cranston murmured, dabbing his mouth with
a napkin. 'Friar, I am sure I do. A face from my past but I
cannot place her.'

'Has she recognized you?'

'No, no. Ah well, what a strange place!' He leaned closer.
'Well, Friar,' Cranston whispered. 'When you were mumbling
your prayers I despatched one of the lay brothers to His Grace
the Regent at his Palace of the Savoy—'

Athelstan abruptly gestured for silence. The table conversation had now changed. Mistress Eleanor was asking about the murders amongst the Wyverns. Abbot Walter immediately assured her that he could not explain the deaths but added that they might be the work of malefactors from the river.

'The Wyverns suspect me,' Richer declared abruptly. 'They think I am waging a feud over the Passio Christi.'

'Are you?'

'You asked me that before, Brother Athelstan. As I answered then, I am a Benedictine.'

'You also served under the Oriflamme banner,' Cranston declared. 'You've been a mailed clerk, yes?'

Richer did not disagree.

'So why have you come here – the truth?'

'I have already explained.'

'Brother Richer is a peritus,' Abbot Walter retorted, shooing off his pet swan. 'He has done excellent work in our library and scriptorium but . . .' Abbot Walter smiled maliciously at Prior Alexander, whose jibe about his beloved Leda he'd not forgotten. 'Perhaps, with all our many problems here, Brother Richer, it's time you returned to St Calliste. I mean,' Abbot Walter waved a hand, 'sooner, rather than later?'

Richer simply shrugged. Prior Alexander, however, sat rigid, his wine-flushed face tense with anger.

'Brother Richer,' Athelstan intervened swiftly, 'which manuscripts . . .' His words were cut off by a sharp knock on the door. A servitor hurried in and whispered into Abbot Walter's ear.

'Bring him in, bring him in,' the abbot insisted. 'Sir John, a messenger – Kilverby's man, his secretarius, Crispin.'

The arrival of the sad-eyed clerk eased the tension. The two ladies immediately rose and said they must retire, as did Prior Alexander who gestured at Richer to follow suit. As they left Crispin was ushered in. He assured Prior Alexander that his eyesight had at least not worsened and he was grateful for all his advice. Once the door was closed, Crispin was offered a vacant seat, Abbot Walter insisting he drank some white wine and eat a little of the cream tart. Crispin did so, muttering between mouthfuls how he and a manservant had travelled by horseback as the river had become swollen and turbulent.

'Never did like the Thames at night.' He cleared his mouth.

'Crispin, what will you do now Sir Robert is so pitifully slain?' Abbot Walter asked.

Crispin shook his head. 'I have sworn to perform some act of loyalty to my dead master. Perhaps I might go on pilgrimage as Sir Robert wanted to do. I could fulfil his vow at Rome, Santiago and Jerusalem. Yes,' he smiled bleakly, 'that's what I should do; after all, my master has gone and Mistress Alesia has her own plans.'

'You'll still be most welcome here,' Abbot Walter reassured him.

Crispin thanked him and turned to Athelstan and Cranston.

'I came here,' he declared, 'because I had to. His Grace the Regent came to our house.' Cranston groaned and put his face in his hands.

'Sir Robert's chamber was not unsealed, was it?' Athelstan asked.

'No, no, His Grace was most strict on that but his temper was very sharp. He had the rest of the mansion searched from cellar to attic but they found nothing. His Grace also sent you this.' Crispin drew from his wallet a small scroll sealed with wax. Cranston snapped the letter open and swore under his breath, forcing Abbot Walter, more interested in his beloved Leda, to glance up sharply.

'And there's more, isn't there?' Athelstan asked Crispin. 'You bring other news?'

'Master Theobald the physician has scrutinized Sir Robert's corpse most thoroughly. Some potion stained his lips and created blueish-red marks here.' Crispin gestured at his own thin chest and sagging belly. 'Master Theobald also declared that the wine and sweetmeats were not tainted but he detected a smell from Sir Robert's corpse which seemed to grow stronger after death: the odour of almonds.'

'The juice of almond seed.' Abbot Walter had now forgotten his swan. 'We have some of that juice here. Prior Alexander would recognize it. I am glad however that the sweetmeats, our gift to Sir Robert, were not tainted but his death is so odd, so curious. Now sirs, please excuse me.' The abbot, dabbing his sweaty, porkish face with a napkin, rose to his feet, sketched a blessing in their direction and, followed by Leda, swept out of the chamber.

Cranston broke the ensuing silence by drinking noisily from his goblet, then held up the Regent's letter.

'Worse and much worse to come, little friar.'

'Sir John?'

'The Regent must be obeyed on this,' Cranston declared. 'Crispin and I will leave for the city. Yes, we'll go now even though it is dark. The city guard will let me through. In truth, I prefer to sleep in my own bed with my plump wife beside me.'

'And me, Sir John?'

'You, Friar, have drawn the short straw on this. His Grace insists that you stay here until this business be finished.'

Athelstan, his cowl pulled well over his head, stood by the gate which led from the abbey gardens overlooking Mortival meadow. It was certainly a morning for a hanging: sombre, grey and mist-filled. The sounds of the abbey remained muffled and distant, be it the clanging of bells, the lowing of cattle or the strident cries of geese and cockerels. Sir John and Crispin had left immediately the night before, the coroner borrowing a mount from the abbey stables. Cranston was visibly shaken by the Regent's apparent temper and, as he whispered to Athelstan in the stable yard where they made their farewells, there was much to reflect upon about this abbey, especially Eleanor Remiet. Athelstan had watched Cranston go. Later in the evening the friar had been given a warm chamber in the abbot's own guest house. There he tried to marshal his thoughts but tiredness overtook him and he fell asleep to dream about his own sojourn in France. Awake long before dawn, Athelstan sang prime with the brothers and celebrated his Jesus Mass in a side-chapel. Now he was here to glimpse the anchorite, who also served as the abbey hangman.

A bell began to toll the death-knell, booming solemnly, announcing to the world that another soul was about to meet its God. The refrain of the '*De Profundis*' wafted on the breeze.

The glow of candle sparked through the swirling mist. Out of this came the crucifer grasping a wooden cross, either side of him the acolytes carrying their capped candles, followed by a thurifer filling the air with incense. Prior Alexander followed. A cowl concealed both his head and face, hands pushed up the sleeves of his gown. He recited the death psalm which was repeated by the group of brothers huddled behind him. The anchorite, garbed in a monk's robe, came next; the thrown back hood revealed a cadaverous, clean-shaven face framed by straggling hair the colour of straw which fell down to his shoulders. In one hand this sinister-looking individual carried a crucifix and in the other a coil of rope. Behind him lay brothers on either side bore a coffin and a set of ladders. The closely guarded prisoner came next, his mask now removed. Athelstan stared at that reddish, furrowed face, scrawny hair and the scars along his neck.

'Fleischer the fisherman!' he exclaimed. The prisoner paused and stared at the friar, who pushed back his cowl.

'Brother Athelstan, you've come to see me dance on air.'

The entire procession stopped. Prior Alexander, intrigued, walked back. 'You know this felon, Brother?' the prior asked.

'Oh, yes.' Athelstan gazed at Fleischer. He certainly knew the fisherman. A bosom friend of Moleskin the boatman, Fleischer sometimes appeared on the shabby quaysides of Southwark to participate in the rich harvest of mischief to be found along its filthy runnels and alleyways: robbery, smuggling and counterfeiting. Fleischer was as attracted to such devilry as Bonaventure to a dish of cream.

'I would like words with you, Brother?'

Athelstan glanced at Prior Alexander, who nodded. The anchorite pushed Fleischer across.

'Your prisoner, Brother.'

'*Pax et bonum.*' Athelstan stared into the glassy, blue eyes of the anchorite. Was he mad, touched by the moon? No, Athelstan reckoned, the anchorite was only agitated. Athelstan also caught the glint of humour in the man's strange, pallid face.

'For a short time he is yours.' The anchorite stood back. 'And then he'll be mine again.'

Athelstan gently led Fleischer out of hearing.

'You want to be shriven?'

'I've confessed,' Fleischer replied. 'Give me your blessing.'
Athelstan did so.

'Will you sing a Mass for me, Brother, that my journey
through the flames won't be too long?'

'Of course.'

'Give Moleskin and the rest greetings.' Fleischer tried to
curb his tears. 'I was born into wickedness, Brother, no mother
or father, alone with all the other rats.' He stared around. 'I
didn't mean to kill the monk but I was desperate. Strange.'
Fleischer ignored Prior Alexander's cough as he shuffled from
foot to foot. 'Here I am,' Fleischer stepped closer, his ale-tinged
breath hot against Athelstan's face, 'being hanged by the Lord
Almighty Abbot – you're here for the murders, to probe and
snout for the killer?'

'You could say that, my friend.'

'Then take a good look at these shaven heads. I've seen the
Frenchman Richer meet boatmen from foreign ships – what
is that, treason? And as for Prior Alexander, he so likes being
with his good friend the sub-prior, even if it means travelling
along a freezing river in a barge. Or shall we talk about those
good monks who don disguises and visit the stews and bath
houses of Southwark? For me retribution is close but theirs is
also approaching. When the great revolt breaks out and it will,
like pus from a sore, believe me, all the Marybread and
Marymeat distributed on a Sunday won't save them. They're
all as rotten and wicked as I am.'

'Scurrilous rumours, my friend?'

'Perhaps, Brother.' Fleischer looked over his shoulder. 'As
for Lord Walter! Sharing the kiss of peace with the Upright
Men who gather at All Hallows won't protect him.' Fleischer
grinned bleakly. 'Ask any of the river people. Anyway, these
mumbling mouses now want to hang me.' He nodded back at
the anchorite, standing like some sombre statue. 'At least they
say he's good. He can do it in a splice – he's not some
cow-handed peasant. Ah well, I'm getting cold and it's time I
was gone.' He bowed his head. Athelstan made the sign of the
cross over him and stepped back as the anchorite came over.

'I would like words with you, sir,' Athelstan murmured, 'when this business is finished. I shall be waiting for you in St Fulcher's chantry chapel.'

The anchorite simply darted a look, grasped Fleischer by the arm and took him back to join the others. The procession reformed. Prior Alexander intoned the opening words of the sequence, '*Dies Irae* – Oh Day of wrath, Oh Day of Mourning, See fulfilled heaven's warning . . .' The sombre sight disappeared into the thick veil of mist. The candle light dimmed, the words faded, nothing but silence. Athelstan sighed, blessed himself and walked back through the murk into the abbey church. All lay quiet. This hymn in stone closed around him, evoking memories of his motherhouse at Blackfriars. Athelstan compared its magnificence with the simple crudeness of St Erconwald's and felt a pang of homesickness. He would love the likes of Huddle, Watkin and all that boisterous throng to come tumbling through the porch. Athelstan reached the chantry chapel. He went in under the latticed screen with its fretted carving and sat down on a stool staring up at the painted window, marvelling at the sheer subtlety of it all. A demon had been drawn into its intricate tracery. Red stain had first been applied to the blue glass whilst the glowing left eye of the fiend had been formed by simply drilling the actual glass. The devil's yellow, spiky hair was depicted against a background of flaming red which reflected the very fires of hell.

Athelstan glanced down at the floor. He must concentrate on why he was here. He must summarize what he'd learnt then revise and draft it as he used to before debating a theological problem at Blackfriars.

Item: Sir Robert Kilverby had apparently retired to his chamber hale and hearty. The Passio Christi was safely locked away in its coffer and kept in that chamber.

Item: No one entered that room. Sir Robert certainly never left it.

Item: No poisonous taint or potion could be found in the room, neither in the wine nor the sweetmeats.

Item: The door to that chamber had to be forced. Members of the household, very hostile to each other, had discovered

Kilverby's corpse. They were certain nothing had been interfered with or taken away.

Item: Nevertheless, Kilverby had been poisoned by some slow-acting potion, perhaps the juice of almond seed. Athelstan was well acquainted with that venom – even a few grains were deadly. Traces of a poison had been found on Kilverby's lips and elsewhere on the corpse.

Item: After Kilverby's two monkish visitors had left, the Passio Christi was placed back into its casket and made secure. Witnesses had seen the ruby returned to its casket, which Kilverby and Crispin had then taken to the chancery chamber. Kilverby surely would have personally assured himself of the bloodstone's security? After all, he alone carried the keys on that chain around his neck. He would have certainly raised the alarm if anything was amiss.

Item: Sir Robert Kilverby was a very rich man who'd undergone some form of conversion. He intended to go on a life-time pilgrimage to Santiago, Rome and Jerusalem. All his business affairs would be left to his daughter and her husband. Kilverby's widow was not his heir, so why should she kill her husband? She profited little except, perhaps, a closer intimacy with her strange kinsman Adam Lestral. Finally, Crispin appeared to be his master's most loyal servant, who was leaving his service anyway. Kilverby's secretarius certainly did not profit from his master's death.

Item: The Passio Christi was, by contract of indenture, to be shown to the Wyvern Company twice a year. Yesterday the Feast of St Damasus was one of those days. However, Kilverby intended the bloodstone to be taken to St Fulcher's not by himself but his trusted secretarius and beloved daughter. Why? Athelstan squinted up at the devil's face on the painted window. Kilverby seemingly did not want to meet the Wyvern Company. Had he learnt something highly distasteful about them? That they had sacrilegiously stolen the sacred bloodstone?

Item: Was Sir Robert planning to leave the Passio Christi at St Fulcher's just before he left on pilgrimage? Was this an act of reparation, for what the Wyverns had done? On the one hand Sir Robert avoided their company but, on the other, he liked to visit this abbey and mingle with its community. Was all this part of Kilverby's conversion?

'But in the end,' Athelstan whispered to himself, 'Kilverby was poisoned in his own locked chamber with no evidence as to why, how or by whom. The Passio Christi has been stolen, but once more without a scrap of evidence to show how this was done.'

Athelstan rose, stretched and paced up and down the chantry chapel, half aware of the distant echoing sounds. He breathed out noisily. Then there were the murders here at St Fulcher's. Again, the friar tried to organize his thoughts.

Item: The Wyvern Company had been comfortably lodged here for about four years. Master bowmen, veterans, they had served the late King and his son the Black Prince. Both King and heir now lay cold beneath their funeral slabs. The crown had descended to the Black Prince's young son Richard, under the care of his uncle the Regent, John of Gaunt, a prince of deep deviousness who wanted that bloodstone.

Item: The old soldiers were lodged here because the Crown generously patronized St Fulcher's. Moreover, because the Passio Christi was held in trust by Kilverby it was he, not the exchequer, who paid for the sustenance of the old soldiers. However, once all the Wyverns were dead, the Passio Christi reverted to the Crown; Kilverby, or his heirs, receiving a generous grant.

Item: Both the Wyvern Company and Kilverby, whatever they thought about each other, were apparently content with this business arrangement. John of Gaunt, however, was desperate for bullion. Could that arrogant, handsome yet so sinister a Regent be assisting all those with claims on the Passio Christi into the darkness?

Item: Who had killed Hanep and Hyde, two experienced swordsmen caught out in the open and cut down? Had Hyde been killed by one or two assailants? Neither of the slain men had been able to defend themselves. Did this indicate the works of a paid assassin, someone either despatched in from outside or hiding deep within the abbey?

Item: And why had they been killed? They'd apparently not alienated any of their confreres. And why should old comrades turn so viciously on each other? There was certainly no evidence of bad blood between them . . . Athelstan paused in his pacing as a group of novice monks padded along the aisle and up into the choir stalls. Athelstan continued his reasoning.

Item: The Lord Abbot with his swan, his niece and the enigmatic Eleanor Remiet, was not exactly a mirror of monastic dedication. Was Isabella Velours his niece or something else? Athelstan was certain she was the former. Moreover, the abbot might be a priest consumed with lusts of the flesh. Some of his monks might frequent the pleasure pots of Southwark but, Athelstan smiled to himself, monks sinned, as did friars. Moreover, just because they were lecherous, did that mean the likes of Abbot Walter were murderers?

Item: More importantly, did Father Abbot go to All Hallows Barking? Was he secretly negotiating with the Upright Men and the Great Community of the Realm? What was really happening at the distribution of Marymeat and Marybread on a Sunday? Then there was Richer, the elegant, sophisticated Frenchman, certainly a man of mystery. Prior Alexander was much smitten with him. Athelstan pulled a face. Such a friendship, like that of David for Jonathan in the Old Testament, was common enough in monastic communities. Richer was the problem. Why was he really at St Fulcher's? To secure the *Passio Christi* or was he a spy? Why did he, according to Fleischer, meet boatmen from foreign ships? What did he receive or give to these people?

'Alleluia, alleluia, *O Sapientia Altissimi* – Oh Wisdom of the Most High.' The lucid voices of the novices intoned one of the Christmas 'O Antiphons'. Athelstan stood, heart thrilling at the sheer passionate beauty of the sound.

'Come,' the choir chanted, 'and teach us the way of truth!'

'Aye,' Athelstan whispered, tears pricking his eyes. 'Come Everlasting Beauty whom we all desire, and will have no peace until we find you.'

Athelstan stood transfixed as the choir moved on to the second 'O Antiphon'. The words, the exquisite loveliness of the chanting evoked so many bittersweet memories of his past – and his present! Athelstan beat his breast. St Erconwald's! His parishioners? The choir and the 'O

Antiphons'? The bustling business of preparing the church for Christmas?

'We need more holly,' Athelstan murmured absent-mindedly.

'Pardon, Brother?'

Athelstan glanced sharply to his right. The anchorite stood in the doorway to the chantry chapel.

'He has gone.'

'And may God give him eternal rest,' Athelstan whispered, crossing himself. 'Poor Fleischer.'

'He made a good end.'

'Nobody makes a good end.' Athelstan walked towards this cadaverous spectre of a man, 'At least not when you're hanged.'

'He died quickly.' The anchorite plucked at the rope belt around his waist, curling one end with his strong fingers, 'It's best that way. If you topple your victim from the highest rung of the ladder the neck snaps, or so I think. Other hangmen strangle their victims. You could say the office for the dead before it's truly over. Anyway, you want words with me, Friar?'

Athelstan indicated the bench against the wall beneath the painted window. The anchorite sat down next to him. Athelstan noticed how the man's fingernails were neat and cleanly pared, though stained with dashes of ink and paint.

'You're a scribe?'

'I am a painter as well as a hangman.' The anchorite shifted and stared at Athelstan with his strange blue eyes. 'I'm also a listener. I sit in my anker house and the brothers slip by me. They often forget I'm there. I hear their chatter and gossip. You're Brother Athelstan, the consummate hunter, a lurcher in Dominican robes who seeks out his quarry. So, what do you want with me?'

'First, who are you? Why are you here?'

The anchorite glanced away. 'I was raised,' the anchorite began slowly, 'at the baptismal font in Sempringham as Giles, that's my real name. My doting parents despatched me to the cathedral school at Ely. I sat with the other scholars in the north aisle with my horn book, ink pen and quills. I studied the Latin of Jerome as well as that of Cicero. I was meant to be a cleric but my sin,' the anchorite bared his lips in a mirthless grin, 'to quote the psalm, was always before me. I fell in love with the wall paintings, frescoes and coloured glass of that cathedral. I would wander to marvel at all that I saw. After my apprenticeship in Norwich I became a painter. I travelled the roads to this church or that chapel. God heaped even more blessings on me. I met my wife Beatrice and she became my helper. We had a child but we still continued to wander the kingdom. I earned very good silver and gold. I was in much demand, be it depicting the *Biblia Pauperum* – the Bible of the Poor for parishioners to learn from, or the single solitary scene, be it a sinner being carted off to hell by a demon in a wheelbarrow or the Assumption of the Virgin. We lodged in taverns and guest houses until the Apocalypse occurred . . .'

'When the waters swept over your head?' Athelstan intervened, recalling the anchorite's interruption of compline the previous evening.

'Too powerful,' the anchorite whispered. 'Still too powerful – such memories! Let me tell you. We were crossing the Weald of Kent; it was early autumn. I left Beatrice and the child to go and buy paint, brushes and pigment. When I returned outlaws, wolfsheads, creatures from the stinking blackness, fiends from the dungeons of hell had attacked our cart, pillaged it, ravished Beatrice then murdered both her and our child.' He paused at Athelstan's sharp gasp.

'Wickedness,' the friar murmured, clutching at the anchorite's arm. 'God have mercy on them, and on you. I shall remember them at Mass.'

'At the time,' the anchorite continued, evenly lost in his own nightmare past, 'I was too full of hatred and vengeance to mourn. I'd done good service for the sheriff of Kent in his castle chapel. I took my family's corpses to him for burial. I also invoked the blood feud and he agreed to help. He raised the hue and cry and issued writs summoning up both the posse comitatus and the shire levies. The outlaws, five in number, were trapped in a wood outside Rochester. They were caught red-handed and immediately sentenced to hang from the Keep of Rochester Castle. You know it?'

Athelstan nodded.

'I was their hangman. I took each of those wicked souls put the noose around their necks and tossed them over. I watched each do the dance of death. My reputation spread. Rochester hired me as its hangman.' He laughed a short, bitter bark. 'I painted their churches and hanged their wolfsheads until I met Alice Rednal.'

'Alice Rednal – I am sure my Lord Coroner . . .?'

'I know Sir John Cranston, Brother; he hired me as Rednal's executioner at Smithfield. I was given a chamber in St Bartholomew's Priory which lies nearby. I didn't just hang her but others. On execution days I would journey from Newgate to Smithfield in the execution cart with those condemned to die sitting at my feet. I also continued to do some paintings; you can see them in St Sepulchre's which stands close to Cock Lane.'

'Alice Rednal?' Athelstan persisted.

'Sorry, Brother,' the anchorite paused, 'you know I should go back to my cell. I want to. I always like to be alone after a hanging. However,' he sighed, 'Alice Rednal! She was the wickedest fiend from the darkest ward of hell. She murdered children, drowned them in the Thames. Sir John caught her and arraigned her before the Justices of Oyer and Terminer where she was condemned to hang. I collected her in the execution cart. No sooner were we out of the prison than she started to mock me. She whispered how, hanging or not, she'd taken quite a liking to me, as those others who'd murdered my wife had taken such a liking to her. I then realized, somehow, she'd been a member of their coven. She named their leader, a malignant called Wolfsbane. I challenged her, claiming she was lying, but it was obvious – she knew so much about them.'

'What was she like physically?'

'Oh, tall with wild, greyish hair. Harsh-faced with a full figure.' The anchorite blinked furiously. 'She also told me something else.' He pointed at Athelstan. 'Is this why I am being brought to the bar for questioning?'

'What do you mean?' Athelstan asked.

'According to Rednal, after I left Beatrice, she and our child were resting under a shade of trees. Beatrice realized she was being watched by Wolfsbane and his coven and as she prepared to flee, a group of mounted archers journeying to Rochester galloped by. Beatrice tried to persuade them to help but they were in too much of a hurry. They mocked her fears and left her to herself.'

'These mounted archers?' Athelstan felt a coldness creeping through him as if from the hard stone around him.

'Rednal claimed they were the Wyvern Company on garrison duty at Rochester.'

'The same who now lodge here?'

'I presume so, Friar.'

'So why did Rednal tell you that?'

'She said they were on duty when I hanged Wolfsbane and his coven. She claimed I should have executed them as well.'

'Is that why you came here, hangman, to pursue vengeance?'

'No, no, let me finish. Rednal, sitting on her own coffin, continued to ridicule me. She pointed out how the world was truly cruel and no one really cared. I slapped her face and told her to shut up. She replied that we would certainly meet again. Anyway, I hanged her at the Elms. I kicked her off the ladder and watched her struggle and twist, then I went my way. Oh yes, thoughts of further vengeance on those archers who refused to help Beatrice curdled and boiled, but then Rednal's ghost intervened.'

'Pardon?' Athelstan turned on the bench.

'I was lodged in my chamber at St Bartholomew's. The door had a small grille at the top which could be opened. One evening, about a week after Rednal's hanging, I heard a knocking. I thought it was a servitor. I crossed and opened the grille. I swear I saw this: Rednal's face all liverish, eyes glaring, stared in at me, her full foul lips moved. "I told you", she whispered, "we would meet again". I slammed the grille shut yet when I opened the door I saw nothing but shadows. Since then I have seen her face again and again peering at me through a dusty, latticed window or from a crowd . . .' His words trailed away.

Athelstan crossed himself.

'Do you believe in ghosts, Brother Athelstan?'

'Yes,' the friar answered. 'Some you see and some you don't.'

'Do you think I am madcap, fey and witless?'

'No, my friend.' Athelstan tapped the man's wrist. 'But you are a painter,' he smiled, 'with wild imaginings, who saw his family slaughtered. You yourself were cruelly baited about this. In the end what is real enough to you is also the truth to you.' Athelstan paused. 'You must anticipate my next question as you would if you faced a magister in the schools. I have asked it once, I do so again. Did you come here to seek vengeance on the Wyvern Company?'

'No, no, Brother, here in this church I swear. I arrived here a broken man. I fled to escape from the ghost of Alice Rednal, to atone for my many sins. I arrived at St Fulcher's to execute certain paintings in the south aisle. Abbot Walter had three prisoners waiting to be hanged. No one would do it so I performed the task.' The anchorite got to his feet, visibly agitated. 'One thing led to another. I told Father Abbot my story. I expressed my desire for peace and he granted me the anker house.' He turned to face Athelstan. 'I continue both to paint and to hang.' He laughed drily. 'Look at me, Brother – do I look like a swordsman? Despite my wild imaginings I'm no fool. You do not confront, challenge or cross the likes of Wenlock and Mahant – cruel men, professional killers who fear neither heaven nor hell. Oh yes, I could tell you more about the dire events here but,' he strode as if in a panic towards the entrance to the chantry chapel then glanced over his shoulder, 'I have much more to say,' he whispered, 'much more to judge, much more to condemn but not for now.'

For the rest of that Advent week Athelstan kept to himself. Cranston did not return but sent a message with Flaxwith that all was well. The coroner had even visited St Erconwald's and announced how 'that coven of sinners' were walking the path of righteousness. Benedicta also despatched Crim the altar boy with similar reassurances. Athelstan truly missed his parish. He thought of appealing to Blackfriars but he knew John of Gaunt, the silver-tongued Regent, would have already convinced Athelstan's superiors that the friar's presence at St Fulcher's was vital for the Crown's interests. Accordingly Athelstan distracted himself, becoming immersed in the daily horarium of the abbey. He stayed well away from those he intended to investigate later: the Wyvern Company, Richer, the abbot and his niece, that anchorite and his grim paintings in the south aisle. Athelstan closely studied these even as he was aware of that eerie soul staring at him through the aperture of the anker house. He also stayed away from the watergate and the nearby gallows where poor Fleischer's corpse was to hang for three turns of the tide. Athelstan did attend the felon's hurried burial in the Field of Blood, that deserted derelict stretch of the cemetery reserved for the corpses of malefactors and vagabonds.

Athelstan merged like a shadow into the rule of the black monks. He woke with them when the sub-prior rang the cock-crow bell in the dormitory and joined the sleepy, lantern-lit procession into the choir. Once there he'd watch the sacristan lay out the purple and gold vestments of the Advent season, trim the great lantern horn above the lectern and go round the brothers in a glow of candle light to ensure none of them had fallen asleep during matins. Sometimes he joined the brothers in their stroll around the cloisters. He learnt a little of their sign language when talking was forbidden, though he was never invited to their chapter where duties were assigned, notices proclaimed and corrections carried out. The food in the refectory was good: fish, vegetables, fruit, cheese, spices, figs and ale with pork pies, capon pastry, apple tarts and all kinds of blancmange being served. On occasions he played nine pins and provoked laughter due to his clumsiness, though he soon retrieved his reputation at the chess board.

At other times Athelstan wandered that forest of stone, constantly aware of arches, columns and pillars all intricately decorated. Statues of saints, sinners, gargoyles and babewyns peered down at him from finely sculptured bushes, trees and foliage where mystical animals such as the salamander and unicorn sheltered. Athelstan became accepted as a fellow brother, though one to be wary of as the purpose of his visit became more widely known. Increasingly however, especially as daylight faded, Athelstan locked himself in his own chamber and tried to make sense of the jumbled bloody events which had occurred since St Damasus' eve. He searched for the root, for the prime cause, to unpick all this tangle, a seminal event which would explain and clarify. Athelstan grew certain of one truth. Kilverby's murder and those of the Wyverns were connected probably through the bloodstone, the Passio Christi. Yet, what was the prime cause of all this slaughter? The *radix malorum omnium* – the root of all evil? Kilverby's pilgrimage to Outremer? But why should that open the bloody gate to the meadows of murder? The only person who might be affected would be John of Gaunt should the Passio Christi be handed over to St Fulcher's but Gaunt, at least according to the evidence, had no knowledge of what Kilverby intended.

Athelstan's puzzlement deepened. On the Saturday before the third Sunday of Advent he locked himself in his own chamber and pretended to be Kilverby. The merchant had sat at his desk poring over manuscripts, just thinking. He'd never left, not even to relieve himself. Athelstan had examined the covered jakespot in the far corner of the chamber. Kilverby had already supped and suffered no ill effects from that. The wine he'd carried in proved to be untainted as had the sweet-meats brought from the abbey. The Passio Christi was securely locked in its casket with the keys around Kilverby's neck. No one had entered that chamber, yet by morning Kilverby was murdered and the Passio Christi gone. How? Why? Athelstan heard a noise, a tapping on the shutters. He rose and walked across to the lantern window. He pulled back the shutters and looked out over the frozen flower garden, its shrubs and rich soil gripped in a harsh frost. Warming his fingers over a nearby chafing dish, Athelstan glanced around and dismissed the tapping as a mere flurry of ice in the snapping breeze. He was about to turn away when a flurry of movement out of the corner of his eye made him start. A cowled figure moved from his left into full view – one of the brothers? The figure knelt as if studying the frozen ground. Athelstan caught the glint of metal as this sinister apparition brought up the arbalest. The friar sprang back, stumbling to the floor as the barbed quarrel whirred angrily above him, smashing against the plaster on the far wall. Athelstan murmured a prayer, sprang to his feet, unlocked the door and hurried out. He almost crashed into Wenlock coming into the guest house.

'Brother,' Wenlock gripped the friar's arm with his maimed

hand, 'are you well? What is the matter? You look as if you are going to shout harrow and raise the hue and cry.'

Athelstan caught his breath as a cold sweat broke out.

'Nothing.' He breathed in deeply. 'Nothing for the moment.'

oOoOo

FOUR

'Jurat: a sworn man.'

On that same Saturday, Sir John Cranston sat in his judgement chamber in the great Guildhall overlooking Cheapside. He eased himself up in his leather-covered throne-like chair and glared around. He'd had tried to make this chamber as comfortable as possible. Triptychs from Genoa celebrating the scenes of the Lord's Passion rendered in glowing colours hung alongside tapestries displaying the Arms of the city and the livery of the Cranston family. He caught sight of the Cross of San Damiano, a replica of the one St Francis of Assisi had prayed before. Cranston stopped his quiet cursing and blessed himself. He glanced at the claret jug and goblet on the polished dresser beneath the crucifix but shook his head. He would not drink, not now! Sir John opened the thick, leather-bound ledger before him and stared at the litany of human weakness and wickedness drawn up for his inspection by Osbert, his chancery clerk, and Simon the scrivener. One long, cream-coloured sheet listed the weapons seized that week: daggers, blades, cudgels and quarter staves, pike staves, crooked billets, pole-axes and halberds. 'London's like a battlefield,' Cranston whispered.

The next folio contained grimmer entries. The murder of a poor girl by a man and his wife just for the clothes the young woman wore. Elena Hellebore, convicted for smashing a chaplain's head after he'd called her a 'tread-foul', a slang term for a whore. Agnes Houdy, who'd strangled a drunk with his own belt so she could have his boots. Henry Staci, for causing the death of Margaret Privet 'other than her own natural death'. Next was William Hammond.

'You're an interesting one,' Cranston murmured. According to the entry William's wife Marisa was burnt to death by a fire caused by the fall of a lighted candle as she and her husband prepared for bed. Both had escaped from the burning tenement but William was so angry at his wife for causing the fire through her own negligence he pushed her back into the flames and tried to flee for sanctuary to St Martin-Le-Grand. Beside each of these entries the scrivener had written 'susp' in red ink – '*suspenditur* – hanged'. The next page listed all the fatal accidents in thc city. A robber at St Paul's wharf who'd been recognized by his victims whom he'd attacked on the Brentwood Road. The outlaw had tried to escape, fallen into the Thames and drowned. Other entries listed victims being killed by a horse, falling timber, scalding water tossed from a window or arrows loosed at Stepney, not to mention the drunk who drowned after jumping into the great sewer near Fleet or the two carpenters who'd tumbled from ladders at the Savoy Palace. The final entry made Cranston groan. He'd returned from St Fulcher's and presented himself at John of Gaunt's inner chamber at the Savoy. The Regent had done his best to hide his smouldering temper. Dressed in red, gold and blue velvet boasting the snarling leopards of England, his fingers and chest glittering with gold rings and a jewel-encrusted collar, the Regent had been both magnificent and munificent. He had filled Cranston's goblet to the rim and personally served the coroner with a dish of sugared fruit and a mazer of sweetmeats. Gaunt had listened attentively, those strange eyes crinkling, full lips pursed, yet his temper was obvious and his message was clear. The Passio Christi had been stolen and he wanted it back. Cranston and Athelstan would achieve that or . . .

'Or what?' Cranston murmured to himself.

He wondered what Athelstan was doing, as well as the strange secrets that abbey held. The Regent had told him little and Cranston was still bemused by Eleanor Remiet. He was sure he'd done business with her before, but when and why?

'Sir John, my Lord Coroner?'

Cranston glanced up. Osbert, his plump, cheery-faced clerk stood in the doorway fingering his lank brown hair. Next to him was Simon the scrivener, pasty-faced with ever watery eyes and dripping nose. Both clerks found Cranston a source of many droll stories though in his presence they acted most dutifully.

'The Deodandum?' Simon asked. 'You must decide on the Deodandum.'

Cranston immediately did. He had the case written out on a piece of parchment before him. In brief, Ralph, Megotta Ugele's husband, had been killed by a runaway horse and cart in Hogweed Lane. Megotta now claimed both horse and cart should not be sold and given to the church, who owned it anyway as a *Deodandum*, a gift to God, but handed over to her as compensation. Cranston decided with a sweep of his quill pen that the widow's needs were more pressing than those of Holy Mother Church. Once done he rose to his feet, pushing back his chair.

'It is Saturday.' He glared at his two minions. 'I have other business. Has Muckworm appeared?'

'No, Sir John,' both men chorused.

'In which case,' Cranston buckled on his war belt, grabbed his cloak and beaver hat and stepped down from the dais, 'if Muckworm rears his ugly head, tell him he'll find me in my favourite chantry chapel immersed in my devotions.'

'The Holy Lamb of God, Sir John?'

'Very perceptive.' Cranston nodded at both men and swept out of the judgement chamber, down the stairs and into the bailey. Scurriers and messengers, all booted and spurred, were readying restless horses, the breath of both man and beast hanging like a clear mist in the freezing air. Cranston pushed his way past these as well as a swarm of clerks, ostlers and ragged scholars whose Goliard song caught Sir John's fancy.

'My desire is to die in a tavern,

Where wine will stain my dying mouth.

All the choirs of angels will chant,

May God be merciful to this man of drink.'

Cranston dropped a coin in their begging bowl and strolled out under the cavernous arch into Cheapside. Evening was due yet business still thrived. The air was thick with a mixture of smells. The sweet fragrances of the herb and perfume-sellers, vegetable and fruit hawkers mingled with the stink from the ordure-strewn cobbles. The fullers' stench was still strong, whilst the wind wafted in the foul odours from the fleshing yards. Cranston donned both cloak and hat as he surveyed the busy stalls and booths. He hardly noticed the drab but smart smocks, jerkins and gowns of the tradesmen, the glossy elegance of court fops with pomanders pushed under their nostrils or the wealthy in their velvet, wool-lined cloaks and sheepskin mittens.

'No,' Cranston whispered, 'where are you my lovelies, all you creatures of the dark?'

Two worlds existed here: one apparent, the other had to be closely studied. Cranston surveyed the crowd. Oh yes, they were here, the night-walkers and dark-hawks, soil-caked and dirt marked, who slept on straw pallets stretched out over tamped-down mud. The coin-fakers and cross-biters, the cozeners, the mumpers, the scolders and sneaksmen in their motley garish rags, pointed hoods and scuffed boots were on the prowl. All these were of the same genus – Newgate birds, who would milk a pigeon to get a drink. Some were obvious, others more hidden as they threaded through the crowd, looking for prey. Cranston recognized quite a few of his 'Lovelies': Mouse-ears with his twitching nose and stuck-out ears, Frost-face, his skin badly gnawed by the pox, Rats-tooth and Spindle-shanks, could all be glimpsed amongst the mad and the bad, the moon-men and the moon-cursers. At the mouth of alleyways clustered even more, the beggars who ate mouldy bread filled with barley straw and drank watered ale and wine so muddy it made them wry-mouthed.

'Ah, well,' Cranston breathed. He moved out from beneath the archway and crossed the broad expanse of Cheapside. He was soon recognized by a gibbet lawyer going down to Newgate to meet an accomplice. 'Cranston is out!' The whisper spread through the crowds. Sir John, one hand on the hilt of his sword, watched both the slime-strewn cobbles beneath him as well as the crowds around him. He glimpsed Matilda the mistress of the maids hurriedly disappear down a runnel with a bevy of her ladies of the night. Alleyway mouths also mysteriously cleared. Foists and nips darted off like sparrows alarmed by a cat. The rag traders, the whipsters, mountebanks and miserere men stooped, crouched and ran back to hide in what Cranston called 'Mumpers' Manor' or 'Castle Conning', the filthy lairs and bolt-holes of these Cheapside cheats. They all feared Cranston. Parson Dumpling, who looked after these malefactors at his Chapel of the Gibbet deep in the slums of Whitefriars, always warned his congregation that Sir John, when the spirit took him, could whistle up his bailiffs and beadles and sweep like the wind through Cheapside, Poultry and the surrounding wards, netting their quarry as a fowler would his birds. Once done, they'd herd all their captives down to the great yard at the Fleet prison. There, as on Judgement Day, they'd begin to separate one flock of goats, those they wanted to question, from the rest, whom they'd leave to graze for a while. Cranston paused – should he do that now? Yet he had enough business awaiting him. Muckworm would soon appear.

'Not today, my lovelies,' Cranston murmured.

He walked on, then stopped by a stall to view a vase made out of clay with a dark green glaze, next to this a jug fashioned out of quartz which Cranston quietly promised to mention to Lady Maud. He fingered some Saracen cloth on the next stall, glanced around and moved on. He inspected the cage on the Tun; this was empty except for a drunk who lay snoring on his back. At the nearby stocks, bailiffs were locking in Plugtail, a notorious cunning man who sold philtres no more useful than a cup of dirty water. He greeted Cranston cheerfully. The coroner responded by ordering the bailiffs to ensure Plugtail was released before freezing nightfall. Outside 'The Holy Lamb of God' lurked the beggars Leif and Rawbum who, despite the cacophony noise from the market place, insisted upon telling Cranston some tale about a priest in Burton-on-Trent who'd exorcized a demon from a blood-drinker back from the dead. Thankfully both were interrupted by a funeral procession, flanked by acolytes and mourners, the deerskin shroud they were honouring sprinkled with ash. Both men, eager for alms, hopped off like crickets, allowing Cranston to disappear into the warm mustiness of one of his favourite resting places. The coroner ensconced himself in the inglenook, ordered the best of ales, a capon pie, a bowl of diced vegetables and today's bread fresh from the bake house. He sat and ate, recalling what he'd seen at Kilverby's mansion and St Fulcher's Abbey.

'Sir John?'

He glanced up.

'*Quomodo non valeat hora, valet mora?*'

'Why is the delay worth so much?' Cranston translated. 'When time is worth nothing?' He extended a hand. 'Draw up that stool!' He visitor, thin as an ash pole, freshly shaven face ending in a pointed chin, scampered to obey. Muckworm sat down, beaming at Sir John, his green eyes sparkling with life, his bloodless lips slightly parted to display what Sir John called 'the blackest teeth in Cheapside'. Yet it was Muckworm's hair which always caught his attention, flaming red and brushed up into long strands held firm by a handful of cheap nard which could be smelt long before Muckworm ever appeared. Dressed in a long brown gown which gave him his name, rumour had it that Muckworm, before he found his true calling, had been a cleric. Certainly every time he appeared before Cranston he quoted a Latin tag for the coroner to translate. Muckworm, however, had one God-given talent which Cranston treasured. He truly was a worm who could burrow into the secrets of any house, tavern, abbey or palace to nose out both its secrets and scandals.

'You want a blackjack of ale?'

'Of course, Sir John, and a warm crust soaked in gravy.'

Muckworm was soon settled, shuffling his booted feet as he gobbled the crust the slattern brought and guzzled noisily at the tankard. He again beamed at Cranston.

'I bring you news.'

'Tell it.'

Muckworm closed his eyes like a gleeman about to sing.

'Sir Robert Kilverby,' his voice low and soft, 'was a fine gentleman. One of his stable grooms is a friend of Hog-grubber.'

'Who? Oh, never mind, continue.'

'Hog-grubber has been a close comrade of mine ever since we spent a week in the Louse House.' Muckworm opened his eyes. 'That's the Fleet prison to you, Sir John.'

'Continue.'

'In the Kilverby household tension smouldered between Sir Robert and Lady Helen but nothing new. Our wealthy Kilverby really truly doted on his daughter. She and her husband, the beloved Edmond, are good, if anyone on God's earth is good. Lady Helen is a Fartleberg.' Muckworm opened his eyes.

'Speak on,' Cranston whispered.

'Kinsman Adam is as slimy as a snake but there's no proof he uses Lady Helen as his left-hand wife. Crispin the clerk has been with Sir Robert since they were both knee high to a buttercup. Finally, Sir Robert was determined to go on pilgrimage.'

'Why?'

'God knows. For some time Kilverby had been on his knees under the Star of the Levites.'

'What?'

'The power of the priests, especially the monks at St Fulcher's. I'll come to those shaven-pates in a short while. Kilverby often went out there. He confided in the French one.'

'Richer?'

'Very good, Sir John, or so I'm told.'

'Why did Kilverby become so religious? What caused his conversion?'

'I don't know. Perhaps like Dives from the gospel, Kilverby feared for his immortal soul.'

He paused as the door to the tavern flew open and a garishly dressed Salamander King, a fire-eater, entered carrying his basket of implements. Behind him trailed two other characters, a dwarf whom Cranston immediately recognized as 'Hop-o-my-thumb', a notorious mountebank, and the other a large, muscular woman, the dwarf's constant companion who, because of her hulking size, rejoiced in the name of 'The Horse's Godmother'.

'Good day, my lovelies,' Cranston growled, getting to his feet.

The Salamander King and his two companions paused and gazed in horror across the tap room at their nemesis.

'Cranston!' Hop-o-my-thumb screeched. All three promptly turned and fled through the door.

'Very good.' Muckworm sniffed. 'This, Sir John, is no buttock shop.' He held up a tankard. 'The labourer is worthy of his hire?'

Cranston ordered the blackjack to be refilled.

'Oh, yes,' Muckworm continued, 'Kilverby wanted to atone for his sins but the pilgrimage would have taken years. Crispin was to join him but his eyes are failing so Kilverby secured him soft lodgings at the abbey. Crispin was deeply opposed to this but eventually became reconciled to it. Now Kilverby is gone. Juice of the almond, I hear. Yes, Sir John, I made careful enquires among the leeches and apothecaries – almond juice is costly. No one from Kilverby's household was observed buying it. I sit and watch, Sir John. I gave the potion sellers careful descriptions of all of Kilverby's kin. Now,' Muckworm gabbled on, sipping from his tankard, 'as for St Fulcher's. Abbot Walter is a great Lord, over-fond of his niece. No, Sir John, she is his niece, from the same sty or so they say.'

'Cruel words.'

'My Lord Abbot waxes fat and well. Those who live under the shadow of the abbey have little love for him, that's why he goes out to All Hallows Barking.'

'All Hallows?'

Muckworm glanced round; the tap room was empty except for two costermongers who'd just entered, drained their tankards and fallen asleep in the far corner.

'The Great Community of the Realm, Sir John. They say its leaders meet at Barking. They call themselves, among other things, "All Hallows".'

'All Saints.' Cranston translated the old English.

'All Saints,' Muckworm agreed. 'They will lead the Community when the earthworms rise up.'

'Sweet angel,' Cranston whispered, 'the fools will all die.'

'True, Sir John, but they are all very much alive now. They threaten to rise with fire and sword on the Day of Reckoning, when the Angel of wrath pours out the vials of God's anger and all the castles of hell release their hordes. They're already drawing up lists of who is friend or foe . . .'

'Protection,' Cranston interrupted.

'Agreed. Abbot Walter goes to All Hallows to meet the Upright Men so, when the revolt begins, St Fulcher's will be spared, which is why the abbot gave the anchorite shelter. He couldn't find anyone to hang the felons he catches. Nobody wants to be seen as Abbot Walter's friend. Memories are long.

Times are hard. Our Lord Abbot is fey-witted. When the great revolt begins, protection or not, St Fulcher's will be sacked.'

'This anchorite?'

'You know him, my Lord – the painter, the Hangman of Rochester, the one whose wits were tumbled after he hanged that evil witch Alice Rednal.'

'Oh yes, I remember her. I also recall him. So he's there. What else?'

'Prior Alexander has a great love for Sub-Prior Richer, who spends most of his time in the library and scriptorium though sometimes he does meet boatmen from foreign ships.'

'Why?'

Muckworm became crestfallen. 'Sir John, I do not know.'

'How did you learn all this?'

'Oh, very simple, Sir John.' Muckworm grinned triumphantly. 'I have a cousin who is a boatman. More importantly, another cousin is a lay brother at the abbey. He serves in the refectory at the prior's table. He . . .'

'And Eleanor Remiet?'

'Nothing, except she looks after the abbot's niece. Now, as regards the Wyvern Company,' Muckworm chattered on, 'the King's own bully boys? Men of blood through and through. Oh, I know you fought in the King's wars but they're different.'

'Did you discover much?'

'All candles burn out, Sir John. I had little time except I did visit the tavern Mahant and Wenlock claimed to have visited on the eve of St Damasus.' Muckworm raised his eyebrows. 'They certainly did. They arrived just before the market horn blew and stayed there feasting at the long table and enjoying the favours of some of the ladies offered by the mistress of the maids. According to my sources, the next morning they broke their fast, went out amongst the stalls then returned late to their abbey.' Muckworm noticed Cranston's disappointment. 'But I did search out one secret. Two of my comrades, I believe you are acquainted with them: Mulligrub and Scapskull.'

'Both gentlemen have graced my judgement chamber, not to mention every stock and pillory post in London.'

'Sir John, they have turned lawful. Do you remember how swift they are?'

'Like rats down a hole.'

'Well, they now serve many of the London taverns as messengers including "The Pride of Purgatory". They said that Mahant and Wenlock were waiting for Geoffrey Portsoken.'

'Don't know him.'

'Oh yes, you do, Sir John, in the bills posted at St Paul's Cross and elsewhere, he is Vox Populi . . .'

'Vox Populi, Vox Dei.' Cranston smiled in astonishment. 'He's a ditch crawler, a hedge creeper, a man who slinks through London and the surrounding shires preaching rebellion and tradition. He calls himself the "Voice of the People and the Voice of God". He was attainted, proclaimed *ultegatum* – beyond the law, a wolfshead.' Cranston sipped from his own tankard.

'What does he have in common with the Wyverns?'

'He used to be one of them. Something happened and he was cut off from their company. Anyway, Sir John, Vox Populi is about to be strangled. He's already appeared before the Justices in Eyre so he'll dance at Smithfield.'

'And now?'

'Lodged in Newgate Hole where the blackness salutes the darkness.' Muckworm drained his tankard and stared around. 'Now, my Lord Coroner, other duties call?'

Cranston dug into his purse and pushed a silver piece into Muckworm's extended hand. 'God go with you.'

'And you too, Sir John.' Then Muckworm was gone.

Cranston sat for a while, staring into the fire. He'd kept an eye on who came into the tap room and was growing suspicious about the two costermongers in the corner. They had, he remembered, entered just after he had, ordered ale and fallen asleep. Cranston entertained a nagging suspicion that they were '*faux et semblant* – false and deceiving', just by their position, lying in a way so they could furtively watch him. The tap room's warm comfort seemed to fade. Cranston rose, buckled on his war belt, donned both cloak and beaver hat then left. Outside he immediately drew his stabbing dirk and, keeping that at the ready, made his way along Cheapside. It was candlelight time. The cold had grown more intense: already the apprentices were busy clearing stalls and booths. He went down Stoat-back Lane, a narrow runnel stretching on to the broad thoroughfare leading to the shambles and the forbidding mass of Newgate.

'The hour of the bat and the screech owl,' Cranston muttered. He just wished Athelstan was with him, not for bodily protection but that strange little friar was always balm for the soul with his shrewd observations and humorous asides. A man in the world but not of it, Cranston reflected, Athelstan was a priest as cunning as a serpent with the innocence of a dove. Cranston made the resolution to seek out the friar as soon as possible and walked on. Lanterns glowed on door posts. Candles flamed behind latticed windows or between the chinks of shutters; these threw some light on the filth-strewn cobbles as well as the narrow doorways and alley enclaves where the destitute sheltered. The coroner made his way around the slime-drenched mounds of refuse where dogs, cats and rats all foraged for morsels. Ahead of him trundled the dung cart and the evening breeze wafted back a smell so putrid Cranston had to cover both nose and mouth behind the folds of his cloak. Despite the poor light he was soon recognized and strident calls echoed like a ball bouncing up the runnel before him.

'Cranston, here! Wary! Wary! Coroner, here!'

He walked on gripping his dagger, shadows slunk away. He was almost at the top of the alley when a beggar woman pushed her ragged boy towards him, his little arms outstretched for alms. Something in the boy's eyes pricked Cranston's suspicions. He dug into his belt wallet and thrust a coin into the boy's scabby hand. The child stepped back and Cranston heard the whispered warning from the shadows.

'Watch your back, Lord Coroner.'

He walked up to the mouth of the alleyway then swiftly turned. Shapes further down just as abruptly stepped back into the creeping shadows.

'St Michael and all his angels.' Cranston murmured a prayer for protection and walked on. He was determined to meet Vox Populi before the day was through. He turned right into the Shambles, the great fleshing market of London. The butchers and carvers were now unhooking the chunks of beef, chicken, poultry, duck, rabbit, venison and ham. The air reeked of salt, blood and messy entrails; even the cobbles glowed red in the dancing light of torches whilst the butchers and their boys seemed like demons in their gore-splattered leather aprons and hats. Beadles and bailiffs thronged to secure their blood-soaked linen packages of free meat. The poor and the needy also clustered, going down on hands and knees beneath the stalls searching for fresh gobbets of flesh, fighting off the curs and cats which also massed to feast in this place of slaughter. Traders and tinkers, selling the rejected to the rejected, shouted for business. Prostitutes, faces all painted, hair dyed and festooned with gaudy ribbons, sheltered together ready to entice customers into what Cranston called their 'Temples of Mercenary Love'. Pimps touted for courtesans, even mixing with a small crowd who'd gathered round a Friar of the Sack. The Franciscan stood on a plinth intoning the office of the dead for the Guild of the Hanged, a pious group of men and women who assembled outside Newgate to pray for those inside condemned to death.

Cranston pushed himself through these and the horde of nighthawks, dark-walkers, gibbet lawyers and mountebanks; all assembled before the great iron prison gates hoping to visit friends within, coins at the ready to bribe janitors and turnkeys. Cranston recognized many familiar faces amongst these Pages of the Pit and Squires of the Sewer, who swiftly drew away as he marched up to the postern door and vigorously pulled at the bell. The door flew open. The bullnecked, grey-faced turnkey took one look and hurriedly stepped aside. Cranston entered that antechamber of hell. He met the keeper in the great yard, showed him his seal and demanded to see the Vox Populi. The keeper, dressed in black like a parson with the sanctimonious face to match, swiftly agreed. Cranston had little time for him. The keeper was a born rogue who, Cranston had often confided to Athelstan, was twice as fit for hell as those he guarded. They entered the murky, main gallery of the gloomy prison. Cranston took the proferred rags soaked in vinegar to cover his nose. The air was fetid, damp and reeking of putrefaction. The walls seemed to sweat slime which gathered like sludge over the flagstone floor. The light was poor. Torches flared, giving off trails of pitch and tar. Tallow candles, cheap and nasty smelling, flickered in niches and crevices. A thriving place for rats, cockroaches and other vermin, Cranston tried to ignore the lice crackling under his boots. They passed chambers and cells where prisoners laden with irons stood with hands outstretched, their pleading for alms almost drowned by the horrid howling and screaming which rang out constantly. They reached the condemned cell – nothing more than a filthy box guarded by a heavy oaken door. Inside it reeked like a midden heap, black as pitch with no light or vent for air. The prisoner was crouched in the corner on a palliasse of rotting straw. Cranston breathed in deeply on the rag as he shouted for lights, two stools and a jug of claret.

'Bordeaux,' he yelled. 'I've had enough of your bloody vinegar.'

The keeper hurried to obey. Once he'd brought everything, Cranston ordered him out, leaving the door open. He sat on one stool, the prisoner on the other, drinking greedily from the goblet of claret. He raised his head, pushing back his filth-strewn hair to reveal the brand mark on his cheek close to where his left ear had been. Cranston studied the dirty face, the tangled moustache and beard; the eyes, however, were bright, not yet bereft of hope or courage.

'Geoffrey Portsoken, known as a Vox Populi.' Cranston lifted his goblet. 'I salute thee.'

'Sir Jack Cranston, I toast thee too, you and yours.' The prisoner took another gulp. 'I'm for the elms at Smithfield, Jack, condemned I was, beaten up by Gaunt's henchmen. Anyway, why are you here? Not to gloat! No, that's not for our Jack, so why?'

'To offer you life.'

Vox Populi mockingly raised the goblet but his eyes brightened. 'Gaunt will not let me skip away from this.'

'Not skip, my friend, walk to the nearest port. Queenshithe will do, ship abroad never to return under pain of hanging, drawing and quartering. I mean that.' Cranston clinked his pewter cup against the prisoner's. 'Out, never to return!'

'I'll need money.'

'The city will pay for you to be shaved, clothed, booted with a water pannikin and a linen parcel of bread and dried bacon. You'll also receive a thin purse.'

'For what – information?'

'The truth, so shut up and listen!''

Cranston spoke swiftly and succinctly about Kilverby's murder, the disappearance of the Passio Christi and the slayings out at St Fulcher's.

'So,' Vox Populi murmured. 'Chalk has gone to his maker, followed by Hanep and Hyde. Chalk will have much to answer.'

'Why?'

'He was a defrocked priest, Sir Jack, a curate from the church of St Peter's-in-the-wood in Leighton Manor in Essex where we all hailed from an eternity ago. It must be,' Vox Populi paused to cough phlegm, 'some thirty years ago now. All of us golden boys, archers swinging off down the tree-lined lanes bound for the glory of France.'

'Very touching.'

'No, Jack, very true. You know how it was. We were roaring boys. About twenty of us at first who answered the King's writ from the commissioners of array; few of us are left now, only me and those hard-hearted bastards out at St Fulcher's.' He stared at Cranston. 'I fought with them. In the year of our Lord 1353, we sealed an indenture with the Black Prince to serve him and him only as the Company of the Wyvern.'

'A small cohort?'

'By then, Jack, we were all skilled archers, master bowmen; we could bring down any bird on the wing or put a shaft through the narrowest window. Experts in the use of yew, ash, the hempen string, the goose-quill arrow.' He wagged a finger in mock anger. 'Some took an oath never to use a crossbow; I still can't. I'm not too sure whether this is true of my former comrades.'

'Your duties?'

'To attend upon the Prince day or night, in peace and war, to be his sworn men and so we were, mounted archers who moved around the battlefield. You've seen the likes of us, Jack. Imagine loosing an arrow with every breath. In battle the Prince assigned us a special duty. We were to seek out the enemy commanders, having first learnt their heraldry and livery. A knight, especially the French, is invariably helmeted and visored.'

'The heat must have been suffocating,' Cranston added quietly. 'Especially with the sun strong in the full fury of battle. They'd open their visors to breathe, to catch some coolness.'

'Aye, Jack,' Vox Populi leaned forward, eyes gleaming, 'and we'd be waiting. We would have an arrow notched, two of us, ringed and protected by men-at-arms. One shaft,' he held a hand up, 'to the commander's face, down he'd fall. You know what happened next: his banner carrier, the standard bearer, would raise his visor in alarm . . .'

'And he would receive the second shaft?' Cranston nodded. 'Both commander and standard bearer brought down in a few heart beats. Disarray amongst the enemy would be intense?'

'And because of that, the Prince loved us, we could do no wrong.'

'Including ransacking an abbey and the theft of the sacred bloodstone the Passio Christi?'

'Oh yes, I know about the Passio Christi being held by Kilverby. You do realize he financed the Wyvern Company with loans to the Black Prince? Oh, yes! Kilverby made a handsome profit. The loans carried no interest but Kilverby took a share in the plunder. Little wonder,' the prisoner scoffed, 'in his final years Kilverby turned to God.'

'The Passio Christi?'

'I was not there, Cranston, when it happened.' The Vox Populi moved, manacles clinking. 'I swear that! After Poitiers, noble prisoners were being taken for ransom. The poor French men-at-arms fled to Poitiers town for protection but they closed the gates against them. They were all massacred. I took part in that, God forgive me. My companions, the seven who found lodgings at St Fulcher's, went on their own campaign of pillage and looting. We later heard the story how they supposedly found a cart full of treasure close to St Calliste Abbey and seized it as the spoils of war.' He shook his head. 'What a find! A beautiful bloodstone, precious items, manuscripts, plates, cups and ewers. Of course I don't believe that. Those

seven pillagers probably scaled the abbey walls whilst the
shaven pates, who'd learnt about the slaughter at Poitiers, were
hiding in their wine cellars. The Wyverns roamed that abbey
like Renard would a hen coop. I am sure they quietly pillaged
the abbey church, found a cart, loaded their plunder on it
and the rest you know. Who could contradict master bowmen,
patronized by no less a person than the King's son?' Vox
Populi paused to finish his wine. Cranston emptied his own
goblet into the prisoner's, who thanked him with his eyes.
'Naturally the French objected. The Abbot of St Calliste rode
out with bell, book and candle to protest but the Prince was
not moved. The abbot cursed the perpetrators but that was war
Jack, who cares?' He paused. 'You've met Richer? His uncle
was the abbot.'

Cranston cradled his empty goblet, very pleased he had
come here.

'And afterwards, what happened to you?'

'I tell you Jack, from the moment the Passio Christi was
taken, those seven became inseparable comrades, a lock within
a lock. I remained an outsider, a stranger. A year later whilst
on campaign, we surprised a French camp. I was eager for
plunder. I cried, "Havoc, havoc!".' He raised a hand to touch
where his ear had been. 'You know the rules of war, Cranston.
To cry havoc is to proclaim the enemy is defeated so we can
turn to plunder. I shouldn't have done it. The fight was not
yet over. The Black Prince said that any other man would have
been hanged; instead I lost my left ear, was branded and turned
out of the company.' The prisoner's voice turned bitter. 'My
comrades gave me little help or comfort. I was in France,
wounded, a beggar bereft of everything, and then a miracle
occurred. French peasants found me cowering in a ditch. I
expected to be hanged or have my throat cut. In fact, they
proved to be true Christians, good Samaritans. They tended,
fed and clothed me. They healed my wounds in more ways
than one, those earthworms, the poorest of the poor! I began
to reflect on the kindness of such people to an enemy. I cursed
the Black Prince and all his coven. I journeyed back to England.
I took refuge in Glastonbury before moving to St Peter's at
Gloucester where I dwelt as a hermit. I forsook the path of

war; instead I railed against the rich and the powerful.' He paused. 'I became a preacher as powerful as Jack Straw or John Ball. I moved from village to village preaching that our day would come. I moved into London. The Upright Men, the leaders of the Great Community of the Realm, invited me into their company. By all the angels don't ask me about All Hallows, the Community or the Upright Men. We always met disguised in deserted copses, clearings or ruins as old as the Romans. We'd sit hooded and visored and never named.' He breathed in deeply. 'I heard of my old comrades lodging like lords at St Fulcher's. I sheltered secretly in some rat's lair near Dowgate. I sent those two rogues Mulligrub and Snapskull out to St Fulcher's with a plea for help but my old comrades never replied.' He coughed. 'Then one night, around All Souls, I was taken by the sheriff's men during an affray in Poultry.' He rattled his chains. 'So, am I free, Jack, or will you play the Judas? Have you come to cry all hail when you really mean all harm?'

Cranston got to his feet, knocking over the stool.

'Oh, by the way,' Vox Populi squinted up at him, 'one last thing. The Great Community have marked you down for death.'

'Like so many others in my long life.'

'I know you, Jack. You'll fight, and you'll survive, but your monk . . .?'

'Friar, and he's not mine.'

'Athelstan, on him,' Vox Populi whispered, 'sentence has not yet been passed.

'Why are you telling me this?'

'Everyone is buying protection, Jack. Kilverby did and so has Abbot Walter. Have you ever wondered why he gave the Wyverns such comfortable lodgings?'

'He had to, the Crown insisted.'

'I've never yet met a monk who didn't try to wriggle out of an agreement. No, Jack, Abbot Walter was only too pleased to have master bowmen in the abbey just in case the Upright Men decided not to be so upright. Can you imagine Jack, seven master archers, their bows strung, arrows notched, loosing showers of barbed shafts at any intruders?' Vox Populi lowered his head. 'Well then, there were six. Now there are four, that's better than nothing. Who knows, Jack, the deaths of my comrades Hanep and Hyde could be the work of the Upright Men, removing the guard dogs before they attack.'

Cranston picked up the stool and sat down. 'Who else would murder them? Some old blood feud?'

'Well, I doubt if the abbot would kill his own watch dogs. The Frenchman Richer? Does he have the skill? Perhaps his infernal Grace the Regent wants the Passio Christi so badly he killed Kilverby and now he wants to annihilate the Wyverns. Who knows what in this vale of tears?'

'Would they turn on each other?'

'Hardly likely. Wenlock is a cripple, captured by the French. They sheared off his archer fingers. He and Mahant, according to you, were in London when Hanep was killed and still out of the abbey when Hyde was slaughtered. I used my last coins to send a message to them. I don't know if they came to meet me. Look at me,' he gestured around the cell, 'a crust of bread would have been a gift from heaven.' Vox Populi stared wistfully into his empty wine cup. 'Now, Sir Jack, your promise?'

Cranston leaned across and seized the prisoner's beard.

'I'll have a word with the keeper. You'll be moved to the common hold. In two days time Master Flaxwith and my bailiffs will collect you, washed, shaved and clothed with a few pennies to spend. You'll be taken down to Queenshithe. If I ever see your face again I'll hang you myself.' Cranston released his grip. 'Goodnight, friend, I will not see you again.'

The coroner left Newgate intent on Cheapside. He had learnt enough. He only wished he could share his thoughts with Athelstan. Undoubtedly the Passio Christi lay at the heart of all these mysteries, but how and why? Cranston was certainly determined to question Crispin and intended do so before the end of the day. The coroner gathered his cloak about him and stared around. The harsh early frost and seeping river mist had already cleared the great concourse in front of Newgate. The Fleshers' stalls had gone, as had all the remains and slops from the day's trade. Torches, braziers and great bonfires flared, drawing in the poor and homeless, who gathered silently in their ragged cloaks for any warmth. Franciscans appeared, moving amongst the huddled groups, dispensing what physical or spiritual comfort they could. Cranston ignored these, more alert to the twinkling light of naked steel or the shapes flitting along the shadows' edge. He was certainly being followed but that was normal. Life had a pattern. Cranston was very alert to that pattern being disturbed.

The city now lay silent, sinking deep into the fierce frost which already sparkled in the fading light. The night creatures were out; these kept to the murky mouth of alleyways or grouped close to the makeshift bonfires the bailiffs had kindled to burn rubbish as well as warm the homeless who brought whatever raw meat or fish they'd pilfered to roast over the flames. The Mendicants of Christ, garbed in robes of dark murrey festooned with the Five Holy Wounds, did their nightly rounds with baskets of stale bread and rejected fruit and fish. A pilgrim, absorbed in his own private devotions, came out of an alleyway dragging a cross in reparation for some sin. Cranston noticed this and trudged on, only stopping to greet bailiffs and beadles he recognized. Cranston was cold, hungry and angry. Kilverby's family could have been more honest with him and he intended to rectify this.

The coroner reached the dead merchant's mansion and immediately gained entrance. He strode in and demanded the household meet him in the solar. Cranston only gave the barest apology for dragging them away from their supper, though he sensed that the deep antagonism between Lady Helen and Mistress Alesia probably marred such occasions. They eventually gathered and sat in the comfortable leather-cased chairs near the fire. Cranston drained the cup of hot posset he'd been given, watching their faces, especially the furrowed, anxious-looking Crispin, who kept blinking and wetting his lips.

'Sir John,' Lady Helen coughed prettily, 'you have more questions?'

'Yes, you,' Cranston pointed at Crispin, 'know your master's business. Years ago he financed the Wyvern Company through loans to the King's son the Black Prince – yes?'

Crispin nodded.

'He took a share of the spoils?'

Again, the nod.

'So he was fervent in his support of such warriors?'

'Of course, Sir John.'

'He profited from their plundering. He held the Passio Christi in trust.'

'Yes.' Crispin's nervousness deepened, 'But that was years ago.'

'Sir John,' Alesia intervened, 'your questions – they're leading to my father's recent change of heart.'

'What change of heart,' Cranston barked. 'Why, when?'

'In the last three years,' Alesia's cheeks had turned slightly red, 'my father grew tired of his life; he wanted to change, to go on pilgrimage, to make reparation.'

'Reparation for past sins, I presume.'

'You presume right, Sir John,' Lady Helen declared. 'My good husband,' she darted a venomous look at Alesia, 'had grown tired of his life.'

'And his marriage!' Alesia snapped.

'How dare you!'

'Ladies!' Cranston bellowed, turning to Crispin. 'Tell me, why did he change now and not five years ago?'

'I don't know, Sir John.'

'According to you,' Cranston declared, 'when he met the Wyvern Company on his journeys with the Passio Christi to St Fulcher's, he grew to hate them, what he saw, what he heard . . .'

'That's not entirely true,' Crispin spluttered. 'Yes, he had little time for the Wyvern Company but he drew close to one of them, William Chalk. Sir Robert often sought Chalk's company. They would walk in the gardens or stroll down to the watergate.'

'Who else was he close to – you?'

'My master kept his own counsel. He was secretive and prudent. He never discussed his personal thoughts with either me or his family. Isn't that true?' Crispin appealed to the others who loudly confirmed his words.

'So he talked to Master Chalk and who else? I mean, if Sir Robert's thoughts had turned to judgement and death, he must have had a confidant, a confessor?'

'Richer,' Crispin confirmed. 'I know that. He was often closeted with him, to be shriven, to be set penances.'

'Such as?'

'Crawling to the rood screen every Friday, alms for the poor, Masses for the dead.'

'And contributions to the Upright Men and the Great Community of the Realm?'

Crispin shrugged. 'Every powerful man in London did and does that.'

'I don't.'

'Merchants are different.' Crispin was agitated. 'He only gave them money for the relief of the poor.'

'You mean a bribe, so that when the doom arrived, this mansion would not be burnt around your heads. Tell me, is there anyone who wanted Sir Robert dead, who would profit from his murder?'

'My father was much loved.'

'Mistress, we all are, once we are dead.'

'Sir John . . .'

'Don't "Sir John" me,' Cranston retorted. 'Are the seals on Sir Robert's chamber still unbroken?'

'Of course.'

'Why didn't he want to take the Passio Christi himself to St Fulcher's?'

'We have answered that,' Alesia replied. 'My father grew tired, weary of it all. He was old. The journey, especially during winter, was hard.'

'No.' Cranston shook his head. 'It was more than that.'

'If it was we didn't know. He didn't tell us.'

'Is that so, Master Crispin? By the way, why was the bloodstone taken at Easter and on the feast of St Damasus?'

'Well, Easter celebrates Christ's Passion and Resurrection; the bloodstone was said to have originated during those three days.'

'And St Damasus?'

'A pope of the early church who wrote an extensive treaty on the Passio Christi, its origins, power and the miracles it worked.'

'And where's that?'

Crispin blew his cheeks out. 'Still held by the monks of St Calliste near Poitiers, or so I believe but,' he hurried on, 'that's why Damasus' feast day was chosen.'

'There is something very wrong here,' Cranston declared. 'Item,' he emphasised his points with his fingers. 'Sir Robert, God assoil him, was a hard-headed merchant. Years ago he financed the Wyverns, a marauding free company in France. He took a share of their plunder. Yes?'

No one objected.

'Item: He held the Passio Christi for years. He'd heard the accepted story but he must have also entertained the accepted doubts. Item: Sir Robert also knew the Wyverns for years? He apparently suffered no scruples. But then, during his visits to St Fulcher's, he radically changes. He cannot tolerate the Wyverns.'

'The influence of Richer,' Alesia broke in.

'Mistress, with all due respect – nonsense. A young French monk from St Calliste? Your father was a very shrewd merchant. He would expect Richer to be biased. No.' Cranston returned to his argument. 'Item: Sir Robert was influenced, like the astute man he was, by something he didn't realize before, hence all my questions.'

'True, true.' Alesia sighed. 'Recently, I'd often come into my father's chamber. He'd be sitting at his chancery desk, nibbling as he so often did at the plume of his pens, the other hand smoothing the wood. He'd be lost in thought as if he was experiencing a vision.'

'What was that vision?' Cranston asked.

The household just stared back at him, shaking their heads.

Cranston shuffled his feet. He was finished here. He felt he had only been told what they wanted to tell him. He rose, gathered his possessions and insisted on checking the seals on Kilverby's chamber. Crispin took him there. The coroner scrutinized the large wax blobs bearing the imprint of the city arms. Flaxwith, as usual, had done a thorough job. The chamber and all the mysteries it held was still securely sealed. Crispin escorted him out but, just before he opened the main door, Cranston grasped the clerk's arm.

'The Passio Christi, could it be sold on the open market?'

'No.' Crispin gently freed himself from Cranston's grip. 'What buyer could ever realize gold and silver on it? He'd certainly risk detection. If he took it abroad the same would happen. Sir John, no merchant would risk sacrilege by buying a sacred relic owned by another, especially the likes of His Grace, John of Gaunt.'

Cranston grunted his agreement and donned both hat and cloak. He strolled out into the icy darkness, smiling to himself as Crispin slammed the door noisily behind him. The coroner had only walked a few paces from the main gate, the porter's farewells ringing in his ears, when a group of hooded, masked men burst out from an alleyway, sconce torches held high. Cranston threw his cloak back, drew sword and dagger, quickly edging round to have the wall against his back.

'Good evening. Not me, gentlemen, surely,' he said hoarsely. 'The King's own coroner? Not here where I will cry "Harrow" and rouse the good citizens.'

The men, five in all, formed an arc blocking his way. None had drawn their weapons.

'Sir John, Sir John, my Lord Coroner.' The voice of the man in the middle was gentle. '*Pax et bonum*, sir. We have no quarrel with you – well, not yet, not here.'

'So you've come to praise me, to wish me well?' Cranston raised both sword and dagger. 'Who are you – envoys from the Upright Men?'

'Two items, Sir John. The Dominican Athelstan. He's at St Fulcher's because of the deaths of those former soldiers?'

'Yes.'

'And their assassin?'

'We don't know who yet, perhaps you or someone you've hired.'

'Everybody is for hire and yes, we have friends in St Fulcher's but they know little.'

'So why ask me?'

'For our own secret purposes as well as to assure ourselves that the Dominican is safe. His parishioners . . .'

'You mean your adherents who happen to be his parishioners?'

'His parishioners are worried. They want to be assured that he's there for a good purpose. Rumour has it that His Satanic Grace, our so-called Regent, has exiled him.'

'That's nonsense.'

'We have your word on that? Athelstan's parishioners do seek reassurance.'

'You have my word, now get out of my way.'

'Secondly, Coroner,' the man's voice remained conversational, 'we would like you to take a message to my Lord Abbot.'

'Go hire Mulligrub or Snapskull. I'm not your scurrier.'

'Please tell our Lord Abbot when you meet him that his payments are long overdue.'

'Payments for what?'

'He'll know and, I guess, so do you, Sir John. We bid you goodnight.' The five men swiftly withdrew back up the alleyway.

Cranston remained where he was – pursuit would be highly dangerous. He sheathed his weapons and stared up at the sky. He certainly would have words with Lord Walter. As for those rapscallions at St Erconwald's, they wanted reassurance? Well, Cranston smiled to himself, tomorrow was Sunday and such reassurance would be his gift.

oOoOo

FIVE

'Moot: a gathering of the people.'

Athelstan spent the remainder of the Saturday before the third Sunday Advent recovering from that mysterious attack. Immediately after that he had met the rest of the Wyverns, who said they'd been looking for him to invite him to a game of bowls. Athelstan reluctantly agreed, studying them carefully. He quickly concluded that the would-be assassin could not be one of them. It would have been impossible for any of them to launch such an attack, dispose of both cloak and arbalest and hurry round to appear with the rest outside the guest house. This conviction deepened as he played bowls, using all his skill to shatter the pins carved in the shape of demons and hell-sprites. Wenlock's hands were too maimed to hold a crossbow whilst the rest, when questioned about their archery, proudly scoffed about using 'a woman's weapon such as an arbalest'.

'The Genoese tried to use them at Crecy,' Mahant explained after a particularly skilful throw. 'Clumsy and unreliable, they were. We have our war bows, our quivers, yard long shafts and bracers, none of us would trust such a weapon.' He clapped his hands against the cold and stared down at Brokersby putting up the pins.

'Why these questions, Brother? We are glad you joined us yet you seem agitated. Has something happened?'

Athelstan shook his head. He made his excuses and wandered off into Mortival meadow. The river mist was thickening muffling even the cawing of the rooks and the strident calls of the many magpies who flashed in a blur of black and white. The grass was still frozen, the ground hard as iron. Athelstan walked down to the watergate. He paused where Hyde's corpse had been found and studied the bloody spots and flecks he had noticed earlier. He opened the watergate and followed the path he'd taken previously. The smattering of blood along the quayside had disappeared. Athelstan stopped, staring out over the river; here and there misty glows of moving light showed where barges and boats made their way through the gloom. Cries and shouts echoed eerily. Athelstan listened for other sounds. He heard a clatter and whirled round, moving away from the edge of the quayside, but the noise was only the gate creaking in the strong breeze. 'I wonder,' Athelstan murmured, recalling what he'd learnt. He made his way back across Mortival meadow and into the abbey precincts where he asked directions from a wizened old lay brother. Chattering like a sparrow on the branch, the monk took him round to the barbican, an ancient, slate-roofed squat tower which served as the armoury. Athelstan pushed the door open; the ground floor was deserted. He glanced around. Weapons glimmered in the glow of a tallow candle, all neatly stacked in barrels and war chests: swords, daggers, halberds, a few maces, war bows, quivers of arrows, shirts of chain-mail, conical helmets, small targes, shields and, hanging on wall-hooks, a range of arbalests and crossbows. Athelstan made his way in. The room smelt of oil, iron and fire smoke. He stood, warming his fingers over a chafing dish, listening to the silence. The air was thick with dust. Athelstan sneezed loudly and a young lay brother, eyes heavy with sleep, tumbled down the stairs leading to the upper storey. The monk stopped halfway down, peering at Athelstan.

'Ah, er, what . . .?' He rubbed his smutty face and came down. 'I was asleep. You're the abbot's guest, aren't you? What do you . . .?'

'I have a question for you.' Athelstan smiled. 'Weapons are distributed from here?'

'Only with the prior's approval.'

'But someone could come here when you are otherwise engaged and help themselves?'

'But who would do that in an abbey?'

'Have any weapons been recently distributed or taken?'

'Oh no, just the execution party who escorted the felon down to the watergate. They carried staves.'

'Has anyone taken an arbalest?'

'No.'

'Are you sure? Have you taken a tally?' Athelstan patted the young man on the arm. 'Would you please make careful search and tell me if anything is missing? I suspect there is.' With the lay brother's assurances ringing like a chant, Athelstan left the barbican. He continued on past different brothers now hurrying to prepare the sanctuary for the Sunday Masses. Athelstan decided to wander, observe and reflect. He found himself out in the main garden and stood watching the wavering wisps of mist. Were the souls of the departed like that? he wondered. Did Hanep and Hyde still hover here unwilling to journey into the light? Did they press his soul? Did they see him as their avenger? He walked across the grass and stood at the entrance to the great maze. The privet hedges, all prickly and leaf-shorn at the height of winter, rose like walls of sharp points at least eight feet high. The trackway into the maze was pebble-dashed, deliberately uncomfortable for all those who wished to crawl on hands and knees to the Pity in the centre. A fascinating puzzle, a place of mystery with its labyrinthine branching paths, Athelstan was tempted. He entered, stopped, then murmured a prayer. He should be more prudent. A twig snapped, sharp and abrupt. Athelstan turned and strolled quickly back. He panicked. The entrance was not where it should be. He paused, remembering how he'd turned left coming in so he must always walk to the right on his return. He did so and sighed with relief when he glimpsed a stretch of frost-gripped lawn. He pulled up his cowl, strolled out then stifled a scream as two figures abruptly emerged from the mist.

'Good day, Brother Athelstan, we glimpsed your black and white robes.'

Athelstan bowed as Eleanor Remiet and Isabella Velours approached. Both women wore thick woollen cloaks, ermine-lined hoods and elegant gloves which stretched past the wrist.

'Ladies,' Athelstan pushed his hands up the sleeves of his gown, 'I have tempted the cold enough. I need some warmth.'

They walked back into the cloisters and crossed the yard into the buttery where fresh bread was being sliced for the waiting platters from the refectory. Isabella, gossiping about this and that, thankfully fell silent as she crammed her mouth with bread smeared with honey. Athelstan chose his slice holding the cold, grey gaze of Eleanor Remiet, who'd hardly spoken a word.

'You've been here since when?' Athelstan broke the uncomfortable silence.

'Since Advent began. We will return to my house in Havering once Epiphany has come and gone, though Abbot Walter says Christmas is not over until the Baptism of the Lord and the commencement of the Hilary Term.'

Athelstan questioned her about her life at Havering. Eleanor's replies were quick and curt. She told him how Isabella was the daughter of the abbot's only beloved sibling, namely herself. Isabella's father had died so she, Eleanor, had become her official guardian. Athelstan sensed the woman's deep dislike of him from her clipped tone, the way her eyes kept looking him up and down.

'You're not overfond of priests or friars, are you, Mistress?'

'Brother Athelstan, once you've met one you have met them all.'

'Except for Uncle Walter,' Isabella broke in and trilled volubly about the gifts she expected at Christmas.

Athelstan listened and wondered how a young woman could be so spoilt and empty-headed. A pampered life, Athelstan reflected, but Eleanor Remiet is different. The woman's face was harsh and severe, yet Athelstan could detect, beneath the layers of age and hardship how, in her youth, Eleanor must have been a most remarkable beauty.

'You'll stay here long, Brother?'

'I hope not.'

'You should go.'

'Is that a warning?'

'Yes, Brother.' She divided a piece of bread with her long, delicate fingers. 'It is a warning. This is a field of blood. We are in the world of men.' She paused. Isabella rose and went across to help herself to ale from a barrel on a trestle near the door.

'Isabella hardly hears what others say let alone understands,' she remarked. 'You be careful, Brother. The old soldiers who are being slaughtered here? Kilverby, whose fingers were in every juicy pie? They've all gone. The Passio Christi has disappeared.' She popped a piece of honeyed bread into her mouth. 'The root grows silently but eventually it erupts through the soil and harvest time always comes.' She rose, brushing the crumbs from her cloak. 'So yes, Brother, I think you should go before the evil flourishing here entangles you.' She nodded brusquely and walked over to Isabella, now gossiping loudly with the lay brother who supervised the refectory.

Athelstan stood reflecting on what she'd said, finished his bread and left. He decided to stay in the precincts. The day was greying and the bells would soon toll for the next hour of divine office. He went across to the library and scriptorium; he stood just within the doorway revelling in the sights and smells. For Athelstan this was heaven. Shelves, lecterns and racks all crammed with books of every size bound in calfskin or leather. Capped candles, judicially placed, glittered in the polished oaken woodwork and silver chains kept precious volumes secured to their shelf or ledge. The windows on either side were sealed with thick painted glass, now clouded by the poor light though some colours still glowed, springing to life in the reflection from the candle flame. Down the centre of the scrubbed, pave-stoned floor ranged long tables interspersed by the occasional high stool and sloping desk where monks worked at copying or illuminating manuscripts drawn from a cluster of pigeon-hole boxes attached to the walls. Covered braziers, perforated with holes, exuded warmth and a sweet fragrance from the herb pouches disintegrating between the glowing coals. Other sweet odours, ravishing in the memories they provoked, mixed and swirled: ink, paper, paints, sandal-wood, vellum freshly honed, wax soft and melting. A hive of learning, the scribes busy with pens or delicate brushes. Athelstan recalled his own days as a novice in the rare world of books, of cleaning a piece of vellum until it glowed white and innocent as a newly baptized soul.

'Brother Athelstan?' Richer was standing before him, his delicate, handsome face all concerned.

Athelstan blinked, shook his head and apologized. Richer demanded that he join him. He took Athelstan down past the tables, pointing out the different books and manuscripts:

theological tracts by Aquinas, Anselm and Albert the Great; the writings of the early Fathers, Origen, Tertullian, Boethius and Eusebius. The abbey's collection of Books of Hours bequeathed by the rich and powerful. The works of the Ancients: Aristotle, Plato, Cicero and Lactantius. By the time they'd reached the end of the library, Athelstan had recovered his wits. The distractions of that beautiful, well-endowed scholars' paradise faded as he followed Richer into the scriptorium. The room was richly furnished with lecterns, shelves and pigeon boxes. Two glowing triptychs adorned either wall depicting St Jerome studying the Bible in his cave at Bethlehem. The far wall was dominated by a huge crucifix with a twisted figure of the crucified Christ beneath the shuttered window. Athelstan, however, was more concerned with the great desk littered with manuscripts and books. Richer had apparently pulled across large sheets of blank vellum together with a napkin from a nearby lavarium to hide what he'd been working on. Athelstan moved towards the table. Richer stepped quickly into his path.

'Brother Athelstan, can I help you? I am very . . .' Richer, now visibly reluctant at the friar's curiosity, relaxed as the abbey bell sounded the next hour of divine office. He tactfully shooed Athelstan back towards the door, voluble in his apologies and promises that Athelstan must return, when he would show him particular books and manuscripts. Indeed, was there, Richer asked, any work the Dominican would like to study? He'd heard about Athelstan's absorption with the stars and St Fulcher possessed a number of valuable treatises by Aristotle and Ptolemy, as well as Friar Bacon's musings? Athelstan smiled his thanks and left.

'Now there's a monk with a great deal to hide,' Athelstan whispered to the carved face of a satyr hiding in the sculpted foliage at the top of a pillar in the passageway outside. 'Oh, he has much to hide. As has Mistress Eleanor. She threatened me and wants me gone from here. Why? What does she hide?'

Athelstan returned to his own comfortable chamber. He did not attend divine office but recited the hours kneeling on a prie-dieu. Afterwards he laid out clean clothes borrowed from the good brothers for the morrow, looked at the readings for the Sunday Mass then lay on the bed letting his thoughts drift. Worries about St Erconwald's, the whereabouts of Cranston, what he'd learnt that day and that sense of brooding danger as he walked this abbey. He fell into a deep sleep and, when he woke, glanced at the hour candle and groaned. Compline must be finished. The abbey was settling for the night. He was wondering if he could get something to eat from the kitchens when the bells began to clang warningly – not the usual measured peals but strident, proclaiming the tocsin. Athelstan grabbed a cloak, thrust his feet into his sandals and hastened out. Others, too, had been aroused. Torches flickered. Lanterns swung in the chilly blackness.

'Fire, fire!'

Athelstan left the yard, following the lay brothers hurrying along the passageways into the courtyard before the main guest house. Few had yet reached the place. Athelstan immediately realized the fire was serious. The doors of the guest house had been flung open and smoke plumed out. Wenlock, Mahant and Osborne were there coughing and spluttering. Athelstan pushed his way though knocking aside restraining hands. A lay brother, a wet cloth across his nose and mouth, emerged from the smoke.

'Brokersby's chamber,' he gasped. 'God help the poor man. I cannot get him out.'

Athelstan seized the rag and entered. Smoke choked the corridor. He saw one door open; the near one was locked. Sheets of fire roared at the grille and the stout oak was beginning to buckle. Smoke scored Athelstan's nose and mouth. Heat and the smell of burning oil closed in. He could do nothing. He retreated to cough and gasp with the rest in the clear night air.

'The building is made of stone.' Richer appeared out of the darkness. 'I understand the door to where the fire started is locked.' He turned to the assembled line of bucket carriers. 'Go round,' he ordered. 'Force the windows. Use dry sand, not water, at least not yet.'

Marshalled by the sacristan, the lay brothers hurried off. Athelstan crossed to Wenlock and his companions.

'What happened?'

'Brother, we do not know. We were aroused by the smoke.' Mahant pointed to Wenlock and Osborne. 'They have chambers on the upper floor. Mine was next to poor Brokersby's. I fell asleep until roused by the smoke and heat.'

'The door?'

'Brother, I hammered on it. The fire was already raging. I saw Brokersby slumped half off the bed. I pushed but the door was locked and bolted from the inside. Brokersby must have done that. I mean, since the other murders . . .'

'So you think this was murder?'

'Heaven knows, Brother! Poor Brokersby! Well,' Mahant turned back towards the smoke, 'the least we can do is help.'

Athelstan walked away. He put his hand in the pocket of his cloak and drew out his Ave beads. He recited a Pater and three Aves even though he was distracted. Brokersby was dead. Athelstan recalled that locked door, the sheer ferocity of the flames and returned to his chamber, convinced the fire was no accident. Brokersby had been murdered.

The next morning Athelstan celebrated his Jesus Mass in a side chapel, broke his fast in the refectory and went immediately to the death house. Brother Odo showed him the mangled, blackened human remains. Brokersby had been consumed by the inferno: his eyes had melted, the flesh shrivelled to mere lumps of congealed fat with scorched black skin clinging to charred bone. All vestiges of clothing and footwear had also been consumed whilst his ring and the silver chain around his neck were burnt beyond all recognition.

'You discovered nothing else?' Athelstan asked.

'Nothing,' Brother Odo replied mournfully. 'He doesn't smell now but when they first brought him in he reeked of oil.'

Athelstan knelt down and sniffed; the stench of oil was still very pungent.

'Brother Athelstan?'

He turned and recognized the keeper of the Barbican, who took one look at the charred corpse and hastily withdrew, indicating with his hand that Athelstan follow. Once outside the lay brother retched and coughed.

'Brother Athelstan,' he gasped.

'The weapons?'

'There's no crossbow or arbalest missing.'

'What?'

'Brother, I counted most scrupulously – the only weapon missing is a sword.'

'Who took that?'

'No one can, no one should without permission of the prior, yet the ledger has no entry. I am sure; I checked it.'

Athelstan thanked him and walked back to the still-smouldering chamber. Only a senior lay brother was present. He explained how the Wyvern Company had moved all their belongings to the abbot's guest house whilst the damage was inspected and repaired. Like Virgil did with Dante, the monk led Athelstan through the devastation. The guest house was built of solid stone. This, and the heavy oaken door sealing Brokersby's chamber, had confined the fire, the greatest damage being to the ceiling and the supporting beams as well as the chamber above. Ignoring the good Brother's warning about the heat, the fiery cinders and acrid smoke, Athelstan insisted on inspecting the dead man's chamber. The fire still smouldered despite the layers of wet sand thrown in. Everything had been consumed or deeply scorched, whilst the stench of oil remained strong.

'Where's the source?' Athelstan murmured.

'Pardon?'

'Talking to myself,' Athelstan replied. 'If I could have a pole?'

The lay brother left and brought one back. Athelstan was grateful that his stout sandals and thick woollen leggings protected him from the floating sparks of red-hot fragments. He began near the door sifting carefully through the debris. He swiftly concluded how the traces of oil were fainter, less congealed and thinner nearest to the door, whilst close to where the bed and lantern table must have stood the oil appeared much thicker.

'Would Brokersby have a night candle?'

'Yes, he did, or so I learnt from his comrades. He had a large stout tallow candle under a metal cap. He liked to keep it burning. He had trouble sleeping. He also took a potion of poppy juice.'

'But a tallow candle would not create the fires of hell here,' Athelstan declared. 'Was there oil in the chamber?'

The monk abruptly turned and walked away. Athelstan thought he'd forgotten him, then he returned with a small stout colleague, his belly round as a barrel.

'Brother Simon might be able to help you.'

'Yes, I can.' The newcomer smiled in a show of near-toothless gums. 'I clean poor Brokersby's chamber. I assure you there was no oil, just a wine skin. That was all.'

Athelstan picked his way over to the remains to the door and examined the twisted lock, bolts and clasps. He studied these closely; they had definitely been rent apart. He glanced back at the shattered, scorched shutters and the open window now drawing off the worst of the smoke.

'We had to force the door,' Brother Simon declared. 'But, of course, it was too late.'

'So,' Athelstan walked out of the room, carefully picking his way, 'Brokersby retired for the night and his chamber was devastated by fire.'

'So it seems,' both monks chorused.

'But we can't find a reason for it,' Brother Simon added.

Athelstan nodded his thanks and left, crossing into the gardens as he tried to deduce what had happened. Both the door and window of Brokersby's chamber had been sealed. The grille at the top of the door was too narrow to pour oil through so how could anyone get it so close to the bed? Had oil been stored there? But how was it ignited? Did the candle topple over? Yet that had probably been planted on a firm spigot with a cap covering it. An unlucky spark? However, that would mean the fire depended on fickle chance, yet Athelstan was certain Brokersby was murdered. The assassin had deliberately flooded the area close to the bed with burning oil. Brokersby may have been drugged with some opiate and woke too late or, mercifully, never at all. So how had it all been achieved? Brokersby, probably frightened, had sealed himself in that chamber. He had then been murdered by a raging fire cunningly planned and contrived. Brokersby had no chance to escape. He had been utterly destroyed along with everything else in that room.

'Henry! Henry Osborne!'

Wenlock and Mahant appeared, stopped and called their comrade's name again.

'What's the matter?'

'It's Osborne,' Wenlock gasped, pulling his cloak closer about him. 'He has disappeared.'

'Disappeared?'

'Disappeared, fled!' Mahant snapped. 'His chamber is empty; he's packed his panniers and taken his weapons. He appears to have left long before first light.

'Why should he do that?' Athelstan demanded. 'Why flee in the dead of night?'

'Because he's frightened,' Mahant snarled. 'Terrified. Hanep, Hyde and Brokersby – all slain.'

'So you think Brokersby's death was no accident?'

'Of course not,' Wenlock retorted. 'Brother Athelstan, a short while ago we were all comrades enjoying the vespers of our life; now we're being hunted in this benighted place.'

'Why? By whom?'

'For the love of God, we don't know.'

'Why do you think Brokersby was murdered?'

Mahant made to walk away.

'If Osborne's fled,' Athelstan added, 'you'll hardly find him here, will you?'

'No, no.' Mahant sighed and came back. 'We hoped he may have just panicked and be hiding close by.'

'Father Abbot is the one who should organize such a search,' Athelstan said. 'You must see him – demand that this happen. Tell him that I too insist on it, but first,' he plucked at Wenlock's cloak, 'my friends.' Athelstan gestured towards the abbey buildings. 'We need to talk but not here in the freezing cold.'

The two old soldiers agreed. Athelstan led them into the grey stone cloisters where they stood warming their hands over a brazier.

'If Osborne has fled, where would he go? Does he have family, kin?'

'I don't think so.'

'I suspect,' Wenlock rubbed his hands, 'he's probably gone

into the city to hide there, perhaps seek out comrades we didn't know.'

'But why should he give up such comfortable lodgings here?'

'The cowl doesn't make the monk, Brother Athelstan. Nothing here is what it appears to be. Never mind all the babbling to God and all the holy incense.' Wenlock shook his head. 'This has become a slaughter house for our company.'

'But how would Osborne live?'

Both men shuffled their feet.

'I think,' Athelstan smiled, 'each of you has his own private monies, the result of years of campaigning.'

'You mean plunder, Brother? Yes, we all have that, some more than others.'

'When I visited your comrade's chambers I found very few coins,' Athelstan offered. 'You took their money, didn't you? I wondered . . .'

'Hanep and Hyde had little.' Wenlock confessed rubbing his maimed hands over the brazier. 'Of course we took whatever coins or precious objects they owned. Better us than our greedy abbot.'

'Would Osborne have enough money to live on?'

'Perhaps.' Wenlock became evasive. 'A skilled archer may still find employment.'

'Let's say he's fled,' Athelstan paused as a monk slipped by pattering his Ave beads, 'because he was frightened. Others might allege that he was guilty of his comrades' murder.'

'Osborne would never kill one of his own,' Wenlock replied in disbelief. 'Why should he?'

'True, I can't think of any reason. Indeed, I can deduce no reason whatsoever for any of your colleagues being murdered. Can you? Has an ancient blood feud been invoked by someone here in the abbey or the city?'

'None, Brother! We cannot think of any and, if there was, why now? Unless it's the Passio Christi?'

'What do you mean? Kilverby held that.'

'He's dead but the Passio Christi was, allegedly, once owned by the black monks. Richer is a Frenchman, a monk of St Calliste, which now claims it. He is a young man, vigorous,

probably trained in arms but why should he murder us? That
will hardly bring back the Passio Christi?'

'I agree,' Athelstan replied. 'What about revenge,
punishment?'

Athelstan let his words hang in the air. Busy warming his
hands, he watched a solitary robin hop across the cloister
garth, pecking furiously at the frost-laced grass. Incense and
candle smoke wafted mixing with that from the bake house.
Athelstan glanced back; both his companions had begun to
hum a song, shuffling their feet in a slow dance and softly
clapping their hands. Athelstan, surprised, stood back watching
these two soldiers, lost in their own ritual, shuffle and clap as
peasants would in a tavern celebrating their harvest. Mahant
and Wenlock, eyes closed, moved clumsily to their own rhythm;
the humming grew louder then faded away with both men
throwing their hands up in the air and exclaiming, 'Alleluia,
Alleluia, Alleluia!' The soldiers opened their eyes and turned
back to the brazier, grinning at Athelstan.

'You monks and priests have your liturgies and we have
ours,' Wenlock explained. 'At the beginning of every battle the
Wyverns always performed their dance; in the evening we did
the same. You understand why?'

Athelstan nodded. When he and his brother had joined the
King's army he'd seen soldiers, veterans of the free companies,
perform such dances.

'But why now?' Athelstan asked.

'Because we are about to do battle.'

'Against whom? Do you really suspect Richer?'

'Why stop with him?' Wenlock sneered. 'Look around you,
Friar, what do you see? Monks? Many of these hail from the
farms, villages and shires around London. They know us, at
least by reputation. Further up the river at All Hallows near
Barking, the Upright Men gather to plot bloody treason.'

'Don't talk in parables.' Athelstan drew closer.

'We're not. You asked us who wants us dead. Your fat friend
Cranston has returned to the city to sniff around. You have
remained here to do the same, so I'll help you. We're old
soldiers. We have served our purpose. Go into the city and
you'll find others less fortunate than us,' Wenlock, white froth

staining his lips, held up his maimed hands, 'starving at the mouth of every alleyway and filthy alcove. You ask us who wants us dead? Well, perhaps His Grace the Regent so that the Passio Christi, when it is found, will fall into his greedy hands. Or again there's Abbot Walter, who'd like to see us ejected from his precious precincts even though, if need be, he would use us against the Upright Men should they attack this abbey. As for Richer – yes? He nurses grudges and grievances against us but there's more.' Wenlock paused, chest heaving, gesturing at Mahant to continue.

'Wenlock and I have talked about this. Now Brokersby is gone and Osborne has disappeared, we thought we'd tell you. We have enemies within and without, Richer, even that anchorite. You and Cranston must have heard the rumours but let him tell you his tale. We have no blood on our hands as far as the anchorite's concerned. We were only doing our duty.' Mahant drew a deep breath. 'As for the rest, the Upright Men and the Great Community of the Realm hate us. You see, Friar, before we came here we garrisoned the Tower, Rochester, Hedingham, Montfichet – indeed, all the castles around London. The shires seethe with unrest. You've heard about the uprisings, the attacks on houses like that at Bury St Edmunds and elsewhere? Well, to cut to the quick, the Wyverns were used by the Crown, the sheriffs, the abbots and other great lords to crush such revolts. We carried out our orders, as always, efficiently.'

'Ruthlessly?'

'Yes, Brother, ruthlessly. The royal banner was unfurled and the trumpets brayed. Any man, woman or child found in arms against us were either cut down or hanged out of hand.'

Athelstan nodded and walked over to a stone bench. The old soldiers joined him, sitting on either side.

'We burnt their villages and farms,' Wenlock continued. 'We crammed their corpses into wells and springs.' He paused, waiting for Athelstan to reply, but the friar just sat listening.

'Don't judge us, Brother! When the rebels burn Blackfriars and your parish church you'll understand. True, we became hated. Undoubtedly here in this abbey we have shaven-pates, kinsmen of those we slaughtered, we know that. We've received dark looks, curses and spitting, signs made against the evil one and that includes Prior Alexander. We hanged one of his beloved kinsmen, no better than a hedge priest, a ranter on the common gallows outside Ospringe.'

'So the Upright Men may have marked you down.'

'Yes, and our Lord Abbot may well come to regret our stay. We suspect that, like many of the great lords, he's raising Danegeld to bribe these traitorous bastards. Friar, you ask us who wants us dead? Well, we've given you a list. Be it John of Gaunt, some madcap monk or an assassin despatched by the Upright Men.'

'And Osborne has fled the danger?'

'Perhaps.'

'And Brokersby – did he take an opiate to sleep?'

Wenlock stood up and glanced down at Athelstan.

'Brokersby took an opiate, some powder grains.' He pulled a face. 'Supplied by the infirmary.'

'Did Brokersby ever keep oil in his chamber?'

'No, why should he?'

'Did he keep the night-candle lit?'

'I think so.' Mahant paused. 'Brokersby, God assoil him, was frightened by the dark but more than that I cannot say.' He waved at Wenlock. 'We should go, perhaps into the city and search for Osborne there.' He leaned down, his face so close Athelstan could smell the ale on his breath. 'But we'll not go today, brother, it's Sunday. My Lord Abbot will be dispensing Marymeat and Marybread to the poor, or that's how he describes it.' Mahant adjusted his war belt.

'Do you suspect us?' Wenlock asked, archly holding up his maimed hands. 'Poor me who can no longer swing a sword?'

'I never said that.'

'We were in the city when Hyde and Hanep were murdered,' Mahant added quietly, 'and fast asleep when the fire started.'

'Did William Chalk,' Athelstan asked, 'when he fell ill, did the good brothers give him ghostly comfort, shrive him?'

'Richer often visited him but, as you know, the secrets of the confessional are inviolate.'

'And Kilverby the merchant?'

'He used to visit us when he brought the Passio Christi. In

the end he let others do that and, when he did come, he avoided us. I don't think he liked us. We were not particularly fond of him.'

Athelstan watched as the two Wyverns sauntered off. Several brothers then hurried into the cloisters carrying baskets. Athelstan stopped and questioned one, who informed him that as it was Sunday Abbot Walter would distribute alms, free bread and meat to the poor clustered before the main gate of the abbey as well as to others at the watergate. Athelstan, recalling earlier remarks about this, decided to follow them. He went first to the main gatehouse, waiting under its yawning arch until the brothers assembled with their baskets at the ready. He followed them through the postern door and was surprised at the throng gathered there. Peasants in their dirt-gained smocks and mud caked boots, men, women and children, their lean, furrowed faces full of desperation, eager to eat. Other outcasts crowded in: wandering beggars in their motley array of rags, hats and footwear; pilgrims, swathed in tattered weather-worn cloaks on which were pinned the rusting badges of the shrines they had visited – Walsingham, Canterbury, Hereford and even abroad to the famous Magdalene shrine at Vezelay in Burgundy or St Peter's in Rome. Beyond these the lepers, clothed in their shrouds, every inch of flesh hidden by swathes of soiled bandages, clustered in a solitary group ringing hand bells or rattling clappers to warn away the rest. Athelstan took two baskets over to them. He blessed both lepers and food, trying not to be affected by the rank stench and the glimpse of scabbed skin. He distributed the bread, meat and fruit, ensuring that everyone received a portion. He smiled at the benedictions and thanks hissed through worm-eaten lips, talking to the lepers about the dangers of the road and the lives they led.

Athelstan moved away and looked around. At first he could see little amiss until the latecomers, hooded and visored, arrived. About a dozen in all, they appeared quickly, took the baskets specially brought out for them and left. Intrigued, Athelstan decided to visit the quayside. He strolled through the now busy precincts and down across Mortival meadow. Outside the watergate another group of monks were dispensing

Marymeat and Marybread. Fewer beggars congregated here, most of them destitute river people clutching their rags tightly against the bitter cold. They reeked of stale fish, dirty water and sweat. Athelstan moved amongst them. He felt both guilty and angry at his church and about the way the world was. He felt the fury well within him as it did sometimes in his own parish at the sheer injustice of it all. No wonder the Upright Men gathered to plot and the Great Community of the Realm, brimming with discontent, moved out of the shadows. Why shouldn't they have their day of doom, fire and sword, revolt and savage attack? Athelstan turned away, blinking, shaking his head at the furious thoughts which pelted his soul. He blamed himself. Perhaps he should be more active and support the Upright Men, give his blessing to the likes of Pike and Watkin. Athelstan then glimpsed the gallows gaunt against the lowering sky, the fragments of rope attached to a hook fluttering in the breeze. Athelstan closed his eyes and recited the first verse of psalm fifty – that is why he never supported them! No matter the misery now, what the Great Community plotted would only make matters worse. The revolt would be crushed. The Lord of the Soil would dominate. They'd whistle up men like Mahant and Wenlock, professional soldiers, killers to the bone, to crush all dissent. Every gallows from here to the Wash would be heavy with corpses.

'Brother, take care,' Athelstan apologized to the fisherman he bumped into. The quayside was now very busy. He also noticed the new arrivals, similar to those grouped at the main abbey gateway. He was sure they were envoys from the Upright Men sent to collect purveyance by their masters; they picked up the special baskets and carried them to a waiting barge manned by four oarsmen. Such was the way of the world, Athelstan reflected. Abbot Walter was paying service to the emerging threat with special provisions for those who lurked away from the light. Athelstan approached Brother Simon, whom he'd first met after the fire in Brokersby's chamber. The friar indicated with his head at the group he'd noticed.

'Brother Simon, who are those men?' Athelstan asked. 'Both you and the poor treat them with every respect. They collect your alms, your charity as if it was their God-given right.'

'Brother Athelstan.' Simon peered up at him. The lay brother put a finger to his lips. 'What do you think?' he whispered, leaning forward. 'The truth, as Pilate once asked, what is the truth? We must, one day, all answer that question – you, me, Father Abbot and the rest, eh?' Simon's face remained passive, his eyes watchful.

Athelstan recalled his conversations with the Wyverns. How the Upright Men had their adherents in the abbey – the sons, brothers and kinsmen of the earthworms, the peasants of the shires who hacked the earth for those who owned it.

'Have you answered your own question, Brother Simon?'

'Time will tell.' The Benedictine smiled. 'Time will tell. Now I'm busy.'

Athelstan walked back through the watergate and stared down at where Hyde had been murdered. The friar stood chewing his lip; there was still the vexed question of Osborne's whereabouts. What had really happened to him? Had he fled? Was Osborne the assassin, hence his escape? Or had Osborne been terrified witless by the murder of his comrades? Yet would he leave their protection – men with whom he'd spent a generation, who'd stood with him in the battle line? Where would he go now?

'I think you're still here,' Athelstan whispered at the shifting tendrils of mist. He repressed a shiver of fear as he searched for a logical answer to his own questions. He was more than convinced, conceding to a growing conviction, a deep suspicion that Osborne had not fled; he'd been murdered, perhaps here in the abbey, but why? Simply because he was a Wyvern or because he suspected something? If he had been murdered why had his corpse been done away with so secretively? Hyde and Hanep were left sprawling in their blood. Did Osborne's murder involve more than one person? He was a soldier who, despite all his fears, could hold his own against the likes of the maimed Wenlock, even if the latter was helped by others. Athelstan fingered the knots on his cord. It would take a group of assassins to overcome someone like Osborne, and then what? His corpse would have to be disposed of. Not an easy task here in this sprawling abbey with its countless windows, passageways and galleries. Any struggle might be seen; the removal of a corpse would attract attention. A group of monks could do that or a coven of assassins despatched by the Upright Men. Someone must have noticed something yet it was now early afternoon. Despite the searches of Mahant and Wenlock, no trace of Osborne had apparently been found, no alarm raised.

Athelstan peered up at the sky. 'Let us say, good Brother,' he mockingly whispered to himself, 'poor Osborne, God rest him, was killed swiftly by dagger, garrotte or poison?' Yes, Athelstan thought, that could be achieved without little clamour but what then? Hyde and Hanep's corpses had been left like chunks of meat. Brokersby's had been publicly burnt to death. So why hadn't Osborne's corpse been found out here in the meadow or somewhere else in the abbey? True, Athelstan continued his line of thought, the precincts could be lonely, desolate at certain times but on the other hand, once the monks were out of the abbey church, scores of them wandered here and there. Traces of violence, certainly corpses, would soon be discovered. 'Where then?' Athelstan murmured to himself. Where do you hide a corpse in an abbey like this? Out in the woodlands? But lay brothers constantly passed to and fro. The abbey owned lurchers; Athelstan had heard them barking in their kennels. They would soon nose out a corpse. Moreover, in this harsh winter an unburied cadaver would quickly attract kites, foxes and other scavengers which would rouse the attention of someone in the abbey. Athelstan tapped the ground with his foot. The soil was rock hard; digging a pit or a makeshift grave would also prove extremely difficult. Athelstan walked slowly back across the meadow. Of course there were the wastelands around the abbey but would a man like Osborne be trapped and killed whilst leaving during the early hours of the morning? The former soldier would not give up his life easily. Even if his murder was swift, with the flash of a blade or a mouthful of poison, the difficulty of getting rid of his corpse still remained. Athelstan paused at laughter from beyond the watergate. Of course there was always the river, yet Osborne would have to be enticed out there in the hours of the night or early morning. Now, given his comrades' brutal murders, Osborne would be highly wary.

Indeed, even if Osborne was killed and his body thrown into the Thames, it would have to be weighted down. Nevertheless, the river was fickle, especially here further east of the city with its large reed beds. Sooner or later his corpse would be discovered.

Athelstan reached the sand-covered bowling ground. The skittles with their carved demonic faces had all been set up, the bowls gathered in their box. Athelstan was tempted to make a cast to see how many he could bring down. Instead he sat on a turf bench, hands up the sleeves of his gown as he considered further possibilities. What if Osborne had truly fled? What if he, for his own secret purposes, was the assassin? Then why and how had he killed Brokersby in such a fashion? The fire had been deliberately started close to the bed in a secure, locked chamber. How could anyone ignite it from outside? The grille high on the oak door was very narrow. A line of oil-soaked string or cord might be used but that left a great deal to chance. The fire, if it was started in such a fashion, would begin slowly. Anyone near that door would be noticed; if not by a passer-by then Brokersby himself. And why had the soldier not tried to escape? Was he so drunk with wine, an opiate or both? Brokersby had certainly been murdered. Athelstan entertained an equal foreboding about Osborne. But where was his corpse? Athelstan glanced across at the crude stone table on which the monks played checkers. He glimpsed the shard of bone used in one of the games. He got up and touched this with his fingers.

'The charnel house!' Athelstan exclaimed. He'd passed this on the other side of the abbey church, those narrow steps leading down to a massive ancient crypt. St Fulcher's had stood for centuries; every so often its cemetery would overflow so the brothers would remove the bones of the long deceased to make room for others. Blackfriars had a similar ossuary, a place much avoided by everyone, a macabre crypt full of dry bones and sightless skulls, reeking of corruption yet an ideal place to conceal a corpse. Most people would be reluctant to explore it. Athelstan startled as a flock of jays nesting in a large oak on the fringe of the adjoining garden burst out in a flurry of shrieks and fluttering wings. Athelstan peered at the oak. Was someone hiding there, watching him? Athelstan took a deep breath. He wanted to question Richer but that could wait. In the meantime . . .

Athelstan reached the abbey church. The choir was filing out. He went round to the north-east corner and the ancient steps leading down to the charnel house. The thick oaken door at the bottom was blackened with age, its iron studs rusting. Athelstan heard a sound behind him; he glanced over his shoulder but there was nothing. He fished into the small wallet on his belt then pulled out the sconce torch from its rusted coping; the torch was dry and fully primed. Athelstan, using his tinder, fired the pitch; the blueish yellow flame fluttered then strengthened. Satisfied it was fully caught, Athelstan lifted the latch and entered the grim mausoleum. He fired the cressets just within the door and gazed round that morbid crypt with its stout, barrel-like columns, fretted arches and mildewed walls. A truly macabre sight, the charnel house was filled with yellowing bones and skulls over a yard high, the air thick with the dust of the dead.

'A place where Mother Midnight lurks,' Athelstan whispered.

The bones had been unceremoniously tossed behind a crude wooden palisade which had been erected to create a path between the pathetic remains of former monks. The ominous words of the liturgy of Ash Wednesday sprang to mind.

'Remember man,' Athelstan murmured, 'that thou art dust and into dust thou shalt return.' Lifting the torch Athelstan made his way through what he called this garden of the dead, past the mound of bones heaped high behind their great wooden casing. He ignored the squeak and rustle of vermin. Bones loosened in the pile clattered down, skulls rolled and bounced to crash against the fencing. Athelstan made his way towards the steps he'd glimpsed at the far end of the crypt. He felt as if he was going through a maze. Torch held out, he scrutinized the gruesome pyre looking for any disturbance, a flash of colour or glint of metal which would indicate something untoward. A disembodied shadow, black and fluttering, flittered past the dancing torchlight. Athelstan's mouth went dry. Others followed, the bats squeaking in protest. Athelstan continued on, now regretting his decision to come down here. He could detect nothing.

Abruptly the door he'd entered opened and shut with a crash. The torches on either side of it were swiftly extinguished but not before Athelstan glimpsed a darting shadow and the glint of steel. Athelstan fled up the path crashing against the wooden palisade. Bones and skulls tumbled down. Behind him echoed the soft slither of boots. Athelstan grabbed a skull, turned and hurled it at the moving shadow. The midnight figure faltered and slipped on some of the shiny bones smashing on to the floor. Athelstan hurried on. He stretched out the torch and glimpsed the steep steps built into the far wall. He turned. The shadow was not yet up and following. Athelstan leaned over the palisade, dragging down more skulls and bones, then he hurled the torch. Blackness descended. Athelstan, however, had glimpsed the steps and the path leading to it. He reached the staircase, sweat starting, and clambered up. He tugged at the door but it held fast. His pursuer was still slipping and slithering along the narrow path, bumping into the fencing. Athelstan desperately beat on the door shouting, '*Aux aide! Aux aide!*' The door shook. Bolts on the other side were drawn and it creaked open. Athelstan pushed the gaping monk aside, turned and slammed the door shut, shoving across the rusting bolts.

'Brother Athelstan, what is the matter?'

The friar turned, leaning his back on the door and stared at his rescuer. 'God be thanked.' Athelstan gasped. He crouched down, arms across his belly, trying to curb the panic seething within him. 'Thank you!' he murmured.

'My friend.' The monk knelt beside him.

Athelstan now recognized Odo from the infirmary.

'What were you doing in our charnel house? I came into the church to set up the funeral trestles for poor Brokersby. I heard the clattering and your shouting. What happened?'

'I was searching for the other one.' Athelstan gasped again, now weak with shock. 'Henry Osborne. I thought I'd search . . .'

'Why look for the living amongst the dead?' Odo helped Athelstan to his feet.

'What do you mean?'

'Brother Fidelis, who guards the postern door in the main gateway? Well,' Odo gabbled on, 'he is getting quite old. He does the nightly vigil and sleeps during the morning. Prior Alexander agreed to that. Anyway, Fidelis declared that Master Henry Osborne, with pack and fardle, weaponed like a man of war, left our abbey in the early hours of this morning. He did not say much. He demanded the postern be opened then he was gone, slipped through like a moon beam. So what happened in the charnel house?'

'Nothing.' Athelstan took a deep breath. 'A frightening, macabre place; I panicked.' Athelstan's eye caught a wall painting celebrating the martyrdom of St Agnes. 'I need to speak to the anchorite.'

'He is not in his cell,' Odo replied, stepping back. 'On a Sunday he always goes for a walk. He says he likes to celebrate the day of the Lord's resurrection in a garden.'

'I am sure he does.' Athelstan, now recovered from his shock, patted the dust from him. He was tempted to seek out his mysterious assailant but that would be fruitless. By now that ominously dark, threatening shape in the crypt would have fled.

'Brother Athelstan, Brother Athelstan.' A servitor came hurrying up the aisle, sleeves fluttering, breathlessly gesturing at the friar. 'You must come!' he gasped, pointing at the door. 'The watergate!'

Athelstan hurried out. He reached Mortival meadow and stopped, speechless. The mist had thinned and there, cloak billowing out, beaver hat pushed slightly back and sipping from his miraculous wineskin, strode Cranston. The coroner was surrounded by a crowd of Athelstan's parishioners who yelled their greetings and streamed across the frozen grass to meet him.

Once Athelstan had recovered from his surprise, staring speechlessly at a grinning Cranston, the parishioners were marshalled into some order. Prior Alexander appeared. He proved to be courtesy itself, offering the largest chantry chapel, that of St Fulcher's, as a meeting place as well as promising that the abbey kitchens would prepare food for Athelstan's guests in the refectory. At first, disorder and dissension reigned.

Different parishioners grabbed Athelstan's sleeve to catch his
attention and divulge juicy morsels of gossip. How Watkin
and Pike had got drunk; all pot-valiant they had challenged
Moleskin to a fight calling him 'a bald face coin-clipper' until
Tab the tinker and Crispin the carpenter had intervened. How
the figures in the crib had been reorganized. Ursula's sow had
been attacked by Thaddeus, Godbless' goat, and so on.
Athelstan half listened to this, quietly relieved that both owners
had not brought their animals with them.

The sheer magnificence of the abbey church soon reduced
such chatter to 'oohs' and 'aahs' of admiration. Huddle
immediately disappeared to study the wall paintings whilst
Tab lovingly caressed the polished carved oak. Ranulf the
rat-catcher had brought his prize ferrets Ferox and Audax in
their cage; he wandered off sniffing the air and poking into
corners. Ranulf's tarred pointed hood, his nose sharp above
yellow jutting teeth, made the rat-catcher look even more like
the rodents he hunted. Athelstan kept a sharp eye on Watkin,
Pike, Moleskin and the rest, whose fingers positively itched
at being surrounded by such wealth. He glimpsed Benedicta,
who had donned her best cloak and hood of dark murrey lined
with squirrel fur. Athelstan smelt her delicate perfume, a
fragrance she once laughingly described as the best of Castile,
a rare soap her husband had bought on his travels. Athelstan
tried not to look into those dark eyes dancing with delight at
seeing him again. One hand grasping his arm, Benedicta
described how Cranston had appeared in the parish like God
Almighty, organizing Moleskin and his St Andrew's Guild of
Bargemen to take them along the river to St Fulcher's. They
had all decided to go. Athelstan glanced around. He noticed
with a twinge of bemused sadness how his little flock had
also insisted on bringing the parish hand bell as well as the
small coffer holding the Blood Book, the parish records and
other important memoranda, not to mention the casket carrying
the keys to the church, tabernacle, sacristy and parish chest.
They apparently trusted no one! Benedicta quietly assured
him all was well even as she studied him closely, flicking the
dust from his robe and gently touching the slight cuts and
bruises on his hands and face. Cranston joined him; his

bonhomie faded as he too scrutinized the little friar from head to toe.

'Not now,' Athelstan whispered, 'let us not alarm our little flock.'

They called back Tab, Huddle and the rest, shepherding them into the chantry chapel with the help of two burly brothers whom Prior Alexander had sent to assist as well as to guide Athelstan's visitors around the wonders of the abbey. Athelstan took his seat in the priest's chair and, with Cranston standing guard at the doorway, the friar delivered a short speech of welcome, then asked how matters stood? Within a few heartbeats he sincerely wished he hadn't. Imelda, Pike's wife, loudly demanded that only members of the parish attend the midnight Mass at Christmas. Cecily the courtesan, who usually brought her own group of Magdalenas to the Mass, was the object of Imelda's spite. Cecily, however, ogling one of the brothers, simply stuck her tongue out and returned to stare dewy-eyed at the bemused monk. Athelstan put the matter to a vote and Imelda's demand was promptly rejected. The friar swiftly moved on to other matters such as washing the baptismal font, the supply of altar wine and bedecking the church with more holly and ivy. Other items of business were raised. Some were voted on; others would have to wait. Mauger the bell clerk, squatting with his chancery tray across his lap, swiftly recorded the items of business; these would be later copied up into the parish ledger. Ursula the pig woman, who had spent her time in a constant mutter, now began to protest at not being able to bring her sow. Pernel the Fleming, threading her red and green hair, loudly hummed a favourite hymn. Meanwhile, Ranulf's ferrets had caught the slither and squeal of vermin and were jumping like fury in their cage. Athelstan decided it was time to finish. He rose, exhorted his little flock to be good and handed them over to the waiting brothers for the promised tour of the abbey.

Once they'd all left singing the praises of Prior Alexander and rubbing their bellies in anticipation of a good meal, Athelstan and Cranston adjourned to the friar's chamber in the abbot's guest house. A servitor brought them bread, cheese, a small pot of delicious preserve and tankards of the abbey's own ale. Athelstan did not wish to eat but washed himself at the lavarium. Once Cranston had broken his fast, the friar tersely informed him about everything that had happened since the coroner had left. Cranston, eyes half closed, heard him out and after Athelstan had finished, reported all he had learnt in the city.

'We need to scrutinize all this logically but first,' Cranston rose to his feet, 'three matters. First, I am staying with you. Secondly, you and I remain close – no more wandering in deserted places.' He glared down at the friar.

'And thirdly, Sir John?'

'We are going to demand an immediate audience with our Lord Abbot. I want the prior and sub-prior in attendance. I want that meeting now with no dalliance or delay.'

Cranston was true to his word and, within the hour, he and Athelstan swept into the abbot's chamber. The coroner immediately ensconced himself on a chair before Lord Walter's desk and smiled falsely at this prince of the church flanked by his two most senior monks.

'My Lord Walter, I want the truth.'

'I always tell it.'

'Good, I expect that from a priest. The Upright Men, the Great Community of the Realm who, we all know, meet at All Hallows, Barking. Do you pay them protection money?'

'I . . .'

'You pay them protection money – yes or no?' Cranston thundered.

'Yes.'

'How much?'

'Five pounds in gold every month.'

Cranston whistled under his breath.

'Don't threaten me with treason, Sir John. I am protected by Holy Mother Church; other great lords also pay the piper.'

'In return for what?'

'As you say, protection. You've heard of the attacks elsewhere. My duty to God and my brothers is to protect this abbey until His Grace the Regent resolves this problem once and for all.'

'And you two know of this?'

Prior Alexander and Richer nodded in agreement.

'As you are about the purveyance given every Sunday to the Upright Men. They take the lord's share of the Marybread and Marymeat, yes?'

Prior Alexander nodded his agreement. Cranston turned back to the abbot. 'So why have the money payments stopped?'

Prior Alexander's mouth opened and shut in surprise. Abbot Walter squirmed in his chair.

'Father Abbot,' Prior Alexander demanded. 'I have seen the accounts. The money was given to you to pass on.'

The abbot sighed noisily.

'Well,' Cranston asked, 'how do you pay?'

'On Sundays, don't you?' Athelstan intervened. 'Or you used to, at the distribution of purveyance before the main gate as well as on the quayside.'

'Why have you suspended payments?' Prior Alexander's anger boiled over. 'Where is that money? Your beloved niece?'

'What I do,' Abbot Walter pulled himself up, 'is my business.'

'When this abbey is burning about our ears it will be ours,' Prior Alexander snapped.

'How dare you!' The abbot turned in his chair. 'How dare you,' he repeated, 'accuse me.' He darted a look at Sub-Prior Richer. 'Put your own house in order first.'

Leda the swan, nestling in her comfortable bed rose, neck out, wings ruffling. A beautiful sight, Athelstan thought, except for that malevolent hissing. Prior Alexander sat tense, his face full of fury. Abbot Walter turned away, murmuring softly to the swan.

'And you, Brother Richer.' Athelstan asked, 'We have reports of you meeting boatmen from foreign ships?'

'So?' The Frenchman shrugged. 'I send letters and presents to my family, my brethren, my kinsmen in France.'

'Including those at St Calliste?'

'Including those.'

'And Father Abbot approves of this?'

'Of course I do,' Lord Abbot interjected, eager to keep Richer's support. 'We communicate rarely with our brothers in France. Brother Richer, however, has close ties to his home community. He has every right to do what he has.'

'Why are you here?' Athelstan insisted. 'Why, Richer, have you come to this cold, lonely place?'

'I've told you. I am a skilled clerk, a copyist, a calligrapher. St Fulcher's library is famous . . .'

'I need to question you on that,' Athelstan interjected, 'but not now. These boatmen from foreign ships? How do you arrange the exact time and place to meet?'

'I often go into the city.' The usually urbane Richer was now flustered.

'As you did on the eve of St Damasus during your visit to Sir Robert? You and Prior Alexander visited the Queenshithe or elsewhere. You made the arrangements then?'

'Yes, yes, Prior Alexander is very understanding.'

'I am sure he is. Your visit with Kilverby . . .?'

'We've explained that.' Prior Alexander spoke up. 'It was a courtesy visit. Sir Robert was not coming to St Fulcher's. There was the business of Crispin being given lodgings here and other minor items.'

'Such as?'

'Sir Robert was a most generous benefactor,' Lord Walter intervened. 'His donations for Masses to be sung helped us build the new hog pen on our farm as well as re-gild some of our sacred vessels. We wanted to assure him that such gifts were both appreciated and well spent.' The reply was rather rushed and from Prior Alexander's face Athelstan concluded that a great deal of such gold and silver revenue stuck to the abbot's greedy fingers. Little wonder Lord Walter's beloved niece and sister lived so high on the hog! Athelstan recalled Isabella's chatter at their recent meeting; he was sure she'd let slip that she had come of age. Was Abbot Walter preparing a generous dowry for his beloved kinswoman?

'Tell me.' Athelstan glanced around. 'Let us establish the times and seasons of all that has happened here.'

'In what way?'

'The Wyvern Company arrived here when?'

'Four years last summer.'

'And you, Richer?'

'I have been here just under three years.'

'And the first fatality amongst the Wyvern Company was William Chalk?'

'That was not murder,' Prior Alexander answered flatly. 'I examined him and so did local physicians. Master Chalk had growths in his belly and groin – I've told you this.'

'When did he fall ill?'

'About eighteen months ago.'

'And who gave him ghostly comfort?'

'I tended to him first,' Prior Alexander retorted. 'Brother Richer later on.'

'Did you shrive him?'

'Of course,' Richer snapped. 'I also gave him the last rites but,' the Frenchman glared at Athelstan, 'Chalk turned to God. You've been through his chamber. You must have seen his prayers scrawled on scraps of parchments pleading for mercy. You're a priest. You know, under pain of excommunication, Brother Athelstan, no priest can break the seal of confession.'

'He must have talked outside the seal.'

'Everything is covered by the seal.'

'You hate the Wyvern Company?'

'You know I do. They are thieves, blasphemers, killers and the perpetrators of sacrilege.'

'So Chalk did not abuse you of that.'

'What passed between us, Brother, is protected by the seal.'

'Where do you think the Passio Christi truly belongs?'

'St Calliste.'

'Is your uncle still abbot there?'

Richer smiled. 'Yes, he enjoys robust health, thank God.'

'And Kilverby,' Athelstan continued, 'he brought the Passio Christi here at the appointed time for the Wyvern Company to view?'

'He used to,' Prior Alexander declared. 'We've told you that.'

'And his relationship with the Wyverns was cordial? After all, he did finance them during the war with France.'

'From what we know,' Lord Walter intervened, 'Kilverby was always distant and aloof but he was amicable enough towards the Wyverns.'

'And this changed?'

'Yes.'

'Why?'

'Sir Robert began to reflect most carefully about them. He changed his opinion of those he once patronized.'

'Encouraged by you, Brother Richer?'

'What do you mean?'

'You know precisely. Did you advise Sir Robert?'

'Of course I did. He was a man much burdened with sin,' the Frenchman replied. 'I shrived him. I gave him ghostly advice.'

'Did he tell you his true opinion of the Wyvern Company?'

'He grew to dislike them intensely. He claimed he'd always believed their story about the Passio Christi but he came to the conclusion that they hadn't found it but stolen it.'

'A conclusion you helped him reach?'

'I didn't disagree with him.'

'Then Kilverby,' Cranston asked, 'stopped bringing the Passio Christi here?'

'Yes,' Lord Walter replied, 'last year it was brought by Crispin and Mistress Alesia.'

Athelstan tapped a sandalled foot against the floor.

'You don't believe us?' Richer asked. 'You think we lie?'

'No,' Athelstan retorted. 'You're not lying but you're not telling the full truth either. Kilverby was a leading London merchant, hard of heart, keen of wit and cunning as a snake. He financed and profited from the Wyverns. He must have suspected their story about the bloodstone years ago so why the change now?'

'God's grace,' Richer declared, 'my counsel.'

'No,' Athelstan retorted, 'something else.'

'Such as?' Richer had recovered his arrogance. 'Why not ask Master Crispin?'

'Did you give Crispin ghostly comfort too, Brother Richer?'

'Master Crispin and Sir Robert were regular visitors here,' Richer replied. 'I counselled Sir Robert but only exchanged pleasantries with Crispin.'

'Can any of you three,' Cranston gestured around, 'cast any light on Sir Robert's murder or the disappearance of the Passio

Christi?' The coroner's question was greeted with muttered denials. 'And the murders here in your abbey?'

'Sir John,' Lord Walter retorted, 'you know as much as we do.'

'And the fire in Brokersby's chamber?'

'Most unfortunate.' The abbot sighed.

'Would he,' Athelstan insisted, 'have any reasons to keep oil in his chamber?'

'Not that I am aware of.'

'And the bedside candle?'

'Visit our chandler, Brother Athelstan,' Prior Alexander replied. 'Such candles are dispensed to all chambers in the guest house – tall, thick, fashioned out of tallow but still the best. They are fixed on a stand with a cap. I don't think such a fire could be caused even if this candle was knocked over. I mean,' the prior flailed a hand, 'such a conflagration.'

Athelstan glanced at Cranston and raised his eyes heavenwards.

'We have to go.' The coroner abruptly rose to his feet, bowed and, followed by Athelstan, walked to the door. Cranston abruptly turned.

'Lord Abbot, your sister Eleanor Remiet – her maiden name?'

'Why, the same as mine, Chobham. She married a Gascon, Velours, then remarried Master Remiet, who also died. My niece is the only child of her first marriage. Is that all?'

'No.' Athelstan pointed at Richer. 'Brother, if I could have a word with you in private.'

The Frenchman looked as if he was going to object.

'Just we two.' Athelstan smiled. 'Sir John will not be present.'

Richer shrugged and followed them out down to the court-yard. Athelstan waited until Cranston was out of hearing and turned.

'Brother Richer, are you an assassin?'

'How dare you!'

'The day Hyde was stabbed to death close to the watergate – you went down there that afternoon. You were seen carrying a sword.'

Richer's lower lip trembled.

'You took a sword out of the Barbican when the lazy brother-in-charge was elsewhere. You took it because of the killings here, whilst the quayside on a lonely mist-filled afternoon could be a dangerous place. You were going to meet a boatman from a foreign ship to give him whatever you really do send from this abbey. I suspect Hyde followed and spied on you close to the watergate.'

'Are you accusing me of murdering him?'

'No, but Hyde had also been followed. The mysterious assassin pierced Hyde's belly and he gave the most hideous scream. You must have heard that. You told your boatman to wait and hurried back to find Hyde dying of his belly wound.' Athelstan paused. 'You really hate those archers, don't you? Did Hyde, an old soldier, ask for the mercy cut or did you see him as the hated enemy? Did you stab him with that sword then carry it back to your friend the boatman?'

Richer refused to answer.

'And then what? Did the boatman take you up or down river so you could make your own way back to the abbey?' Athelstan drew closer. 'You're a very dangerous man, Brother Richer.'

'Am I? A Benedictine?'

'You came here undoubtedly with a letter of recommendation from the Abbot of St Calliste, but he's your uncle. Are you really a monk, Richer, or a knight, a mailed knight in the guise of Benedictine, a man with one mission to secure the return of the Passio Christi?' Athelstan paused. 'I wonder, Richer . . .'

'What?'

'Chalk? Did he fall ill from some malignant ill-humour or did you cause it with some poisonous potion? Did you prepare him for death then parade the horrors of judgement before him?'

Richer stepped back. 'Friar, I do not know what you are talking about. Whatever I am, whatever you are, I know the law. Where is your proof, your evidence?' Without waiting for a reply Richer turned on his heel and left, slamming the door behind him.

Athelstan walked across to Cranston.

'An upset monk? What did you say?'

'Not for the moment, Sir John.' Athelstan stamped his feet against the cold. 'It's time I rejoined my flock and shepherded them back to the watergate. Many thanks, Sir John.'

'For what?'

'You know what.' Athelstan grasped the coroner's hand and squeezed it. 'They wanted to see me. I wanted to see them but it was not just that, was it? You told me what happened outside Kilverby's mansion. The Upright Men questioned you about me being held here against my will. The Upright Men have many adherents in my parish; they'll report back that I am safe and well. I just hope they remain so. Anyway, it's time they were gone. We will talk later tonight.'

oOoOo

SIX

'Hoodman blind: blindman's bluff.'

Athelstan found his parishioners well away from the abbey. They had seen the glories of the church and were full of stories about the strange anchorite who'd swept by them like some baleful cloud to hide himself in his anker house. They had all supped well in the refectory on fish stuffed with almonds, lentil soup, rich beef stew, blancmange, sweet cakes and as many blackjacks of ale as they could down. Now, rosy cheeked with merriment, they had gathered around the new hog enclosure to stare at the abbey's herd of fierce, snouting pigs with hairy, bristling ears and greedy maws. Powerful animals with quivering flanks and muscular legs, the hogs had turned their great enclosure and the surrounding stys into a reeking quagmire of cold, hard mud and steaming droppings. The hogs, aroused by the noise and chatter, crashed into the sturdy stockade much to the enjoyment of Athelstan's parishioners who relished it, as Watkin slurred, better than any bear baiting. Athelstan, wary of these ferocious beasts, coaxed his little flock back up into the church. Cloaks were put back on, only to be taken off as Pike the ditcher announced he wished to personally inspect the abbey latrines.

At last, as the shadows crept from the corners, order was imposed. Athelstan lined them up. He glimpsed the bulging pockets in cloaks and gowns and guiltily realized that his parishioners had probably left little in the refectory and that included tankards, platters and anything else which moved. He led them down to the darkening quayside and, having given them parting words of advice, delivered what he called his most solemn blessing. He sadly watched the two barges manned by Moleskin and his comrades disappear into the mist, the good wishes of his parishioners carrying eerily towards him. Athelstan turned and walked back to where Cranston stood waiting for him by the watergate.

'Very well,' Athelstan breathed, 'let us return to my chamber. I suggest you take the one next to it. We'll have something to sup. Let the bells of the abbey clang for divine office. Sir John, God has more pressing work for us. He wants us to search out the children of Cain and bring them before the bar of his justice.' Athelstan escorted Cranston to the buttery then back to his warm chamber. He bolted the door, prepared his writing tray and stared at his portly friend now sitting bootless on the edge of the bed.

'Item:' Athelstan began, 'The murder of Kilverby and the disappearance of the Passio Christi? Any thoughts?'

Cranston shook his head.

'Neither have I.' Athelstan sighed. 'We are assured that chamber was secured locked and no one entered or left. Nevertheless, Kilverby was poisoned, the Passio Christi taken. We know the merchant was visited earlier that day. He showed the two monks the Passio Christi which was to be brought here on the morrow. The bloodstone was displayed in the solar. Kilverby, escorted by Crispin, then took it back to his chamber. Everything must have been in order. The bloodstone was locked away. We know that, we saw the locked coffer. Kilverby kept the keys round his neck. The chancery was also secured. Kilverby joined his family for supper before returning to his chamber. Only then does hell's black spy, the killer, manifest himself, or herself.' He added wistfully: 'Certainly some hell-born soul contrived a trap which created this mystery.'

'I talked to Crispin,' Cranston declared. 'I did the same with Jumble-guts.'

'Who?'

'One of my spies along Cheapside, called so because his belly rumbles like a drum. Both Crispin and Jumble-guts sing the same hymn. It would be almost impossible, as well as highly dangerous, to try and sell the bloodstone on the open market.'

'So why was it stolen in the first place?' Athelstan exclaimed.

'My mistake, Sir John. We should discover as much as we can about that sacred ruby but . . .'

Athelstan picked up his quill pen, stared at its plume then the point, dipped it in the ink and became lost in his own thoughts.

'Friar?'

'I'm thinking about the attacks on me, Sir John. No,' Athelstan shook his head, 'I cannot say much. I can only remember fragments that I cannot properly explain.'

'Such as?' Cranston demanded.

'Oh, just who was where when that crossbow was loosed. The speed with which my assailant entered the charnel house and extinguished those torches just within the doorway.' Athelstan shook his head. 'Never mind. What we do have in this abbey is the Wyvern Company disliked and barely tolerated. Abbot Walter may have confidence in their presence if his abbey is ever attacked, yet I am sure he would like to rid himself of the old soldiers. They're an embarrassment and possible provocation to the Upright Men who may have dispatched assassins to kill Hanep, Hyde and Brokersby. Our abbot is supposed to pay the Upright Men protection money, but for his own secret reasons, has withheld this.' Athelstan stroked his face with the plume of his quill pen. 'By the way, Sir John, you say you recognized Eleanor Remiet?'

'I did, I'm sure.' Cranston tapped his feet on the floor. 'God send me his grace. I recognized her face but it's years, decades ago.' He glanced up. 'Why do you ask?'

'At first I wondered if Isabella Velours was the abbot's mistress. Of course that's not true. However, I believe she is not his niece but his daughter.'

'What?'

'Nor do I believe Eleanor Remiet is his sister.' Athelstan continued: 'Although I accept she's Isabella's mother. I am sure if we made careful search in certain parish and manor records we'd uncover a legion of lies regarding those precious three.'

'We could do that.'

'Come, Sir John, it would take months. Moreover, Lord Walter's private life is not our concern, even if our abbot doesn't give a fig about anything except that swan and his two women.'

'You've little evidence for what you say.'

'Sir John, why should the abbot be so concerned about his niece? No, Isabella is his daughter and, more importantly, she has just come of age and . . .'

'Needs a dowry,' Cranston breathed.

'Hence the money to the Upright Men being drained away along with whatever else Abbot Walter can seize.'

'Do you think the Wyvern Company found out about Isabella?'

'I doubt it.' Athelstan stopped writing the cipher he always used to record his thoughts. 'Quite honestly, I don't think the Wyvern Company give a fig about Isabella being Abbot Walter's niece or his daughter. They are more concerned about themselves.'

'And Prior Alexander?'

'Basically a good man with sympathies for the common folk. The reception of my parishioners was his work. I must thank him. We know one of his kinsman, a hedge priest, was hanged out of hand by the Wyvern Company. Prior Alexander may want revenge. He is still vigorous, able to wield a sword. He dislikes the Wyverns, whilst he was here when all three died.' Athelstan put his tray aside, rose and stretched.

'Do you think he suspects the truth about Isabella Velours?'

'Perhaps, but Lord Walter can also trap him. Prior Alexander has, I believe, an inordinate love for Richer. The truth behind that relationship is difficult to discern but I suspect Prior Alexander indulges Richer. When they go into the city the prior is willing to take his young friend down to the quayside to search for foreign ships. Indeed,' Athelstan sat down, 'it is Richer who is the key to this mystery. He was sent here, I am certain, by his uncle, the Abbot of St Calliste, to retrieve the Passio Christi. Has he suborned Prior Alexander in order to achieve this? Perhaps. Did he or both of them kill the old soldiers including Chalk? I cannot say. What I am certain of is that Richer lies at the root of this. Look,' Athelstan got to his feet, unbolted the door and stared out. The gallery outside was deserted. He could hear the plain chant from the church as the full choir intoned the psalm: 'The Lord trains my arms for war, he prepares my hands for battle.' Yes, he does,

Athelstan reflected, closing the door. 'Sir John, look at the facts. Kilverby once financed the Wyvern Company. He held the Passio Christi without protest. Time passes. Death beckons. Kilverby wants to prepare for judgement. The Wyvern Company move here. Kilverby visits them but he encounters Richer. He also meets another man frightened of approaching death, a defrocked priest, Master William Chalk. Oh yes, he was, remember?'

Cranston nodded.

'To move to the arrow point. Apparently Richer put the fear of God into both men, especially Kilverby. He points out the terrible sacrilege which took place after Poitiers. Kilverby breaks from the likes of Wenlock. He wants nothing more to do with them. He'll do penance, perform reparation, give up his luxurious life and go on pilgrimage. On the very day he departs he will make decisive restitution. He will leave the Passio Christi at a Benedictine Abbey.'

'But that doesn't explain his murder?'

'No, Sir John. It certainly does not. Moreover, as you discovered during your last visit to Kilverby's mansion, what did compel this hard-headed merchant to change, to want to rid himself of a sacred bloodstone he'd blithely held for years? Richer's persuasive tongue? I don't think so. In my view Kilverby saw or heard something which literally put the fear of God into him and that's what Richer exploited so successfully. However, what that was and how Kilverby came to be murdered? I admit, there's no logical answer to either of these questions.'

'And the murders here?'

'Again, I cannot see any logic behind their deaths. Hanep and Hyde were killed when Wenlock and Mahant were absent. Wenlock's maimed hands are an impediment, though Mahant is a master swordsman. They were all sleeping when Brokersby was burnt to death and Osborne, by all accounts, has fled the abbey. All three murders demonstrated the Wyvern Company are very vulnerable. Perhaps that's why Osborne fled. The Wyvern Company can no longer protect itself. As for who is the assassin? Prior Alexander? Richer? Both of them or someone else? The anchorite is certainly skilled in violent

death with his own grievances against these former soldiers.'
Athelstan picked up another quill pen, dipped it into the ink
and made further entries. 'As regards to the deaths of the first
two Wyverns, well, it could be the work of an assassin
despatched by the Upright Men. It's Brokersby's death which
intrigues me. Why the raging fire?' He put the pen down.
'How was that oil not only poured into a locked chamber but
so close to the bed?'

'Brother,' the coroner sighed, 'my eyes grow heavy. I must
adjourn and reflect. I also need to despatch certain letters to
the city. I want them to go at first light.' Cranston walked over
and gripped Athelstan's shoulder. 'No wandering this abbey
by yourself little friar, promise me.'

Athelstan did. Cranston put on his boots, picked up his
cloak, made his farewells and swept from the chamber . . .

The anchorite had been dreaming about his days as the
Hangman of Rochester. He woke in his anker house bathed
in sweat and sat listening to the sounds of the abbey. Compline
had been sung. The monks had shuffled out. Candles and
lantern horns had been snuffed; only the occasional light
gleamed but these solitary taper flames did little to repel the
darkness. The anchorite peered around. The smells of the
church, beeswax, burning charcoal, incense and that strange
mustiness still swirled. The anchorite crossed himself, knelt
on the narrow prie-dieu and stared up at the crucifix. He'd
had a good day, cheered by the sight of Athelstan's parishioners. During his long walk he had planned more frescoes
and wall paintings but now the day, was gone, night was the
mistress. He strained his ears for other sounds – nothing! The
abbey church had yet to be locked. The sacristan and his
entourage still had to make their nightly patrol to ensure all
lights were extinguished, doors secured, especially after the
peace of the abbey had been so deeply disturbed. The anchorite
had quietly marvelled at the shocking news. Brokersby had
been visited by fire whilst Osborne had apparently fled. Was
this God's justice? Perhaps it was. After all, why should such
killers be allowed to end their days in peace?

The anchorite rose and paced his cell. He paused at the

whispering outside the anker slit. Was she back? Trying to control his fears and the icy tremors piercing his belly, the anchorite crept towards the slit then recoiled at the pasty white face which suddenly appeared there.

'Hangman of Rochester,' that spiteful mouth hissed, 'are you not ready to pay?'

'Pay? Pay?' The anchorite gasped. 'Pay for what?'

'Blood money, surety for what you've done. Strip yourself of your wealth. Leave it on the ledge, the profits you have made. Money for Masses . . .'

The anchorite retreated. He plucked up the coffer crammed with gold and silver coins. For peace, he thought, I'll surrender this, a shimmering cascade through that slit to buy peace from all this. The anchorite grasped the coffer even tighter. He felt his stomach drawn like a bow string. If only she'd go and leave him alone! He glimpsed movement at the anker-slit, a trail of scraggly hair. Was she gone? He startled as the door was pushed and rattled against its bolts. The anchorite opened his mouth in a silent scream. The door shook again, a threatening rattle. Agnes Rednal was trying to break in! He dropped the coffer and hurled himself at the door screaming and cursing, banging with his fists, pleading for that hell creature to leave him alone.

The following morning after his dawn Mass, Athelstan heard about the disturbance at the anker house. He was divesting in the chantry chapel assisted by Brother Simon, who'd acted as his acolyte and altar boy.

'Screaming and banging he was,' Brother Simon exclaimed. 'The sacristan had just entered the church when it happened, a man possessed or so they say. Our anchorite is haunted by demons.'

Athelstan thanked Simon. Curious, he made his way down to the anker house and tapped on the door.

'Who is it?'

Athelstan glanced at the slit and glimpsed the anchorite's long white fingers grasping the sill.

'Brother Athelstan, friend. I wonder if all is well? I mean no harm. If you would like to speak?'

To his surprise he heard the rattle of chains, bolts being drawn and the low door swung open. Athelstan bent his head, entered the anker house and straightened up. The anchorite immediately knelt and asked for his blessing. Athelstan gave this and stared around. The cell was rather large, apparently a disused chantry chapel – its wooden screen had been removed and a wall built across the gap. A comfortable, sweet-smelling chamber with bed, chest, coffers and a lavarium; a table stood under a window of clear glass, beside it a lectern then a prie-dieu with pegs driven into a wall on which to hang clothes. A small brazier warmed the air with scented smoke whilst a five branch candle spigot and a lantern horn provided more light. The anchorite, still agitated, invited Athelstan to the chair while he drew up a stool and gazed expectantly at the friar.

'What happened?' Athelstan asked.

The anchorite told him. When he'd finished Athelstan shook his head in disbelief.

'And this has happened before?'

'Oh yes, Brother, I always see her, at least in my mind's eye. I always did but now, during these last few weeks, she comes here demanding vengeance and blood money.'

'Blood money?' Athelstan scoffed. 'For what?'

'For her death.'

'Well, what money?'

The anchorite rose, went into the shadows and returned carrying a casket which he unlocked with a key from a ring attached to his leather belt. Athelstan gasped at the mound of glistening coins, good, sound silver and gold. He grasped a handful, weighing it carefully before putting it back.

'My inheritance,' the anchorite explained, 'after my parents died, as well as what I've earned over the years both as a painter and hangman. Remember, I am allowed all my victims' goods while some pay well for their going to be brisk.' The anchorite paused, muttering a prayer. 'Brother, why am I being haunted? If she wants blood money should I give it to her?'

'She demanded that last night?'

'Yes, she did and I nearly agreed.'

'Look,' Athelstan took the coffer from the anchorite's hands and placed it on the ground, 'demons walk, we know that. The Lords of the Air float by in hordes. Devils whisper in corners and all kind of darksmen roam the wilderness of the human soul. Ghosts cluster close before our mind's eye or, indeed, to our physical senses. Nevertheless, I've never heard of a ghost demanding money. Moreover, why does she only appear when the abbey falls silent and deserted?'

The anchorite stared back, unconvinced.

'You have eerie imaginings, my friend,' Athelstan continued. 'Undoubtedly the death of Agnes Rednal haunts you but not her soul. Please,' Athelstan smiled, 'trust me.'

The anchorite just kept staring, face all haggard.

'You have eaten and drunk?' Athelstan asked gently. 'Refreshment, as Sir John says, is good for the soul as well as the body. I promise you, I will plumb these mysteries which brood so close to you.'

'And those other mysteries, the murders here?'

'My friend,' Athelstan gestured round, 'we still stumble and fall.'

'I heard about your panic in the charnel house. Brother Athelstan, tread warily here.'

'You said something similar when we first met. You told me you had things to say,' Athelstan added. 'You still nurse grievances against the Wyvern Company about your wife and child?'

'Yes, my poor family.' The anchorite rubbed the side of his head. 'Sometimes I see them as I do Agnes Rednal.' He glanced up pitifully. 'That's what I wanted to confess last time. My deep loathing for those soldiers yet I did not kill them.'

Athelstan stared at the man's strong, claw-like hands.

'You have the strength and skill,' Athelstan murmured, 'you are deeply troubled.'

The anchorite sprang to his feet then sat down face in his hands.

'True, I am deeply troubled. Agnes Rednal crawls on to my bed.' He pointed at the ledger resting on the desk. 'I describe my dreams, my visions. Brother, I cannot distinguish between what is real and what is my imagining.'

'Friend,' Athelstan replied briskly, 'you live in this anker house, you're close to God. You are, I believe, a good man of troubled soul though your wits remain sharp. So answer my questions. Keep with the land of the living. Help me to pursue justice.'

The anchorite sighed and took away his hands.

'Your questions?'

'Good. You came here when?'

'About three years ago.'

'Did you ever talk or converse with the Wyvern Company?'

'What do you think? I voiced my resentment of them. Once, shortly after my arrival, they came here to gape and stare. I told them who I was and what chains bound us together from the past.'

'And?'

'They just protested and walked away. They stayed away except for Chalk, who fell ill. I saw him here with Sub-Prior Richer; they sat in the shriving pew close to the Lady chapel. Of course all I could glimpse was him kneeling at the prie-dieu and the monk in the shriving chair. At the time I laughed to myself. I hoped Chalk would confess his sins against me and mine. I prayed such offences would thrust themselves up like black, stinking shrubs in his midnight soul.' The anchorite breathed out noisily. 'God forgive me, he must have done. One day Chalk, his face as white as his name, came and knelt outside my door. He begged my forgiveness for what he had done. He confessed it was a memory, something which happened on a summer's day, a few heart beats when he'd been a soldier and didn't give a fig about anyone. Oh, I forgave him, I had to. For his penance I asked him to pray for me and mine every day. He promised he would.' The anchorite pulled a face. 'Apart from that the Wyvern Company kept their distance except, strangely enough, Ailward Hyde. On the day he was murdered, he came into church. He was worried. He stopped to look at my paintings. He'd done this before. I shared a few words with him then something alarmed him. A figure crept in down near the Lady chapel. I heard a clatter as if a weapon was dropped. Hyde was also curious and followed in silent pursuit.'

'Who was this figure?'

'I don't know; perhaps a monk. Anyway, Hyde took off in pursuit but someone else followed him, I'm certain of it. I glimpsed a black monk's robe then it was gone, that's all I can say.'

Athelstan nodded understandingly. 'But let us go back, my friend: Kilverby, was he shriven by Richer?'

'Yes.'

'And what about Kilverby's clerk, Crispin?'

The anchorite blinked and shook his head. 'I saw Crispin, he often came here with his master. I noticed nothing untoward except one afternoon early last summer, around the Feast of the Baptist. Kilverby arrived at St Fulcher's to pray before the rood screen. Crispin was with him. They, like many people, forgot about me as they strolled up and down the south aisle. On that particular day they were arguing.'

'About what?'

'Oh, Crispin coming to lodge here at the abbey. Crispin was respectful but insisted that he too should leave with his master. Kilverby strongly objected to this, saying Crispin's eyes were failing. Crispin then said something rather strange: "I don't want to live back here again".'

'I am sorry?'

'I listened more attentively. Apparently, many decades ago, Kilverby and Crispin studied here as novices, though both later left. I heard similar gossip amongst the brothers. Anyway, Kilverby tried to lighten Crispin's mood, teasing him about being left-handed and how the Master of the Novices had tried to force him to use his right. The merchant reminisced how Crispin used to be punished for that as Kilverby was for gnawing on the end of every pen or brush. He and Crispin laughed at the foibles of this monk or that. Abbot Walter's early days were mentioned, some gossip or scandal about him, but their voices became muted and they moved on.' The anchorite rose and paced up and down the cell. He paused, tapped the crucifix and glanced down at Athelstan.

'Brother, I am lost in my own puzzle of dreams and fears. I see things. I overhear conversations but there's little else. When we first met I had so much to say; I was being threatened. True, at first, I rejoiced in the deaths of Hanep and Hyde. Now I am beginning to wonder. So much hate, so much resentment all because of deep, hidden sins.' He paused. 'Brother?'

'Yes?'

'I would like to leave here. Would St Erconwald have an anker house?' He kicked the coffer. 'I have the money to pay for its construction. I could help your painter.'

Athelstan was about to refuse but softened at the man's pleading look.

'Friar!' Cranston's booming voice echoed along the south aisle.

'I must go.' Athelstan rose. 'As for your request, let me see.' The friar left the anker house and found Cranston had moved across the church to admire a scene painted from the Book of Daniel about Susannah facing her lecherous accusers.

'Sir John, good morrow.'

'And the same to you, little friar. I've heard Mass, I've broke my fast. What . . .' He paused as Wenlock and Mahant, their cloaks glistening with wet, came up the aisle. Athelstan noticed the daggers pushed into their war belts. Men of violence, Athelstan reflected, yet they looked cowed, Mahant especially, his hard eyes now red-rimmed, his cheeks unshaven.

'We are leaving,' Wenlock declared, 'no, no, not for good.'

'I hope not,' Cranston retorted. 'You'll stay here. I sent a lay brother into the city. I've asked the sheriff to issue writs for the fugitive Henry Osborne.'

'He's not a . . .'

'Master Wenlock, he is. Osborne fled from here by night. He could be the assassin we are hunting.'

'Never –'

'Everyone,' Cranston insisted, 'including both of you, are suspects, Osborne even more so. His description will be proclaimed in Cheapside, posted on the '*Si Quis*' door at St Paul's as well as its Great Cross. If Osborne does not surrender himself in ten days he will be declared *utlegatum* – an outlaw, a wolfshead.'

Mahant glanced sharply at Wenlock, who simply shook his head.

'Just as well,' Mahant muttered. 'It's best if he's taken.'

'Why?' Cranston demanded.

'Osborne was our treasurer,' Wenlock explained. 'I am sorry. We did not mention this before. When he left Osborne took most of our gold and silver with him. We are going into London to search for him ourselves.'

'Why there?' Athelstan asked.

'Osborne is not a country bumpkin,' Wenlock replied. 'He also likes the ladies. Perhaps we'll find him in the stews or some other brothel.' Wenlock shrugged. 'Athelstan, Sir John?'

Both men bowed and left.

'I'm not too happy,' Cranston whispered, 'I would like everyone to stay where they are but so far we have little proof to detain them, yes?' Cranston's gaze travelled back to the painting of Susannah. He walked up to it, stared hard for a while then abruptly jumped up and down like a little boy. 'Lady Purity!' he exclaimed. 'Lady Purity, also known as "Mistress Quicksilver".'

'Sir John, are you madcap?'

Cranston pointed to the picture of Susannah then grasped Athelstan firmly by the shoulders, his blue eyes blazing with good humour.

'Eleanor Remiet,' he whispered, pushing his face close to Athelstan. 'Eleanor Remiet be damned! She's Lady Purity. Athelstan, I know London. What you told me about the anchorite? I certainly remember him as an excellent hangman. Nor can I forget that murderous harridan Agnes Rednal whilst Wolfsbane was a demon incarnate. They've all crossed my path. I've certainly crossed theirs and others. Do you recall Alice Perrers?'

'The mistress of the late King Edward, she stayed long enough by his corpse to strip it of rings and every other precious item.'

'Living like a nun now out in Essex.' Cranston chuckled. 'Oh yes, I've met them all, little friar, the good, the bad and the downright wicked.'

'And this Lady Purity?'

'Stare at the painting of Susannah, Friar, gaze at her face. I've been studying it since I arrived here this morning. I know that face! This fresco was executed many years ago but the painter certainly used someone as his image.'

'Eleanor Remiet?'

'Look and judge.'

Athelstan did. Cranston snatched a flaming cresset from its sconce and held it up to illuminate the beautiful face shrouded by a mass of golden curls, the downcast eyes, the graceful way that Innocent from the Book of Daniel kept her cloak about her naked body. Athelstan stared, fascinated by the compelling beauty of the woman's face and the more he looked his doubts began to crumble. The artist, whoever he was, had used the woman now calling herself Eleanor Remiet as his mirror for this biblical heroine. To be sure, Remiet was now old, her face ravaged by time, but a hidden glow of beauty still remained in those haughty features and Athelstan could detect the same in the wall painting before him.

'Sir John,' Athelstan stepped back, 'you are correct. Who was this Lady Purity?'

'A great courtesan of Cheapside. I used to woo her from afar. She certainly wasn't for the likes of young Jack Cranston, freshly inducted into the Inns of Court, oh no, but I adored her from a distance, worshipping at her altar. I did all I could to discover more about her.'

'And?'

'Lady Purity, as she called herself, reserved her favours for the great ones of the land. She also acquired a rather sinister reputation.'

'As?'

'As a cozening blackmailer who, when it suited her, could threaten a cleric with a summons to the Archdeacon's court or an errant husband with the wrath of his wife. She earned money swiftly and smoothly in both her callings, hence her nickname, "Mistress Quicksilver". As for her title, "Lady Purity",' Cranston laughed, 'well, that was because of her pious ways, at least publicly. In her youth she was a great beauty who acted so innocently, so decorously, you'd think butter wouldn't melt in her mouth. She was the toast . . .' Cranston walked away as shouts and cries from outside rose and fell. Athelstan remained rooted to the spot, lost in his own wild tumble of thoughts.

'As I said,' Cranston continued, coming back, 'she was the

toast of Cheapside. Athelstan, you were right about her relationship with our abbot, that's what started me thinking.
Eleanor Remiet is not the abbot's sister but his leman.' Cranston
chuckled to himself. 'She is definitely the mother of the lovely
Isabella who, of course, is the abbot's natural daughter,
certainly not his niece. They are, in the eyes of God, though
not Holy Mother Church, husband, wife and child. Lady Purity
or Mistress Quicksilver, whatever her name, will have her
claws very deep into our Lord Abbot. She will demand the
best sustenance and purveyance for both herself and her
daughter. In her youth, saintly Susannah or not, Lady Purity
had a hunger for gold and silver. The passing of the years and
the needs of young Isabella will have only whetted her appetite
as sharp as a knife.'

'Which would explain why the abbot stopped paying the
Upright Men?'

'Aye, and God knows what else he has misappropriated. I
think it's time—'

'Not yet,' Athelstan gripped Cranston's sleeve, 'not yet
my Lord Coroner, let me first reflect; there are other
matters . . .'

Athelstan broke off as the hubbub outside grew. He and
Cranston went through a side door into the porch. A group of
brothers were gathered round a barrow being pushed up the
path. Exclamations rang out, the monks, jostling each other,
blocked Athelstan's view of what was in the barrow. They
parted and Athelstan groaned in sheer pity at the horror piled
there, the long graceful neck now twisted, the glorious white
plumage piled in dirty disarray – Leda the swan! Athelstan
stopped the barrow and stared down at the once magnificent
bird.

'How did it happen?'

'Hanged! Hanged!' Brother Simon pushed his way through.
'We found Leda hanged on the gallows near the watergate.'

Athelstan sketched a blessing over the dead bird.

'Abbot Walter will be distraught,' one of the brothers
exclaimed. 'He will mourn as if for a loved one.'

'Aye, but does he love any of us?' another added.

The question was greeted with silence.

'Who? How?' Athelstan asked.

Another monk passed Athelstan a parchment script with the phrase, 'Answer a fool according to his folly' scratched in red ink. Beneath this, 'The Upright Men'.

'The Upright Men,' Athelstan murmured. 'Where will they flee on the day of judgement?' He looked at the rough, chapped faces of the brothers who stared stonily back. 'Jerusalem,' Athelstan added sadly, 'will not be built on earth.'

'But Babylon and its proud princes can be brought as low as hell,' a lay brother retorted.

'Like this,' Athelstan pointed at the dead swan, 'do you know what the great philosopher Anselm said? "Cruelty to God's creatures comes directly from the evil one". Leda was,' Athelstan continued softly, 'a manifestation of the glory of God.' He stood aside. 'Your Lord Abbot needs to be informed.' Athelstan returned to Cranston, still standing in the porch, and told him what had happened.

'Abbot Walter is a fool. Athelstan, please excuse me, I've other business to attend to. We'll then meet and confront Abbot Walter and his Lady Purity.' Cranston strolled away.

Athelstan watched him go and decided to visit the library. Immediately as he entered two of the monks sitting in their carrels swiftly rose. Courteous, gracious and welcoming, Athelstan sensed they were under strict instruction to keep him occupied, whilst a third brought Richer from the scriptorium. Athelstan informed him about the swan. The Frenchman raised his eyes and murmured a prayer.

'I am sorry,' Richer lisped, 'but at the present I've other business to deal with. I will see Father Abbot in due time. I have decided,' Richer gestured around the library, 'much as I love it here, to return to St Calliste, as Lord Walter said, sooner rather than later, probably in the next few days.'

'I am sorry,' Athelstan shook his head, 'that will not be possible.'

'What do you mean – I'm a priest, a Benedictine, a citizen of France. I—'

'Brother Richer, you could be the kinsman of the Archangel Gabriel. If the Crown of England decides that you must delay your return to France until this business is cleared up then that must be so. No harbour master will allow you out of this realm without proper licence. Now, do you have information here on the bloodstone, the Passio Christi?'

Richer, all flustered, waved the friar to a carrel under a window, further light being provided by a covered candle. Athelstan sat and patiently waited until Richer brought a book, a copy of a work Athelstan recognized from his own order's library at Blackfriars, 'The Book of Relics', a compendium describing the great relics of Christendom and their location. Athelstan opened this and found the entry for the bloodstone, short and succinct, telling him very little more than he already knew. Athelstan stared at the entry and leafed through the pages. A bell sounded. The monks, busy over their manuscripts, paused, rose and filed out. Athelstan glanced down the library. The door to the scriptorium remained closed. Richer had not left. Athelstan extinguished the candles, closed the book and moved into the shadows, searching the shelf from where Richer had taken 'The Book of Relics'. Athelstan was sure there must be more information than just a few lines in a general compendium.

So hidden in the darkness, Prior Alexander did not see Athelstan as he flung open the library door and hurried down, knocking at the scriptorium and entering even before Richer could reply. Athelstan edged out of the corner and softly approached as near as he could. The prior had not bothered to close the door behind him. He heard Richer ask if Prior Alexander had seen 'that friar – more of a ferret than a priest?' Athelstan smiled at that. Prior Alexander ignored the question and began a tirade, highly irate at the prospect of Richer leaving so soon. The prior lost all control, shouting at Richer, asking if he cared, and demanding he tell him the reason why? Athelstan felt guilty yet he stayed, listening to what was really a passionate lovers' quarrel. Richer tried to defend himself, explaining how he had to go, but the prior was besides himself with jealous rage. The argument grew more heated. Athelstan braced himself as he heard a stool crash over, Richer yelled that the prior let go of his arm. Athelstan was about to intervene when the library door rattled. The friar hastily stepped back into the shadows. A servitor entered, clumsily slipping and slithering on the polished floor, loudly shouting how the Lord Abbot demanded the immediate presence of both his prior and sub-prior in his chamber.

The altercation in the scriptorium swifty subsided. Both monks left, followed by the agitated servitor loudly lamenting how the Lord Abbot was stricken at what had happened to poor Leda. Athelstan waited until they'd gone and stepped out of his hiding place. He was about to continue his searches when he heard Cranston shouting his name. Athelstan sighed and walked to the door. The coroner stood at the far end of the portico gallery which ran down to the library, patting the shoulder of the stranger standing next to him as he gestured at Athelstan to join them.

Once he did, Cranston introduced his eccentric-looking visitor, Bartholomew Shoreditch, commonly known as the firedrake 'for his skill, knowledge and expertise with all forms of fire'. The firedrake was a short, dumpy man clothed entirely in dark red including his cloak, cowl and soft Spanish boots. He preened himself like a peacock as Cranston went on to explain how the firedrake was one of his confidants, much respected by the London guilds, especially the chandlers, wool and coal merchants not to mention the great lords of the Guildhall. The firedrake was all neat and precise in his actions with closely shorn greying hair, his snub-nosed face clean-shaved and oiled. The firedrake definitely loved all things glittering. Rings shimmered on his fat fingers. Around his neck hung a collection of gold and silver chains adorned with medals depicting martyrs such as St Lawrence the Deacon who'd been grilled to death over a slow fire.

'He used to start fires himself, did little Bartholomew,' Cranston explained, 'until his uncle Jack caught him, pilloried him, put him in the Fleet prison and gave him a lecture he'll never forget all the God-given days of his life. Isn't that right, my lovely?'

'Truly, Sir John.' The firedrake extended a hand gloved in a gauntlet of blood-red velvet studded with imitation diamonds. Athelstan grasped this.

'I've now seen the error of my ways, Brother. Good to meet you, Sir John often talks about you.'

'What exactly do you do?' Athelstan asked when the firedrake released his hand.

'I am a journeyman, Brother. I advise my many customers and clients about candles, fires and chimney stacks as well as the storing and charging of faggots, the properties of oil, the difference between waxes, coal and charcoal, not to forget the careful preservation of cannon powder.'

Little wonder, Athelstan thought, the fellow looked so prosperous, especially at this time of year.

'Brokersby's death?' Cranston declared. 'The firedrake wants to discover what happened.'

Athelstan took their guest out into the precincts. The abbey was still disturbed by the cruel death of Leda. No one interfered when Athelstan escorted the firedrake to the guest house to inspect the charred, derelict chamber. The firedrake moved swiftly. He scrutinized the floor, walls and ceilings, concentrating on where the bed, table and candle had stood. He opened his pannier, donned a leather apron, took off his gauntlets, crouched and sifted amongst the ash, dust and fragments, letting them run through his fingers whilst questioning Athelstan on what had actually happened and what he had learnt. The firedrake picked up a piece of charred leather rim and the blackened remains of what looked like a stopper to a wineskin. He held these up.

'You are correct, Brother Athelstan. The candle provided the spark but something else started the fire, yet how that was done I truly don't know. Look,' he pushed back his sleeves, 'can I talk to the abbey chandler? Afterwards just leave me – out of friendship for you and Sir John, I will do what I can.'

Athelstan agreed. He took the firedrake across to the abbey chandlery. At first the brother responsible was wary and suspicious but the firedrake's enthusiasm swiftly charmed him and soon both were immersed in discussing the properties of wax and which were the most important to use. Athelstan left them to it and joined Sir John sitting on a turf bench overlooking the abbey herb gardens. For a while they sat in silence. Athelstan thought about the swan, the ugly warning behind its brutal death and that painting of the beautiful Susannah. He recalled the anchorite all agitated and fearful.

'How times change, Sir John.'

'What do you mean?'

'Lady Purity,' Athelstan asked, 'otherwise known as Mistress Quicksilver – that was her reputation?'

'I am as certain of it as I am sitting here.'

'Then, Sir John, I want you to seek an urgent interview with Lord Walter, I mean now. The woman calling herself Eleanor Remiet must also be present.'

'The abbot's private life is not within our writ, Friar.'

'He certainly needs to be warned about the Upright Men.'

'Undoubtedly.'

'And his doxy, his leman, needs to be counselled on the evils of blackmail.' Athelstan grinned at the surprise on the coroner's face.

'Please,' Athelstan squeezed Cranston's hand, 'let me collect my thoughts. All will be revealed.'

The coroner rose and strode off, clapping his hands against the cold. Athelstan went into the abbey church. He lit a candle before the lady altar and stared up at the subtle carving of the Virgin and Child, an excellent copy of the famous Walsingham Statue. Athelstan earnestly prayed three Aves for wisdom then left. By the time he reached the abbot's lodgings, Mistress Eleanor, haughty face all flushed, was being ushered in to join Lord Walter sitting disconsolate by the hearth, three white downy feathers on his lap. He greeted them dolefully, motioning to the other chairs. Athelstan and Cranston sat down, both expressing their deep regrets on the death of Leda. Abbot Walter, face still tear-streaked, nodded as he stroked the feathers. Mistress Eleanor just sat to the abbot's left, impatiently tapping the arm of her chair.

'You asked me to come here,' she blurted out. 'Why, what is the matter?'

'It's a long time,' Athelstan replied quietly, 'since Sir John saw you, Lady Purity, also known as Mistress Quicksilver.' Athelstan's words were greeted with a stunned silence. The friar gazed at the woman. She must be past her fiftieth summer but he could see that once, when her skin was smooth, her cheeks full and soft, her lips ripe and red, she must have been a truly remarkable-looking woman.

'I don't know what . . .' Abbot Walter ceased his crying, the white feathers floating down to the floor.

'I do.' Cranston grinned. 'You were a monk here, yes, Abbot Walter? Prior then abbot? In your earlier days you hired an artist to execute a wall fresco celebrating the vindication of the chaste Susannah and you asked your leman, your mistress to be the image. I recognized that face eventually.' He turned to the woman. 'Lady Purity, when you entered the Inns of Court with this or that great noble, I worshipped you from afar. Despite the passage of the years I still glimpse what I once revered.'

The woman forced a smile, fluttering her eyelids at the flattery.

'Now, Lord Walter,' Athelstan declared, stilling the abbot's protests, 'we are not concerned about your private life. My Lord of Gaunt and the Archbishop of Canterbury might be but that is a matter for them. Nor am I concerned that Isabella may be your daughter not your niece, a love child, yes? Conceived late, my Lady, raised by you and supported by Lord Walter with help from the revenues of this abbey? I advise you not to challenge that. As I've said, your private life is your own. However,' Athelstan added, 'cozening blackmail is another.'

'How dare you!'

'Oh, Mistress, I dare and will dare again.'

Eleanor made to rise.

'The anchorite!' Athelstan exclaimed. The woman promptly sat down. From her fleeting expression Athelstan knew he'd hit his mark.

'What is this?' Abbot Walter pleaded.

'Agnes Rednal. The anchorite believes he is haunted by the ghost of a wicked woman he hanged. Now that poor man has all sorts of imaginings. You, Mistress, learnt his story from Abbot Walter. You are hungry for gold and silver. After all, your daughter Isabella needs a rich endowment if she is to gain a wealthy suitor. The anchorite has a box crammed with gold and silver. Well,' Athelstan lifted his hands, 'you know all this. Deny it and I'll ask Sir John to arrest you, abbey or not, whilst I search your chamber for a box of face paints, a

wig of wild hair, as well as the black Benedictine robe you
wear when you flit like a bat through these supposed holy
precincts after darkness has fallen.' Athelstan glanced quiz-
zically at her. 'According to the anchorite, these apparitions
of the real Agnes Rednal only began recently. Of course they
did. They coincide with your arrival here for the festive
season.' Athelstan gestured at the abbot now drained of all
pomposity. 'I cannot prove your guilt in all this but you,
Mistress, stand charged. You could be arrested. While you
lodge in Newgate, Sir John will conduct a most thorough
investigation into your real origins. You dreaded this moment,
didn't you? You're sharp-witted, Mistress. Your relationship
with Abbot Walter is very secretive. Your face being taken as
an image for that painting so many years ago would, I am
sure, have been protected by all kinds of subterfuge. Now,
Sir John acts the bluff officer of the Crown but he has a most
prodigious memory . . .'

'True, true,' Cranston whispered.

'You must have become very alarmed when he began to
stare so closely at you.' Athelstan spread his hand. 'You hoped
it might be something passing until you realized we'd be
staying here for some time. That's why you warned me to
leave.'

The woman swallowed hard and just stared back.

'Did you also try to terrify me with a quarrel from a
crossbow?'

'Never!' Eleanor now looked genuinely frightened. Abbot
Walter gave a strangled cry.

'Of course His Grace the Regent will get to know.' Athelstan
continued: 'In time he would undoubtedly inform your
superiors, Abbot Walter, not to mention the Archbishop of
Canterbury.'

The abbot looked pale enough to faint. He cleared his throat
and tried to speak.

'Don't, Walter.' The woman leaned across and patted his
hand, 'What is the use? The truth always emerges, especially
when you don't want it to. Yes, Brother Athelstan, Sir John,
I was Lady Purity in my early days, a great beauty, a courtesan
sans pareil. I feasted on delicacies; I was clothed in silk and

satin. Men fought for my favours but my heart was always given to Walter Chobham, Sub-Prior of the Benedictines at St Fulcher's. Yes, I'm depicted as Susannah in that painting but those were my green and salad days. Age withers us. The years stale. Your body fails – mine certainly did. I was ravaged by the pestilence. An even greater surprise occurred in my last years, just before my courses stopped: I became pregnant with Isabella. Both pregnancy and delivery were difficult and by then all real traces of my beauty were gone. Walter has stayed faithful to me, especially now Isabella has come of age. Yes, I am desperate for her, for me. If Abbot Walter dies what will happen to us?' She took a deep breath. 'True, Walter told me the anchorite's tale. I heard of his wealth stored in that coffer,' she stroked the side of her face, 'so I became Agnes Rednal.' She smiled icily at Athelstan. 'I assure you, Brother, it was desperation not greed which prompted it, nothing but a game to secure his wealth.'

'A cruel game, Mistress, one that ends now, yes?'

'Of course. And what else?'

'Nothing, Mistress.'

'As for you,' Cranston gestured at the abbot, 'I urge you to be most prudent; the Upright Men have sent you a warning.'

'What can I do?'

'Be vigilant. As for my part,' Cranston added, 'well, leave that to me.'

'The Wyvern Company will be of use,' Abbot Walter added desperately.

'True,' Cranston agreed, 'but that brings me to my last question. Is there anything you haven't told us about the murders here?'

'Sir John, Brother Athelstan, I swear I know nothing. Yes, I have failed, I have sinned. I am locked in my own deep worries about Isabella and Eleanor. All I can say is that I fervently regret allowing Brother Richer to come here. Why? I cannot say. Only after his arrival did Sir Robert Kilverby change.' The abbot picked up the fallen feathers. 'Perhaps,' he mumbled, 'perhaps it's time I resigned my post.' He put his face in his hands and began to sob.

You're crying through your fingers, Athelstan thought.

You're not penitent but plotting, nor have you told me the full truth. Athelstan rose to his feet. He stared around that luxurious chamber and remembered the lepers out in the freezing cold beyond the gate, those others on the quayside, numb and starving. Fleischer being dragged off to be hanged whilst the abbot who ordered it lived his own dissolute life. The thought of Fleischer in his boat watching the abbey made Athelstan pause. Fleischer! Those poor river people! Of course!

'Athelstan, are you well?' Cranston also rose to his feet.

'Sir John, a moment with you alone. My Lord Abbot, Mistress,' Athelstan gave them the most cursory of bows, 'please stay here.' Once outside the chamber Athelstan grasped Cranston's sleeve. 'Sir John, you've sent messengers from here to the city, yes?'

'Of course, you know I have.'

'Sir John, I beg you. Fetch Prior Alexander and Richer here now, I mean now. By the way,' Athelstan again grabbed Cranston's sleeve, 'you could, if I wanted it, obtain a list of grants made by the Crown to this abbey?'

'Of course.'

'Very good. Please go, I shall return to Father Abbot.'

Lord Walter still sat slumped in his chair, his mistress, one hand on his arm, gazing pitifully at him. Athelstan went and stood over both of them.

'The anchorite,' he warned. 'I do not know, Mistress, if what you did was solely your work or both of you, but it stops now.'

She nodded, her haughty face all worried.

'As for you, Father Abbot, I cannot and will not condemn you except exhort you to reconcile yourself to God and,' Athelstan leaned down threateningly, 'tell the truth when I ask.'

Athelstan walked away and stared at one of the gorgeously painted glass windows. He silently chastised himself for his mistake and wondered how many more he had committed; he vowed to take each scrap of knowledge and pursue it to its logical conclusion. Behind him the abbot murmured to his mistress. A knock on the door a short while later ended this. Cranston, Richer and Prior Alexander entered. Both monks protested at the peremptory summons but Cranston ordered them to sit. Athelstan quickly composed himself. He would not question them but present the arguments which now tumbled through his mind.

'Brother Athelstan,' Prior Alexander declared, 'we are here.'

'So you are.' Athelstan turned and smiled. 'Robert Kilverby and Crispin, his secretarius, were also here.'

'I . . .?'

'No. I mean years ago. They were novices here. Lord Walter, you're of the same age, you must remember them.'

'I do,' the abbot replied slowly, 'but what has that got to do with all this?'

'They were novices here.'

'Yes, I was an assistant to the novice master, I . . .'

'Did anything singular happen to them?'

'No, they were both the sons of London citizens. Kilverby was special. He had a sharp mind and keen wit, he excelled in logic and debate.'

'And Crispin?'

'Oh, he was called "the Silent One", sometimes "Sinister", because he was left-handed. He was often punished for that. The novice master said he must change.'

'And did he?'

'No.'

'Were both men happy?'

'Kilverby more than Crispin.' The abbot scratched his head. 'I believe he hated being here. Both young men publicly declared their intention of not taking minor orders and left. Kilverby soon made his name as a trader, an astute merchant. Crispin became his helpmate. Kilverby rose to be an alderman, a leading member of the guild, a banker, a trader in every kind of commodity, much patronized by the Crown.'

'And you can see no link between Kilverby's novitiate here and his mysterious death?'

'No.' Abbot Walter's voice was clipped; he glanced nervously at Prior Alexander.

'Brother Athelstan,' Richer asked, 'what has this got to do with me, with us?'

'Oh, everything,' Athelstan sat down. 'Prior Alexander, go
to your chancery and bring me the list of all the items seized
by the Wyvern Company from the cart they found so oppor-
tunely on a country lane near the Abbey of St Calliste.'

'There isn't such a—'

'Don't lie.' Athelstan saw the deep flush in the prior's face.
Abbot Walter simply groaned. Richer glanced longingly at the
door.

'It is abbey property,' Abbot Walter blustered.

'In which case,' Athelstan declared, 'I could ask all three
of you to join me and Sir John, the King's officer, in the
muniment room at the Tower where such a list, I am sure, is
recorded on a memoranda roll of the exchequer or royal
chamber. Now,' Athelstan sighed, 'that may take some time
– days, weeks – but I am sure we can secure you comfortable
lodgings in the Tower until that list is traced. After that,'
Athelstan continued remorselessly, 'the Crown might decide
to hold an inventory on what goods donated to St Fulcher's
actually remain here? Silence!' Athelstan pointed at the abbot.
'Do not make a bad situation worse. I doubt if much remains.
Most of the goods seized by the Wyvern Company from St
Calliste have been despatched back to France by you, Richer.
You sent these items by this cog or that ship. You weren't
sending messages. Why should a boatman from a foreign cog
come down here?' Athelstan gestured at the door. 'You have
servants, lay brothers, not to mention the river folk who would
leap at the chance to earn good coin by taking letters to this
ship or that. You were sending precious, sacred items which
could only be entrusted to certain people. Prior Alexander,'
Athelstan spread his hands, 'Sir John and I are waiting for
that list. I want it now.'

Prior Alexander glanced at the abbot who simply fluttered
his fingers.

'Do as he asks,' Eleanor whispered. 'Walter, do it, we have
to.'

'The list,' Athelstan insisted.

The prior rose and swept out of the chamber. Athelstan glanced
across at Sir John, who sat cradling a goblet of wine he'd poured
from the jug on the great open dresser. Athelstan rose and walked

back to the window where the winter light still picked out scenes from St Benedict's life at Subiaco. He was aware of the silence behind him as he prepared his indictment. Richer was wily and subtle: a spider who'd entered this abbey and spun his web cleverly, adroitly drawing in the likes of Kilverby and William Chalk but who else – Prior Alexander? Athelstan wondered about Osborne and then his own desperate flight through the charnel house. Had that been Richer? Was the Frenchman determined to prevent his probing even if it meant murder?

'I have it.'

Prior Alexander had returned to the chamber. He carried a calf skin ledger inscribed with the title *'Dona Recepta* – Gifts Received'. Athelstan leafed through the yellowing pages, tied to each other and the strong spine with reddish twine. Athelstan recognized it as a true document over which these deceitful monks could not deceive him. The *'Liber Donorum Receptorum* – the Book of Gifts Received' was an important record of any religious house. It provided the day, month and year of every gift received, along with the donor's name. The record had to be kept because every religious house had a special day when Masses were offered for the intentions of all such benefactors. More importantly, it was a document drawn up years ago over which these monks had no control. Prior Alexander offered to help. Athelstan shook his head.

'I know where to look,' he murmured and took the book across to the window. The battle of Poitiers had been fought in 1356. Athelstan moved to January 1357 and scrutinized the entries, quietly marvelling at the generosity of lords, merchants and other patrons. At last he found the entries under 'Rex Angliae, King of England' or 'Edwardus Princeps Walliae, Edward Prince of Wales'. Athelstan studied the list of about sixty items 'found on a cart near St Calliste': candlesticks, triptychs and crucifixes, missals and other sacred items such as a small tabernacle, gold and silver cruets then the entry he'd been looking for: *'Liber Antiqua, Liber Passionis Christi'* – An old book, The Book of the Passion of Christ'.

'Very well,' Athelstan lifted his head, 'I would like to see all these items now.'

'That's impossible!'

'Of course it is,' Athelstan retorted. 'How many of these items have now been returned to St Calliste?' He closed the book. 'Prior Alexander, stop looking offended, it's not honest. Sit down.' Athelstan rejoined Cranston. 'I shall tell you what happened,' Athelstan continued. 'The Wyvern Company's plunder was handed over to the Crown within a year because all the items were sacred. They were then granted to St Fulcher's, some twenty-three years ago.' Athelstan tapped the book. 'You cannot erase or change these entries. A few years ago the Abbot of St Calliste decided it was time to get his property back. Did he exchange gifts with you, Abbot Walter? Or was it bribes?' Athelstan asked. 'So that his beloved nephew Richer, the skilled copyist and illuminator, could visit St Fulcher's on an extended course of study? He would definitely work for this privilege, being given the position of Sub-Prior.' Athelstan stared at the Frenchman who looked relaxed but poised. 'I cannot prove this but the Abbot of St Calliste also learned as he would through the chatter and gossip of his order, how the remnants of the Wyvern Company were now at St Fulcher's. What an excellent opportunity! What a prize! To recover everything lost as well as wreak vengeance on the sacrilegious English who'd dared plunder the great Abbey of St Calliste with such impunity.'

'Are you, yet again,' Richer demanded, 'accusing me of murder? Where is your proof, your evidence?'

'Seeds grow, stalks thrust up,' Athelstan retorted. 'Gathering time always comes, Richer. You definitely arrived here to right a whole series of wrongs and, to begin with, God was good. You must have even thought St Benedict himself had intervened on your behalf.'

'Explain!'

'You know full well. One of the Wyverns, William Chalk, fell ill; a defrocked priest, he desperately wanted to make his peace with God. You Richer, with Prior Alexander's conniv-ance, wormed your way into that man's soul. I am not accusing you of breaking the seal of confession but you used the second miracle which presented itself. Kilverby was also undergoing conversion. Like the subtle cozener you are, you struck hard and fast. Kilverby realized that the free company he'd financed in France were sacrilegious thieves and he'd profited from them. Worse was to come. He learnt that the Passio Christi, the sacred bloodstone, had been blasphemously stolen and he was also part of that. He was under God's doom.' Athelstan shook his head. 'I admit, I confess. I still do not fully understand Kilverby's motives.'

'I am sorry?' Prior Alexander's voice seemed hoarse and dry.

'Richer, you are persuasive. Kilverby had his doubts but something other than your honeyed words influenced both him and Master Chalk.'

Richer half-smiled, as if he was playing a chess game and was acknowledging a cunning opponent.

'Anyway.' Athelstan sighed. 'Kilverby asked what could he do? He distanced himself from the Wyvern Company. He probably promised you the bloodstone. Of course all this did not happen at once. I suspect it took almost the first two years of your stay, Richer, before you were able to reap your hidden harvest and send it home.' Athelstan glanced quickly at the abbot and his woman; their fearful faces showed he was close to the truth.

'Which was what?' Prior Alexander asked.

'Oh, you all know. Kilverby offered reparation of a different kind; influenced by Richer, he made very generous donations to this abbey on one condition.'

'Which was?' Prior Alexander whispered.

'All the goods plundered from St Calliste were to be gradually returned. You, Abbot Walter, agreed to this in order to swell the coffers of your beloved kinswoman. Prior Alexander, you cooperated out of your great love for Richer . . .'

'I . . .'

'Please, Brother, why lie? What you feel is not my business.' Athelstan pointed at the Frenchman. 'Richer, you were delighted. You weren't sending messages home but the objects listed in this 'Book of Gifts': cruets, crucifixes, sacred items not to be entrusted to simple river folk but specially selected emissaries who, with Prior Alexander's full connivance, you met with on your visits to the city. I'm sure most of these objects are now gone.'

'We could prove . . .' Prior Alexander protested but his voice faltered.

'What?' Athelstan moved in his chair. 'How you still have these items? Of course you could produce a crucifix, cruets, a triptych and claim they were those from St Calliste. One chalice looks like another, yes, but,' Athelstan tapped the ledger, 'give me the *"Liber Passionis Christi"*.' His invitation was greeted with silence. 'Well,' Athelstan declared, 'where is the Book of the Passion of Christ? I suspect it's a manuscript written by Pope Damasus – yes? This too has gone back to France. Richer gave it to some trusted envoy on a foreign ship, well?'

'The book has been returned.' Prior Alexander was flustered. Trying to regain his dignity, he glanced sharply at Richer. 'The book has been restored to its proper owner.'

'With the permission of the Crown,' Athelstan asked, 'did you make a copy?' Athelstan demanded, 'Well, did you?'

Richer simply spread his hands, Prior Alexander slipped further down his chair.

'There's no *"Liber"*, no copy,' Richer muttered.

'I might insist on searching this abbey, including your chamber, Richer.'

'You can't . . .'

'We can and we might,' Cranston retorted.

'The Passio Christi,' Athelstan asked, 'do any of you know where the bloodstone is?'

'No,' Richer's voice was restrained, 'I swear, no!'

'The Passio Christi,' Athelstan got to his feet, 'and the book about it hold the key to all this mystery, and the question which lies at the very heart of it: why did Sir Robert change so radically? There was more to that than his own scruples or your eloquence, Richer.'

'I cannot help you on that!'

'Never mind.' Cranston rose and stood over the Frenchman. 'You, Brother, whoever you may be, are confined to this abbey. Any attempt to flee will be construed as a treasonous act.'

'I'm a Frenchman.'

'And His Grace, King Richard,' Cranston thrust his face down, 'also claims to be King of France. Richer, you are confined to this abbey under pain of treason. Brother Athelstan?'

The coroner and friar stepped out of the chamber. Once they'd left the courtyard Athelstan paused.

'Perhaps we should begin now, Sir John.'

'Begin what?'

'Our search!'

Cranston agreed. He and Athelstan adjourned to the library. Richer joined them. Athelstan told him to stand aside, yet even as they searched Athelstan realized they would find nothing amongst this precious collection of books. Richer was cunning. Should they, Athelstan wondered, demand that the sub-prior's chamber also be searched? But, there again, the Frenchman was now alert to the danger. Moreover, although the *'Liber Passionis Christi'* might prove very useful, its disappearance did not prove Richer, or anyone else, to be an assassin or a thief. Athelstan sighed as he placed the last book, a copy of Lucretius, back on the shelf.

'Sir John, I'm ready!' The firedrake in all his garish glory marched into the library. Cranston smiled at Athelstan and both followed this eccentric character out through the cloisters to Mortival meadow where the abbey chandler waited.

'I've everything prepared.'

The firedrake pointed to a barrel with a capped tallow candle on its upturned end. The firedrake struck a tinder, sheltering its flame against the boisterous cold breeze. The wick flared into life. The firedrake hastily withdrew. The tongue of flame danced even though it was protected by the concave-shaped cap. Cranston stamped his feet impatiently; almost in response the candle dissolved in a burst of angry, spitting flames. Small tongues of fire shot up to land, hissing like snakes on the frost-hardened grass. The top of the dry wooden barrel caught light, flames licked down its side already smouldering from the spits of fire. Soon the entire barrel was alight. Athelstan thought the flames would die but then a fresh burst flared up, angry shoots of fire leaping so swift and fierce the entire barrel was soon reduced to blackened wood crumbling away in fiery fragments.

'You see.' The firedrake was almost dancing with glee whilst the abbey chandler beamed at the dying fire. The monk abruptly remembered what he was doing and hurriedly pulled a more mournful face. 'That's how Brokersby died,' the firedrake declared.

'Do explain,' Cranston insisted.

Athelstan sniffed the grey-black smoke and walked closer to the dying fire. The tang of oil was strong, needle-thin rivulets of smoking blackness scored the frozen grass.

'Very simple.' The firedrake breathed in the smoke as if it was the very incense of heaven.

'Then keep it so,' Cranston retorted, 'and brief. I'm freezing.'

'Come, come,' the chandler insisted on taking them back to his own work shop, a large chamber which reeked of oil, cordage and wax. He made them sit on stools around a brazier which sparkled just like a ruby. Athelstan, clutching the cup of posset the chandler served, ruefully wondered on the whereabouts of the bloodstone.

'Very simple.' The firedrake held up a large tallow candle. He turned this upside down tapping its base. 'You hollow this out and pour in oil, perhaps add some salt-petre powder, the type used by the King's newfangled cannons – you've seen them at the Tower?'

Cranston grunted.

'Reseal the candle with a wax plug and you have nothing less than a vase of oil.'

'If you light the wick,' Athelstan agreed, 'the flame burns down, the wax dissolves and the conflagration begins. The lower the oil sits in the hollowed-out candle, the longer it takes.'

'I've seen it done,' the chandler observed ruefully. 'Sir John, as coroner, you must have encountered tallow-makers, candle-fashioners who use cheap materials within a shell of wax?'

'I have,' Cranston drank from his posset cup, 'which explains why the guild's regulations are so stringent against such a practice.'

'That and more,' the firedrake explained. 'This barrel was as dry as tinder. Inside it was a small pouch of oil. The false candle was perilous enough but the oil would make it truly dangerous. You must have seen conflagrations; people forget how fast flames can move. I've seen fires in dried forests course swifter than a fleeing deer. Burning oil is even worse.' He waggled a finger. 'Very dangerous – it turned our candle into a fountain of spitting flame.'

'So,' Athelstan drained his cup, 'somebody entered Brokersby's chamber. They placed a wine skin, one full of oil sprinkled with salt-petre, under his bed. The tallow candle was replaced with a false one. Brokersby either lit it or let it burn as he was accustomed to. He retired to bed, his belly full of wine, an opiate, or both. The candle eventually disintegrated in a shower of flame which would swiftly reach the pouch of oil hidden away.' Athelstan crossed himself. 'The bed was of dry wood, linen sheets and woollen blankets, ideal fuel. Brokersby may have woken and tried to stagger out of danger but the fire was all around him. The oil-rich flames would have turned him into a living torch. My friends,' Athelstan rose and bowed, 'I thank you heartily but your hypothesis leaves one tantalizing question.' He stared down at them. 'Why? Why kill any soul but especially why like that, the artifice, the subtle cunning, why?'

Cranston escorted the firedrake, rewarded with good silver, back to the watergate. Athelstan took to wandering the abbey. He felt agitated. The buildings seemed to crowd in around him. The statues and carvings appeared to draw closer, making him more aware of sightless eyes, stone smiles and frozen glances. He became acutely alert to the dappled light, the black alleyways and the yawning mouths of corridors. Bells tolled. Monks slipped here and there on different duties. Athelstan sensed a change: their mood was colder, more distant. Bony white faces peered suspiciously out at him from hoods and cowls. Brothers turned and whispered to each other as he passed. Athelstan entered the church to pray before the lady altar. Afterwards he went and stood before the anker house but the anchorite was either asleep or pretended to be. Athelstan returned to his own chamber and tried to clear the fog of mystery behind the disappearance of the bloodstone and these horrid murders. Were they all connected? Athelstan wondered. Or should he look at Kilverby's murder as separate from the rest? The Passio Christi did link Kilverby to the Wyvern Company. Another tie was Richer. Athelstan curbed his frustration. Ideally, Cranston should seize the Frenchman and hoist him off to the Tower for closer questioning. Richer however was a cleric, a monk. He would plead benefit of clergy and, within the day, every churchman in London would be stridently protesting.

oOoOo

SEVEN

'Placitum: a case heard before a court.'

N ext morning, after a troubled sleep, Athelstan celebrated a late Mass. As he divested he wondered if he
should escape the abbey and return to St Erconwald's
for the day. Outside in the aisle the brothers were preparing
their own crib, bringing in lifelike statues and arguing about
whether the abbot wanted the Three Kings immediately or
should they wait until the Epiphany. Athelstan was about to
help when he glimpsed an inscription carved along the rim of
the chantry altar. He swiftly translated the Latin. He was about
to close his eyes in thankful prayer when he heard his name
being called. Prior Alexander, unshaven and red-eyed, his black
robe stained and blotched, pushed through the gossiping
brothers to inform Athelstan that Cranston required him
urgently near the watergate. Athelstan collected his cloak and
writing tray and hurried down across Mortival meadow, pleas-
antly surprised by the change in the weather. The mist had
lifted. The clouds were thinning and the weak sunlight gave
the meadow a more springlike look. On the quayside Cranston,
cloaked, booted and armed, stood with Wenlock and Mahant,
similarly attired. The old soldiers looked heavy-eyed as if
roused from an ale-sodden sleep. Moored along the quayside
was a high-prowed barge with a covered awning in the stern.
The prow boasted a snapping pennant of dark blue fringed
with gold displaying the insignia of the Fisher of Men, a silver
corpse rising from a golden sea. The barge was manned by
six oarsmen dressed in black and gold livery – these were the
Fisher of Men's coven, outlaws and outcasts who'd rejected
their own names and rejoiced in being called Maggot,
Taffyhead, Badger, Brick-face, Gigglebrazen and Hackum.
Standing on the barge was Icthus, the Fisher's principal
assistant, dressed in a simple black tunic, a strange creature

who took the Greek name for fish, an apt enough title. The
young man had no hair even on his brows or eyelids whilst
his oval-shaped face and protuberant cod mouth made him
look even more like a fish. Icthus raised a hand in greeting as
Cranston broke off whispering heatedly with Wenlock and
Mahant.

'Osborne's been found,' Cranston declared, 'or at least his
corpse, naked as he was born, throat slit from ear to ear.'
Cranston waved at the waiting barge. 'The Fisher of Men
requires an audience. Wenlock and Mahant are coming with
us whether they like it or not.'

They all clambered into the barge. Icthus in a high-pitched
voice ordered the oarsmen to push away and soon they were
out, the rowers bending and pulling back in unison. The river
was thankfully calm though busy with fishing smacks, bum
boats and market barges all taking advantage of the break in
the weather. Mahant and Wenlock sat fascinated by Icthus and
his companions. Cranston tersely explained how the Fisher of
Men was a retainer of the mayor and city council. The Fisher's
task was to roam the Thames and drag out the corpses, the
victims of suicide, murder, or accident.

'A common enough occurrence,' Cranston confirmed. 'He,'
the coroner pointed at Icthus, who sat with his back to them
crooning a song to the rowers, 'has one God-given gift: he
can swim like an fish whatever the mood of the river.'

'Where was Osborne found?' Wenlock asked.

'Down river,' Cranston remarked, 'trapped amongst some
reeds. Icthus believes he was thrown in somewhere between
the abbey and La Reole.'

'We have his assurance it's Osborne?' Wenlock shifted his
gaze from Icthus to Cranston.

'We shall see,' the coroner replied. 'Apparently not only
was the victim's throat slashed but someone used a hammer,
or a rock, to pound his face into a soggy mess of blood, bone
and tattered flesh.'

'Sweet Lord,' Mahant whispered, sitting squashed in the
semicircular stern seat, he leaned down and gently touched
the hilt of his sword for comfort.

Cranston nudged Athelstan and pointed to a flock of birds

which seemed to cover the corpse dangling from a crude gallows on a sandbank.

'That reminds me – Leda the swan. Do you really think the Upright Men hanged that poor bird?'

Athelstan recalled what he'd glimpsed in the chantry chapel that morning.

'Leda was hanged,' he replied evasively, 'by someone with a deep hatred for my Lord Abbot.'

'That must include,' Wenlock declared, 'virtually most of his community and everyone outside it.'

Athelstan, reluctant to continue the conversation, stared round the awning at the other barges passing close as they moved in towards the quayside. Athelstan studied them and glimpsed Crispin, Kilverby's secretarius, sitting huddled in the centre of one skiff staring directly at the Fisher of Men's barge. Athelstan swiftly drew back. Crispin was apparently heading for St Fulcher's. Athelstan wondered what urgent business brought him back to the abbey? Icthus, in that eerie voice, abruptly called out commands. The barge rocked as it turned and came alongside a deserted wharf just past La Reole. They disembarked and made their way up to what was variously called, 'The Barque of St Peter', 'The Chapel of the Drowned Man' or 'The Mortuary of the Sea', a single storey building of grey brick with a red tiled roof. The corporation had built this so all the corpses harvested from the Thames could be laid out for inspection and collection by relatives; if not recognized, they were placed on to the great cart standing alongside the Barque and taken to some Poor Man's Lot in one of the city cemeteries.

The mortuary fronted the quayside, on either side ranged the wattle and daub cottages of the Fisher of Men and what he termed 'his beloved disciples'; others called them 'the grotesques'. Athelstan stared up at the vigorously carved tympanum above the wooden porch showing the dead rising from choppy waves to be greeted by the angels of God or the demons of Hell. Beneath this ran the words: 'And the Sea shall give up its dead'. On the right side of the door hung the great net which the Fisher of Men used to bring in the bodies, above it another inscription: 'The deep shall be harvested'.

On the left side of the door a proclamation boldly proclaimed the prices for recovering a corpse. 'The mad and insane – 6p. Suicides – 10p. Accidents – 8p. Those fleeing from the law – 14p. Animals – 2p. Goods to the value of £5: ten shillings. Goods over the value of £5, one third of their market value'. The Fisher of Men was seated beneath the sign, his bald head and cadaverous face protected by a leather cowl edged with costly fur. A thick military cloak shrouded his body from head to feet, which were pushed into the finest cordovan riding boots. The Fisher of Men rose and greeted his visitors in fluent Norman French and, turning specifically to Athelstan, lapsed into Latin. He asked the friar if he would give him and his 'beloved disciples' a formal blessing before leading them in their favourite hymn, '*Ave Maris Stella* – Hail Star of the Sea'.

Athelstan, as always, was tempted to ask the Fisher about his past, his knowledge of Latin and the classics. Cranston, however, had warned Athelstan how this harvester of corpses was most reluctant to reveal any aspect of his past, be it stories about once being a leper knight or a merchant who had visited the court of the Great Cham of Tartary.

'Well, Brother?'

'Of course, of course.'

The Fisher of Men turned to Icthus, who produced a hunting horn and blew a long haunting blast which hastily summoned the members of that strange community to kneel on the cobbles before 'The Barque of St Peter'. With Cranston and the others looking on, Athelstan delivered the blessing of St Francis.

'May the Lord bless you and protect you.

May he show you his face and smile on you.

May the Lord turn his face to thee and give you peace.

May the Lord bless you.'

When Athelstan finished he sketched a cross in the air and intoned the '*Ave Maris Stella*', the rest of his singular congregation merrily joining in, chanting the Latin hymn learnt by rote to the Blessed Virgin Mary. Once the 'Amen' had been sung, the Fisher of Men clapped Athelstan's shoulder and led him and the others into the Sanctuary of Souls, a rectangular lime-washed chamber. On a dais at the far end stood an altar draped with a purple and gold cloth, above it a large crucifix nailed to the wall. The Fisher's 'guests', as he described the corpses plucked from the Thames, were placed on wooden trestles, each covered with a shroud drenched in pine juice. The stench, despite the herbs, was sharp and pungent, a sombre place of haunting sadness. Athelstan blessed the room even as Icthus and two of his companions came around him swinging thuribles, anointing the air with sweet smoke. The Fisher removed the shroud covering one corpse. Athelstan immediately gagged at the sight and grasped the proffered pomander. Cranston and the two soldiers cursed until the Fisher of Men loudly tutted. The face of the corpse, already bloated liverish by the river, had been reduced to a reddish-black pulp, the nose and lips fragmented into a grotesque mask. The body was naked, the muscular torso, legs and arms streaked with old wounds. Athelstan stared closely; he could not be certain who it was.

'Osborne,' Wenlock murmured. 'It's Osborne.' He turned to the Fisher of Men. 'How did you know?'

The Fisher lifted the arms of the corpse, he pointed to the wrists marked by the bracers now removed and the deep calluses on the arrow fingers of the left hand.

'We keep our eyes and ears sharp. We read and learnt the description Sir John posted at St Paul's Cross and elsewhere. How you were seeking Henry Osborne, former master bowman, who fled without permission from the Abbey of St Fulcher. Where would such a man flee, we asked? We heard about the deaths at the abbey so when Icthus fished this corpse from the reeds, throat cut, face all disfigured, corpse stripped, we wondered. I examined the wrists, which the archer braces would usually cover, the fingers worn by years notching a bow . . .'

'Where did you find him?' Cranston indicated for the cadaver to be covered.

Athelstan didn't wait for the answer; he took a deep breath on the pomander and walked back to the door. He glanced over his shoulder. Wenlock and Mahant stood apart, hiding in the murky light of that grim place. Cranston was helping with the funeral cloth whilst the Fisher of Men and his acolytes gathered around all pleased, eager for their reward.

'God forgive me,' Athelstan murmured, 'for my lack of thought.' Clutching his writing satchel, he walked back to the trestle. He took out the small phials of holy oils and insisted on anointing the corpse whilst he whispered the words of absolution. He tried to ignore the brutal remains which once housed a living soul, concentrating on the rite whilst the bile bubbled at the back of his throat. Once finished he gratefully strolled outside to the fiery heat from a huge brazier where the rest were already warming themselves. Wenlock and Mahant, now vociferous, informed Cranston how they no longer wished to reside at St Fulcher's. Cranston warned them that, until he was finished, they could either stay there or be lodged in the Tower and that applied to anyone else involved in these dire events.

'You must also surely,' Athelstan added tactfully, 'see to the burial of poor Osborne? He should be interred next to his comrades at St Fulcher's?'

The two old soldiers, hands extended over the glowing coals, just glared back at him.

'You, Magister.' Athelstan turned to the Fisher of Men. 'How long do you think Osborne's corpse was in the water?'

'He was discovered just after first light,' that gleaner of the dead replied, 'in a reed bed. We think he must have been there for at least a day. More importantly, we know where he came from.' This stilled all conversation.

'Osborne was murdered,' the Fisher of Men declared stoutly, 'on Sunday evening. The weather is too cold even for an old soldier to camp out. In addition, if you know the flow and pull of the river you can deduce where his body fell in.' He rubbed his hands together.

'Where?' Wenlock snapped. 'Let's not play games.'

'My friend, I am not! Listen, Osborne needed shelter. The only place providing that between here and St Fulcher's is the great riverside tavern, "The Prospect of Heaven".'

Cranston nodded in agreement.

'After we found the corpse I sent one of my best scurriers, Hoghedge, who has a nose for tap room gossip. Minehost at the "Prospect" clearly remembered an old soldier armed, carrying his bow not to mention a fardel and panniers, who hired a chamber very early on Sunday morning. He called himself Brokersby.'

'Brokersby?'

'That's what he called himself. Anyway, Minehost recognized an old soldier when he saw one. His guest kept to himself then, later that Sunday, this individual settled all accounts, took his baggage and walked down the towpath towards the river.'

'And?'

The Fisher clicked his tongue noisily.

'That is all I can tell you.'

'Osborne left St Fulcher's.' Athelstan turned to the dead man's companions. 'He sheltered at that tavern under the name of Brokersby for most of the day then left. Can you tell us why?'

Both men just shook their heads.

'He did not contact you?'

'Of course not,' Wenlock retorted. 'Nor do we know why he'd go there. We thought he'd hide deep in the city.'

'Did you find any of his possessions?' Wenlock turned to the Fisher of Men who just waved back at the Sanctuary of Lost Souls.

'Naked we come into the world,' that strange individual intoned, 'and naked we shall surely leave.' The Fisher smiled at the coroner. 'Sir John, if there's nothing else?'

Cranston and the Fisher of Men walked away from the rest, disappearing into one of the cottages. A short while later Cranston emerged carrying a scrap of parchment, a receipt for the exchequer to account for the monies he had paid to the Fisher of Men. Cranston, Athelstan and the rest clambered back into the barge and, with the cries of farewell from that bizarre community ringing out over the water, the 'Charon of Hades' as the barge was called, took them back along the river. Cranston however insisted that they stay close to the bank and pull into the narrow quayside close to 'The Prospect of Heaven'. He asked them to wait, swiftly disembarked and strode off up the towpath towards 'The Prospect'; its great timbered upper storeys and black slate roof could be clearly glimpsed from the barge. Wenlock and Mahant followed and, cloaks wrapped about them, walked up and down, whispering between themselves as they tried to keep warm. Athelstan studied both of these. The two old soldiers were unusually taciturn and withdrawn. Were they fearful, anxious? He tried to catch the essence of their mood, their souls. Would they also flee? But, there again, Osborne really hadn't. He'd simply assumed his dead comrade's name and moved a short distance down the river. Athelstan took out his Ave beads and fingered them. 'The Prospect' was an ideal place to hide. A ramshackle sprawling tavern along the Thames where merchants, travellers, pilgrims and river folk ebbed and flowed like the water itself. So, why had Osborne really left St Fulcher's? What was he doing at that tavern? Why had he left? How had he been so swiftly overcome, his throat slashed, his corpse stripped of everything, his face pounded beyond recognition before being tossed like rubbish into the river?

Athelstan turned as Icthus and his oarsmen broke off from the hymn they were softly chanting and pointed excitedly as the war cog, its prow and stern richly gilded, sails billowing, the armour and weapons of its crew twinkling in the light, rounded a bend in the river. The cog, 'The Glory of Lancaster', was surrounded by small boats eager to sell provisions and even the joys of some whores gaudily bedecked and crammed into a skiff by an enterprising pimp. The sight of the cog made Athelstan think of Richer. Was the Frenchman responsible for Osborne's death? Richer with his many emissaries from foreign ships? Had Richer persuaded Osborne to flee with a promise of safe passage abroad then killed him, but why? Was it to do with the truth behind the theft of the Passio Christi or even where it was now?

'Nothing!' Cranston almost jumped into the barge, hastily followed by Wenlock and Mahant.

'Nothing at all.' Cranston squeezed into the seat. 'It's as the Fisher of Men said. God save us, Athelstan, I tell you this.' He raised his voice. 'Osborne will be the last person to flee.'

On their return to St Fulcher's Athelstan discovered the reason behind Cranston's statement. The coroner had been busy and his messages into the city had borne fruit. The watergate and every entrance into the abbey were now guarded by royal archers, men-at-arms and mounted hobelars. The same, Cranston declared as he strode across Mortival meadow, patrolled the fields and woods beyond the abbey walls whilst the cog they'd glimpsed had taken up position off the abbey quayside.

'There will be no more secret meetings, leaving or goings,' Cranston insisted as they reached the guest house. 'Everyone, and I mean everyone, will stay where they are.' The coroner's edict was soon felt. Cranston relaxed it a little, allowing carts of produce, visitors, beggars and pilgrims, as well as individual monks, to come and go but the royal serjeants had their orders. Everything and everyone were thoroughly searched. The protests mounted. Wenlock and Mahant tried to leave claiming they hoped to secure lodgings in the city along Poultry. Cranston refused them permission. Abbot Walter, still shocked and surprised at the truths he'd had to face as well as the death of his beloved Leda, retreated to his own chamber with his mistress and daughter. Prior Alexander and Richer, however, were furious. They both confronted Cranston and Athelstan as they broke their fast in the buttery. The two monks were joined by Crispin, who bleated he should journey back to the city, claiming he had urgent business with Genoese bankers in Lombard Street. Cranston heard them out, cleared his throat and ordered all three to shut up and listen.

'You,' he pointed with his finger, 'all of you are suspects in this matter.'

'How dare you?' Richer's handsome face reddened with rage. He fidgeted with the hilt of the silver dagger in its embroidered sheath on the cord around his waist.

'Oh, I dare,' Cranston replied evenly, 'that's the problem, my friends. This abbey is like a maze of alleyways. People scurry about bent on any mischief, even monks who go armed.'

'I am fearful,' Richer retorted, 'the Wyverns hate me. Men are being murdered.'

'Which is why you are all suspects?' Athelstan smiled. 'Anyone associated with Sir Robert, the Passio Christi or the Wyvern Company must hold themselves ready for questioning either here or the Tower. That includes you, Master Crispin. I would like you to stay here at least for a day.'

'Why?' the clerk protested.

'Because I am determined to finish these matters,' Athelstan declared. 'Don't worry, this applies to everyone else. Sir John, I am sure, has issued instructions that all members of Sir Robert's household be confined to their mansion.'

'Are you so close to the truth?' Prior Alexander asked.

'Very close – we always were,' Athelstan retorted. 'We are just frustrated by lies and evasions and that includes you again, Master Crispin. You knew full well that Sir Robert was spending lavishly, bribing the monks of St Fulcher to send back treasures to St Calliste, and that you and Sir Robert were once novices here. That Sir Robert was not going on pilgrimage but fleeing. I am sure all his accounts are in order.'

'I don't . . .'

'Please don't lie,' Athelstan warned. 'Sir Robert was not coming back. He did not intend to leave the Passio Christi here but take it back to St Calliste himself, or so I suspect.' Athelstan brought the flat of his hand down loudly on the table. 'So yes, we may be close to the truth, though gaps remain. Consequently you will all stay here until we finish. Now, sirs, we would like to finish our meal. However, before I do, one last question, Master Crispin: what are you actually doing here?' Athelstan jabbed a finger at him. 'Again, no lies. You came to find out what was happening?'

Crispin nodded. 'True,' he sighed, 'the mansion in Cheapside is now surrounded by archers. I had to discover what was going on.'

'Now you have,' Athelstan replied. 'So, all of you, please go.'

'Are we close to the truth?' Cranston asked once their visitors had left.

'Yes and no, my Lord Coroner. Yes in the sense that we have the keys but we don't know which keys fit which locks. We are now dependant on time and three other factors: first, and I must reflect on this, a vigorous search of this abbey, including Richer's chamber, might be of use. Secondly, matters proceed apace. Another bloodletting might take place and the killer might make a mistake.'

'And the third?'

Athelstan took a deep breath. 'God also demands justice. I pray he gives it a helping hand.'

Athelstan returned to his chamber whilst Cranston decided to visit the serjeants in change of the royal archers. The friar locked himself away listing time and again all he knew. He found it difficult to make any progress on the bloody affray here in the abbey except on two matters. First, when Hyde was murdered near the watergate, Richer ran back to see what had happened. Driven by his deep hatred for the Wyvern Company, the Frenchman thrust his sword deep into Hyde's belly but . . . Athelstan paced up and down. Surely Richer must have glimpsed the assassin who'd fled, certainly not through the watergate where Richer and the boatman were doing business, but across Mortival meadow, even if it was to hide in one of the copses? If the assassin had been one of the Wyvern Company, Richer would have been only too pleased to point the finger of accusation, so was it someone else? Someone he recognized? A monk from this abbey? Prior Alexander? Secondly, Athelstan could not forget the attack on him in the charnel house, the speed with which his assailant had opened the door and doused those sconce torches. As regards to Kilverby's death and the disappearance of the Passio Christi? What if Kilverby himself had removed the Passio Christi, locked the coffer and put the keys back around his neck knowing full well the Passio Christi was safe elsewhere? Athelstan could make no sense of this so he returned to listing his questions, trying to construct a hypothesis which he could push to a logical conclusion. Frustration, however, got the better of him. Athelstan visited the church to pray and, when Cranston returned, listed his unresolved questions for the coroner.

'And yet, little friar,' Cranston sat on the edge of the bed, 'we cannot keep this abbey under siege for weeks. What do you suggest?'

'Tomorrow,' Athelstan replied flatly, 'bring your archers into the abbey. I want the library cleared. Prior Alexander and Richer must be detained and their chambers searched. Of course,' he added despairingly, 'they may well have anticipated that and be prepared. I suspect they already have, so, for the moment, let us eat and retire early.'

Athelstan rose long before dawn. He felt refreshed and resolute. He was determined on what he must do and, if he had to face the wrath of the Benedictine order, the bishop of London, not to mention the displeasure of his superiors at Blackfriars, then he would accept that. The church in London might scream in protest at the ransacking of an abbey by royal troops and the questioning of its community in the cold chambers of the Tower. Nevertheless, what more could he do? Richer had to be seized. Athelstan waited until dawn then went down to celebrate his own Mass. He was drawing this to a close, about to pronounce the '*Ite Missa*' when the bells began to toll the tocsin, a harsh discordant clanging which shattered the sleeping silence. Athelstan hastily divested and hurried down the aisle. Others were doing the same; even the anchorite left his cell to join the few brothers who'd been busy in the church. Outside the greying murk was broken by the dancing glow of torches and bobbing lantern horns. Monks clamoured about the reason for the tocsin until Brother Simon, face and hands all muddied, screamed something about a dreadful scene down near the hog pen. Athelstan seized the lay brother. Simon was frantic, his robe, face and hands caked with blood-encrusted mud.

'Two of them,' Simon gasped, 'horrible to see! The hogs have mauled them!'

'Who?' Athelstan pleaded.

'Richer,' Simon gasped, 'Richer and one of the Wyvern Company. Prior Alexander is sobbing like a child. You must come, you must come!'

Athelstan reached the hog pen on the farm to the north of the abbey. Others were also gathering. Abbot Walter, swathed in a great woollen cloak, face all stricken, rested for support on the arm of a young novice. Prior Alexander was kneeling between two rolled deerskin shrouds soaked in blood. The prior was distraught. He knelt on the hard cobbles, keening like a distraught mother over her child. Other monks, booted and armed with iron-tipped staves, were driving the hogs back to their sties. Wenlock appeared resting on the arm of Brother Odo, the old soldier was dressed only in his night shirt, stout sandals on his feet, a cloak about his shoulders. He looked as

pale as a ghost. He approached the shrouded corpses then
turned away to vomit and retch violently. A brother whispered
how Wenlock had been sick all night. Once he'd been taken
away, Athelstan asked for the deerskin shrouds to be opened.
He took one glimpse at the mangled corpses and walked away
fighting to control his own stomach. Cranston also arrived and,
accustomed to such horrors, he knelt and examined the remains
of both cadavers.

'The hogs feasted well,' the coroner murmured. 'They ate
the soft fat first, face, belly and thighs.'

Athelstan forced himself to look. Both bodies were reduced
to a hideous, reddish-black mess, no faces or stomachs, just
hunks of meat with the ragged remains of clothing and boots.
Athelstan glimpsed the bracer around the tattered wrist of one
of the corpses, the remains of a boot and war belt.

'Mahant!' he whispered. 'It must be – but why? How?'

Between the corpses glittered the silver knife belonging to
Richer. The coroner rose to his feet, clapping his hands for
silence.

'Take the corpses to the death house,' he ordered. 'You,' he
pointed to Brother Odo, 'clean what is left of them then report
to me. Father Abbot,' he turned to Lord Walter, 'the hogs have
eaten human flesh, they are deodandum – they must be given
to God and slaughtered. You,' he pointed at a royal serjeant
of archers who'd also arrived, 'bring your best bowmen, the
hogs are to be destroyed, their corpses burnt. No, no,' Cranston
stilled the abbot's protests, 'the hogs must be slaughtered.'
The coroner gazed up at the brightening sky. 'At Nones I, Sir
John Cranston, King's coroner in the City of London, will
hold an official Inquisitio Post Mortem in the nave of the
abbey church. If you are summoned, you must present
yourselves.'

Athelstan nodded in agreement, whispering his own advice,
which Cranston quietly promised to act on. Athelstan then
plucked at Sir John's cloak. 'Now, my Lord Coroner,' he urged.
'Let us waste no time. We must search Richer's chamber and
that of Mahant – there's nothing further to be done here.'
Athelstan acted swiftly. Nobody objected. The monks of St
Fulcher were no better than a flock of sheep terrorized by

some mad dog. The divine office and the dawn Masses were
forgotten as the nastiness of what had occurred seeped like a
filthy mist through their community. Abbot Walter seemed
frozen in shock. Prior Alexander, distraught and frantic, was
taken to the infirmary. Athelstan, murmuring a prayer of
apology, seized the opportunity. He and Cranston found
Richer's chamber and conducted their search. Athelstan soon
realized his earlier suspicions were justified. Richer had anticipated their arrival. One of the braziers in the corner was caked
with the feathery remnants of burnt parchment.

'He destroyed what he had to,' Athelstan commented. 'He
was preparing to flee. Nothing remarkable here, just possessions
you would expect of a Benedictine monk: psalter, Ave beads,
triptychs and personal items. Except . . .' Athelstan, who was
on his knees, drew a leather pannier from beneath the bed.
He unbuckled the straps and took out the two small but thick
books; one was obviously of great age but the other, bound
in fresh calfskin, was recently done, its pages soft and creamy
white, the ink black and red, each section beginning with a
title, the first letter of which was framed in an exquisitely
jewelled miniature. Athelstan put this down and picked up
the old book; its cover was of hardened plates covered in
leather and embossed with fading Celtic designs. The pages
were stiff and greying with age though held fast by tight
binding of strengthened twine. The ink was a faded black.
Although the letters were beautifully formed and clear, the
Latin was almost classical in its construction and composition.
Athelstan turned to the first page and the '*Prologua* – the
Introduction' and swiftly translated the author's description:
'A true narration of the origin, history, powers and miracles
of that most sacred bloodstone, the Passio Christi, as drawn
up on the instruction of Pontifex Damasus in the second year
of his Pontificate . . .'

'Friar?'

Athelstan stared up at Cranston.

'God has sent his angel, Sir John, one of the dread lords of
heaven. He wants justice to be done.' Athelstan put both books
back into the pannier. He and Cranston then went to the guest
house. A sleepy-eyed servant showed them Mahant's chamber,

its latch off the clasp. Inside the room looked as if Mahant had left in a hurry. Chests and coffers lay opened, clothes spilling out, weapons thrown on the bed, its sheets and coverlets disturbed. Cranston and Athelstan made a thorough search but only found remnants, relics, mementoes of the past, nothing Athelstan could place as part of this mystery. Mahant's chamber, despite its apparent disorder, seemed as if it had already been cleared of anything untoward but by whom? Wenlock was in the infirmary so was it someone else? Or Mahant himself? He voiced his suspicions to Cranston.

'So you think someone came here before us?' Cranston asked. 'I suspect Mahant himself did this – he was preparing to leave,' he grinned, 'which is understandable.'

Later that morning the abbey became more settled. Athelstan through a now very subdued Abbot Walter, ordered divine office to be suspended until the Inquisitio was finished. Cranston set up his court before the lofty rood screen of the church. A table was brought with the abbot's throne-like chair for Sir John. Athelstan borrowed a stool and laid out his writing tray with freshly sharpened quills, brimming ink pots, sander, pumice stone, wax and freshly scrubbed sheets of vellum. Brother Simon, who'd called those summoned at Cranston's behest, was given the duty of sacramentarius. He would proffer the Book of the Gospels for witnesses to take their oath before they sat on the stool on the other side of the table facing the coroner. Candles were brought and lit, braziers fired to full glow and wheeled close. Athelstan intoned the '*Veni Creator Spiritus*'. Cranston delivered a short barbed speech declaring how he was 'the King's officer in these parts with full power to hear, judge and terminate'. He then had to deal with an objection from one of the senior monks who, on behalf of the abbot, delivered the ritual protest that royal power could not be exercised on church land. Cranston politely heard him out and replied that such matters of law were not for him or his court; the abbot would have to appeal direct to the royal council.

'By which time,' Cranston whispered, sitting down on his chair, 'Gabriel will have blown his horn for the end of days.' Cranston shouted for all to withdraw except those

summoned and the proceedings began. The coroner moved
swiftly, Athelstan carefully noting what was said. The two lay
brothers in charge of the hog pen were summoned first. They
described how they had come out at first light to find the hogs
highly agitated, snorting and casting about as if, in the words
of one of their keepers, they were possessed by a legion of
demons. The massive sty where they were usually confined
for the night was barred by a great half-door. Cranston nodded
and said he'd seen this. The brothers thought some fox or
other night predator had climbed over this into the sty so they
unbarred and opened the half-door. The hogs, now being
slaughtered, one of brothers added mournfully, were so frenzied they had to drive them off with staves. Eventually, after
the entire herd had spilled out into the great pen, they noticed
blood on the snouts, flanks and legs of some of the hogs so
they took lanterns and went back into the sty.

'At first,' one of the brothers shook his head, 'we didn't
believe it. Two corpses horribly mauled. We dragged them out
but even then the hogs tried to attack. We drove them off,
placed the mangled remains outside the pen and raised the
alarm. We then examined the dead and realized one was a
monk from the remains of his clothing: robe, cord and sandals.
The other was an outsider, Sir John. Most of his clothing,
except for his belt and shoes, had been shredded.'

'And the knife?'

'We found it in the straw glistening in the light of the
lantern.' Athelstan stooped down and picked up the elegant,
silver-hilted knife still encrusted with blood.

'And you cannot say,' Athelstan asked, 'whether this knife
was used on one or both of the victims or was it just stained
when the hogs tore their corpses apart?'

'Brother Athelstan, both men must have been dead, or nearly
so when they were cast into the sty.'

'Why?'

'Hogs will attack children, even a man, but they can be
driven off. It's only when they become frenzied and their
victims are helpless that they will feast.'

The monks who worked in the scriptorium and library then
presented themselves. They could say little about Richer or

what he was working on. Athelstan recalled the great table in the scriptorium which the Frenchman deliberately covered up; now he knew the reason why. Cranston questioned the brothers regarding the previous evening. They all reported that Richer had Prior Alexander's permission not to attend divine office. Instead he stayed working in the scriptorium long after dark. They'd glimpsed the glow of candle and lantern horn through the window but more than that they couldn't say.

'Richer was working on copying the *"Liber"*,' Athelstan murmured once the monks had left. 'And when he finished, he placed that and the original in a pannier, returned to hastily hide them in his chamber, then left to meet whom?'

Cranston just pulled a face. Master Crispin was called next. The secretarius was sullen, openly resentful at being kept in the abbey. Once he'd taken the oath on the Book of the Gospels he admitted he was shocked at the horrid deaths.

'And where did you spend your sleeping hours?'

'In my bed, Sir John. I wish to be free of this place. I never liked it. I know nothing of these deaths.'

'Murders,' Athelstan broke. 'Murders, Master Crispin, heinous slayings for which someone will undoubtedly hang. You're on oath – do you have anything else you can tell us?'

'No.'

'Then, sir, go back to your chamber and wait.'

Prior Alexander came next. He looked woebegone and exhausted, face unshaven, eyes red-rimmed with weeping. He mumbled the oath and slouched like a broken man on the stool.

'He's gone.' The prior lifted his head. 'Beautiful Richer.' He heaved a deep sigh. 'My friend, oh . . .' Prior Alexander seemed unaware of his surroundings or to whom he was talking. 'He was a butterfly in many ways. I knew his only task here was to secure the return of everything plundered from St Calliste, including that bloodstone. God knows,' Prior Alexander screwed his face up, 'the curse that ruby carries, now he and one of the Wyvern are dead, murdered.'

'By whom?'

'God knows, Sir John. I would suspect the Wyverns but one of them died with him, perhaps they fought . . .'

'Richer hated them, yes?'

'Of course.'

'Enough to meet one of them at the dead of night and attempt to kill him? After all, Richer was armed with a dagger?'

'Why there?' Prior Alexander pleaded. 'Why in the hog pen?'

'Why indeed,' Athelstan answered. 'Prior Alexander, you loved Richer.' Athelstan put his pen down. 'I do not wish to know to what extent or in what way but he came here to reclaim plundered property. Richer arrived at St Fulcher's once his uncle at St Calliste knew the Wyverns were here. He turned the minds of Master Chalk and Sir Robert to the truth about the Passio Christi?'

'Yes.'

'He persuaded Sir Robert to bribe your Lord Abbot for the secret return of those items.'

'Of course. You know our Lord Walter, he and Judas would have been true blood brothers.'

'You hate your abbot?' Athelstan insisted. 'You regard him as venal, pampered and corrupt.'

Prior Alexander did not answer.

'He made it clear that Richer would soon leave, after all, there was little else for him to take back to France except the "*Liber*". Is that why you killed the abbot's pet swan Leda and hanged it on the abbey gallows? You wrote that threatening message which is nothing more than a translation of a quotation inscribed along the edge of an altar in one of your chantry chapels. You made it appear that the threat came from the Upright Men because you sympathize with them, hence your anger against Lord Walter for stopping payments to them.'

'The swan – true I strung the bird from the gallows,' Prior Alexander shook his head, 'but I never killed it. Richer found it dead in the abbot's garden. The swan died, Brother Athelstan, like all his pets do, from overeating. You saw how he constantly fed it morsels from his table, sweetmeats, sops of wine, cream, and fragments of marzipan. The arrogant fool was more concerned at appearing to be the swan's lord and master than the man who should protect it. For God's sake,' the prior scoffed, 'do you think I would kill some hapless bird out of spite? Don't you know anything about Mother Nature? Swans are not to be fed such a surfeit of richness. I hanged the corpse as revenge but I did not kill it.'

Athelstan sensed the prior was telling the truth.

'Do you know what passed between Richer and Sir Robert?' he asked. 'What really turned the minds of a ruthless city merchant, not to mention a professional killer like Chalk, to repentance and reparation?'

'I know nothing about Richer's conversations with Master Chalk or Master Crispin.'

'He talked with the latter?'

'Of course, when Sir Robert sent him here.'

'Did you treat Crispin for his eye sight?'

'Yes, I used to be the infirmarian here. I'm skilled in dealing with infections of the eyes but there was little I could do. Years of straining over memoranda books had taken their toll.'

'Do you think Richer killed the Wyverns?' Cranston asked.

'I heard you found Osborne's corpse, or at least the Fisher of Men did,' Prior Alexander murmured. 'It's possible,' he confessed bleakly. 'Richer did hate them. He was young, vigorous and, by his own admission, skilled in arms. He performed military service before he entered the novitiate.' Prior Alexander became more composed.

'And you know nothing about the murders amongst the Wyverns?'

'Nothing. My only concern was that Richer stayed. Sir Robert paid the monies. The abbot released the items plundered from St Calliste. I allowed Richer to go into the city to arrange those meetings with envoys from foreign ships. Does it really matter if precious objects were returned to their rightful owner? Abbot Walter was happy and Richer was content, whilst I was only too pleased to help.'

'The "*Liber Passionis Christi*", which we now have – you should have told us the truth.'

Prior Alexander just glanced away.

'Well?'

'Abbot Walter, and on this I agreed with him, declared that we must have a copy so that if a royal inquisition ever took place on the goods from St Calliste, we could produce like

for like, at least show we had a copy of that valuable manuscript. Richer seemed very pleased with that. He personally
supervised the copying both in the scriptorium and his own
chamber.'

'Tell me.' Athelstan paused. This mystery was gathering
like a boil about to bust its venom. 'In your own mind Prior
Alexander, and this is very important, did Sir Robert secretly
plan to bring the Passio Christi not to St Fulcher's but across
to France and personally return the bloodstone to St Calliste?'

'No.' Prior Alexander shook his head vigorously. 'I truly
do not know what passed between Richer and Sir Robert except
Kilverby, that cunning merchant, had a change of heart. He
certainly told me, on the very afternoon before he died, when
Richer and I visited him, how he would leave the bloodstone
at St Fulcher's and that would settle his conscience. He'd give
it back to the Benedictine order. However, which monastery
or abbey housed it was not his concern.'

'Richer would have left now that the "*Liber*" was copied?'

'Yes.'

'And you resented that. I know you argued hotly about it.'

'Of course we did! Why, Brother Athelstan, are you saying
I killed my beloved friend?'

'Lovers argue; they can even kill.'

'We were not lovers in that sense,' Prior Alexander whispered, eyes all fierce.

Athelstan held his gaze. 'So how did you, Prior Alexander,
spend yesterday evening and the early hours of this morning?'

'I attended divine office. Well, I had to; for the rest I stayed
in my chamber.'

'Waiting for Richer?'

'Yes, Brother Athelstan, waiting for Richer. He told me he
intended to work late. I waited and waited,' Prior Alexander's
voice broke, 'but he never came.'

Athelstan looked at Sir John, who'd sat with his eyes half
closed throughout this interrogation.

'We need keep Prior Alexander no longer,' Athelstan
murmured. 'He can leave and bring Wenlock before us.'

Wenlock was helped to his seat by one of the lay brothers;
the old soldier looked pale, simply dressed in his nightgown,

a cloak around his shoulders. He clutched a bowl explaining that he still felt nauseous and had been vomiting since yesterday evening.

'It may have even caused Mahant's death,' he murmured immediately after taking the oath.

'What?' Cranston sat up in his chair.

Athelstan stopped writing.

'Yesterday evening,' Wenlock wearily explained, 'Mahant came to my chamber. There was a platter of sweetmeats, just three or four left. I offered some to Mahant but he refused. I was hungry and ate them all. We were discussing Osborne's death. I began to feel sick. I vomited into the jakes pot. Mahant believed, and so did I, I still do, that the sweetmeats were poisoned or tainted. Mahant began drinking. He grew hot against Richer. He blamed the Frenchman for all the ills which had befallen us. He cursed him.' Wenlock paused, fighting back the urge to retch. 'He vowed to confront Richer, make him pay for what had happened. I thought it was the wine talking. By then I did not really care, I was vomiting so much. Mahant asked if I wished to go to the infirmary, I said no and he left. I stripped off my clothes, put on my nightshirt and lay on the bed.' Wenlock paused. 'God assoil him, that's the last time I saw Mahant alive. I woke in the early hours, my belly raging like a bubbling pot. I was freezing to death. I left my bed, put on a cloak, went down to the infirmary and hammered on the door to speak to the infirmarian. He made me drink water with some herbs infused. I fell asleep there, not waking until the tocsin sounded.'

'You feel better?' Athelstan asked.

'Certainly, the retching has stopped.'

'And you never saw Mahant after you fell sick?'

'No.'

'Do you have any explanation why his corpse and that of Richer should be found in the hog sty?'

'Brother Athelstan, I wish I did.' Wenlock clutched his stomach. 'Perhaps he and the Frenchman confronted each other.'

'In that place, in the dead of night?'

'Brother, I wish I knew.'

'Were you and Mahant planning to leave St Fulcher?'

'Of course. We had already moved some of our possessions to "The Pride of Purgatory" tavern. We were also preparing to petition His Grace for safer lodgings. We invoked the memory of his blessed brother the Black Prince. Can you blame us?' Wenlock insisted. 'We'd become no better than hogs for the slaughter here.' He smiled at his own grim joke. 'Sir John, Brother Athelstan, if you've finished . . .?'

Cranston let him go. The infirmarian was summoned but he could add little. He confirmed Wenlock's story. As regards to the two most recent murders, he explained how both corpses were so badly mauled it was impossible to determine what had happened. The royal serjeant, captain of the archers, came last. He reported how the hogs had been slaughtered and, following Cranston's order, both the sty and the pen had been scoured for any items but they'd found nothing. He left, followed by Brother Simon. The abbey church fell silent.

'So?' Cranston asked.

Athelstan rose, collecting together his quill pens and scrolls of soft vellum.

'One last person.'

Cranston followed Athelstan down to the anker house. They heard movement within, a shape moved. The anchorite looked out, shifting to get a better view of Cranston.

'I know what has happened. Now you have come down to question me. Sir John, I believe we have met. I shall never forget—'

'Agnes Rednal.' Cranston came up close to the anker slit. 'You and I have hanged London's worst.'

'And the kingdom is the better for it.'

'Agnes Rednal,' Athelstan intervened. 'She will never visit you again.' He peered through the slit. 'I assure you. I have laid that demon. She will only walk in your nightmares, though a prayer before sleep should take care of that. Look, why not come out and greet Sir John?'

'Brother Athelstan, I have left my cell enough over the last few days. I have nothing to say about these dreadful slayings. The church is locked an hour after compline, I cannot leave. I saw nothing. I heard nothing . . .'

Athelstan touched Cranston on the arm. They strolled back up the aisle.

'I wonder,' Athelstan whispered.

'About the anchorite?'

'Yes. Those grievances he nursed against the Wyverns, though nothing against Richer or so I believe. I just wonder why he would not allow us into his cell or come out of it. Does he have something to hide? As for leaving this church, he could always creep out through the charnel house.'

Cranston and Athelstan cleared the judgement table and walked out into the Galilee porch. The friar stared up at a carved stone boss displaying a demon with a grinning monkey's face.

'Enough is enough, Sir John,' he declared, 'all this questioning must end. I'll retire to my chamber and study the "*Liber*". I must discover why Richer wouldn't show it to me. You, my learned friend, are always welcome provided you let me share some of your refreshments.'

Back in his chamber Athelstan placed the original '*Liber*' on the table and carefully scrutinized the different chapters. He soon realized the bloodstone was a very precious relic. The ruby's history stretched from its formation to its collection by Joseph Arimathea and its long journey round the ancient Roman empire until it passed into the hands of the early popes. The history was disappointing. However, when Athelstan began to read about the alleged power of the bloodstone, the punishments inflicted on those not worthy to handle it as well as its miraculous curative powers for those who regarded it as a sacred relic, Athelstan's heart skipped a beat. The '*Liber*' proclaimed powerful warnings against any sacrilegious handling; little wonder Kilverby changed. Indeed the '*Liber*' explained why Richer was so zealous in pursuing the bloodstone's return, his hatred for the Wyverns and his influence over William Chalk. The defrocked priest must have come to view his own painful, lingering disease as a just punishment from God for what had happened in France. The list of miracles also made Athelstan think and reflect deeply. Eventually the friar prepared his pen and ink pots, smoothing out a piece of vellum after staring distractedly at a finely drawn triptych celebrating the life of St Benedict's sister, the holy Scholastica.

Once he had collected his thoughts, Athelstan began to construct a logical argument. Kilverby's murder was relatively easy. Athelstan's hypothesis was that when the merchant died he must have known the bloodstone was safe. It was logical. Kilverby held the bloodstone. He sat in his chamber for some-time before he died yet he did not raise the alarm or express any anxiety about it being missing. Athelstan developed this argument then returned to fill in the gaps. On one occasion the friar left going through the now silent abbey to check the records in the muniment room behind the chapter house. No one objected. Divine office remained suspended until matins the following morning whilst the good brothers had been truly overawed by Cranston's display of power. Athelstan's queries and questions were soon answered and he returned to his studies. He finished what he called his Kilverby thesis; a few minor gaps remained but Athelstan believed he had enough to hoodwink then trap the killer.

The friar pulled across a fresh piece of parchment and began what he entitled 'The Abbey Thesis'. He listed the murders beginning with those of Hanep and Hyde. He could now explain these, then he turned to Brokersby's. He scruti-nized earlier notes and found the entries he was searching for. Osborne's death was relatively easy to explain whilst the logic behind that also accounted for the murders of Mahant and Richer. Nevertheless, though he had the bricks to build, the mortar and cement were a little more difficult to find. There were gaps which had to be filled: the chasing, flitting shadow which had pursued Hyde; the mysterious crossbow man: the ugly incident in the charnel house: a proper, logical account of Richer and Mahant's death and how they were overcome and killed by the same assailant. Athelstan kept working on his hypothesis. Cranston knocked on the door and brought in a platter of food and some ale. Athelstan ate and drank, absent-mindedly fending off Cranston's questions until the coroner, muttering he might as well be singing to the moonbeams, left for his own chamber. At last Athelstan made his decision. He crossed himself, rose and went out and knocked on Cranston's chamber. The coroner was already preparing for the night.

'Sir John,' Athelstan made the coroner sit on the edge of the bed, 'I know you to be honest – your face and your mood are easy to read, so don't question me.'

Cranston sighed noisily.

'Tomorrow morning at first light you and I, together with Master Crispin, are off to Kilverby's mansion to confront an assassin. Whilst we are gone you must have archers, two to each person, guarding the abbot, his mistress, Prior Alexander, Wenlock and the anchorite. These archers must not leave their charges not even for a second. In fact, you should put your clothes back on and do that now. Master Crispin must also be protected until we leave tomorrow . . .'

oOoOo

EIGHT

'Judicium: judgement.'

Athelstan sat at the late Sir Robert's chancery desk and smiled around at the dead merchant's assembled household. He, Crispin and the coroner had left St Fulcher's just after dawn, risking their lives on a choppy, misty Thames. Thankfully Cranston had commandeered one of the great barges which had brought the archers so they had all huddled in their cloaks in its canopied stern. The secretarius had asked the reason for the haste. Athelstan simply assured him that the journey was essential. Mercifully, it also proved brief and without incident. They'd arrived in Cheapside and roused Kilverby's household, Cranston brushing aside all objections. Whilst the coroner assembled everyone, Athelstan carefully examined the seals on Kilverby's chamber; none of these had been interfered with. He broke them and had the chamber door unlocked. The chamber was dark, cold and musty-smelling. Candles were hastily brought, braziers wheeled in. Now with Cranston guarding the door, Athelstan lifted the empty casket which had once contained the Passio Christi. He also kept the palette of pens close to him. During the preparations he'd carefully scrutinized these.

'Brother Athelstan,' Lady Helen snapped, 'why are you here?'

Athelstan ignored her and tapped the casket.

'Sir Robert, on the eve of his murder, knew this was empty.'

'But . . .' Alesia interrupted.

'Your father also mistakenly thought the bloodstone was in safe hands.'

'Whose?' Crispin spluttered.

'Why yours, sir! I have brought you back here, Master Crispin, to confront you, to show you proof, to accuse you of the heinous murder of your master Sir Robert Kilverby, here in his own chamber.'

Exclamations and cries greeted his words. Crispin, hands shaking, sprang to his feet protesting. Cranston, hiding his surprise, strode forward and forced the clerk back on to his stool.

'You're a murderer,' Athelstan accused, 'and you'll hang for it.'

'I am not—'

'You are what I say. All of you,' Athelstan stared around, 'listen carefully, especially you, Master Crispin, because your life, and indeed your death, depend on it.' Athelstan took a deep breath, staring hard at Crispin's fearful face. 'I shall be succinct. I shall try not to repeat what you already know. Sir Robert had grown rich; he'd also become frightened of impending justice. In his heyday he'd held the Passio Christi as merrily as he had gleefully taken a share of all the plunder of the Wyvern Company in France. However, dreading the fast approaching day of judgement was only the beginning. In his visit to St Fulcher's he also met Richer, a monk from St Calliste, sent to England with the specific task of reclaiming everything looted from his own abbey, especially the Passio Christi.' Athelstan paused. 'Richer was undoubtedly eloquent but he had something more powerful, the "*Liber Passionis* – the Book of the Passion of Christ*", a most detailed description of the bloodstone – drawn up by no less a person than a saintly pope. Richer swore Sir Robert to secrecy, as he probably had William Chalk, and let him read that singular manuscript. Now the "*Liber*" clearly describes the history, power and properties of that most holy relic. The "*Liber*" specifically states every insult and injury to the Passio Christi provokes divine judgement. Richer played on this. He harassed Sir Robert's soul until the merchant asked for forgiveness. Now Kilverby's mind was fertile soil. Lady Helen, I apologize for this, though it is well known: Sir Robert's marriage to you was not as happy as he would have wished. Perhaps he saw that, as well as the death of his beloved first wife, as all part of divine judgement.'

'I do not think . . .'

'My Lady,' Athelstan smiled apologetically, 'that is only one strand of the close, cloying web which snared your late husband's soul. He became fearful that other misfortunes might befall him – why not? Crispin, his loyal secretary, was losing his sight and what would happen if anything dreadful befell his beloved heir and daughter – you, Alesia?'

The young woman just stared back, tears welling in her eyes.

'Sir Robert, guided by the subtle Richer, decided to do penance.

'Surely,' Kinsman Adam broke in, 'Sir Robert would not be so easily influenced.'

'Why not?' Athelstan retorted. 'Read the "*Liber*" and you'll see the long litany of curses and their effects. As I have said, Richer could not only point to Kilverby's life, the death of his first wife, his second marriage and Crispin's blindness, but to the Wyverns. They told me they had no families; their wives and children now lie cold in the clay. A curse? Surely! Not to mention Chalk's illness and Wenlock's maimed hands. Were the rest any better? Hanep, unable to sleep, wandering the abbey at night? Brokersby feeding himself on opiates? Richer may have included the dotage of the old King, the fate of his son the Black Prince who contracted that malevolent disease in Spain and wasted away, leaving the kingdom to a mere child.'

'Not to mention the failure of the war in France,' Cranston added mournfully.

'Richer could,' Athelstan continued, 'argue all this was due to the bloodstone. Sir Robert had all the evidence he needed. He decided to bribe Abbot Walter to send back the plunder taken from St Calliste. He also paid for a copy of the "*Liber*" to be made. He was making it very clear how, before he left England on his pilgrimage of reparation, he would return the bloodstone, not to its rightful owners outside Poitiers, but at least to another Benedictine abbey.' Athelstan paused, picked up the quill pens and examined them carefully. He wondered if Crispin already suspected what he was going to say. 'You, Crispin,' Athelstan glanced up, 'hoped to join your master on his journey; a lifetime of love and loyalty merited companionship on such a pilgrimage but your sight is failing after years of poring over Kilverby's ledgers and account books. You were already receiving treatment from Prior Alexander with all the skills and knowledge he'd learnt as the abbey infirmarian. He actually achieved very little. So, instead of going with your master or even staying here in this comfortable mansion, Sir Robert, thinking he was acting kindly, insisted on you taking up a corrody at St Fulcher's.'

'I accepted that.'

'Nonsense, Crispin, you only pretended to. You'd served as a novice at St Fulcher's. You hated that place. You also grew to hate your master for giving you such short shrift after decades of loyal and faithful service. Hatred is the soil where murder thrives as vigorous as any shrub. Into that midnight garden wormed the serpent Richer. Sir Robert must have told him all about you. Richer was pleased. He wanted the Passio Christi either to be given to him or returned directly to St Calliste. On that, however, Sir Robert was insistent: the bloodstone would not leave England.'

'Yes, yes, you are correct,' Alesia broke in. 'My father told me that the bloodstone should be handed back to its rightful owner yet he was fearful of the Lord Regent's wrath falling on me if he fled to France with the bloodstone.'

'Quite so,' Cranston declared from where he stood near the door. 'The Crown's lawyers would have spun a fine tangled trap of treason.'

'Richer turned to you, Master Crispin,' Athelstan continued. 'Only God and you know what was offered: a huge bribe, freedom to settle down quietly in France, not to mention the opportunity of exacting revenge on your hard-hearted master who apparently no longer cared for you? Oh, Richer was cunning and devious. He would smear all that with righteousness. He would argue how Sir Robert should be rightfully punished for his share in what had happened. You, Crispin, would not only be the divine instrument for that but also do great good. You would return the bloodstone to its rightful home. Unbeknown to Sir Robert, you and Richer secretly plotted his murder.'

'Murder?' Crispin protested. 'Me, how can I buy poisons?'

'I never said you did. Richer gave them to you. He was sub-prior in an abbey where the abbot was lost in his own concerns, where the prior was pliable as soft clay in the potter's hands. St Fulcher's is a treasure house of potions and powders. Either on the eve of St Damasus when he visited here or sometime before, Richer handed over these poisons to you: hemlock, henbane, nightshade or the juice of almond seed, perhaps all four. You certainly knew their properties.'

'I do not.'

'Yes, you do. I have studied the muniments at St Fulcher's. You are left-handed, Crispin, a matter I shall return to. When you were a novice, the master was frustrated by this, he would not allow you to work in the library, scriptorium or chancery so you became an assistant to the abbey apothecary.'

Crispin, all agitated, his face ashen and drawn, could only shake his head.

'Now,' Athelstan persisted, 'on the eve of St Damasus, the day of his murder, Sir Robert entertained Prior Alexander and Richer. He met you all in the solar?'

Alesia nodded, all watchful.

'He put the Passio Christi back into its casket and returned here to his chancery chamber.'

'Yes,' Alesia replied. 'Crispin, you went with him.'

'How long were your father and Crispin absent?'

'Not for very long, we were all preparing for supper.'

'Precisely,' Athelstan replied. 'However, back in his chamber, Sir Robert was preparing to lock the bloodstone away. You, Crispin, intervened. You have read the "*Liber*". You knew about the recuperative powers of the Passio Christi, especially round the Feast of St Damasus. How someone inflicted with a disease of the eyes should hold the precious bloodstone against their head? The "*Liber*" lists all such practices. You, Crispin, begged Sir Robert for such an opportunity to hold the precious relic against your own eyes. You pleaded as a loyal and faithful servant for help from the bloodstone. I am sure Richer coaxed you to ask and, perhaps, Sir Robert to consent. You may well have asked for this before. I am sure you did and your master agreed. On that particular evening you would point out that the bloodstone might soon pass from your master's hands to others who might not be so obliging.

Sir Robert approved. He gave it to you in trust for the night. You would, and he agreed, ask for the matter to be kept confidential. You took the Passio Christi and Sir Robert simply locked the coffer. Why should he object? In the morning the bloodstone would be returned by his faithful servant. Crispin certainly wouldn't tell anybody. Neither would Sir Robert – why should he? You all adjourned for supper.' Athelstan paused. 'However, Crispin, you had planned a subtle death for your master. He would not survive the night to ask for the bloodstone back.' Athelstan lifted the writing tray, gesturing at the quill pens. 'I've studied your master. He was right-handed. He constantly nibbled at the quill plume. You prepared the pens left in this tray that night. You coated their plumes with the poison at your disposal; they were richly drenched in some noxious potion. Sir Robert would, as he was accustomed, nibble and chew at the quill plumes. He would absorb the poisons, small tinctures at a time but the mixture would, over hours, wreak their effect.' Athelstan picked up a quill pen lying on the writing palette. 'This is the proof. You thought you were safe, Master Crispin. You did not care. You had removed the poisonous quill pens you'd first laid here but, in fact, you were sealing in your own guilt. You made one miscalculation: the arrival of Sir John and myself. This chamber was secured. You could not rectify any omission.' Athelstan held up the three quill pens for all to see. 'Are these nibbled and chewed? No. More importantly, Crispin, you are left-handed. I am right-handed, I hold the quill such and the point on the right side of the pen becomes worn, yes? These, however, have been used by a left-handed writer.' Athelstan turned all three quill pens, tapping their worn edges.

'Sir Robert,' he added. 'Even when he was in the novitiate he was known for chewing the end of his pens. He laughingly referred to this, Crispin, when you and he were once strolling up the south aisle of St Fulcher's abbey church. You were overheard by the anchorite who shelters there. Mistress Alesia, did you not tell me the same?'

'It's true,' Alesia whispered, 'my father always chewed the ends of his pens, a mannerism he couldn't give up despite my scolding.'

Others murmured their assent. Crispin undid the cord of his cambric shirt as if he couldn't breathe properly.

'But we all came in here that morning,' Lady Helen demanded. 'Nobody moved anything, I am sure.'

'Are you?' Athelstan replied. 'Look, Crispin is Sir Robert's clerk. He has an ink horn and quills strapped to his belt. It's one of the first things I noticed about him.'

'He always carries pens,' Alesia declared, 'he always has ever since I can remember.'

'It was the same that morning,' Athelstan agreed. 'You all came in here. You were distraught and distracted. Crispin, the faithful clerk, moved to Sir Robert's desk. Why shouldn't he rearrange the pens? He makes the exchange in the twinkling of an eye. He leaves these quills, the ones he has used himself, and takes the poisoned ones which, I am sure, he immediately burnt.' Athelstan paused, letting the silence deepen.

'But surely,' Lady Helen now spoke directly to Athelstan, 'he must have realized the mistakes he had made?' She paused. 'Of course.' She answered her own question. 'It was too late. Crispin never expected, as you said, this chamber to be sealed with all the evidence in it.'

'Crispin's eyesight is also poor,' Athelstan declared. 'He may have failed to realize the full implications of what he'd done. Once Sir Robert's corpse was discovered, he was committed to the heinous lie he had to live. Perhaps he delayed gnawing on the ends of the replacement quill pens until it was too late. Or did he panic, frightened that one of you would note such act so closely associated with his master rather than himself? What he'd done was certainly settled by this chamber being sealed. However,' Athelstan pointed to the ashen-faced clerk, 'only he can say. But remember, for Crispin, Sir Robert's death was only a means, a device to get his hands on the bloodstone and keep it.'

'It must be true,' Kinsman Adam whispered. 'Sir Robert would only have entrusted the Passio Christi to someone in this room, someone he trusted implicitly, there's no other explanation.'

'Don't accuse me!'

'I do, Crispin,' Athelstan declared. 'True, I do not have full

proof but I possess enough to present a bill of indictment.
You'll be arrested and lodged in Newgate. The Regent's
torturers will demand your presence at the Tower. They'll
interrogate you day in and day out. They will not let you die,
though there'll be times when you pray that they do so.
Confession or not, you'll be judged a traitor for having stolen
Crown property. You will also be condemned as sacrilegious
and excommunicate because the Passio Christi is a sacred
relic.' Athelstan held Crispin's terrified gaze. 'In the end you'll
suffer the full penalty for treason. You'll be drawn on a hurdle
from the Tower to the Elms at Smithfield. You'll be half hanged,
disembowelled and castrated. You will die the enemy of both
church and realm. You'll never be allowed to enjoy the fruits
of your foul act.'

'A full confession,' Cranston came up and softly placed
both hands on Crispin's shoulders, 'and the return of the
bloodstone and you can expect a swift, merciful death. Your
soul purged of all sin.'

Crispin swallowed hard. He tried to speak but couldn't form
the words.

'Please,' Alesia pleaded, 'for any love you have for me,
Crispin, confess because the odds press heavily against you.'

Crispin bowed his head and sobbed, a heart-rending sound.
Athelstan steeled himself. This man had deliberately and maliciously killed another human being. He had betrayed his master
who, despite all his faults, had meant him well.

Crispin lifted his head. 'It is,' he confessed, 'as you say . . .'

Athelstan sat in the inglenook of 'The Port of Paradise', an
ancient tavern which, Cranston claimed, was built in the time
of the present King's great, great grandfather. A claim,
Athelstan stared round, which he would not challenge. The
lowering beams of the tap room were black with age, the onions
and cheeses hanging in nets from these exuded a tangy smell
which offset the stench of gutted fish drying outside the main
door. Athelstan bit into the freshly baked manchet loaf smeared
with honey and sipped at the ale which the barrel-bellied
Minehost had proclaimed to be the best in London.

'In which case I'd hate to taste the worst,' Athelstan

whispered, putting the blackjack on the floor beside him. Cranston had promised he wouldn't be long. Athelstan stretched his hands out to the blaze. The leaping flames in the great hearth reminded him of the Passio Christi. Crispin had confessed and then, with Cranston as his guard, had gone down into the garden at the rear of the mansion where he had cunningly hidden the bloodstone amongst a pile of ancient sacking.

'Beautiful,' Athelstan murmured to himself. He'd handled the bloodstone, big as a duck's egg, as Cranston had described it. Turning the ruby Athelstan had marvelled at what appeared to be shooting flames of fire within; these caught the light and dazzled even more. Athelstan was wary of most relics. He'd seen the most ludicrous venerated, the worst being a pile of straw miraculously preserved from the stable at Bethlehem. For all his scepticism Athelstan had appreciated the sheer beauty of the bloodstone. Its unique glow alone would convince many that it had been formed by Christ's precious blood and sweat. Athelstan had returned it to its coffer, nestling the ruby amongst the soft blue samite. Crispin had then repeated his confession which virtually agreed with every aspect of Athelstan's bill of indictment. Crispin also admitted that his mind had been turned by his intense dislike of St Fulcher's, the powerful resentment he felt against Sir Robert and how subtly Richer had played on this.

'Once Richer died . . .' Crispin paused at the exclamations this provoked from the rest of the household.

'Oh, yes,' Athelstan intervened. 'Richer has gone to a higher judge in a way he did not expect.'

'Whatever his death,' Crispin continued muttering as if to himself, 'he deserved it. Now he is gone what can I do?'

'All finished.'

Athelstan glanced up. Cranston towered over him, his head and face almost hidden by the great beaver hat and the folds of his cloak.

'Crispin is lodged in Newgate and the bloodstone lies in the great iron chest at the Guildhall.'

'But the bloodstone,' Athelstan added, getting to his feet,

'has not yet finished its work. We must now confront the act which began this bloody mayhem, "the *Radix Malorum* – the Root of all these Evils".'

As soon as Athelstan returned to the abbey, he sent Cranston with two archers to bring Wenlock to his chamber. The veteran had apparently recovered from his belly gripes, the colour returning to his ruddy face. He was dressed for travelling in thick woollen jerkin and leggings, riding boots on, his maimed hands hidden by gauntlets.

'Sit down,' Athelstan ordered, 'you'll be going nowhere, Master Wenlock, except to Newgate then on to be hanged at Smithfield. Don't lie,' Athelstan ordered, 'but sit and listen. Take off your gauntlets, Wenlock, that's right; let us see your maimed hands. You were caught by the French?'

Wenlock, eyes watchful, glanced over his shoulder at Cranston standing by the door.

'You know I was,' he retorted.

'You were punished, maimed for being an English master bowman,' Athelstan continued. 'Did you and your coven see this as just punishment for stealing the Passio Christi?'

'I did not . . .'

'You did,' Athelstan retorted flatly. 'Your story about finding a cart near St Calliste piled high with treasure, its escort having fled, is a lie. Many have regarded it as such, but now we have the truth. Wenlock, you stole that bloodstone. You pulled it out of its tabernacle, out of its shrine. You stole that and the "*Liber Passionis Christi*", probably chained to a nearby lectern together with other sacred items. Your later capture and maiming by the French may have provoked some fears in you and your company. Wenlock, I have read the "*Liber*": it curses any sacrilegious act against the bloodstone. The "*Liber*" boldly proclaims, with fitting examples from its past, how the hands of such a perpetrator would wither like dry leaves. Look at your hands, Wenlock, they have shrivelled. You lost your skill as a master bowman though I suspect you have enough grip, perfected over the years, to wield a dagger or club.'

Wenlock stared above Athelstan's head, lips moving as if memorizing something.

'Matters changed when you came to St Fulcher's, even more

so when Richer arrived here as sub-prior. He was ruthlessly dedicated to recovering all the property stolen from St Calliste. He was well placed to do this because he had at his disposal a looted item which you probably overlooked, the "*Liber Passionis Christi*". Kilverby also came here. He was vulnerable, growing old, becoming frightened of impending judgement. Using the "*Liber*" as evidence, Richer converted that merchant but then seized on an even greater prey, your old companion William Chalk.'

Wenlock just snorted derisively.

'I am sure that's how Richer regarded Chalk,' Athelstan countered, 'a defrocked priest, a man growing old and fearful. Richer counsels Chalk. He shows him the curses against those who have sinned against the bloodstone. Chalk may have even come to see his own malignant disease as God's judgement on him. In the end Chalk confesses. Of course Richer is protected by the seal of confession but I suspect Chalk began to chatter. The sub-prior certainly used Chalk to influence Kilverby; he hoped the same would happen amongst your coven with all their memories and hidden guilt. You, Wenlock, the recognized counsellor of the Wyverns, sensed the danger now emerging. Chalk and Kilverby were both victims of Richer's subtlety – who would be next? Who knows? Richer might eventually persuade Brokersby, Hyde or Hanep to go in front of a King's officer, Sir John Cranston or any other Justice and, on surety of being pardoned or even rewarded, confess what really happened at St Calliste so many years ago. Of course your story about finding that cart was always doubted but matters would radically change if a full confession was made. Once one of your coven did that, others would soon follow. They would swear that you, not them, stole the Passio Christi; perhaps you were helped by Mahant and only protected by the others. In the end you know how such matters proceed?'

Wenlock simply smiled to himself.

'In the final conclusion,' Athelstan continued, 'you'd be cast as the thief, your maimed hands as proof of divine judgement. Once such a confession was made public, the church would declare you excommunicate and insist that the Crown use the full rigour of the law against you. His Grace the Regent would, despite any personal feelings, be forced to act or suffer similar ecclesiastical punishment.'

'What proof do you offer?' Wenlock snarled. 'I was away from here when Hanep and Hyde were killed.'

'I will come to that in a while.' Athelstan shifted on his stool. 'You,' he pointed at Wenlock, 'were fearful. Chalk's confession, Richer's presence, Kilverby's alienation from you emphasized the real danger. In a word you persuaded Mahant to go with you, why or how I don't know. Perhaps Mahant had assisted you in your sacrilege. Perhaps you threatened him that, if you were accused, you would implicate him in your confession. You decided, and so persuaded Mahant, that it was best if all your old companions died. Of course there were other motives. You'd use your comrades' wealth as a bribe; perhaps they owned more than we ever suspected. You talked of a common purse and claimed Osborne held it. Another lie. I suspect you do and half of such money is better than a sixth.'

'I was not here!' Wenlock shouted fiercely, though Athelstan glimpsed the fear in those watery blue eyes. 'I was not here,' he repeated, 'when Hanep and Hyde died.'

'Oh, but you were.'

'I was in London.'

'No, you and Mahant went to London. You lodged at "The Pride of Purgatory" tavern. You made great play at revelling and feasting there. You ogled the ladies and loudly mentioned how you were waiting for your old friend Geoffrey of Portsoken, now known as Vox Populi. In truth you didn't give a fig for him. You probably knew full well that he'd been taken up by the sheriff's men.' Athelstan paused as the abbey bells boomed out their summons to plain chant. 'Sir John,' he asked, 'how long would it take two able bodied men to walk from Cheapside to here?'

'Less than an hour.'

'Which is what you did,' Athelstan accused. 'You left that tavern probably disguised in the black robes of a Benedictine, you'd easily secure such gowns. With your shaven heads and stout sandals, you appeared what you wanted to be, two monks returning late to their abbey. Who would know? You left that tavern with its many entrances in the dead of night. You walked through the darkness. Once here you were able and fit enough to scale the abbey walls, drop into the grounds and make your own way to the guest house. Hanep was your first victim. If he came out for one of his midnight saunters all to the good, if not you'd strike some other way. Of course Hanep did and died swiftly for doing so. You then returned to London disguised. No one would really notice you coming or going at the dead of night. "The Pride of Purgatory" tavern is busy with many entrances and exits, that's why you chose it. You can slip in and out as easily as you did. You then prepared for your next victim. You also purchased an arbalest or crossbow, I am sure of that. I don't believe that nonsense about never using one. You might despise it but that's not the same as never using one. Mahant was a master bowman – he was skilled enough.'

'We would never . . .'

'Yes, you did,' Athelstan snapped, 'or at least Mahant bought one on your orders. He confessed how he used it against me.'

'What do you mean?' Wenlock's shock was obvious. He sat gaping at Athelstan, who spread his hands.

'In a while,' Athelstan murmured, determined not to glance at Cranston, 'you and Mahant returned to St Fulcher's late in the afternoon on the Feast of St Damasus. You stealthily entered this abbey, probably disguised as Benedictines. I have learnt, even from my short stay here at the dead of winter, particularly with the mist seeping in, how members of this community pass unobserved all garbed in black, hoods or cowls pulled forward.' Athelstan ignored Wenlock's mocking sneer. He sensed this killer was truly frightened behind his scoffing front. 'You waited near the guest house. You would have chosen any of your coven but Hyde appeared. Mahant, with you trailing behind as guard, followed Hyde into the abbey church. Hyde glimpsed Richer and set off in pursuit, curious at why this Frenchman was armed and where he was going. In a word, Mahant killed Hyde near the watergate then fled across Mortival meadow, its mist shrouded bushes and copses provided an ideal place to hide. Mahant was very clever,

disguised in the robe of a Benedictine monk. If Hyde had been
alerted and turned round, Mahant could have simply reverted
to being the old comrade wondering what was going on. Hyde
paid for his trust in you. Of course you did not wish to be
implicated in his death so once Hanep was dead, you both left
the abbey then reappeared in your own guise at the abbey
gates which, you thought, would place you beyond
suspicion.'

Wenlock's sneer had disappeared. He was now openly
nervous, looking around as if searching for any weakness in
the allegations levied against him.

'Sir John is behind you,' Athelstan observed, 'and this guest
house is now ringed with men-at-arms.'

Wenlock just blinked and breathed in deeply.

'Brokersby surprised you, didn't he?' Athelstan continued.
'Admitting in my presence and that of Sir John how he was
drawing up his own chronicle. God knows what he was writing.
Was he also making a confession? Had William Chalk gossiped
to him as well as to others?'

'Brokersby was fey, madcap,' Wenlock jibed.

'Perhaps he was or perhaps he was converted,' Athelstan
replied. 'After all, like Hanep he couldn't sleep at night. Did
his past come back to haunt him? Is that why he had to take
an opiate before he could sleep?'

Wenlock refused to answer.

'Whose idea was it,' Athelstan asked, 'to tamper with the
night candle, scoop out the tallow, fill the void with oil,
sprinkle in a few grains of salt petre then reseal it? Was it
yours, Wenlock? Did you also put the small pouch of oil
beneath Brokersby's bed when you came to wish him goodnight? Oil is easy to obtain for a man like you who's lived
all his life stealing from others. You and Mahant acted the
Judas. You wished the heavy-eyed Brokersby goodnight but
insisted he lock the door behind you as protection against
that mysterious assassin stalking you all. Poor Brokersby!
He never realized this murderer was you and your comrade-
in-sin, Mahant. In fact, Brokersby sealed himself in his own
coffin. The candle dissolved. The spitting fire caught the oil
in his room and everything in it, including his chronicle, was

consumed by the inferno exactly as you wanted.' Athelstan paused as Cranston lifted a hand and came up behind Wenlock.

'You're an old soldier, a professional killer,' Cranston remarked, 'you have taken part in sieges where oil and salt-petre are used to undermine walls. You're well acquainted with their effects.'

Wenlock still refused to answer.

'Osborne's killing is also no longer a mystery,' Athelstan persisted. 'He must have been genuinely fearful. You and Mahant exploited that. Osborne would have only been too pleased to flee this place for what he thought was a safe refuge, "The Prospect of Heaven". You told him to lodge there under Brokersby's name just in case a search was made. Late on Sunday afternoon, when Sir John and I were busy with my parishioners, you moved to the second part of your plan to remove Osborne. You probably told him to leave "The Prospect" and wait for you at some deserted spot along the river. Did you promise that you'd meet him and all three of you would flee? That you were staying in the abbey to finish certain affairs and once completed you and Mahant would join him there? Well?'

'Friar, you tell a good tale.'

'A murderous one and no fable. You and Mahant killed Osborne. He was vulnerable, unsuspecting. You slit his throat, smashed his face with a rock or some weapon, stripped his body, stole his possessions then tossed his corpse into the river. If the Fisher of Men had not been so observant, Osborne's corpse would have rotted away beyond recognition. He would be proclaimed as missing, even depicted as the assassin both for past crimes and any still to be perpetrated.'

'What do you mean?'

'You know full well. You and Mahant planned to use Osborne as your cats-paw, at least for a while until this bloody tumult died down.' Athelstan paused. 'You and Mahant made a mistake. You said Osborne was your treasurer. You claimed he may have disappeared with the common purse.'

'And?' Wenlock mocked.

'At no time, apart from a general question, did you mention

this during our journey to and from the Fisher of Men – or indeed whilst we were there. No concerns about the great amount of gold and silver Osborne was allegedly carrying. Of course the truth is he was carrying very little except for his weapons and a few personal possessions. You are probably the treasurer – and a great deal more.'

Wenlock simply raised his eyebrows.

'You are a murderous soul. You are steeped in blood, you thirst for it. You never intended Mahant to live. He recognized that, which is why he left a sealed confession.'

'He didn't, he couldn't . . .' Wenlock's voice faltered.

'How do you know that?' Athelstan demanded. 'You truly have no fear of God, do you? I am not sure when you planned to kill Mahant but there was one other death you and Mahant plotted: Richer the Frenchman.' Athelstan paused, wetting his lips. 'Thanks to William Chalk, Richer now had the full truth about the seizure of the Passio Christi. A very dangerous man, Richer the Frenchman, who had entered your world and turned it upside down. For that he had to be punished as well as silenced. Mahant would certainly agree – why not? His soul was like yours, black as midnight. Two nightmares in human flesh who kill whenever they wish.'

Wenlock's cheek muscles twitched as he fought to control what Athelstan considered to be a truly murderous temper.

'You hunted Richer. You waited as he left his chamber to meet Prior Alexander. You and Mahant attacked. A swift blow to the head then, under the cover of dark, you both carried his body away from the abbey precincts to the hog pen. The swine were confined to their sty. You cut Richer's throat and tossed his corpse over the half-door. No one would know how or why he died; the mystery would only deepen because he died alongside a member of the Wyvern Company. You then decided it was also opportune to rid yourself of Mahant. You waited out there in the hog pen, close to the sty. For one brief moment, a few heart beats, Mahant turned his back on you. Maimed hands or not, both together can lift a dagger, in this case Richer's – you plunged or drove it deep into Mahant, a killing blow followed by another. You then threw his corpse into the sty and fled.'

'I was ill, vomiting.'

'Wenlock, you are a liar, you went back to your chamber. You changed. You made sure you removed all traces of your murderous foray. Only then did you act the part of the old soldier, pathetic in his night shirt, suffering from belly gripes.' Athelstan paused. 'Do you remember telling me about that first attack on you near the maze? How you were rescued by others? Of course there was no attack, that was just part of the web you and Mahant were beginning to spin, a sham fight with your accomplice Mahant acting as the assailant. At the time you told me how you had a great interest in herbs, that's why you were out in the garden. You'd use such knowledge to protect yourself. You drank some concoction, harmless enough, to cause a mild disturbance of the belly to make it look as if you were genuinely sick – but only after the murders of Richer and Mahant.'

Wenlock was staring down at his maimed hands.

'Wenlock!'

He did not move.

'Wenlock!'

He lifted his head, hatred seething in those watery eyes.

'You despise both church and state, don't you?' Athelstan leaned forward, determined not to show any fear. 'That's why you pillaged St Calliste. You have no compunction about committing sacrilege or murder. You hunted me as well.' Athelstan ignored the fleeting smirk. 'Actually very clever, especially the first attack. Mahant rattled the shutter of my chamber, probably with some pebbles. I opened it and he loosed that crossbow barb. He nearly hit his mark. I suspect Mahant was skilled enough with the arbalest. Of course it's not the war bow of which he is a master; his possible inexperience saved my life. Or was it only meant as a warning to frighten me off? I left that chamber. You and others of your coven were outside in the passageway. You asked me to join you. You acted the smiling Judas, asking me questions, delaying me so by the time I got outside Mahant had joined the rest. You tried again in a more deadly fashion in the charnel house. You were hunting me, waiting for an opportunity. I was stupid enough to provide one. You and Mahant had listened to me, watched me and decided I was dangerous. I might not be misled by your farrago of lies. I might discover the truth behind the murders. You and Mahant decided I should die. I would have done so if it hadn't been for God's good grace. I wondered then at the speed with which my assailant entered the crypt and doused those torches. Of course there were two, not one intruder, which explains it. I thank God I escaped.'

Wenlock gave a final look around the chamber as if he was still searching for any gap or weakness.

'Master Crispin stole the Passio Christi,' Athelstan added softly. 'He poisoned his master. He's confessed. He'll be spared the torture, the full rigours of a traitor's death.'

Wenlock sighed deeply.

'We will visit "The Pride of Purgatory" tavern,' Athelstan added. 'We'll seize your possessions, all the money you and Mahant have stored there. You've tortured enough men in your life to know what to expect.'

'Did Mahant really leave a sealed confession?' Wenlock murmured. 'Where? To whom?'

'We'll produce that when you are arraigned.'

'You have further proof, witnesses?'

'We'll produce those,' Athelstan repeated, 'when you are arraigned before the King's justices.'

'A swift death,' Cranston urged.

Wenlock began to hum a tune, shuffling his feet in a strange macabre dance. He stopped, smiled to himself then lifted his hands in a token of surrender.

'I knew I was cursed,' he remarked, 'when the French cut off my fingers. I knew it was only a matter of time. Are you promising me a swift death?'

'Swift,' Cranston repeated.

'The anchorite must do it.' Wenlock glanced over his shoulder at the coroner. 'I've hanged enough to know what will happen. I don't want to dance for an hour, twitch and jerk, soil myself while I'm choking. The Hangman of Rochester will ensure it takes no more time than a Gloria.' Wenlock forced a laugh. 'You're right, Cranston, I've seen men tortured.' He blew his cheeks out. 'I won't reply, Friar, to what you've laid against me. You've said enough, there's little to add. I plead guilty. I have no more to say . . .'

Athelstan stood in the narrow nave of St Bartholomew's Priory in Smithfield. The church was deserted except for the Guild of the Hanged who clustered before the Great Pity just inside the main door. They knelt, pattering their Aves for the two men being hanged at the Elms only a short distance beyond the great lychgate of the priory. Athelstan half listened to the swelling murmur of the crowd thronging around the soaring scaffold which brooded over Smithfield. The Regent had insisted that both Cranston and Athelstan witness the execution of the two criminals they'd trapped and caught. The coroner was now on the scaffold together with the Hangman of Rochester garbed in black, his head and face hidden by a blood-red visor. Athelstan moved over to pray before the gilt-edged tomb of Rahere, King Henry's jester who'd founded both the priory and the nearby hospital in fulfilment of a vow he'd made to St Bartholomew in Outremer.

'God's jester,' Athelstan prayed, eyes tightly shut. 'Have great pity on Crispin and Wenlock. Show even more loving mercy on their poor victims. Eternal rest . . .' Athelstan broke off at the great roar which echoed through the church. 'Eternal rest,' he continued, 'give them all.' He pleaded, 'And let perpetual light shine upon them.' He remained kneeling, locked in fervent, desperate prayer.

'It's over, they've gone!'

Athelstan opened his eyes. Cranston and the anchorite stood in the doorway of the church.

'Swift?' Athelstan asked.

'Like that!' Cranston snapped his fingers.

'For such small mercies,' Athelstan whispered, getting to his feet, '*deo gratias.*' He walked down the nave. 'Although not over Sir John.'

'What do you mean?'

'It never is,' the anchorite declared, hood and visor now pulled back.

'It never is, is it, Father?'

Athelstan smiled at both of them. 'Abbot Walter needs to

do a great deal of explaining, so does Prior Alexander. His Grace the Regent must decide on what to do with the Passio Christi . . .' Athelstan spread his hands.

'Father,' the anchorite stepped forward, 'could I move my cell to St Erconwald's? I cannot stay in that abbey.'

'You could hang half of his parish,' Cranston joked.

'Not now, and you,' Athelstan pointed at the anchorite, 'you have a name, Giles of Sempringham, yes? I shall call you that. So,' Athelstan rubbed his hands, 'let us go back to "The Holy Lamb of God". Let us sit before a roaring fire. Let us revel in all God's comforts and rejoice in the approach of the feast of the birth of God's Golden Boy.'

'Oh sweet words, lovely friar,' Cranston breathed.

All three left the priory. Athelstan turned his face away so as not to glimpse those two corpses hanging black against the bright December sky.

oOoOo

HISTORICAL NOTES

Bloodstone is of course a work of fiction but it is based firmly on historical fact. By 1380 the war in France had turned into a disaster; the great victories of Crecy and Poitiers had been reversed. Edward III slipped into his dotage, attended by Alice Perrers, who later died in something akin to the odour of sanctity at her retreat in Essex. The Black Prince preceded his father leaving a mere child, Richard II, as his heir. (The sobriquet 'Black Prince' was in common use by 1378.) Real power was vested in the cunning and subtle John of Gaunt who sowed a bitter harvest for Richard to reap.

French privateers became a real threat both in the Channel and along the south coast. However, the real menace emerged in London and the surrounding shires. The Great Community of the Realm and the Upright Men reflect the radical movement which later exploded into the Peasant's Revolt of 1381; this nearly brought Gaunt, and indeed the Crown, to its knees. For a few days the whole kingdom teetered on the edge.

The strange doings at St Fulcher's should not be regarded as exceptional. St Fulcher's, of course, is a fictitious abbey but, for example, the attempted theft of the Crown Jewels from Westminster in 1303 revealed a seemingly rich underbelly of corruption at that famous Benedictine house which included theft, blackmail, midnight orgies and violence. It ended with the abbot and a hundred of his monks being shut up in the Tower!

The underworld of medieval London and its strange and eccentric characters are all based on original documents. The 'scam' involving tallow candles was common enough and led to some fairly fierce conflagrations.

The trade and constant squabbles over the possession of relics was extremely vigorous; these included both the weird and the wonderful, be it a napkin which once belonged to Our Lady or the Crown of Thorns placed on Christ's head. The bloodstone is an accurate example of this trade in relics which religious houses held and venerated to attract pilgrims as well as their cash.

The Free Companies who fought in France were greatly feared and English bowmen were renowned for their skill and speed. At least two Popes excommunicated all members of such marauding companies. The French did, according to some sources, maim the hands of captive English archers – which may have been the origin of the famous 'V' sign. The use of a 'sniper' archer was common enough, for example in the death of John Howard, Duke of Norfolk, at the battle of Bosworth in 1485. In all other matters I have striven to be faithful to Athelstan and the strange world through which he moved.

Paul Doherty, 2011
www.paulcdoherty.com